Praise for *Bi*
by

"Oh, wow! I can't even describe how much I love that book. Scarlet Avery hats off. It was my first reading from you, but I can definitely say, not the last you are really good!"

—Daniele Charlotin

"Scarlett Avery has fogged up the windows with this one. Princess Brielle and business mogul Easton are one hot couple. This love story is sweet, daring, and steamy. Great chemistry."

—Amazon Customer

"Fantastic plot! Very exciting story! I loved it!"

—Patti

"Holy Hotness! I couldn't put this down!"

—Susanne

"Such a great story! Brielle's mother was atrocious! I loved how the story had a bit of everything, steamy, funny, drama!"

—Mariah

"I loved the characters and the way the story just sucked me in!"

—Jacymay

"I haven't read a book by Scarlett Avery that I haven't loved! This one was a little bit different… in a good way. I refuse to give away anything about the book, unlike others. Go read this for yourself. You'll be glad you did."

—Lisa Dyer

"This book, I must say, is my favorite from this author. Easton was, to me, a great lover for his virgin princess."

—Lin9153

"Great read! As usual, Scarlett Avery writes another bestseller!"

—Melody

"Another great, heartwarming love story that's hard to put down!"

—Donna Vitarelli

"Love it, love it! I literally could not put it down. It had drama and passion, and chemistry!"

—Rachel Pearson

"This book is amazing! The characters are so vivid and the story is compelling. This story is emotional and wonderful!"

—JG

"This book was the right amount of hot, sexy goodness that I absolutely love!"

—Bridget J.

"I love the way that Easton protects and cares for Brielle but at the same time unleashes the woman he knew she truly was meant to be!"

—Jan

"Scarlett Avery has done it again! She comes up with the most amazing stories with the HOTTEST alphas! There's no better hero for this princess than Easton!"

—Barbara VanDeVelde

"Steam, intrigue, and suspense!"

—Angela Tyler

BILLIONAIRE FACTOR
Easton

Scarlett Avery

Edited by John Hudspith

Proofread by Ali Skrzypiec

Publisher's Note: This is a work of fiction. Names, characters, places, and incidents are a product of the author's imagination. Locales and public names are sometimes used for atmospheric purposes. Any resemblance to actual people, living or dead, or to businesses, companies, events, institutions, or locales is completely coincidental. This book is for sale to adults over 18.

Billionaire Factor—Easton © Scarlett Avery
ISBN 978-1-77498-007-1

Get the BILLIONAIRE FACTOR—EASTON Storyboard

Join my mailing list and grab the Exclusive Secret Chapter or Storyboard for this romance.

Great extra goodies. Hot deals. Zero spam.

www.RomanceBooksRock.com

Foreword

PLEASE NOTE: This USA TODAY Bestselling romance was first published as Royal Lust. It's also been previously released as The Billionaire and The Princess and Undeniable Crush. The characters are the same. Their story is the same. We just have a new title and a new cover.

—Scarlett

About the Monarchy in this Royal Romance

Princess Brielle Elise Madeleine Strasberg of Exton is from the Kingdom of Belzer.

Belzer is a small, but rich European country. People living there are Belzerians. Since Belzer was once ruled by Britain, many still speak with the British accent and use British spelling. Belzer was also once ruled by Sweden, hence the many cultural similarities.

Princess Brielle is 4th in line to the throne.

Princess Brielle's mother is Princess Janika Levyna Strasberg of Blackcheldale.

Her dad is Prince Janek Tomás Strasberg of Blackcheldale.

Her grandfather is Prince Joachim Christophersen Strasberg of Durhamderry and her grandmother is Princess Birgitta Eloida Strasberg of Durhamderry.

Her great-grandfather, and current ruler of Belzer, is King Dagget.

Her cousin is Princess Blakely Willow Victoria (Lilo) Strasberg of Gyllenhielm (Lilo's father is Brielle's uncle).

The other princes, princesses and royals in the book are easy to understand.

Enjoy!

About this Story

A woman at my level is expected to marry within her rank.

But that's not what I want. I want my best friend's older brother.

Billionaire Easton Winchester might not have a drop of royal blood running through his veins, but he carries the key to my heart.

I should be able to choose the one I spend the rest of my life with. Instead, I'm promised to a cold-hearted man I absolutely despise.

Refusing this marriage could mean losing it all. Accepting it, could mean losing my soul…

CHAPTER 1

Easton

"I'm finally here," I mumble as I get off the elevator. Even in your own private jet, the flight from Tokyo to New York is a bitch.

Since my eyes are glued to my phone as I turn the corner, it's only when I see a pair of polished black military boots near my front door that I pull my gaze up. A pair of blue eyes dart at me with laser precision. I nod at the woman standing guard in front of my Central Park penthouse. She recognizes me immediately. She nods back and her sharp gaze softens. Thank God, I'm a friend and not a foe.

"Good evening, Officer Pavlova," I say, sliding the phone into the inside pocket of my suit jacket.

"Good evening, Mr. Winchester. It's always good to see you again," the tall brunette with a closed face says. She's adorned in her trademark black suit and white shirt. Of course, the earpiece is a standard accessory.

"Same here. You're alone tonight?"

"Yes, sir. This is a routine visit, sir. One bodyguard can hold the fort," she says with a noticeable Russian accent.

I already know that, but I get a kick out of asking the question.

"My sister is in there with your protégé?" I point my thumb towards my door.

"Yes, sir. They've been in there for a few hours now."

"Girls," I snicker.

"Indeed," Officer Pavlova says.

"Let's go see what kind of trouble Sienna has stirred up in my absence."

"Miss Winchester mentioned you wouldn't be back until tomorrow."

"Technically she's right. But since everything wrapped up sooner than expected, I decided to come back early and surprise her."

"In that case, have a good evening, sir." She offers me a tight nod.

"Officer Pavlova," I return the favor.

With my colossal fortune, I thank God that I don't need a shadow or two tailing me twenty-four-seven—I just need security on special occasions. That said, when one shows up at my door, I know that my sister's best friend isn't too far away.

I shake my head and roll my eyes as I fetch the key to my penthouse. Before I even open the door, I can hear thumping and bombastic sounds blaring through the surround sound speakers of my home. Sienna can't live without music.

I step inside, drop my suitcase and throw the keys on the side table. I undo my tie and fling it, so it lands right next to the keys.

I'm just about to call my sister's name when I hear a screeching yelp.

"Oh my God, Sienna!" a voice shouts over the vocals of the latest pop star sensation playing full blast. "Have you lost your ever-loving mind, or is the music so loud I misunderstood you?" *What's going on?*

Just like that the music stops.

Thank God.

"Bri, hear me out," Sienna pleads.

It sounds like the girls are in the small office located downstairs.

"This is far-fetched even for you!" Brielle bellows.

Yes, that's right. My sister's best friend is Princess Brielle Elise Madeleine Strasberg of Exton. Her family rules over Belzer—a small, but powerful European country.

"It makes perfect sense, Bri—"

"Sienna, there isn't anything you can say that will help me forget you just suggested we attend a dirty virgin orgy where we'll be the *pièce de résistance*."

What the fuck?

Not that it's my habit to eavesdrop, but this I have to hear. I walk as quietly as possible and post myself near the door that's ajar.

"It's not a virgin orgy—"

"Virgin auction? Same thing."

Jesus Christ.

"It's not," Sienna argues. "You're twisting things."

"I see. It's just a slutty party where one is supposed to throw all caution to the wind and give up one's inhibitions? Am I close?"

"Bri, the Innocente Ball of Venezia is like an updated version of a debutante ball. For socialites only."

"Same thing. For the love of God, Si. What were you thinking? It's absolutely unbecoming of us to do such a thing." Brielle dives into Sienna like the US military uses water as a weapon to slice through IEDs to prevent them from exploding.

"It's not. It's a gala. A very posh one. It just so happens that all the women are virgins and all the men are wealthy and successful Dot Com trailblazers and business moguls from around the world, and they're looking for a wife."

Where is that coming from? I've always made it my mission that Sienna wants for nothing.

"You're a complete nutter if you think I'll go along with it."

Thank God Princess Brielle has a good head on her shoulders.

"Bri—"

"The whole point of this debauchery party is for us to get taken advantage of because of our status by some teenage geeky nerdy coder—with zero charm and zero social skills—who made a little money like yesterday. Those blokes can't shag a woman any other way, but at your little kinky ball, we're easy bait. They can then claim to have bagged an aristocrat—like me—or a little rich girl—like you."

"Well, technically, other than the revenues from my dessert blog, I don't have much to my name."

"Wash your mouth out with soap. The revenues from your blog are far from paltry."

"I'm doing okay."

"You're doing more than okay. You've been voted number one in the Top 3 dessert blogs by *Saveur* magazine's 'Saveur 100' awards. And BBC Foods named you number two 'dessert blog to watch'—right after famed dessert maven Jewel Bishop. And loads of other international publications have given you accolades since you started the blog."

"I'm pretty proud."

She should be. She's done a kick ass job with that blog.

"All that to say my brother is the rich one," my sister laughs.

"That may be the case, but I doubt there's anything in this world he would refuse you. He's done an incredible job taking care of you."

Sienna laughs. "He's pretty amazing as far as big brothers go. He's definitely a keeper."

"I agree. Easton is an amazing man. You're lucky." *Is that longing in her voice?*

There's a long stretch of silence before Sienna speaks again. "I never heard you talk about my brother that way. That's kind of weird."

"In what way? I was just agreeing with you," Brielle argues.

"In any case, back to the ball. You have it all wrong. The whole point of it is for us to control who gets our cherry."

Brielle was right. Sienna has lost her goddamn mind.

"Well, my cherry is fine just the way it is and no geeky coder will get close to it."

I bite off a smile.

"FYI, those men have more than just a little money and they're well past their teenage years. They're grown men sitting at the helm of colossal empires. According to the website, the guys need to have a net worth north of half a billion to attend. So, your cherry will be in good hands." *I'm baffled to hear my sister talk like this.* "No chance you're getting it popped by a prick with a few measly million in his bank account," my sister laughs.

I fail to see the humor in this.

I ready myself to barge into the office to put an end to this stupidity, when Brielle says, "And going back to your point. How is paying twenty-five thousand dollars to lose said cherry being in control? It's selling out."

Excuse me?

"It's for charity, Bri," my sister says.

"I'll just wait until I get married. My husband should be the one popping my cherry. That's how women in my lineage have been doing it for centuries."

And just like that, I can only think of Brielle's pussy.

And my mouth on her sweet and untouched pussy.

And me licking her from her clit to her tiny puckered hole—also virgin, I presume.

Damn.

And gorging on her until her juices are coating my mouth.

Yes, I'd take good care of her virgin pussy.

I can just imagine dipping my very big and hard cock inside her unclaimed pussy. How tight it must be. She's going to clench around me like a vise.

Is it wrong to admit that I just want to paint her royal ass with my cum?

Am I breaking some kind of law by wanting to corrupt a princess in the best possible way?

Fuck.

I press the palm of my hand against my erection, desperate to relieve the ache there.

It's been too long.

"And that's worked really well for your parents." Sienna's words snap me back to reality. "You're the one who keeps saying that they're absolutely miserable and barely look at each other—let alone talk to each other."

"That may be the case, but your pop-my-cherry party is wrong. Scandalous even," Brielle says.

"I disagree." *No one can ever accuse my sister of not being headstrong.* "Do you really want to marry a guy your iron-fisted mother chooses for you? Do you want to give him your virginity?" *Fuck, I'll take Brielle's virginity.* "I understand waiting for someone you've selected as a husband. Even then, I think it's important to test the merchandise beforehand."

Who the hell is that woman? What kind of Kool-Aid has Sienna been drinking?

"The last thing you want is to discover on your wedding night that your new husband is nothing more than a prat—as the Brits say—who doesn't know the first thing about pleasuring you. I bet that would've been the case of those blue-blooded boys your mother was pimping."

"You know very well that it's a no-go with the three princes my mother was pushing down my throat."

That's good news.

"There will be a fourth one, Bri. And if Mommy runs out of options, she'll force you to marry one of your distant cousins. That woman is determined," Sienna counters. "It's a sin that even nowadays your parents get to decide who you spend the rest of your life with."

So wrong.

So very wrong.

Brielle lets out a long sigh. "That's the way it's been done in the Belzer dynasty. I don't think I have a choice in the matter. Dad is far more flexible about it, but Mum seems to have a vendetta to settle. She won't stop with her, *'If I had to marry a man that was chosen for me, so do you'*, and her *'Some traditions need to be upheld or else it turns into anarchy'*."

"That's absurd," Sienna volleys.

Is it ever.

"And God forbid she'd marry me off to a man who isn't from Belzer or a neighboring country. It could taint the lineage," Brielle says with a tinge of sarcasm.

"My God that's absurd!" Sienna bellows.

"I agree. You're so lucky. You Americans don't have to deal with such aristocratic nonsense. You get to marry whomever you want."

"Plead your case again." *Sienna the consummate negotiator.* "You're too young to settle and way too beautiful."

Hear, hear.

"Nothing I say gets through to Mum. She's steadfast in her mission."

"What if you meet the one, Bri? What if you fall in love? That should trump everything else… even your crusty old royal Belzerian rules."

My sister is such a sappy romantic.

"And I'm supposed to meet *the one* at this virgin auction party?"

"The Innocente Ball of Venezia *gala*," my sister stresses, "will put us face-to-face with strong men. Decisive men. Powerful men. Alphas." *How the hell does she even know what that means?* "Hunks who know how to take control and train you in the bedroom. Or any other room for that matter."

Huh?

"Train me? I'm not a circus animal, Sienna," Brielle snaps.

She's grown into a feisty woman.

"Bri, you're a virgin. You're like a puppy. This gala is what you need so you don't end up being completely awkward and inept when you do meet *the one*."

For the love of God.

I've been leaving my sister to her own devices. That needs to change.

"You can keep your cherry intact if you choose to. The money we pay to attend will be put to good use. Worst case, it will be a fun getaway and a hell of a party."

Brielle doesn't respond.

"Invite your cousin Lilo to tag along," Sienna sweetens the pot. "It'll be the three of us"

"This sounds like a disaster in the making, Si."

"Okay, I didn't want to bring out the big guns—"

"What now?"

"You remember Countess Sigrid Klarskov?"

"Of course. We went to boarding school with her baby sister Carlyle at Wycombe Abbey."

I sent Sienna to the UK to pursue her studies after she hit puberty. I needed to make sure someone kept a watchful eye on her as my company was exploding.

"Where do you think Sigrid found her hot filthy rich blond god of

a husband? The one who happens to be the military's first in command and best friend to the newly appointed young King Lars Ehlers of Vianden?"

"Really?"

"And you and I both know she's madly in love. Ditto for him. Carlyle has never been able to shut up about how she wanted what her big sis had."

"I didn't realize that's how they'd met."

"I ran into Carlyle a few weeks ago and we got to chatting about men. That's when she told me in confidence over coffee and apple pie. Sigrid attended the ball five years ago—at the first ever gala—and the rest is history," Sienna reveals. "He's not a royal, but he comes from a wealthy family. And may I point out there isn't anything shabby about sexy Vladimir Sekelj."

"No, there isn't. I wouldn't mind one of those. Vladimir is very handsome," Brielle says.

"Personally, I'm hoping to bag a caveman at the gala."

A caveman? What kind of trash has my sister been reading?

Brielle explodes in laughter. *At least someone finds this amusing.* "Now, you've completely lost it. Most of us are looking for a prince and you're looking for a beast?"

"Sweet and gentle guys make great friends. Not great lovers and they'll certainly not hold your attention as husbands."

"Says the girl with loads of experience," Brielle sneers.

"Well, not exactly. I'm as much of a virgin as you are, but a girl can fantasize."

At least she hasn't allowed a dipshit to take her innocence.

"You kill me, Si."

You and me both.

I thought I was doing an okay job as a surrogate parent, but after hearing this conversation, I feel like I dropped the ball. Big time.

How do you talk to your little sister about men, sex and love?

Love?

Like I know anything about that.

It goes without saying that I've given her the basics, but how do you delve into things deeper?

"The Innocente Ball is a weekend extravaganza taking place in two weeks. By the time I found out about the event, tickets were sold out, but lucky for us, Carlyle spoke to Sigrid. Her big sis has connections."

"Carlyle is going?"

"No. She said she's holding off on love until she finishes medical school. You and I don't have that kind of pressure."

"You're pushing your luck, Sienna."

"Maybe, but there are three tickets with our names on them if you and Lilo decide to come along."

Brielle remains silent.

"I can't go alone, Bri. I'm not that brave. Come on. It'll be fun!"

I rub a hand down my face, scratching the dark five o'clock shadow on my chin I'm still sporting from Tokyo, wondering how the hell I'm going to approach this. Sienna is a handful. Stubborn like a freaking mule. A bit of a hellion who loves to rattle the status quo. I can't blame her. I've built an empire by doing just that. That said, Sienna is a special breed of mischief-maker. She's twenty going on who knows what? She thinks she knows it all and good luck proving her wrong.

Time to put an end to this.

"Knock, knock, knock. I'm home," I announce.

I walk inside the office and freeze.

Holy.

Hotness.

I drink in every line of the princess' slender body in shock.

Other than a few glimpses of her on photos Sienna shared with me, I haven't seen Brielle in person in months.

I can't believe how much she's changed.

For the better, of course.

"Easton!" my sister shouts, running towards me waving her hands above her head.

"Hey, sis," I say, catching her and picking her up in my arms.

She's this tiny little thing that weighs nothing.

"What are you doing here?" Sienna asks.

I drop to her feet. "A brother needs a reason to come home?"

Well, one of my many homes, that is.

"No, not at all. I'm so happy to see you," she cheers jumping into my arms again.

"I'm happy to see you too, kiddo."

I drop her to her feet again and turn my attention to the gorgeous blonde standing there with her fingers interlaced. She's always impeccably dressed, but she's more beautiful than the last time I saw her. If that's even possible.

I bow slightly at the neck. "Her Royal Highness Princess Brielle. Your Grace," I say, taking a step towards her. "It's been too long," I add, meeting her sparkling gray eyes.

"Don't be daft, Easton. You know you don't have to do that," she laughs.

I can't hold back my grin.

It's a bit frightening how much I like the sound of my name on her lips. It could easily become my favorite word… right after *please*.

"In the presence of royalty, one must follow proper protocol," I joke. "Even when you've known said royalty for years."

"You're incorrigible," she says.

"I try my best, Your Highness." I smile.

She rewards me with an unrestrained belly laugh. Those joyful notes reverberate right through me.

If she were mine, I'd do everything in my power to hear that sweet laugh every single day of the week.

But she isn't.

Damn.

I open my mouth to speak, but pause for a beat, looking for my words. I settle for, "You're fine." *Shit. Not quite.* "I mean you're in fine form, Brielle."

That's still not what I wanted to say.

More like…

I could swim in those big gray blue eyes for the next century and never come to shore.

I can't believe how cock-stirringly stunning you've become.

You make a grown man want to drop to his knees and worship your fine royal self.

As classy and demure as that pink dress is on you, I bet my fortune it would be much sexier on the floor.

Dare I assume the lingerie matches the color of the dress? Or do you prefer virginal white? Personally, I'm okay either way.

Yeah, that's just a snippet of the inappropriate thoughts bouncing around my head.

Should I be ashamed?

Perhaps.

But her beauty makes it hard for me to think straight.

My eyes drop to her feet.

Jesus Christ.

My cock hardens.

Those nude-colored high heels are killing me.

Damn, woman.

Why was I not born a royal? It would make this attraction a hell of a lot easier.

It's only when my eyes travel back up to hers that I realize she's staring at me. When my gaze shifts to my sister's, it's evident that she shares the same bewildered look as her best friend.

Shit.

My eyes shift back to Brielle. "Is it okay for me to say that?"

"Hmmm… well, yes… I guess."

Why is it only now that I take note of the melodic harmony of her voice? It's almost symphonious and a little reserved—very much like the princess herself. The best way to describe the Belzarian accent is to think of Rebecca Ferguson or Alicia Vikander. It's incredibly arousing.

"Good," I nod.

"Thank you for the compliment." The shyness that colors her voice is so endearing.

"It's more than a compliment. I speak the truth."

"Wow," she averts her gaze.

"Why are you two acting so strange?" Sienna asks with a frown.

"Strange? What are you talking about?" I ask.

"Yeah, like you are right now," Sienna retorts waving a finger at us.

Brielle bats her eyelashes furiously as her face turns beet red. She takes a step back and I do the same.

"So, what are you two up to?" I ask casually.

Of course, I'm tripping all over the princess.

In my defense, my sister's best friend has blossomed since the last time I saw her four months ago at Sienna's twentieth birthday. That said, she's been the star of every single one of my filthiest dreams ever since I threw my baby sister an all-girl birthday party to end all birthday parties in Miami. I still remember how shocked I was when Brielle showed up in a yellow bikini. The way her perfect breasts and her ass were displayed was a work of art. Honestly, that thing was so outrageously sexy it needed to come with a warning and two bodyguards.

"Nothing much." Sienna is quick to answer.

I beg to differ.

"Brielle was over because YSL Beauty sent her an enormous box filled with their latest makeup collection," Sienna says approaching us. "She needed a model so that she can take photos for her popular beauty and fashion blog and of course, I volunteered. Look. She did my makeup," Sienna closes her eyes.

"Ah, I see," I say.

"You like?"

"The blue eye shadow looks good on you, sis."

"I like it too. The best part is I get to keep the palette. Brielle is testing the new lip colors," my sister says.

As much as I struggle, I can't seem to hold Brielle's gaze. Instinctively, my eyes fall to her plump red lips. *Damn.* They're the sweetest thing I've seen in a very long time. *Do they taste as good as they look?*

"You were born to wear red," I tell her. That's all I can manage without compromising myself.

Her cheeks go pink again, making her eyes appear a shade of deep violet instead of their usual sultry gray. I love it when she blushes like that. So much so, my cock goes rigid with approval.

"I'm not sure I would dare to wear it other than to play around with," she reveals.

"You should dare."

Her tempting mouth slides into a sly smile.

I return the favor and catch her staring at my mouth.

"How long are you in New York for?" Once again, Sienna breaks our connection.

"I'll be here for a while. I haven't spent nearly enough time with you as I'd like. It's important for me to remedy that."

"Oh, really? A while?"

"Yeah. Business will always collide with my life, but I only have one sister."

"Oh, yeah. Of course," Sienna mumbles.

I narrow my gaze at her. "You look worried, Sienna. Will my presence put a kink in any of your plans?"

"Not at all." She shakes her head vehemently. "You know me. It's all about school and my blog. Nothing exciting."

"I'm glad to hear that."

My sister turns her attention to her best friend. "Come on, Bri, let's go up to my room so we can finish this makeup."

"Sure."

The two of them gather their things and head towards the door.

Brielle sneaks a quick peek over her shoulder as she trails behind my sister. I respond with a cocky side grin and a wink. When she finally turns her head, my eyes land straight on her ass.

Jesus Christ.

The princess has filled out nicely.

Very nicely.

I crank my neck from left to right, trying to dislodge the knot that's sprung up.

My cock is a lost cause.

Double damn.

I need a glass of bourbon. Right the fuck now.

CHAPTER 2

Brielle

"Will that be all for the evening, Princess?" Officer Pavlova asks as we ride the lift to the twelfth floor.

My cousin Lilo and I live in a spacious two-story rented penthouse in Hudson Square—not far from the Hudson River. The Thayer Hersey Court is an extremely secure and fairly secluded fortress—that meets our parents' rigid standards. We live there with our ladies-in-waiting, aka chaperones, aka royal nursemaids. Our four guards—two for me and two for Lilo—have their own penthouse across from ours.

"Yes, Officer Pavlova."

"Officer Stanton and Officer Kerr will take over the guard."

"Thank you."

"Of course, Your Grace. Have a good evening."

"Good night, Officer Pavlova."

She answers with a nod before heading to her penthouse.

"Good evening, Iyanna," I say when I step inside the penthouse.

"Princess!" She gets up from the sofa and runs towards me. "You're back!"

"I am. Is Lilo back yet?"

"Not yet. Lady Philippa is upstairs if you need her."

"Thank you, but I really need to speak to Lilo."

"I'm sure Princess Blakely should be back any minute."

"Good."

"How did it go, Princess?" Iyanna asks.

"YSL Beauty will be pleased with their upcoming feature," I smile.

"Are you sure you don't need another willing soul—or should I say, face—to try on more makeup? More photos can never hurt."

"I think I have it covered… pun intended," I wink.

"Pity."

"Next time. This palette was more suited for a brunette than a redhead like you. Not to mention the luxury makeup company sent me so much stuff I could literally gift the entire city and still have some left over to spread some joy back home. Don't worry, I have more than enough goodies for you to choose from."

"Yeah!"

She makes me laugh. As if she doesn't already have a chest full of makeup samples.

"How was your day?" I ask as I head to the kitchen.

I drop my nude-colored Gucci Marmont handbag and laptop on the granite counter on my way to the refrigerator. I pull out a small bottle of Evian and lean against the closed fridge as I crack open the cap and take a few sips.

"Well, 'tis the season when people are planning parties, galas and events for late spring and summer months, therefore that was a top priority for the day. I also took care of picking up a slew of pretty evening dresses from Melinda Jacobs. She'd love for you to wear one of her designs at one of your upcoming events. Conrad Stockwell will send a courier tomorrow to your office with his summer collection."

"Noted."

"And of course, the chef was here to prepare food for the week and the cleaning lady came in. The penthouse is fully stocked up and properly sanitized. All in all, it was a very busy day. I couldn't even carve out enough time to catch a quick hot yoga class. It was work, work, work."

"You're the best, Iyanna."

"Tell me something I don't already know, Princess."

We both laugh.

"Thank you for taking such good care of me."

"It's an honor and a privilege, Princess."

Lady Iyanna Hoffräulein is my right-hand woman. She's twenty-two and unmarried. She takes care of my personal and my business life. She helps tend to everything I want and need. I guess a more modern title would be private secretary or personal assistant, but since we're encrusted in old aristocratic traditions, she's my lady-in-waiting. Lady Philippa de Habsburgs does the same for my cousin Lilo, except for the business part.

"Well, I should go upstairs and finish writing my blog posts. I still need to crop the photos I took of Sienna," I say, heading towards the stairs.

"Oh, your mum called. Several times." I stop dead in my tracks and slowly turn around. "She's been trying to reach you all evening. Apparently you silenced your phone." Iyanna gives me a knowing look. "Princess Janika says it's important. Something to do with your future."

"There was a lot to do at Sienna's," I offer.

"I'm sure, however the princess made me swear on my future heirs that I'd get you to call her before the end of evening. As you know, I plan on having lots of babies. In other words, mummy dearest is expecting your call, Princess."

"Bollocks."

* * *

I pace around my bedroom wondering how I might be able to escape to Russia without anyone knowing. I did study with Alena Sharipova—her multi-billionaire father dominates the steel industry in her country—maybe she can hide me out.

What—or who—does Mum have up her sleeves now?

I keep pacing.

Of course, I could drag this on, but it would only get Iyanna in trouble.

"Just do it," I tell myself for encouragement.

With trepidation filling my heart, I put my big girl knickers on and make the call.

"Hi, Mum, it's me," I say when she picks up.

"Finally. Where in the world were you?" *Notice, no hello or hi.* "I've been trying to reach you since five o'clock New York time. It's ten now. It's not the wee hours of the morning in Belzer?" she barks.

"I was at Sienna's."

"Doing what?" she demands.

I close my eyes and breathe deep through my nostrils. It's going to be one of those conversations. "She volunteered to test the new—"

"Oh, Brielle." She lets out that sigh. You know, the one she uses when disappointment is painted all over her face. "When will you quit daydreaming?" There's a slight slur in her speech. I wonder how many vodka martinis she's already had. "You're wasting far too much time on that silly beauty and fashion blog of yours," she reprimands.

PoshStyle.com is anything but silly. It exploded into the stratosphere two years ago when I correctly predicted which designer Patrice—Britain's King Albert Patrick David II's youngest granddaughter—would wear to her big eighteenth-birthday bash. I had an unfair advantage since we went to boarding school together and my blog had already become an obsession. Patrice flew to New York to seek my advice. I was so flattered. When I got over the shock, I suggested a few designers that would suit her curvy body. She gave me an exclusive when she had locked down her decision. Since then, I've been riding high. My blog is one of the only things I control in my life. Dad gets a kick out of it. He's proud of me and encourages me to keep pushing forward. Mum thinks it's a futile exercise. Frankly, I don't care what she thinks, but unfortunately, for now, I'm still very much dependent on my parents.

"I love what I do and it's in line with my degree in fashion," I argue.

"Well, it's about to end soon."

"What do you mean?"

"The reason I insisted on speaking to you is because I found you a proper suitor."

"What?"

"A husband, Brielle," she snaps.

"Shouldn't we take a respite given your last three failed attempts?" I ask with a tinge of effrontery. Okay, maybe that was like a bucketful, but she's royally pissing me off.

"I misjudged those princes. This one is different." She also said that for the last two. "This one is a winner. You and Prince Haakon Lurköping of Wallon will form a beautiful couple."

I suck in a horrified breath. "Prince Haakon?"

"Yes!" *Yuck.* "He's of proper age—"

"He's thirty-three. I'm only twenty."

She ignores me. "He's blue-blooded, you caught his eye and we share neighboring countries. He'll be ascended to the throne of the Kingdom of Brihon in six weeks, replacing his ill grandmother. That means it's prime time for him to take a bride. Marrying him would make you a queen, which would only be good for our surname and the heirs you'll bring into this world."

And that should be enough for my happy ever after?

"Why can't I find my own husband?" I insist stubbornly. "British royalty has evolved—"

"Good for the Brits."

"But it works for them. Why can't it work for us?" I cry out.

"The Brits and their royal divorces. What a farce!" She lets out a mocking laugh. "That's so unbecoming of nobility and certainly not something we want to emulate. The same applies to marrying people from common lineage. Ridiculous." That mocking laugh again. "Belzerian Royals don't get divorced; we endure."

And she certainly holds a PhD degree on the subject.

"I want to find the right one," I retaliate.

I don't want to endure. I want to love and be loved.

"We've already been down that road, Brielle. Even if I had a temporary lobotomy and I was inclined to indulge you, your flaky tart of a cousin killed any chances of that ever happening," Mum says.

"So she rushed into things."

"Rushed?" The sarcasm is dripping from that one word. "Princess Aloisia met an American fool at the Rio Carnival last year—a simpleton from common class without a dime to his name from the hippy state of Oregon. Shagged him. Claimed he was her best ever, therefore she needed a daily dosage of his manhood. Married him—even though she barely knew his surname. Ignored her parents' request for a prenup. She even fed us the line that she was in love—with a capital L. She professed it was forever. Pure rubbish. As we all know, four months after her mockery of a wedding, she asked for a divorce. That's not rushed, Brielle. That's stupidity."

"It was a lapse in judgment." To be honest, it was a colossal debacle, but I'm not ready to cave in. "The rest of us shouldn't have to pay for Aloisia's mistakes," I retort.

"Enough!" my mother shouts. She's as imperious-sounding as ever. "I will not allow you to bring shame to our family's name like your cousin did."

"But—"

"You'll be twenty-one soon. My parents chose your father as my husband. I had little say in the matter. I'm just keeping up with tradition. If Prince Haakon doesn't meet your expectations long-term, a vodka martini always does a smashing job. And to think, vodka is a family business. You don't have to pay to drown your sorrows. It's delivered to your door on command."

Wow.

To this day, I don't know what scars added up to the vitriolic and rancorous woman I know as my mother.

"Mum—"

"It's already been arranged."

That sentence is worse than a slap in the face. To be honest, it feels like a guillotine.

"What?"

"You heard me. You'll meet Prince Haakon when he comes back from his official tour of Australia, New Zealand, Indonesia and Papua New Guinea. We spoke right before he left a few hours ago. Three weeks from now, we'll have an official dinner in Belzer." Panic stabs through my heart. "Soon after that, we'll announce your engagement. Enjoy your little blog while it lasts."

I don't have time to rebuke. She's already hung up.

I sit for what seems like an eternity, staring at my phone, allowing myself to register the ache of discouragement—the finality of it all.

Someone, please, kill me now.

* * *

"Knock, knock. It's me!" my cousin says before walking into my bedroom.

"Oh, hi, Lilo. How was your day?"

"Too much homework and not enough time. And yours?"

"Okay," I sigh.

"Why the long face?" she asks sitting across from me on my bed.

"I don't know if I have the heart to talk about it," I tell her.

"What are you talking about, Bri? We tell each other everything," Lilo stresses.

She's right.

Princess Blakely Willow Victoria Strasberg of Gyllenhielm is not only my cousin, she's my best friend. We're the same age—we were born two weeks apart. I came first—and since neither of us have siblings, we grew up like twins. Because we're inseparable, it was unfathomable for one of us to study abroad and leave the other behind, hence why Lilo and I went to boarding school in the UK. Since then, it's been Lilo, Sienna and I against the world—like the Three Musketeers. When Sienna declared she wanted to return to New York to attend a prestigious cooking school, Lilo and I followed. We ended up pursuing our University degrees in the US.

"I just had a dreadful conversation with my mother."

"And what does Princess Janika Levyna Strasberg of Blackcheldale demand of you this time?"

There's humor in her voice and I can't help but smile.

"She's found number four."

"Another loser prince?"

"No. Apparently, he's perfect for me."

Lilo rolls her eyes. "Wasn't that her motto for the other botched attempts?"

"I reminded her of that, but she insists this one is different."

"And who is she marrying you off to this time?"

"Prince Haakon Lurköping."

"Yuck!" The expression of revulsion on my cousin's face speaks volumes.

"My sentiments exactly."

"Your mother is truly the worst matchmaker known to mankind. Not that I approve of this arranged marriage ridiculousness, but other mums have done a far better job for their daughters than yours."

"In her view she simply misjudged the last three."

"Seriously? So Prince Haakon is her chosen one? Puh-lease. Rubbish. The man has an appalling reputation. Sure, he seems to have calmed down lately since he rediscovered God—so he claims—but it still looks like smoke and mirrors to me. Like a giant Hollywood production."

"I'm not convinced of the act either," I say.

"I don't care how many recent photos there are of him hugging starving African children with tears in his eyes, he's still a manwhore."

"I don't find him attractive in the least."

"He's ugly, Bri!"

We both laugh.

"You should have the right to your own heart," Lilo says with a heavy sigh.

"I agree, but unfortunately, we were born into a royal family with a name and all the stupid responsibilities that comes with it."

"Utter rubbish," Lilo says.

"Nevertheless, I have three weeks to warm up to Haakon the manwhore because from the sound of it, my mother will do everything in her power for us to get married before the kingship falls on his shoulders."

"What?" Lilo's eyes bulge out of her skull. "That's only a month and a half away."

"It appears so," I say defeated.

"Why is your mum rushing this? Did Prince Haakon offer her a pot of gold or better yet, another source of endless vodka?"

Lilo's sense of humor can be slicing.

"My guess is it's a little of both." I pull my lips down in a sad smile.

"Bri, I understand about traditions, but your mum almost seems to be using your future wedding as a vehicle for her own wasted dreams and aspirations."

"Ya think?"

"Something happened before your parents got married. What? No one will ever tell us, but why else would a beautiful and eloquent woman like your mum turn to vodka as her only friend?" Lilo says crossing her arms over her chest. "There's a story there, I would bet my collection of designer shoes on it."

I can't help but laugh. Lilo and her shoes.

"I wish I were in Sienna's shoes," I confess. "She isn't bound by anything."

"I must admit I envy that about her," Lilo says. "She has total control over her life, her heart and her fanny."

Lilo's comment shocks me.

"Where did that come from?"

"What do you think will happen on your wedding? Haakon will pop your cherry and you will have no say in the matter. He's been with countless slutty women—escorts even. And you can only have one man for the rest of your life? I don't see how that's fair."

I let her words hang for a few long seconds.

"Well, there might be a way for me—us—to have control over who takes our innocence."

"What have you been drinking, because that doesn't even make sense," she frowns.

"It's Sienna's idea. I thought it was preposterous at first, but after the depressing conversation with my mother and your comment, it might not be that crazy after all. Sure, Mum will be infuriated, but I wouldn't mind rattling her world. Since she's always quick to remind me how much of a disappointment I am, why not go all the way?"

"Now you have my attention." Lilo rubs her hands furiously together.

"It's slightly rebellious," I warn.

"Brielle, we've been groomed since birth as aristocrats, which means there's a very long list of five million things we should never do. We're twenty. If we are to do something crazy and completely out of character, now is the time."

"You really feel that way?" I press.

She turns her hands so her palms face the ceiling. "I hold a different pill in each hand. A blue one and a red one. Prince Haakon is the blue one. Whatever Sienna has inside that devious mind of hers is the red one. Which one do you choose?"

CHAPTER 3

Brielle

"Ladies, we arrive in the Floating City as girls and we'll leave as women," Sienna says walking out of the bathroom. "Show time in sixty minutes!"

"Love, love, love the dramatic eyeshadow," Lilo exclaims when she catches Sienna's reflection in the dresser's mirror. "And the vampy lips," she says turning around.

"I asked Brielle to make me look like a femme fatale."

"My cousin knows makeup. She did a smashing job."

"She did," Sienna agrees.

Lilo turns her attention to me. "Si looks every bit the temptress."

"Thank you," I say. "I aim to please."

"Once the mask is off, I want to look my best for my caveman."

Lilo snickers.

I turn around to face my best friend and roll my eyes at her. "You and your beast."

"Yup. As God is my witness, I shall find him," she brandishes her little fist in the air.

"She can be such a drama queen," I tell my cousin as if Sienna is no longer standing in the luxurious suite.

"Go on. Make fun at my expense. See if I care. This weekend is epic. Once we've had a taste of a real man, we'll be able to discern between a good fuck and a bad one. My money is on marrying the good fuck."

"You have that option. We don't," I remind her.

"Well at least tonight, you have a little control," Lilo winks.

"What she said," Sienna says pointing her makeup brush at my cousin.

"I don't know if I have the courage, Si," I admit.

Sienna drops her makeup brush on the dresser and takes several steps until she's standing in front of me. I'm not that tall, but she's even shorter than I am so she has to tilt her head back so our eyes meet.

"What was your mother thinking?"

"It's a business transaction for her," I say, doing my best to suppress a bout of anger.

Sienna shakes her head despairingly. "It's a crying shame, if you ask me." Her eyes are burning with something I've never seen before. "To a man like Haakon you'll always be just a pretty little prize, because by marrying you it'll bring him the adulation and respect he craves—after all, you might only be fourth in line to the throne, but your kingdom is far richer and more powerful than his. The ginger prince will never see beyond what you can do for him—he's too selfish for anything else." Sienna lets out a snort. "God, the man is as shallow as the bald spot on the top of his head." She lets out a long sigh. She then takes my hands in hers and squeezes hard. "I wish your mom had selected someone a lot more worthy of you."

I wince inwardly at her words, averting my gaze. "Me too," I say in a small voice.

"So, about tonight… put your royal panties on and go for it. If you spend an exciting evening talking to a sexy guy, that counts for something. If you can't wiggle your way out of marrying Haakon-the-soon-to-be-king-but-still-a-manwhore," Lilo and I laugh, "at least you'll be able to hold onto this magical night forever."

"And who knows? Maybe you'll catch the eye of a hot prince from a neighboring country, therefore making Mummy Janika happy *and* you'll end up with a dreamy prince," Lilo says longingly. "The best part is you get to leave Belzer and your mum can't pick on you anymore."

"Oh, trust me, she'll come and visit as often as she can just to torment me."

"Hold up!" Sienna lets go of my hands. "Wait, wait, wait, wait, wait." She lifts her left hand up like a royal guard.

"What?" Lilo and I ask in unison.

"Hot? Prince? Those two words don't belong in the same sentence unless we're talking about the royals from the Kingdom of Anders. Now that's some serious eye candy. I'd sell a vital organ for an evening with one of those tall and husky Slavic aristocrats," Sienna says dramatically.

Lilo and I laugh. It doesn't take long for Sienna to join us.

"No offense, but the guys in your circle aren't exactly fitness models," Sienna says when she regains her composure. I can't argue with her. "I can't really think of one that's attractive. Even the ones who did their military service don't look that muscular or strong. Frankly, they look like boys. Not men." Her gaze bounces from mine to Lilo's. "Tonight, we'll meet plenty of hotter-than-hell-please-pop-my-cherry contenders."

"So elegantly put," I snicker.

"We didn't travel all the way out here to pussy foot around *le fait accompli*."

I roll my eyes at the pun.

"She's right," Lilo says. "At fifty thousand dollars to attend, I certainly hope these men know what they're doing."

I just look at her amazed.

"What?" she frowns. "You wanted to do something slightly rebellious, well, here we are in Venice."

I nod, not knowing what to say. After all I'm the one who dragged her here. Until the moment we landed at Venice Marco Polo Airport a few hours ago on a private plane, I was certain I wanted this—daringly choosing the red pill over the blue one. Now that we're an hour away from standing face-to-face with a group of powerful and mysterious men, butterflies have taken residency in my stomach, making me question my sanity.

"Lilo is right. We paid twenty-five grand. The men paid double that. These guys are serious. No dicking about."

"Amateurs, please refrain," Lilo chimes in.

"Exactly," Sienna agrees. "You get something out of it and so does he. The charity bit is bonus."

"Are you seriously comparing this weekend to *quid pro quo*, Sienna?"

"Bri, I'm simply saying everyone gets what they need."

I shake my head at her. "Just go fetch your dress. Lilo and I are here, aren't we? You've already done a banged-up job selling this event. No need to layer on more. While you're all ready for the ball, we have yet to finish our makeup. Go," I command shooing her off.

"Okay, okay. Let me run downstairs to make sure the hotel staff was able to clean off that tea stain on my pretty dress. See you soon," she waves before heading out the door.

"Now that Sienna is gone, I can open up," I say when the door slams shut.

"Open up about what?" Lilo asks, her puzzled gaze meeting mine.

"Can I be honest?"

"That's a weird question," she says scrunching her nose.

"There's someone I haven't been able to stop thinking about."

That look of confusion is replaced by sheer excitement. "Oh! A boy?"

I shake my head. "No. He's all man."

"Even better," she says rubbing her hands furiously together. "A prince?"

"No, a king in his own right."

"Single?"

"As far as I know."

"Older?"

"Much."

"Oh, Bri. Look at you."

I blush.

"You like him?" Lilo asks.

"What's there not to like?" I say longingly.

"Then what are you bloody doing here, Bri? If you've found *the one* and he's of noble blood, why look for someone else?"

"He's not *the one* and his kingship is in the business world."

"Hmmm. So he isn't blue-blooded?"

"Alas, no, but there's so much more to him. He has more in his little finger than those three stupid princes Mum forced me to meet. And it goes without saying that he leaves Haakon in the dust."

"He sounds amazing."

"He is, Lilo. He's so smart—brilliant, even—well-traveled, gorgeous beyond words and his chocolatey voice is sexy. And then there's his contagious sense of humor. He's so charming and he always puts me at ease."

"And why is it only now that I hear of this attraction for this perfect older man?" she swats my arm.

"Because it's only now that I'm willing to admit it to myself," I tell her.

"Is it someone I know?"

I don't respond immediately.

"Who is it, Bri?"

I might as well get it over with.

"Tonight, I hope to meet a handsome and gallant man who will sweep me off my feet. *His* little sister is looking for a caveman and a beast who will train her."

Lilo's eyes widen like saucers and her eyebrows hit her forehead as realization sets in.

"You can't be serious."

I nod.

"Easton Winchester?" she asks.

"Yes," I say, biting my lower lip.

"Does Sienna know?"

I shake my head vehemently. "No and you can't tell her."

"Your secret is safe with me." Lilo crosses her heart for good measure. "So… is this mutual?"

I give her a one-shoulder shrug. "For all intents and purposes, I'm not even sure he notices me other than as one of Sienna's best friends… although the last time I saw him, there was something there."

"Details," Lilo demands.

"Two weeks ago, when I was at Si's place and she announced her desire to attend this ball, Easton was also there. He had arrived early from Tokyo. When he walked into the small office, I nearly stopped breathing. A man shouldn't be allowed to look that good in a suit."

“He wears them so well,” Lilo agrees.

“If I’m an open book, I should admit that he caught my eye a long time ago.”

“Do tell,” Lilo encourages.

“Remember Sienna’s eighteenth birthday?”

“God, yes. Easton booked a whole island near Ibiza for a three-day weekend just for Si’s girlfriends.”

“That’s when he stopped being her big brother and started to become that hot American guy I longed for. I noticed furtive glances, but I thought it was all in my head. But after that, when we were all back in New York and I’d be at their penthouse, he would always make a point of chatting me up—more than before. I relished the attention. Then Si’s nineteenth happened—”

“Another weekend extravaganza with only her big brother as the sole boy and guardian in Portofino, Italy.”

“Exactly.”

“May I point out—and I’m interested in him—the man has a body to die for. Definitely hot fitness model material. But I digress.”

Lilo is hilarious.

“Well, Portofino was three days of me ogling at him whenever I could and hoping to God that none of Si’s other friends caught his interest.”

“You spent quite a lot of time chatting with him at Si’s birthday a few months ago when he flew us all to Miami for another sun-filled bash. I didn't want to bring it up because you hadn't brought it up. I thought I was reading too much into things,” Lilo says.

“Well, by the time we flew back, I was completely under his spell. I was so enchanted that I found myself doodling his name in my notebook,” I admit.

“Wow, Bri, this is huge. There must be a connection between the two of you because I didn’t notice him paying attention to anyone else. Sure, he was nice to me like a big brother would be, but with you, it was different. Now I know why.”

“I think he was flirting the last time I saw him.”

“You think?”

“I'm fairly certain of it.” I hesitate. “Okay, he was definitely flirting.”

"Now we're getting somewhere. I want the scene-by-scene."

"When he approached me to greet me, it's as if it was just the two of us in that office. His gaze traveled down my body, taking its sweet time and turning an innocent inspection into a blatant statement of interest. No one has ever looked at me that way. Lilo, I swear heat flared in his eyes. It only lasted an instant because it didn't take long for Sienna to remind us that she was still standing there. Just like that his searing gaze turned impersonal, but I saw it. I felt it."

"Wow."

"He said and I quote, *'You look fine'."*

"Dear Lord." Lilo fans herself. "That's definitely interest, Bri."

She says that as if she had a world of experience in the matter.

"It was too brief," I lament.

"What next?" she asks, giddy.

I look at her as if she has two heads.

"Nothing. We're from two different worlds. It's ridiculous to think that anything can come out of my juvenile crush."

"But you don't know for sure," Lilo disputes.

I open my mouth to say something, but I pause. After a few beats I dare to say what's on my mind. "If I had a fairy godmother and she could grant any wish," I pause again.

"Yes, I'm listening," my cousin presses.

"I'd want a man like Easton to take my innocence."

My cousin's gaze doesn't waver from mine. For a few long seconds we just stare at each other.

"*Like* Easton *or* Easton?"

CHAPTER 4

Easton

"I can't believe this event has been going on for five years and it's only now I hear of it," Thor says trailing behind me.

After a spectacular dinner in our luxury suite, all three of us stroll towards our private lounge.

"Same here," I say. "I still think I'm officially insane for crossing into the land of the delusional, but I'll be damned if I let my baby sister and her friends be taken advantage of."

"I don't blame you. I would've done the same thing," Harlen says.

"Which one is our lounge again?" Thor asks.

"La Cittadella," I say.

"We just passed it," Harlen says.

All three of us turn around and retrace our steps.

When we enter our assigned lounge, it's as opulent as the rest of Castello del Bernardeschi—the four-hundred-year-old castle an hour away from the main city where the event takes place.

"What a fitting setting!" Thor says walking straight to the bar. "On the rocks?" he asks lifting a bottle of Scotch.

"Yes!" Harlen and I answer in unison.

After serving the two of us, Thor strolls over with his glass in hand. "Cheers, mates! Here's to a great night," he says sitting down on a sleek black chair.

The castle is ancient, but the décor is very modern.

"Cheers!" Harlen and I parrot.

"Although I'm on duty tonight," Thor shoots me a knowing look. I chuckle. "I hope that tomorrow I'll be able to play. So many options. So little time," he smiles.

"Thanks again for doing this, buddy," I tell him. "I know it was last-minute—"

"Nonsense, mate. It's an honor," Thor smiles.

Multi-billionaire Thoren Lidström, also known as the King Who Lost His Kingdom, and I go way back. Had it not been for his father's disgrace, he'd be ruling over the Kingdom of Wintbourg. Instead, Thor has become one of the most astute businessmen I know. His headquarters are in the Big Apple, but he does business all over the world.

My eyes meet the friend sitting next to me on the couch. "You too, Harlen."

Harlen Whitford is another buddy of mine who was willing to drop everything after one phone call to help me out. He's also exceedingly rich. He and his twin brother are dubbed the kings of short selling. The way they leverage financial down turns is legendary. To top that, they're masters at picking up on the public's uneasiness around an election and the impact on the stock market. In other words, they have a nose for detecting when things are about to go belly up.

"Not a problem at all," Harlen says. "It's good to get away from Manhattan. I work way too hard for my own good."

"Hear, hear," Thor and I agree.

"I might not be that lucky tomorrow night since so much will happen tonight, but what a perfect place to find an untouched submissive," Thor says.

"I'm already on a mission for tonight, but I see your point," I say.

"A few lucky high-rollers will be able to find someone to mould at will. Not that I'm complaining, but I wish it were me. There's nothing quite like a virgin," Thor says.

"Maybe it's just me, but virgins don't do it for me," Harlen says. "I like my girls with a little experience. It makes the whole thing that much more enjoyable. I'm not interested in breaking anyone in. Too complicated. Too messy."

"I can't say it was at the top of my hit list, but sometimes in life something happens that changes your whole perspective," I say.

"You blokes are missing out," Thor says. "You'd be the first one to whip her, spank her, choke her, cuff her—God, seeing the red marks on her little wrists is so hedonistic. And of course the *pièce de résistance*, fucking her and owning that pussy in a way no man ever will," he says. Yeah, Thor's brand of edginess is slightly hard-core. "There's nothing quite like dipping your hungry cock with angry veins popping with excitement and pre-cum already dripping inside a young woman's warmth knowing full well when she comes for the first time, it'll be all over you. And then, there's the blood." He closes his eyes for a beat like he's praying. "It's a gift she can only give once. When you finally come and explode deep inside her, it's like climbing Everest barefoot." Thor pauses, his eager gaze bouncing from mine to Harlen's. "Once you've given her a respite, the lesson continues, mates."

"There's more?" I chuckle.

"Easton, you need to get your cock serviced—and fast—if you ask that bloody question," Thor says with the arch of an eyebrow.

"You're taking this way too seriously, Thor."

He ignores me.

"Putting a woman on her knees before you and watching her take your big cock inside her mouth for the first time is enough to awaken the alpha in even the wimpiest beta males. Once you come, spewing your release down her throat and admire as she struggles to swallow, you take her in your arms, flip her over and fuck her with dominant force and unwavering resolve. As you boys know, I demand complete surrender from my conquests."

"Same here," I say.

"Is there any other way?" Harlen chuckles.

Not that I needed the incendiary visual, but that little dirty tale helped my cock remember exactly how long it's been since it's been inside a woman. Too fucking long. Sienna's twentieth birthday party definitely cooled things down for me. Fantasizing over Brielle's pert tits and ass has become a habit I can't break.

"Fuck and I forgot the smell of a virgin. Sublime," Thor adds. "Bloody hell," he says shaking his head.

"Fuck," Harlen says.

"Shit," I growl. I shift in my seat to allow for my thickening cock. Everything feels so impossibly tight down there.

"I've been traveling extensively," Thor continues, "and business is growing so fast I can barely keep up, therefore my fist has been my companion for the past week and a half. My cock is desperate. I brought an indecent stock of condoms with me because tomorrow night, I'm unchained. I'll fuck as many unclaimed virgins as I can. Two or three at a time, even."

Jesus, he's killing me.

The ice rattles in my glass as I gulp it down, hoping the cold drink will tame the volcano burning inside me. *Damn.*

"Thor, we need to change subjects before I embarrass myself," I say looking down at my bulging crotch. "I only came here with one tuxedo. I can't soil it. Not yet anyways. The night is still young."

All three of us chuckle.

Since I arrived at the hotel, I've been trying to ignore the blood flowing to my groin without my permission. No matter how many times I command my cock to behave, it's in vain.

"It's a good thing there's an ironclad NDA that will keep most of the unadulterated stories out of the rag papers and websites. I'm also a big fan of the no-mobile policy. No photos. No proof of debauchery," Thor says.

I frown.

"What?" Thor asks, a glint of malice flashing in his eyes. "You said to change subjects."

"So you go from talking about cocks and virgin pussies to legalities?"

"I bet your dick is no longer on alert."

"Fuck off."

CHAPTER 5

Brielle

As Lilo, Sienna and I take a step inside the ballroom, a whole fleet of butterflies erupts in my stomach.

Wow. I'm really doing this.

I wish my pulse would stop fluttering so frantically.

I guess Lilo feels my trepidation because she squeezes my hand into hers. I smile, but then remember she can't see it.

We make our way through a crowd overflowing with well-dressed and beautiful people. The Venetian masks covering our faces only add to the allure.

Considering the venue, it's no wonder the lavish party takes place in a ballroom that's still decorated in homage to a long-gone era. It's decadent, with its high ceilings, massive windows, pristine white Italian marble floors, and an incredible night view of twinkling lights against a dark sky, gardens and a stunning fountain. The modern touches here and there are typically Italian. The soft classical music playing in the background is the bow that wraps it all. It's so enchanting, it's like being in a fairytale story.

This is very promising.

"My God, the place is packed," Sienna says.

"It's wall-to-wall." I'm still scouring the room, half over-whelmed and half bewildered.

"Everyone looks so elegant, but they have nothing on us," Lilo says. "You came through for us, Bri. Our dresses stand out."

"It's good to know people in high places," I laugh.

Since we didn't want to draw attention to a fairly hefty charge on our credit cards, I made a few phone calls to some of my favorite designers who have always been pleased with their features on my fashion blog. In a matter of a few days, I had three stunning evening gowns delivered to our penthouse. I absolutely love mine. Sienna looks like a classy siren in her glittery, blush gown. The V showcases her ample breasts. Lilo could stop traffic in her red bombshell dress. She looks so glamorous and statuesque.

"Do you see *our* guys?" Sienna cuts to the chase.

"No, not yet," I say stretching my neck.

"Well, they can't be that far," Sienna says.

"I still can't believe we've already caught the eye of a few suitors. When did that happen?" Lilo laughs.

"It must've happened when Sienna declared she *needed* Italian dessert or else she'd die and we all came rushing down to the restaurant to satisfy her sugar craving."

"Don't lie, Bri. You enjoyed the desserts as well."

"That's beside the point, Si."

"You must be right," Lilo nods. "I'm surprised Officer Pavlova didn't deter whomever is behind this. She's impossible to miss and she gives off that don't-mess-with-me vibe when she's on duty."

"I told you guys, we're dealing with *real* men. Not boys. Not even your badass bodyguard could derail them from their mission to secure our affection." Only Sienna would come up with that explanation.

"These men must be something else," Lilo muses.

All three of us were shocked beyond belief when we got a knock on our door as we were slipping into our high heels. A bellboy was standing at the door with three boxes containing different colored orchid corsages. Each box was labeled in a clever way that made it easy to know which flower belonged to which girl. Since our suitors don't know our names yet, they used our hair and eye color. Brilliant!

"I just hope mine is cute. They may all be rich, but we don't know what's hidden underneath that mask. It could be scary," Sienna says.

"What happened to your need for a caveman?"

"The gesture is so sweet and unexpected, I can live without a caveman for one night," Sienna says.

Lilo and I laugh.

Ditching our bodyguards, as Sienna suggested, was impossible. We pondered long and hard on how to go about attending the ball without raising any suspicions. Iyanna saved the day.

We may refer to her as officer—because it's more incognito—but former Lieutenant General Vika Yanina Pavlova is one of the few women to have served in Spetsnaz—Russian Special Forces. She's also the one supervising our three other bodyguards. Colonel Evgenia Sotnikova served under Officer Pavlova. They're still in touch. Colonel Sotnikova was assigned to Prince Haakon's grandmother's security. After four brief months, she quit. Apparently, she saw and heard things she just couldn't live with. Iyanna told Officer Pavlova of my mum's ridiculous decision and it's my lady-in-waiting's idea that we simply come clean with her. Officer Pavlova was too happy to stand guard and even stand back for the ball. Our parents think we're on a three-day weekend art trip with Lilo in Venice for one of her school projects. We'll be back in New York by Monday afternoon with no one the wiser.

"Do you see any men wearing—" Sienna cuts her sentence short. "Oh, shit."

"What?" Lilo and I ask.

"There are a few guys over there. Crap they're coming our way." Sienna jerks her head towards the right of the room. Although effective, her gesture isn't very subtle. "None of them has a flower matching our corsages. This doesn't bode well."

"Oh no. What do we do?" Lilo asks almost panicked.

"Ladies, calm down. Remember, we have final say. We can simply curtsy without taking the hand that's extended to us—it's part of the guidelines for evening. The guy will get the message and move on."

"Right. I'm so nervous I forgot," Sienna says.

"Thank God one of us still has her head on her shoulders. My heart is beating so fast with excitement that it's affecting my thinking," Lilo laughs. "Oh look, those guys are heading to that group of women over there."

"Oof. We dodged that one."

The fact that Sienna whips her hand in front of her mask makes this even funnier.

"Good. We won't need to ditch them when our guys arrive." Lilo is very invested now.

"Maybe we should stand near the bar. It's a landmark," Sienna suggests.

"Brilliant idea, it might be easier for them to spot us," Lilo says.

"I disagree. I think we should hang near the entran—" I freeze when I turn around. "Oh, God," I wince.

"Those are our guys." Siena says nearly jumping up and down.

There's no mistaking it.

Three very tall men adorned in perfectly fitted tuxedos stand in front of us. Each one of them is wearing a flower pinned at his lapel that matches our corsages—orange, blue, and yellow. My guy stands to the right. The blue orchid against the black tuxedo is arresting. Since they're wearing the obligatory masks, it's impossible to know what they look like, but everything about their body language screams supreme confidence.

There's no turning back now.

CHAPTER 6

Easton

Thor, Harlen and I are just polishing off our third drink, doing our best to pretend that Thor's incendiary words aren't still hanging thick in the air when the soft music playing in the background stops.

"Gentlemen, may I have your attention." Our eyes shift up to the ceiling where the voice with the British accent just spoke. "My name is The Skull—you'll soon see why—and I'm your MC for tonight. It's nearing eight o'clock. We'd appreciate it if you could all make your way to the main ballroom so that the festivities can start." Skull's deep voice resonates through the speakers.

"We've been summoned, mates." Thor says meeting my gaze.

"Let the party begin," Harlen says.

"It's about time," I say, standing up. "Come on," I wave my friends over as I rush to the door.

Yeah, I'm eager. For good reasons. Very good reasons.

When we step outside the lounge, a sea of tuxedos and ornate full-face masquerade masks greets us. The crowded hallway is like a scene out of a Hollywood production. We all look alike. Other than the masks and our height, you wouldn't be able to differentiate between us.

My friends and I follow an army of eager men until we hit a grandiose room that is already packed with women dressed in stunning gowns. Already men are in search of a partner. No time to waste.

"Can you smell it, gentlemen?" Thor says over my shoulder.

I shake my head. I don't bother slowing down my stride, I already know Thor isn't done.

"The smell of innocence… just before it dissipates. My mouth is already watering."

There you go.

I stop and turn around.

"You haven't forgotten that you're on duty tonight, right?" I remind him.

"Of course not. I already acknowledged that earlier when we were in the lounge. Relax. I'm simply enjoying the scenery. There's nothing wrong with that."

"As long as we have an understanding."

"I'm not one to renege on his word, mate. You know that full well."

These must be the most uncomfortable contraptions in the world. Still, from the tiny slits on his mask, the steadfastness of his sharp blue eyes peers through.

"Good," I say. "You guys remember what you have to do?"

"Absolutely!" Harlen is the first to respond.

"Loud and clear, mate," Thor says.

"Glad we're all on the same page."

"Come on, man. Thor is right. Relax. Everything will go as planned."

Yeah, I'm a little on edge. There's a lot riding on tonight. There's an equal chance for everything to run smoothly as there is for things to blow up in my face. That said, I know for sure Thor and Harlen have my back.

"Thanks for saying that. There's a lot at stake," I say.

"Of course there is," Harlen sympathizes.

"Can we keep walking now?" Thor asks in a flippant voice.

I just shake my head before taking a step forward. The man is incorrigible.

"I love the shy way these virgins move," Thor throws over my shoulder.

Once again, I halt my step and turn around to face him.

"Buddy, you have to stop calling them that," I tell him.

"That's what they are. That's why every bloke here paid fifty thousand big ones—and upon your request that includes our mate

Harlen and I," Thor says patting our friend's shoulder. "Deal with it. You want this as much as I do… if not more," Thor challenges.

"I need to teach my baby sister a lesson," I quip. "This is about setting her straight."

Harlen chuckles.

"Sure, keep telling yourself that. It's a clever cover up, but I know you too well, mate," Thor quips.

"Yeah, buddy, you aren't fooling anybody but yourself," Harlen chimes in.

Harlen and Thor were surprised by my urgent need to attend this ball. In the end, I had to fess up about my royal lust. After giving me a hard time, they were more than willing to be my wingmen. We go way back, it's no wonder I can't pull a fast one on them. I'm doing a shit job at pretending I'm unaffected. Even I know that.

I won't bore you with the number of times I've jerked off since finding out about Brielle's plans to lose her virginity. I couldn't help but stroke every morning and every night thinking of burying my face in her pussy before claiming her innocence.

The idea of Brielle, long legs wrapped around an asshole who won't appreciate her, infuriates me.

Frankly, I can't explain why, but I'm livid.

I have no rights to her.

No claims.

No titles, no blue-blooded heritage and surely no kingdom.

But here I am, fifty thousand dollars lighter and playing God by interfering with this evening's outcome.

Knowing that Brielle is so close is intoxicating. The chase that will start soon to locate her in the crowded ballroom already has my pulse jackhammering.

"The noble thing to do is to walk away. Like she's even in my league—" I pause. "But I'm not going to allow her—or her cousin or my sister—to get eaten up alive by wolves." I pause again. "If the princess wants to be 'trained', I'll gladly sacrifice myself as her ringmaster." My words send a surge of blood to my already painful cock.

"Well said, mate. Spoken like a true alpha. Now, let's go get you a princess," Thor play punches my arm.

"Let's do this," Harlen says.

"Damn right," I say.

I turn around and I barely take a few steps than I stop in my tracks again.

Three sirens stand before us.

My eyes are riveted to the angel wearing an orchid around her wrist in the same vibrant blue shade as the flower pinned to my lapel.

CHAPTER 7

Brielle

The man wearing the orange orchid steps forward, bows slightly at the neck and extends his hand. Sienna curtsies and takes the hand that's offered to her.

Wow.

The man wearing the yellow orchid does the same. Lilo responds exactly like Sienna did.

Oh, God.

I'm the only one left.

My heart jumps into my throat.

It's one thing to have courage when you have partners in crime, but now I'm alone, I'm as frightened as a kitten.

The tall and commanding man still standing there takes a long step to the right. He's now in front of me. Contrarily to his friends, he bows from the waist with his right hand against his heart.

Very gallant.

After a short beat, he lifts his head up and extends his hand.

With bated breath, I place my hand into his.

The contact is electrifying.

In fact, it sends a shockwave coursing throughout my body. It's like nothing I've ever experienced in my life.

Who is this mysterious suitor?

The man leads me to the other side of the ballroom with a quick step. I turn my head to locate my cousin and Sienna. There are so many people, I can't see them. *Bollocks.*

"Wait. My friends," I babble.

He answers by squeezing my hand before bringing it to his lips. The gesture is incredibly comforting—even with the mask. My moment of slight panic dissolves when I remember that all the men here have been thoroughly vetted and if anything were to go wrong, I can always run like the wind to officer Pavlova's room. So, I will my nerves to settle.

You can do this.

I stand side-by-side with the tall man who's made his intentions known early in the game. I'm still too petrified to smile, but I guess it doesn't really matter since he can't see my face.

Little by little more men find partners. In our case it was easy, but I wonder what prompts the other couples to pair up. Chemistry, I guess. They do say two souls vibrate at the same frequency. I wonder if it would've been the case for my suitor and I had the flower not come into play.

Suddenly the soft music playing in the background stops.

"Ladies and gentlemen welcome to the fifth Innocente Ball."

The room claps loudly.

"As some of you know, my name is The Skull and I'm your babysitter for the evening."

The MC's comment solicits roars of laughter.

"In all seriousness, no one here needs my help. It's clear by what I see. All of you have found a match. Bravo."

The crowd claps again.

"I'm sure you've all read the guidelines. Ladies, when the masks are off, you get three chances to say yeah or nay. After the third suitor, you'll have to sit on the sidelines."

I can't help but look up at *my* man. He looks down at me. I smile shyly behind my mask.

"Do not despair if you aren't able to find a soulmate. It simply means you'll be able to party like it's nobody's business because the music will keep playing on and on until five in the morning."

The crowd shouts a collective, "Yeah!"

"For those lucky ones, the gentlemen have already reserved a private room. We're an intimate group of one hundred. This should be a night to remember. Have fun boys and girls, but play safe. Always.

Don't forget it has to be mutual. No, means no. If we have to remove one of you men from the ball, we won't do it with kid gloves. One of the many security guards lining the walls will unceremoniously throw your arse out on the street like a vulgar vagabond. Are we all clear?"

A few men shout, "Yes!" Others yell, "Hell, yeah!"

"Good. It's time for the big reveal. Remove your masks. Ladies, you have fifteen minutes to confirm you're happy with your match or find a new one. After that, the party kicks off," The Skull says.

Yikes! This is it.

Please let him be handsome. Please, God.

CHAPTER 8

Easton

I was ready to look for her high and low, but I didn't have to. Even in this massive ballroom it seems that we're attracted to each other like magnets.

Is it serendipity?

Nah.

I'm from the school of thought that believes you create your own luck in life.

This encounter was meant to be. I made sure of it.

After The Skull's command, many of the attendees reveal their faces to their partners. You can hear a symphony of, "oohs," and "aahs," and the occasional, "I'm so sorry."

Once I've confirmed that my friends have put my plan into motion, I shift my attention back to Brielle. She removes her mask with shaky hands.

What a vision.

I can fully appreciate the whole package.

Her blonde hair cascades seductively over her shoulder, which only emphasizes her goddess-like body. Her makeup is on point. Her stunning one-shoulder gown accentuates her eyes. The vibrant shade of blue is stunning. The beading shimmers as bright as the diamond chandeliers hanging from her ears and adds a touch of opulence to an otherwise classy dress. The design reveals her beautiful alabaster skin. I just want to run my tongue from shoulder to shoulder tasting every inch of her. My eyes zoom in on her chest. *Damn.* That cut-off on top of her left breast that reveals a glimpse of skin makes me want to leave all good manners at the door. *Fuck.* As my gaze travels down her slender curves and past that indecent slit that runs up her leg, I nearly lose my shit when my eyes drop her to her feet. Her dainty toes painted in hot pink peer through a pair of skyscraper strappy silver high-heel sandals.

Dear God, what are you doing to me? I'm only a man.

I hope my silent prayer brings me the resolve I need to remain a gentleman, but one more glimpse at her tells me that it's unlikely I'll be able to resist her.

As Brielle waits patiently, her eyes shift nervously, looking around the ballroom. I suspect she's searching for her cousin and Sienna. I don't rush her. Eventually, her gaze falls onto me again. She lifts her eyebrows, almost coaxing me to remove my mask, but I make her wait a little longer.

"I'd love to know what you look like," she says after a few long seconds.

Unrushed, I grant her wish.

Slowly, I remove the Venetian mask.

"Good evening, Princess," I say when my eyes meet hers.

"Ha!" she takes a step back. "Easton?" she utters incredulously.

"It's good to see you, Brielle."

Her eyes glitter with excitement.

"Thank God it's—" She blushes furiously.

I take a long step forward and close the gap between us. Our bodies aren't touching, but there can't be more than an inch between us. "Finish that sentence," I order.

She averts her gaze.

"Tell me," I press.

Her blue eyes bore into mine. "Thank God it's you," she says softly, her chest heaving up and down.

"Really?"

She nods. "Really."

I can't help but grin.

"Good."

Her eyebrows knit together and her face contorts into a question. Her excitement is quickly replaced with worry.

"What is it?"

"How did you know we'd be here?"

"Two weeks ago, upon my return from Tokyo, I overheard you and Sienna talking right before I entered the office. A few searches later, I knew everything I needed to know about this ball. After that, I reached out to a few people I know. By my fifth phone call, I had secured a spot for my friends and I despite the fact that this weekend was completely sold out."

"Are your friends going to… you know… I mean, the theme of this gala is…" She waves her fingers between us, but words don't come out. "Oh, God, I can't even say it."

"You're absolutely precious. To put your mind at ease, no. Both your cousin and my sister are in good hands. My buddies are just going to babysit them for the evening. Nothing more. The only difference is Sienna will get the lesson of a lifetime. My friend Thor is more than willing to oblige."

"You know about her caveman fantasy?" she asks, her eyes enormous.

"Alas, there are certain things that can never be unheard. That's one of them."

Brielle laughs. "She's something else."

"Yes, she is. But she's all that I have left and I love her to pieces."

"You're a great big brother."

"That's sweet of you to say. I try my best."

I take a step back, needing to take her in again. My eyes comb the length of her body. "Princess, you went from being pretty to becoming the poster child of outrageous sexiness in that dress," I say admiringly.

"Thank you." Her coquettish smile doesn't go unnoticed.

"I'm merely speaking the truth."

She swings her gorgeous mane over her shoulders before placing her hands at her waist. She extends her left leg out like an invitation. In that stunning dress, Brielle's legs look like they go up to her neck. *Wow.* She looks like a Degas painting I've seen in the Louvre—unreal and impossibly elegant.

"It's a lot more daring than what I'd normally wear, but I figured everyone would be a stranger tonight. The plan was to play the role of vampy temptress and get away with it."

I can't help but growl.

In this moment, Brielle is no longer Sienna's best friend.

She's no longer an untouchable innocent princess.

This seductress standing in front of me flashing sass like it's going out of style is ripe for the taking and I sure as hell will be her conqueror.

My balls feel like lead weights in my pants.

I shift from left to right in the hopes of allowing a little more room for my hardening cock. I have to. If not, I'll be dragging her by the hair to my reserved room right this minute and not letting her out until sunrise.

I move closer and without permission, I lace my fingers through her golden hair forcing her eyes up to mine. This close, her expensive perfume lingers in the air between us.

"That dress looks like it was designed for sin." Her cheeks flame up. "Thank God I didn't have to challenge any other man to a duel over that dress… and your honor. Just so we're perfectly clear, I would've in a heartbeat," I smile.

"I'm in good hands then," she smiles back.

"You're in very good hands."

We hold each other's gaze exchanging far more than words could ever do.

The music starts, signaling the beginning of the party.

I let go of her mane and ask, "May I have this dance?"

"With pleasure," she curtsies.

I envelop her in my arm and start moving to the soft notes of the classical music. She's so tiny compared to me, but she fits perfectly in my embrace. Her slender body is so soft and so delicate against mine.

"I have no idea how to dance to this," I admit after a valiant effort.

As much as I try, I move awkwardly to the beat. It's true, this is a historic setting, but I didn't expect this kind of music.

"To be honest, neither do I. It's a bit of an odd choice considering the crowd," she observes.

A few minutes into this melodic dance and the DJ scratches a record, bringing the music to a halt.

"This isn't the sixteenth century," he shouts into the mic.

The crowd grumbles.

"How the hell are you guys supposed to leave it on the dance floor to that vibe?"

A chorus of voices cheers in agreement.

Brielle and I grin at each other.

"My name is DJ Boiler Room and I'm coming to you straight from the Big Apple. NYC in the house!"

The crowd roars.

"I've earned my name—and reputation—by being a badass motherfucker when it comes to pushing crowds to the brink. Are you ready to bring the house down?"

People lose it.

"Boys and girls, show me what you're made of," DJ Boiler Room shouts before changing the music.

"That's more like it," I smile when a more current beat hits.

"Yes! This song is a few years old, but it's a great one to move to."

"I don't recognize it, but the mix of English pop and Latin beat is perfect."

To my surprise Brielle starts swaying her hips left to right. My eyes are fixated on her. You'd think I'd never seen a woman's body in my life. When her hands travel up to her hair and her eyes close, I know I'm in trouble. It's like she's in some sort of trance. I'm willing to bet a lot of money and proclaim that from the rolling of her hips and the way she moves so beautifully to the music, there's a lot more to this prim and proper woman than meets the eye.

"You rob me of all my words," I say over the music.

Slowly, she opens her eyes. The lustful veil I read is a giveaway that she's still inebriated by the spicy rhythm. "I find that hard to believe," she responds.

I daringly reach for her waist and pull her towards me until her body slams against mine. I exhale a warm puff against her neck, whispering, "You say that because you have no idea what you do to me."

I pull back slightly to watch her reaction.

Astonishment gleams in Brielle's eyes.

"If you only knew," I insist.

She looks up at me with a cheeky smile pulling at her lips. "So you *were* flirting the last time I saw you?"

"Unashamedly so," I smile wide.

She laughs.

"You're okay with that?"

"Very much so," she nods.

I couldn't have asked for a better answer.

"I'm not sure Sienna will."

"Why don't you let me worry about my little sister?"

She nods. "Okay."

When the chorus hits again, I slide one hand down the small of her back, resting it right above her ass. We're so fused together, I can practically hear her heartbeat. She looks to the left, then to the right before pulling her eyes up to mine. I suspect she's trying to assess if anyone else notices how close we're dancing. The couples around us are too busy doing their own thing to pay attention to us as bodies gyrate unabashedly on the dance floor.

Fueled, I up things by several notches. Brielle doesn't flinch as my dancing becomes more suggestive. On the contrary, she mirrors my actions. With every beat, her hips rock at the same tempo and her body bumps into mine.

Fuck.

I lean into her. "Your beauty leaves me in awe."

She shivers.

I'm enraptured by her bewitching spell. The air is filled with an indescribable energy that causes my already hard cock to pulsate.

"You're dangerous, Easton."

I chuckle. "Good dangerous?"

She bats her long dark lashes at me and it's with Herculean strength that I don't crush her lips and claim her mouth in front of an audience.

"Yes," she says so low it comes out as a whisper. Had my eyes not been fixated on her mouth, I wouldn't have heard her.

The music moves from one incendiary track to another and each new sexy song surges the blood in my veins. The expansive room feels like a freaking sauna. My white shirt sticks to me like a second skin. Even my tuxedo jacket feels drenched. The temperature of the room is one reason why I'm heating up.

She's the other.

This woman is doing things to me and I haven't even kissed her yet.

When the song fades out, the DJ speaks again. "Boys and girls, all that hip shaking should've gotten you all warmed up. Let's make it mellow. I want to see you blaze up the place. If this duet doesn't do it, I don't know what will."

The music changes to a sexy and sultry melody.

Unable to resist, I run a lingering finger from the tip of Brielle's chin down to the cut off on her breast. Her gaze follows my finger. When she pulls her lower lip between her teeth, I swear I'm a breath away from coming. When her half-lidded eyes lock with mine, it only adds to the hedonistic nature of the moment. I soak in the heat emanating from her body. I'm completely lost in this song. And in her.

When the chorus hits again, I grind my hips into her stomach allowing her to feel how she affects me. Her eyes widen and she catches her breath. I'm sure she's surprised by my not-so-subtle move, but she does nothing to put distance between us. So I do it again and again and again.

She even moans for me.

And I'm so fucking hard it hurts.

CHAPTER 9

Brielle

Easton is my mystery man?

Thank you God for answering my prayer.

He claimed me before any other man could.

This evening is a dream so far.

The suggestive way we've been dancing together blows my mind. We're both flushed and sweaty. It's so sexy. I'm not sure what's come over me, but I like this brazen girl. I like her a lot.

Every time our eyes meet, I forget to breathe.

When Easton pulls me close and presses his thick bulge against my stomach, digging into my flesh without an ounce of shame, I whimper. For the first time in my life I know what a man feels like and for some inexplicable reason, my body responds in a way that I don't understand. My lady parts clench uncontrollably, sending a flurry of delightful pulses coursing through my body. It's so delicious and so wrong at the same time. *How can that be?*

As we sway to the seductive song, Easton leans into me and whispers in my ear, "God, you're so fucking sexy." When his tongue slides into my ear, I swear I'm going to pass out.

My nerves are dancing wild, sending waves of tantalizing pleasure to parts of me that have been dormant until now. Until Easton.

Then I catch the lyric of the song, *'I'll be yours for a thousand lives.'*

Just like that my bubble bursts.

No, no, no, no.

Suddenly, I snap out of his gripping spell.

Dangerously hot Easton Winchester.

My best friend's much older brother.

An American without a drop of royal blood in his body.

A man my mother will never approve of.

A man whose world is oceans apart from mine.

A man I can never have.

It's one thing to give up your innocence to a stranger, it's a very different one to lose it to a man you want more from.

This is doomed before it even begins.

"Please," I gasp placing both hands against his firm chest before pushing away from him.

"Are you okay?" he asks concerned.

"This is too much. I need a minute. I'm just going to run to the loo."

"I'll come with you."

I shake my head. "I'll be right back," I blurt out before running out of the ballroom.

"Wait!"

I don't.

I run.

God, I can't even think straight.

I rush past a few security guards and turn the corner. I zoom down a corridor, my mind still consumed by Easton Winchester. In my heedlessness, I bump into someone.

"Oh, God, I'm so sorry," I mumble.

"No, not at all. It's my fault for not paying attention. Did I hurt you?" the stranger asks.

"No. I'm okay."

"You're more than okay," he smiles down at me. "Have you not found a match yet? I'm still available."

He's old enough to be my grandfather.

The flame of interest burning in his eyes is predatory. Nothing like Easton's.

"I have. We're a perfect match." *Strip away my title and unshackle me from these stupid old-fashioned constraints imposed on me against my will, and we are.* "I was just going to powder my nose," I explain.

"Pity. Well, my loss. Have a good evening, sweetheart." The way his eyes run up and down my body makes my skin crawl.

I turn around and race away.

I continue down the corridor until I hit a set of stairs. I look up and see a sign pointing to the loo.

Thank God.

When I hit the last step, I stumble.

Bollocks.

I scramble back to my feet, pick up my little silver evening bag, lift the tail of my pretty dress, hook it over my folded arm and keeping moving.

I only allow myself to exhale when the loo door closes behind me.

I let my head fall against the door. With my eyes closed, I flash back to the sexy man I just ran away from.

Why, God?

Why give me a gift I can't keep?

A tear trickles down my cheek as I envision myself on my wedding day standing next to Prince Haakon—a man I'm sure I'll never be able to respect, let alone love. Panic strikes as I see him hovering over me as he takes something from me I'm sure he's taken hundreds of times before from other women.

This is so unfair.

"Enough!" I scold myself.

I need to channel Sienna's advice.

I need to embrace tonight.

If this is my only chance with Easton, I don't want to waste it moping around about my loveless future.

A future that will eerily mirror my mother's.

With a determined step, I move to the sink to assess the damage from my exuberant dancing. My makeup is no longer perfect, but the rosiness of my cheeks makes up for it. Carefully, I pat some cold water behind my neck, hoping it will help clear my head and cool me down. Once I no longer feel like a volcano is about to erupt inside me, I touch up my makeup and apply a fresh coat of lipstick. In no time, I step out of the loo.

As I retrace my steps down the corridor, I take note of the multiple closed doors. Heading towards the stairs, I hear a loud moan coming from my right. The door is ajar, and I can hear movement inside.

"Oh!" a woman yells.

Is she okay?

Quietly, I approach the room and press my face to the crack of the door. The room is dark, but the light seeping from the corridor and the window facing me allow me to see what's happening.

Dear God.

A man is on his knees with his face buried between a woman's opened legs. They're both naked. The way her fingers tangle in his hair make my cheeks flame. Suddenly, the man gets up and places his knees on the mattress. In this position he's not only flashing his butt and his crack at me, but I can make out his long manhood.

That's obscene.

The sight is like a shock to my senses. I've never seen a man naked before. I know a lot about sex, in theory, nothing in practice. I'm fully aware porn exists. It's just not something I'd ever watch. Hence, this is the first time I've ever seen real sex.

The heat from my cheeks travels south. Way south. My body reacts viscerally to the X-rated sight in front of me.

Mother of God.

My body is tingling, nipples hardening against my dress and the palpitation of my heartbeat is so hard, I can barely hear.

What's happening to me?

I really should step away and leave these people to their privacy, but I don't. I just stand there, eyes wide and I stare.

"God," the girl gasps. "That's so good."

I'm not sure what's going on, but it must be something else if she's reacting that way. I allow my mind to wander and imagine what it would be like to be that girl. Of course, in my fantasy, Easton would be the one making me moan.

With a sudden movement, the girl jerks her body off the mattress.

"Yes, yes, yes!" she cries.

What am I doing? I shouldn't be watching them.

Petrified that I might get caught, I take a long step back just to hit a human wall.

"Peeping?"

I immediately recognize Easton's voice.

I'm mortified.

If the floor could open up right now and swallow me whole, it would put an end to this humiliating moment.

Slowly, I turn around already knowing that guilt is painted all over my face.

I shake my head vehemently. "Err… no," I whisper. In my nervousness, I trip over those two words.

There's another moan from inside the room. This one is much, much louder.

"I want your virgin cunt to come all over my face," the man inside the room says.

"Oh, yes, big daddy," the girl pants.

"Give it to me, baby girl. Squirt all over my face." *What does that even mean?* "Let me drink your sweet pussy juices," the man commands.

Blimey.

My eyes widen and I swallow hard at the provocative words.

Easton grabs my hand and drags me towards the stairs.

I don't protest.

Once we reach the bottom of the stairs, he turns around to face me. He places his strong hands against my shoulders. Just like before, the contact is electrifying.

His coffee-colored irises are laser focused on me, making it impossible for me to avert my gaze. "I never would've pegged you as a voyeur," he says.

"A what?" I grasp for the words.

"Someone who likes to watch others in their most intimate moment, beautiful."

God, he has such a sexy smile.

"I-I thought she needed help," I mumble awkwardly.

Easton's patient grin grows wide. "By the sound of it, I'd say he has it under control."

My face turns red.

My only response is to hang my head in shame.

Easton places two fingers under my chin and lifts my head until his eyes lock into mine.

"Are you embarrassed?"

I nod.

"There's nothing wrong with watching." His dark brown eyes stare straight into mine. There's so much strength, power and determination in them. It's the gaze of a man who commands respect. A man I could easily love given a chance. "You hear me?" His question snaps me back to reality.

I'm not sure I understand it all, but I nod.

"Between you and I, I think they wanted to be caught."

"They did?"

"Why else would they leave the door ajar? Some people like to have an audience. It's all part of the game."

"In that case, that's one show I'm unlikely to forget anytime soon."

Easton lets out a deep laugh. The joyful rumble is contagious. Soon I join him. That laugh is quickly becoming one of my favorite things. Along with everything else that's so attractive about this tall, dark, gorgeous and kind man.

"You said it was too much before you escaped," he says when his laughter subsides. "I'm sorry for being too forward—"

"I'm not used to the attention," I explain. "Don't get me wrong. I'm very flattered. It's just all new to me."

"I find that hard to believe." He borrows my words from earlier, eliciting a smile from me.

"Security guards and a thriving dating life tend not to go hand-in-hand. Officer Pavlova and Officer Stanton scare most men off."

"Luckily, they like me and I'm not afraid of them."

"They've known you forever."

"Exactly, which gives me an unfair advantage... like tonight."

"What do you mean?"

"Officer Pavlova knows I'm here. She also knows about my buddies."

"When did that happen?"

"I arrived early and sat in the lobby. The baseball cap helped me hide in plain sight. Since I gave Sienna my blessing to charge the three tickets and private jet to my Black Amex, I knew when you'd arrive. I waited and when all three of you came downstairs to the restaurant, I approached Officer Pavlova."

I laugh.

"Sienna and her sweet tooth."

"Do you want to know why I'm grateful that dessert is my sister's weakness?" The timbre of his voice is so deep and rich.

"Yes," I whisper.

"It allowed me to get the green light from your officer."

He grabs my wrist and pulls me close, knocking the wind out of me when our bodies collide.

I love being this close to him.

Easton leans in. Unexpectedly, he brushes his lips against my forehead, my temple, my nose and my cheek. *My God, I'm going to melt.* "I've reserved a room for the two of us. It'll be more intimate and we can get to know each other better. I hope you'll join me."

I lift my gaze to his. We stare at each other wordlessly. With each breath, my heart thumps loudly against my chest.

It takes me a heartbeat to consider his invitation. "I'd love to."

CHAPTER 10

Easton

It took me a while to catch up with Brielle. When she ran away from me, a desperate soul who hadn't found her match ambushed me thinking she had a chance. Duchesse Léonie Jolie Duquette Joubert cajoled and begged, but I remained unaffected. *Sorry, babe. I found my perfect match.* After letting Léonie down easy, I ran after Brielle. By the time I reached the massive doors, she was nowhere to be found. Thank God, one of the security guards noticed a veil of blue and a cascade of golden locks floating away in a rush.

Imagine my surprise when I caught her watching another couple in the throes of passion.

Poor kitten. She got lost and ended up with a crash course in perversion.

I drag Brielle by the hand past couples cooing at each other in the hallway and even a few daring souls already making out in plain view before taking a right and rushing down a deserted hallway all the way to a set of elevators. When we reach the fourth floor, my pulse is already thumping. By the time the door to our room closes behind us, I'm so fucking hard, I can barely stand it. No matter how horny, a man should remain a gentleman.

"Please, make yourself comfortable. Have a seat, I'll be right there," I say, turning on the lights.

She sashays elegantly towards the couch.

Fuck.

The teasing sway of her slender hips as she glides away from me is pure torture. The delectable offering of her ass under the blue flowy fabric of her dress begs to be kissed, kneaded, licked and worshipped.

Then it hits me.

Every delectable part of this woman has been untouched.

Jesus.

“Do you want something to drink, beautiful? I wasn't sure what you liked, but I figured champagne was a safe bet.”

“Champagne would be lovely.” Once again, I’m completely mesmerized by those gray eyes as they drift back to me.

“Two glasses of bubbly coming right up!”

She laughs.

“This suite is magnificent,” she says her eyes scouring the room. “Then again, everything about this palace is striking. Old world history, Italian modern aesthetics and sophisticated furnishings all wrapped up into one.”

Although impeccably decorated, the room has been kept to the strict minimum—a sitting area, a bar and a massive bed. Everything one needs for an unforgettable evening.

“Well said.”

It doesn't take long for me to return with our drinks.

“Here you go.”

“Thank you so much,” she says, taking her champagne.

I undo the button of my tuxedo jacket and take a seat right next to her.

My gaze slides longingly up and down her body, doing little to hide the fact that I linger on her chest before I catch her gaze again.

She blushes under my inspection.

I lift my glass. “Here's to new beginnings.”

“Indeed!”

We both clink our glasses before taking a long sip.

I drop my glass on the marble coffee table and lean back against the couch. She mirrors my motion.

“Here we are.” I break the silence.

“Indeed,” she repeats. “The princess and the American king of the financial world.”

That makes me laugh.

"So tell me. Who is Princess Brielle?"

"You've known me since I was twelve."

"No, I know Brielle, the girl. The breathtaking beauty sitting next to me?" I shake my head. "I don't know her at all."

"For one, I'm completely petrified right now."

"You're petrified of me?"

"I'm petrified that you'll blink and realize that I'm nothing more than a naïve girl."

"Newsflash, every woman attending this gala *is* a naïve girl."

"Good point," she laughs shyly.

"Tell me something else."

"As you know, fashion is my thing, as you Americans put it—"

"And you excel at it."

"Thank you for saying that."

"I mean it. What you've done with your blog is very impressive. It's transcended from being a hobby to becoming a real influencer."

"It's my escape."

"Now, what would a pretty little thing like you have to run away from?"

"My mum's obsessive quest to find me a suitable husband before I turn twenty-one," she says.

"Why is she rushing it?"

"I guess she can't wait to have an ally in her miserable existence."

"Ouch. Those are harsh words."

"They're justified, trust me." She sticks out her chin and narrows her eyes. The determination on her face speaks volumes.

"Maybe your parents are going through a rough patch," I offer.

She shakes her head vehemently. "I doubt it. It's a lot more than that. I don't think I've seen them exchange more than two sentences in the last year. For the past decade they've been living separate lives. Forget about sleeping in different beds. They each occupy opposite quarters of our big manor. In the meantime, Mum is preaching the sanctity of marriage. She's already presented me to three princes in the last few months—each more inept than the other."

"You didn't like any of them?" I ask.

Oh, don't get me wrong. That's great news for me, I'm simply curious.

"After a scandal went viral, it became apparent that Prince Pim van Rijsselberghe of Tourzel might not be a suitable match. He came with a much older and very married royal mistress, a brood of bastard children and an impressive manhood that was the talk of all the gossip papers and sites."

"Ah, yes, I've heard of the twenty-three-year-old skinny prince with the massive fourteen-incher." That boy puts most men to shame.

"Right," Brielle blushes.

"Who else was on your mom's hit list?"

"Prince Pavus Havilliard of Kostroma. He prefers older royal daddies to princesses, but of course, he's in the closet. And Prince Aaryn Hawkmoon of Wendolen proved that he was a filthy pig on our first date when he tried to grope my breasts."

"Yikes."

"Exactly. A parade of inadequate suitors."

"Wouldn't you be much happier if you were to pick your own man?"

"According to my mother, happiness is a myth commoners tell themselves to justify their subpar existence."

I don't even know what to answer to that.

"Given the laughable results, has your mother put the let's-marry-Brielle project on ice?"

She shakes her head. Her shoulders slump. "No. In the next few weeks she wants me to meet Prince Haakon."

"He's a jerk. He'll never treat you as you deserve to be treated, Brielle," I half-growl.

"Everyone knows that except my mother."

"Have you met Haakon before?"

She shakes her head. "Never. And I have no desire to meet him. I'm sure he'll turn out to be as bad as the previous three princes."

I bring my hand to her cheek and stroke it softly. The touch doesn't match the inexplicable anger boiling inside me. When she leans into my touch, it dissipates the fury. "Is that why you're here tonight? You want to rebel?"

"I want to have a say in something in my life."

"Were you really willing to offer your virginity to a random stranger?"

My question startles her.

She offers a one-shoulder shrug. "If I have to marry Haakon, then I won't allow him to steal every part of me," she says.

"I sympathize, but you're too precious to give up such an important part of you that way."

"I want to marry for love, Easton." That comes out like a plea. "I want to choose my own husband."

"And so you should."

The air shifts between us, becoming thick with want and words not yet said. I search her beautiful face, my gaze falling to her full mouth like I can't tear my eyes away.

"So, under the royal layers, you're pretty normal."

"Yeah," she lets out a soft laugh. "Those unicorn stories are a myth."

I know she means that as a joke, but I'm way too turned on to even chuckle. Instead, I scoot closer to her and lean in.

"It's our little secret," I whisper in her ear.

"I like sharing a secret with you," she says.

You can bet that I read a whole lot into that sentence.

"So do I." I pause for a beat. I'd do anything to wipe away the sadness from her face. "If I could snap my fingers and make anything you desire happen, what would it be?"

"Anything?"

"Anything."

"I'd love, even for one day, to be Brielle. A girl. Just another meaningless face in the crowd. No guards following me like shadows. No unrealistic expectations. No pressure. I doubt that would ever happen, but I wouldn't have to be on my best behavior either if I didn't want to. I could even be a slob. In other words, it would be total freedom." Her answer comes without hesitation.

"What if I could make it happen?"

She pulls away from me. "I thought you were at the helm of a very successful global finance company. Do you also moonlight as a wizard?"

"If I grant your wish, would you come away with me?"

Her eyebrows hit her forehead. "You're serious?"

"Very much so. Well, minus the slob part."

She explodes in laughter.

"What say you, Her Royal Highness Princess Brielle. I'm sorry, I mean *meaningless* Brielle?"

"You're serious?" she repeats.

"Your wish is my command."

She grins like a kid who gets to have two desserts instead of one. "I would in a heartbeat."

"This game is going so well. You're telling me all the right things."

She laughs.

"Now tell me something *very personal* that you've hidden from everyone—even yourself," I challenge.

"Well…" she bites her lower lip.

"You have my undivided attention, beautiful," I tempt.

"Something in my brain switched when I turned seventeen."

"How so?" I frown.

"Suddenly, I started finding my best friend's big brother outrageously attractive."

"Really?"

"Yes."

"That's a naughty secret, Princess."

"Am I allowed to have naughty secrets?"

"You're allowed to have as much naughtiness as you desire."

"I don't know if I can handle more than that."

"I think you're wrong."

For a few long seconds, we just grin at each other.

"May I turn the tables?" she says waving her index finger between us.

"Of course."

"Who is Easton Winchester?"

"The truth?"

"Absolutely." Her eyes sparkle with mirth.

"A man who's been dying to kiss you for a really long time."

"Oh."

"You asked," I tell her.

My fingers brush her inner forearm ever so lightly. Her body trembles under my touch sending a rush of electricity coursing through my veins.

"God. I've never felt like this before," she whispers.

"Like what?"

Her eyes scour my body again, pausing to linger on my chest. "Like the barest touch turns my entire body ablaze."

"Something tells me that I could get addicted to touching you."

She brushes her golden hair behind her shoulders exposing her flawless ivory skin.

Is that an invitation?

"Are you..."

She averts her gaze.

"Are you... you know..."

"Am I going to take your virginity?"

"Yes."

My gaze locks on her. "It's yours to give once. Do you want me to do the honors?"

She nods shyly.

"I want words, beautiful. I want to hear you say it."

"Yes, Easton. I want it to be you."

"You're sure about that?"

"I am."

My cock swells.

"To answer your question. No, not tonight I won't."

"You don't want me?"

Her innocence intoxicates me, calls to the most feral depths of me, the part that needs to own her.

Claim her.

Ruin her.

My hand dances up my arm, tracing the crease where her elbow bends.

She lets out a low whimper.

"Oh, Brielle, if you only knew how much I want you."

"Then I don't understand."

Thor was right.

You can smell her chastity.

Fuck.

I bet I could lose myself in the heady scent of her innocent pussy for days.

This is truly a gift from God.

"I won't take that part of you here in this room. I don't care if that's the point of this weekend. It cheapens the whole experience, in my view. When I do fuck you," she shivers at my words, "it'll be because you'll want it as much as I do. You'll be ready. And it will be at my place—somewhere you'll feel safe. Somewhere I can take my time and make it memorable for you."

"Oh. Okay," she nods. "How do I know when I'm ready?"

"There's so much for you to learn and when you do, you'll know," I tell her.

"Are you going to teach me?"

"Do you want that?"

"Very much so," she taunts with a cheeky smile.

"Then we should jump right into lesson number one."

"I hope it's not a hard one."

Not as hard as I am right now.

"Nah. It's as easy as pie."

"Okay."

"Have you ever been kissed, Princess Brielle?"

"No, never."

"That right there is a crying shame. No, scratch that. It's a matter of national security."

"You're hilarious."

I tilt her head, bring my lips beside her ear, and whisper, my hot breath caressing the side of her face as I do, "May I be the first man to kiss you, Princess Brielle?"

"That sounds very f—formal," she stammers.

"You're right. In that case, may I kiss the hell out of you before I fucking die?"

She nods.

I take her lips in a slow and tender kiss before pulling back.

I can't remember the last time I was this gentle with a woman.

Her lips are everything I'd fantasized—soft, plump, delicious. She tastes like a sweet angel before a big bad wolf taints her.

"I love watching your porcelain skin turn pink, and I love knowing I can make you feel this way."

"That was amazing."

"And to think it was a mere prelude. I can't help but wonder what your tongue tastes like," I say. "Is it okay if I kiss you hard?"

She responds by gripping the lapel of my tuxedo jacket.

"That would be a yes?"

"That would be a definite yes."

I fist her hair and tighten my grip as I pull her body against mine. With one hand cupping her jaw, I let out a fierce growl before crashing my lips against hers. My eager tongue parts her lips and slides into her mouth.

It's with urgency that I taste her.

Control her.

And relish how beautifully she surrenders to me with a shiver of delight.

My skin prickles as my tongue explores her mouth, my lips working against hers.

Her earlier shyness has dissipated and it's with a lot more confidence that she returns my kiss.

Jesus Christ.

I respond by ravishing her mouth with such passion, you'd think I'd never kissed a woman in my life.

"I could get used to kissing you like this."

"I'm already there," she says.

Fueled, I take her right hand into mine. I spread our fingers and slide our hands down my body until she's cupping my straining cock. I close my hand over hers allowing her to feel all of me.

"Oh, God," she sobs inside my mouth.

"Brielle."

She swallows nervously. "You're so hard."

"It's because you turn me on. You've got me so worked up, I can't think straight."

"I don't even know how that's possible," she breathes hard.

"Is this the first time you've touched a man?"

Her eyes go wide, her cheeks flushing. “This is the first time I’ve done anything with a man.”

Pride washes over me.

A much larger part that is unwilling to admit that I’m turned on as hell by that revelation.

“You like feeling me?” I tilt my hips forward and grind my cock against her hand.

“Yes. It’s a bit… perverted.”

“It’s supposed to be.”

“Are you as big as Prince Pim?”

I have to coax myself not to laugh at her question.

“Fourteen inches is a monstrosity. A nine-inch cock is a far more respectable offering.”

Her lips tremble.

I won't lie. It ignites something in me.

Her vulnerability is like a drug.

“I want to do bad things to you, beautiful.”

“Don't hold back.”

Her eyelids are heavy, shadowing her pupils.

I move my hand away from my cock. To my surprise she doesn’t move hers.

Good.

My princess is under my spell.

My hands roam over her dress until I find what I’m looking for.

The hiss of her zipper follows as I pull it down. Without being coaxed, Brielle tilts her head back so her neck is exposed as I push her dress down far enough to expose her breasts. A few extra tugs and her tits are on full display.

“Fuck, you’re not wearing a bra,” I marvel.

My cock throbs and pulses at the sight.

“I couldn’t with this design.”

“Thank you, God.”

She laughs.

“Your breasts are magnificent, beautiful.”

“They aren’t too small?”

“Is that insecurity I hear?”

“Maybe.”

She isn't a double D, but she fits nicely into my palms. What more can I ask for?

"They're perfect to me and that's all that matters. You hear me?"

"You're not just saying that?"

"I would never lie to you. And I doubt there's any part of you I wouldn't find less than perfect."

"You have a way with words, Mr. Winchester."

"When it comes to you, they seem to roll off my tongue."

My hand reaches for her breasts. With my eyes boring into hers, I trace circles around her rosy nipples. They pucker with each revolution.

"Oh, Easton."

She sticks her chest out as if silently begging for more.

So I give it to her.

I pinch her nipples rough enough that she yelps.

"Too much?"

"That hurts so good."

I do it again. Harder this time.

"The pain arcs up my spine and down to my—" She doesn't finish her sentence.

"Your what? Say it."

"My lady parts," she says softly.

"That's cute, but I don't understand what you mean." Yeah, I'm pushing her out of her comfort zone.

"You know." She frowns and tilts her head sideways.

"No, I don't."

She frowns harder and purses her lips.

"I'm still stumped," I tell her.

"Down there."

"You mean your pussy?"

She nods shyly.

"Say the word."

She blushes.

"I want to hear that word, Brielle."

"I don't think I can."

"Let me explain something to you. I don't intend on eating your *lady parts*, I plan on ravishing your pussy. You either want to know how that feels, or not. The choice is yours."

She considers me for a few seconds.

"Pussy," she says so softly I barely hear it.

"What was that?"

"Pussy," she repeats louder.

"That wasn't so bad."

"I don't think I've ever said it."

"Tonight is a night of firsts."

"Yes," she smiles.

"So what about your pussy?"

"I love how it feels when you pinch my nipples."

"You're the sexiest dirty girl I've ever had the pleasure of corrupting."

Her eyebrows hit her forehead. "Did you just call me a dirty girl?"

"When we're together, that's what you are, Brielle. Look at you taking pleasure under my hand. Only a dirty girl would do that."

"Oh, God, that's dirty, pun intended."

I grin at her as I lean in to kiss her breasts, my tongue flicking at her nipple. "You don't even know how to spell the word yet."

My mouth waters when I shift my gaze to her pink nipples. Unable to help myself, I pull her right breast into my mouth while cupping her left one with the palm of my hand.

Fuck.

"God, you're fucking exquisite," I breathe against her skin.

"Your mouth…"

Her head lolls back as my tongue laps roughly across her hard nipples.

"I bloody love your mouth."

I chuckle. "I don't think I've ever heard you swear," I say pulling my head back.

"No one has ever done anything like this to me before."

"Sweetheart, you better fasten your seatbelt. This ain't nothing."

Without giving her time to process what I just said, I circle her areola, before my teeth graze at her peaks.

She lets out a heavy sigh.

"You're mine, Brielle," I growl. "Not Haakon's. Not any other fucking prince's. Mine. All fucking mine." I lick harder with each declaration. She moans, a cross between pleasure and agreement.

"Say it," I order.

"Oh, God."

"Wrong answer."

"You're killing me."

"I know. Now give me what I want."

"I'm yours, Easton."

"Good girl. And don't you dare forget it."

CHAPTER 11

Brielle

"I won't," I pant.

My heart pounds, my body shivering at his sweet assault.

I'm so distracted by the feeling of his demanding lips against my breasts, heightened by the prickly brush of his 5 o'clock shadow on my skin, that I don't even know how I managed to speak those simple two words.

When his eyes flash back up to mine, I see something I've never seen before in a man's gaze. I don't even know how to put it into words.

Easton's brown eyes grow darker. Nearly ebony.

More dangerous.

More ominous.

More hypnotizing.

What I read in those sultry eyes makes me tingle from head to toe.

"Good girl," he says again and those rich brown eyes of his make a slow tour of my face.

Oh, God, I wish it were easier to breathe around him.

As Easton studies me, I admire his gorgeous face. He has high cheekbones and a strong jawline, complete with dark stubble that's been carefully groomed. The contrast with his skin serves to highlight how outrageously handsome he is. Think of it as shading on an art drawing you'd expect to find at the Metropolitan Museum of Art in New York.

He narrows his eyes. “Talk to me. What's going through your pretty little head?”

His question catches me off guard.

I don't answer immediately.

“Here's how the game works, Brielle. I ask you a question, you answer it. And oh, don't lie to me.”

“I-I was wondering how it would feel to run my hands over a man's stubble—”

“A man’s?” he grins.

“Yours.”

“Better.”

I smile wide.

“As I was saying, I was wondering what it would be like to feel the roughness against my fingertips and my palms.”

“Do you know where my stubble would feel really good?”

His voice is deep, like it’s coated with a sinful layer of dark chocolate. And don’t get me started on that American accent.

“No.”

“Between your thighs as I kiss your milky skin.”

“Oh, God.”

The words are so raunchy, I close my eyes for a beat.

“That got to you, didn't it?”

I nod shyly.

“Is your pussy dripping wet at the very thought?”

I moan, loudly.

Mother of God.

“Easton, your mouth.”

“We've already established that I have a very dirty mouth.” Something about his playful yet dominant personality makes me want him more than I did before. “Now answer the question.”

I can't bring myself to say the words.

“Brielle,” he presses.

“I-I am.”

That's an understatement.

“Let’s check.”

To my utter amazement, Easton slides his hand under my dress.

"Oh, what do we have here?" he says stroking my pussy over my knickers.

My cheeks flame up so much, I have no doubt they could start a small forest fire.

I open my mouth to respond, but words don't come out.

The sudden sweltering heat in this room, my drenched knickers and the naked desire veiling this man's eyes are a potent combination. So much so, it renders me silent for a few seconds as my brain desperately struggles to catch up with my body.

When his finger slides under my lace underwear, I swear I'm going to die.

"Dear God, dear God, dear God," I chant when he plunges that finger inside my wetness.

It's so filthy.

So wrong.

So debased.

So why in the world does it feel so good?

"Oh, my sweet little Brielle is all sticky."

Your sweet little Brielle is about to combust.

"Tell me, beautiful," he says sliding his finger in and out of me, "do you like what I'm doing to you?"

I have to bite the inside of my mouth to keep from shouting.

This is so unfair. How on earth does he expect me to focus on his question when he's corrupting me this way?

"I'm waiting."

"Yes. It's… it's incredible."

Easton moves closer to me, leaning in as though he wants to speak into my ear. His breath is hot on my neck and cheek. The expensive scent of his cologne is enough to force a groan from deep in the back of my throat.

"Do you pleasure yourself, Brielle, when you're alone?"

I shake my head and then remember his command. "No. Never."

"Are you telling me that your little—"

"Mother of God!" I yell when his finger strokes my clit.

"Brielle, you have a protruding clit," he says.

"A what?"

"You have a large clitoris."

"Is that a deformity? Is something wrong with me? Am I a monster?"

He explodes in laughter.

"You're so adorable." He drops a soft kiss against my lips before saying, "Not at all. It simply means that I'll help you see God faster."

I blink my confusion. "I don't understand."

"You have a larger clit than most women so yours is more sensitive."

"And that's not a bad thing?"

"It's a very good thing for you. Chances are your orgasms will be much more intense."

Easton's words have me gasping, my head spinning.

"Oh, gosh."

"Do you remember that couple going at it in that bedroom?" The glimmer in his brown eyes is potent.

"I do."

"Do you want to know what big daddy was doing to his baby girl?"

My heart does a back flip at his proposition. "God."

His fingertips settle on my jaw before drifting along my throat and down between my breasts. His voice is a thick growl when he says, "No, Brielle. I'm looking for a yes or no."

CHAPTER 12

Easton

My eyes bore into Brielle's as I wait for her answer.

"Yes, I want to know."

"In that case, I think it's time for lesson number two. It'll be easier if we move to the bed." Without giving her a chance to answer, I circle my arms around her waist and ass and lift her up. With a determined step, I walk both of us to the oversized bed.

I drop her to her feet with as much care as if she were a delicate crystal sculpture.

When I step back, she brings her hands up to her breasts.

"Are you hiding your beautiful tits from me?"

"I feel so exposed."

"That's the point. Your breasts are way too magnificent for you to ever hide them from me. You hear me?"

"You think so?"

"Have I not told you that I would never lie to you?"

That does it.

"Okay," she says with a huge smile on her face.

I undo my bowtie, remove it and slide it inside my pocket. I then slip out of my tuxedo jacket and fling it to the side so it lands on a chair in the corner of the room.

"Get out of that dress," I command as I take a seat on the bed. "It's too pretty for me to ruin."

"Okay," she repeats. The tremor in her voice suggests that she's nervous.

With trembling hands, Brielle slides her elegant blue gown down her body until it pools around her ankles.

"Jesus Christ," I mutter.

I groan at the sight of her slim, creamy legs.

She might be braless, but her panties make up for it. Brielle is wearing a pair of all-lace blue high-waisted panties. None of my prior conquests have ever worn anything like that. It's chaste, yet naughty. The sight is a tempting greeting.

"Those are so fucking sexy on you."

"Thank you. They're French."

"Bless the French," I nod amazed.

She laughs.

"Off," I order waving a finger. "If I touch them, I'll rip them to shreds."

My eyes are fixated on her perfectly trimmed triangle of curls as she lowers her panties. My mouth is already watering.

"You're a natural blonde from head to toe."

That elicits a series of giggles from her.

"I've been a blonde my entire life."

"Some things change as you get older," I wink. "Come here."

I grab her behind the neck and with a forceful tug, I bring her lips to mine. She's so short that even in her high heels, I can easily reach her mouth. Our tongues dance together for several beats until I break our kiss and travel down to her neck. She gasps. When I bite and suck the skin there, she purrs. Her hands claw at my shoulders, and I grunt when her fingernails dig into my skin.

"Easton," she whimpers between kisses.

"You're mine," I remind her.

She's such a passionate little virgin.

Groaning into her moans as I kiss her fiercely, I let my hands slide down her back until I cup her ass and squeeze hard.

"I can't wait for you to come all over my thick, throbbing cock, but for tonight, my tongue will have to do."

She jerks. "What? No. I can't do that. That's wrong."

"I thought you said you wanted to know why baby girl was losing her mind in that room."

"I didn't realize that's what big daddy was doing to her. I don't think I can go through with it."

"You'll be singing a different tune soon," I say. "Let's try it and if you really don't like it, I'll stop."

"O-okay."

"Good." *More like fucking amazing.* I pat the mattress next to me. "I want your ass right here," I tell her.

She bends over.

"What are you doing?"

"Removing my heels."

"Have I told you to remove them?"

She knits her eyebrows in confusion. "No, but—"

"Your butt on the bed. The heels stay glued to your feet."

After a moment of hesitation, she does as she's told.

"Slide up."

She obeys like a good little girl.

"Now, spread your legs open, Princess."

Her legs fall open so beautifully.

I lean in and shut my eyes as I inhale. "Fuck, Brielle. Your heady scent is amazing."

"Easton, you keep saying things that are making me dizzy."

"I know."

I reach out and drag a finger from the bottom of her pussy lips all the way to the top. She cries out at the contact.

"You're so incredibly wet and it's all for me."

"This is so erotic," she says.

"I agree," I flash her a languorous smile.

I keep running a finger up and down her pussy with my eyes locked onto hers. Her perky pink nipples harden like pebbles under my heated gaze. Unable to contain myself, I lean in and wrap my lips around her left one.

Goddamn, I love having those in my mouth.

I give her tits the attention they deserve. I'm unwilling to rush things. Once I've had my fill, I kiss her one more time slowly.

"Oh, God, you're sliding off the bed—"

I grin sinking to my knees. "Open wider for me."

Jesus Christ.

I've never seen anything more beautiful in my life.

I move in and inhale her sweet innocent scent once more.

"I'm going to smell you on me well after I'm done ravishing you."

She pants, breathing hard as she looks down at me.

"No more talking. I'm going to make you mine," I warn, my mouth inches from her untouched pussy.

I dart my tongue out and drag it through her slit.

Her entire body stiffens and she attempts to clamp her thighs closed.

"No you don't."

She looks down at me warily.

"Relax, beautiful," I cajole. My powerful hands grab her thighs and push them apart. "I want you to stay like this."

For a few long seconds her heavy breathing is all I can hear in the room.

"Okay," she says before squeezing her eyes shut and dropping her head against the mattress.

"Eyes on me."

"Okay," she repeats.

"Good girl."

I resume my mission.

My tongue slides deep inside her, lapping at her and pushing in and out of her wetness in a frantic cadence.

"Dear God," she sobs.

Her fingers tangle in my hair as my tongue flicks her big clit.

Damn.

That's one little drug I won't be able to do without.

"Jesus, Mary, Joseph and all the saints up above!" she shouts.

I ravish her like a starved wolf, lapping at her eagerly, growling as I drink her juices. Overtaken by this adulterated wantonness, I slide my right hand down to my crotch and stroke my lengthening cock through my pants.

She moans as my tongue pushes even deeper.

When her eyes squeeze shut, I halt all movements.

She lifts her head off the mattress. Her disheveled hair, running mascara and smudged lipstick are the greatest homage to what I'm doing to her.

"Easton," she pants. "You stopped."

"You closed your eyes," I deadpan.

"I'm so sorry. What you're doing to me—"

"I'm bringing you pleasure."

"My body is reacting to you in a way my mind is still struggling to understand."

"Stop thinking. Just feel," I tell her. "Okay?"

"Okay."

I resume devouring her pussy.

The thought that no man has ever had his mouth here is so fucking hot. As I cross the line between pain and pleasure, I slide down the zipper to my pants. My cock throbs hard through my boxer briefs with such insistence you'd think I was trying to fuck the mattress. I close my hand tightly around my cock groaning as I fist it up and down. My tongue continues to swirl over her fat clit, enjoying every revolution. With my free hand, I slide two fingers inside her tight hole and curl them forward stroking her inner walls. Not once do I stop skating my tongue over her clit.

"Oh, sweet Jesus," she hisses.

I've fucked other women with protruding clits before, but nothing like Brielle's. Hers feel like a ripe little cherry against my tongue.

"Oh, God yes," she prays.

I look up and notice to my amazement that her right hand is cupping her tit. The way her pink nipple pokes between her fingers makes the visual even more erotic.

I let go of my cock so I can use both hands to pull her lips apart. It's time to make her fat clit my sole focus.

Fuck, that little gem is amazing.

As her sobs grow more urgent, I fasten my lips around her clit and suck with earnest, trapping it between my lips. She tastes so sweet I can't help but go crazy.

"Oh, oh, oh," she chants.

She's so loud, I wouldn't be surprised if they heard her in the ballroom. The thought does little to slow me down. On the contrary.

The louder she gets, the more I suck and the more my mouth makes lewd noises. I don't even have to tell you how desperate my cock is.

Suddenly, Brielle's hands clamp against my head and her hips start to tilt back and forth.

That's it, beautiful, take what's yours.

My greedy tongue moves faster. I bring both hands up to her breasts. With a slow and steady cadence, I knead her tits enjoying her roundness in my hands. Wanting to give her more, I close my index fingers and thumbs around her nipples and pinch hard.

"Ha!" she gasps. "Oh, my God!"

I lick, suck and fuck Brielle's princess pussy with my mouth adding more and more pressure on her nipples.

"This is so good. Don't stop, Easton."

Not a chance, beautiful.

"Hmmm. Ahhh. Hmmm," she hums.

I'm about to lose my Goddamn mind.

"I can't breathe," she chokes. "God, what's happening to me?"

I pull away from her pussy just long enough to say, "You're nearing the edge. You're about to experience your first orgasm."

"Easton, I—"

"Give it to me, beautiful," I husk. "I want to know what *my* Brielle tastes like when she comes inside my mouth."

I close my mouth over her fat clit and apply just enough pressure to elicit an orgasm from her.

"I'm having a heart attack. Oh God, I'm having a heart attack," she shouts her head turning from left to right against the mattress. Her cascade of blonde locks stick to her sweaty face. What a beautiful sight.

I give a hearty suck, apply pressure with my tongue.

"Easton, Easton, East—"

She explodes.

She writhes and bucks.

And she comes screaming her head off with her juices flooding my mouth.

My brand marking her body.

And my name on her lips.

My Brielle.

Forever untouchable.

Until now.
Until me.

CHAPTER 13

Brielle

My eyes peer open from a groggy sleep.

I turn my head to the right and notice with disappointment that I'm alone in the huge bed.

I try to sit up, but my body won't have it.

It's like I'm completely lethargic.

"Do you always sleep like a rock after a night of never ending orgasms?" I ask myself with a laugh.

"Up you go," I coax myself. I listen to hear if he might be in the shower, but there are no noises coming from the en suite bathroom.

"Easton?" I call out.

No answer.

"Easton are you in the living room?"

Still no answer.

He left me here without saying goodbye?

No way.

Unwilling to fight with my body, I decide to linger in bed a little longer. I pull the covers over my head and close my eyes. I'm just about to fall asleep when I hear the lock click followed by the door opening. I sit up like an arrow. When I do, I forget that I'm as naked as the day I was born.

"Well, good morning to you too, beautiful," Easton grins stepping into the bedroom. His eyes zoom straight to my breasts.

My eyes flick up at him then down to my nakedness. *Bollocks.* "Good morning," I mumble shyly as I fidget with the sheet to cover up.

"Didn't we talk about that last night?" he asks with a raised eyebrow. "Why are you hiding from me?"

It's only now that it hits me. He's still wearing the same trousers as he was last night along with his well-cut white shirt. Since I'm not as overwhelmed as I was last night, I'm able to relish the sight of his bare chest peeking through the loose opening of his shirt.

Definitely hot fitness model material.

"You like what you see, beautiful?"

That arresting smile could make any girl lose her mind.

"I thought you had gone back to your room to change," I say.

"Without telling you?"

I shrug.

"That would be very ungentlemanly of me." His eyes lower to the grip I have on the white sheet.

"I much preferred the view you greeted me with earlier."

"I—" I pause. "I've never slept naked before. I'm really not used to exposing myself like this."

"Seriously?"

I nod. "Where I come from that would be considered obscene—vulgar even. A princess always wears a nightgown to bed."

Easton approaches and sits next to me. He reaches out and grabs the back of my neck forcing my forehead against his. Even early in the morning, his body radiates heat. "*My* princess always sleeps naked and she never, ever tries to hide the tits I love so much—or any other delicious part of her—from me. Got that, beautiful?"

I blush.

Is it wrong to admit that I absolutely love when he says I'm his?

"Got it." With a boost of confidence, I let the sheet slide off my body.

"Much better," he winks. "Give me a minute." He pulls away from me and walks to the window. When he opens the blind, I cover my eyes. *God, that's bright.* "You just got up?"

"Yes."

"If you're still in bed, I gather you didn't read my note?"

"What note?"

Easton drags a chair over. He drops his iPhone on the bed. He then kicks off his shoes, sits down and stretches his long legs out on the bed. "I stuck a note on the bathroom mirror to let you know that I'd be right back."

"I opened my eyes just a few minutes before you walked in."

"No worries. You were tired. I gave you a good workout last night."

I can't help but laugh.

"I just didn't want you to get the wrong impression when you woke up to an empty room. I guess that bombed."

"Thank you for doing that. That's so sweet. Have you been up long?"

"I've been up since five o'clock—professional hazard."

"What time is it now?"

"It's eight thirty. Believe it or not, there are tons of people still roaming around the gardens and the hallways in their party clothes. The place is still buzzing. Seems like a lot of people pulled an all-nighter."

"Wow. So I won't feel too awkward making my way back to my room in my gown."

"Nope. You'll fit right in."

We both laugh.

"How are you feeling this morning, Brielle?"

"Honestly?"

He slides his feet off of the bed and rests his folded arms against his legs. His eyes bore into mine. "Always."

"I feel bad."

Easton's eyebrows knit together. "Why? I made you come four times last night."

"That's the problem."

He frowns again. "You lost me."

"You refused to teach me how to pleasure you. I feel greedy. I took and I didn't give back."

He lets out a boisterous laugh.

"Are you pulling my leg right now?"

"It isn't fair. I should also be allowed to learn how to make you lose your mind… like you did with me."

"So it was good for you?"

"Good doesn't even start to describe it. It was mind-blowing and core-shaking all at the same time."

"I love hearing you say that."

There's so much tenderness in his voice.

"I know I said it last night, but I'm so glad it was you. I'm grateful you overheard our conversation. I doubt I would've taken it this far with any other man."

Easton flashes me a warm smile. "I've wanted you for so long, last night was a dream come true." His revelation leaves me speechless.

He gets off the chair, sits on the mattress and reaches out encircling me in his arms. I drop my head against his muscular chest. It's incredible how safe I feel.

"Part of my job as your lover is to make sure you're taken care of first."

My lover? That sounds so... hot.

"I've never had one of those before."

He explodes in laughter again.

"You're such a breath of fresh air, Brielle."

"Well, I'm not lying. You're my first *lover*."

"I suspect I'll be your first for a lot of things."

"You will," I say shyly. "And to that point, shouldn't I learn how to reciprocate?"

"Well, if you're so keen on it—"

"I am."

"I like your spirit, kiddo," he says. "Let's spend the next two days doing just that."

"We're going to stay locked up in here for the next two days?"

"God, no. I'd never dream of confining you in a small room. Come to Elba with me. It'll be our little oasis."

I pull away from him. "Where?"

"It's a small Italian island off the Tuscany region. I booked a private plane. It's a short flight, so we'll get there and still have time to enjoy the sun and the beach."

"Are you serious?"

"You said you'd love to be Brielle, just a girl, even for a day. I'm giving you two."

"You're amazing!" I cheer jumping into his arms. I cover his face with soft kisses my excitement overflowing.

"You aren't too bad yourself."

"Will it be just the two of us?"

"Almost."

"Are Sienna and Blakely coming?"

"Nah, that's too many people."

"You're not giving me much to go by."

"I didn't want to shake things up too much, so there's a little caveat to your fantasy."

"I'm afraid to ask."

"I booked Officer Pavlova into a nearby hotel. She won't stay with us, but she won't be too far. I want to play it safe. I've already talked to her and she's okay with that."

"How did you pull that off?"

"Yesterday when I talked to her, I made sure to grab her Italian phone number and her room number. This morning, I rang her up and we met for coffee."

"No wonder people say you can move mountains."

"Well, I've been known to make things happen."

"You mean you've made the impossible happen. I never thought I'd be able to get away like this."

"Believe it."

"Wow… just me and my lover," I grin.

He grabs me in his arms and sits me on his lap so forcefully, I yelp. The contact of his trousers against my naked pussy has my eyes rolling in the back of my head. *God.*

"I like that word on your lips."

"Me too," I admit. "Oh shoot."

"What?"

"What about Sienna and Blakely? And your mates? Isn't it wrong to just abandon them like this?"

"I still have to talk to my sister about her brilliant idea to attend this gala." He shakes his head with an eye roll. "I suspect you'll want to speak to your cousin and Sienna. I'm sure they'll have a million questions for you," he chuckles. "As for my buddies, I talked to them after my conversation with your officer. Thor—who was too eager to *train* Sienna—"

"What?" I shout. "I thought you said nothing would happen."

"Nothing did. Thor knows I'd rip his balls off if he tried anything. He simply introduced Sienna to what it really means to be with a caveman. Let's just say that her wrists will be sore for the next few days from the handcuffs."

My eyes widen like saucers. "That sounds fairly hard-core."

"And that was Thor's softer side."

"Oh, God."

"Sienna asked for it."

"That's true," I laugh.

"In any case, Thor and Harlen—who danced up a storm with your cousin last night—are both willing to continue playing babysitter for the next two days. On Monday, they'll fly back to New York on Thor's private jet. Officer Pavlova called in Officer Kerr to watch over your cousin. I'm paying for the flight. She should be here in the next few hours."

He's incredible. I can't believe he's set all this in place while I was playing Sleeping Beauty.

Sienna and Blakely won't believe the night I had.

Wait a minute.

I can't give them the scene-by-scene.

The idea of revealing what I shared with Easton to my two best friends fills me with dread. We've always been quite open with each other, but I'm the first to have had a steamy encounter with a man. Not to mention, how do I share with a woman I consider a sister-friend when the man in question is her big brother?

"Someone is overthinking. What's going on in my Princess' pretty little head?"

"You read me like a book," I complain.

"You're biting on your lower lip. That's a dead giveaway that you're nervous about something."

"What do I tell Sienna and Blakely?"

"As much as you're comfortable with. I'm not ashamed of anything we did last night and I hope it's the same for you."

"It is."

"I'm happy to hear that, beautiful."

I smile.

"I'm just uncertain what to tell Sienna. What are you going to tell her?"

"That I gave in to my long-time infatuation and kissed the girl."

"You will not tell her that," I laugh, swatting his arm.

I expect him to laugh, but his face is dead serious.

"I will. It's the truth. I have no intentions on revealing the intimate details, but I want my sister to know that last night wasn't a one-time thing between us. There's so much more I want from you, Princess Brielle Elise Madeleine Strasberg of Exton."

I'm dumbfounded by his words.

I can't believe a man like Easton Winchester would feel that way about me.

I'm staring at him like a deer caught in headlights when he leans in and captures my mouth into his.

I moan into his kiss.

Alas, he pulls away too quick.

"You look surprised," he says.

"I am."

I'm just about to bring up my parents' certain opposition and this impending dinner—and potential engagement—with Prince Haakon, but I don't. If I can live out two days of bliss, why would I ruin it for myself?

"Then let me show you how I feel about you."

I nod. "Okay."

"Good," he smiles. I'm taken aback by the vulnerability behind his boyish grin. "I booked a private villa at the Capodimonte Resort," he says. "They know me well there. I often book the entire hotel annexed to the villas for meetings with prospective European investors. It's secluded, opulent and complete with our own private swimming pool."

"That sounds amazing, but I didn't bring a swimsuit or beachwear."

"I'm in the same boat. We have plenty of time to go shopping before liftoff."

"Wow," I shake my head amazed. "You laugh in the face of obstacles."

"Damn right."

Does that include Prince Haakon and my mum?

"We're really doing this," I say.

"We are, beautiful," he says with steadfastness. "I would've done anything to make this come true for you."

My heart tugs in a way that's completely unfamiliar to me and tears sting my eyes. I plaster a brave smile on my face before hiding it in the crook of his neck.

This is such a joyful moment, I don't want him to read my sadness.

CHAPTER 14

Brielle

"Yippee!" I shout with my hands above my head.

I'm so elated that I'm standing up in the convertible luxury sports car Easton is driving like a racecar champion.

Yup, I've thrown caution to the wind.

For the next two days I can be me.

I can experience exciting things without worrying about being reprimanded for wanting to be a lowly commoner.

I don't have to adhere to any stringent code of royal conduct other than what my morals dictate.

Take that, Mummy.

"Elba, here we come!" I shout louder.

Easton smiles up at me.

"We've barely landed and already you can't contain yourself."

"Do you blame me?"

"That smile on your face is why I did this," Easton says.

My God, this man is wonderful.

The flight across Italy from one coast to the other was magnificent. In a little over an hour, we went from overlooking the Adriatic Sea to gazing at the Tyrrhenian Sea. Italy has always been one of my favorite destinations and now I have an extra reason for loving this country so much.

After a short jaunt from Venice and a boat ride from Piombino to Portoferraio, we're driving to our villa. Officer Pavlova is right behind us in a rented Range Rover. Easton hired a driver for her since this is also her first time on the island.

Officer Pavlova was waiting for us when we arrived at the private jet. As I boarded, she winked at me. I thought it was something in her eye, but later on when Easton was in the loo, she quietly approached me and said, *"You deserve the better man. Not the one with the title, lineage, or blueblood. The one that will make you his queen, no matter what."* I was dumbfounded. She's usually so stoic. It's sobering to see that even she knows that Principe Haakon is a big mistake.

Telling my two best friends about this new chapter in my life was one of the scariest things I've done in a long time.

Once Lilo was over the shock, she hugged the living daylights out of me, telling me how happy she was that I was boldly willing to go after the guy I've been crushing over for so long.

My stomach was tied up in knots before I spoke to Sienna. I was so afraid of how she'd react. Imagine my relief when she started crying tears of joy, saying that now we're *real* sister-friends.

"We're going so fast!" I shout again.

My palms are facing the wind. My hair is flying furiously behind me.

I feel so free.

So unburdened.

So unshackled.

What a treat.

"What did you expect, baby? I've got the pedal to the metal of an Aston Martin V8 Vantage," Easton winks shifting gears.

I sit back down and buckle up my seatbelt.

"In Belzer, the Mercedes Benz is the car of choice for the Royal Family," I say, combing my hair with my fingers before pulling an elastic around it. "Daddy broke with convention when he upgraded to a Maserati Quattroporte earlier this year. Mum accused him of going through a midlife crisis. He told her that if she keeps talking his ear off, he'd upgrade her for a newer model and he won't try to hide the affair like he has done in the past. Of course, neither of them knew I overheard them arguing. Again."

Easton's head whips around to the right so he can stare at me. "Shit. Your parents have a horrible relationship."

"They do."

"Did they ever love each other or even like each other at the beginning?"

"I wonder. There are so many scars on both sides, but neither of them is willing to see it. So instead, they've made driving each other mad an Olympic sport."

"That's not the kind of life you want," Easton says in a grave voice.

"I don't know if—"

"No, listen to me, Brielle. The stories about the three inept princes were amusing, but we're talking about your future here. Your happiness. Pardon me for saying this, but your parents are a terrible example of what consists of a good marriage."

"I know." *Believe me I do.*

"My parents were so much in love, it was ridiculous. Sienna blocked out a lot of things after they were killed in that tragic car accident—as you know, she was only seven when we lost them—but I was already eighteen so I was lucky enough to witness it. Dad would bring Mom flowers just because. And Valentine's Day was a veritable treasure hunt. Dad would hide tons of gifts all over the house and Sienna and I would help Mom find them. Mom always cried like a baby when she found the last one. Dad bought the same number of gifts as the years they were married."

"Valentine's Day is a day Mum's claws come out with a vengeance. No matter what you say or do, she jumps on you like an enraged tiger and she chews you up. The staff dreads that day. Daddy always finds a reason to be on a business trip."

"Jesus Christ."

"Tell me about it."

"I'm not sure if it's in the cards for all of us to experience the love my parents had, but your parents' relationship is the type that kills people slowly by eating them alive."

His words are a wake-up call.

"I don't want that, but I don't have the strength to stand up to them. Mum especially. Daddy isn't in a rush to marry me off. He laughed at my mum's failed attempts telling her I was young—to which, Mum reminded him she was eighteen when she was forced to marry a man she didn't choose. That's usually when he shuts up and goes hide somewhere in the manor."

"Find the strength." His tone is firm. "You have to fight this, Brielle!"

CHAPTER 15

Easton

"What a perfect meal to end a perfect day," Brielle says popping the last bite of the veal dish into her mouth.

"I agree."

After Officer Pavlova did the rounds and felt comfortable that our nine-bedroom villa was secure, she was off to her hotel. The Range Rover had barely driven off and Brielle and I quickly changed and ran to the pool. We spent the afternoon swimming, talking, kissing and lounging. The snack we ate upon our arrival is long gone. This sumptuous dinner hits the spot nicely.

"From the arancini served in a creamy béchamel sauce, to the saltimbocca, this is a meal I'll remember for a long time."

The chefs at the Capodimonte Resort don't joke around when it comes to food.

"Those stuffed rice balls we had as an appetizer were addicting. The veal and prosciutto dish was equally delicious," I agree.

"Between the wine, the food, the idyllic temperature and the exceptional lover"—her gray eyes glimmer—"I might never want to leave Elba," she says.

"If that's what you want, Princess, you know I'll make it happen."

She flashes me a side-glance as if she's actually considering my offer.

"Don't tempt me," she finally says after a few long seconds.

If I wanted to lock her up and prevent her from ever running away from me, I would do it without hesitation, but I'm an alpha, not a backward thinking brute. I want this to come from her. I don't want to force it out of her. She'll get there.

"More wine?" I ask.

"Yes, please." I reach for the bottle of Morellino di Scansano and top up her glass before serving myself.

"A whole day of *far niente*. What a dream."

"And we get to chill out—and make out—all day tomorrow as well."

"I'll drink to that… especially to the latter," she winks. "C*incin!*" she cheers.

"C*incin!"* I parrot.

We both take a long sip of our bold red wine.

"This is truly exceptional."

"I couldn't agree with you more. Italians, like the French, know their wine."

"Americans are formidable wine producers," she argues.

"We are. Cali rocks," I laugh. "Ready for gelato?"

She gives me a one-shoulder shrug.

"Is that a yes or no?"

"Let's wait for dessert. Is that okay?"

"Your wish is my command, Your Grace." I even add a little head nod, but to my surprise she doesn't laugh.

I lean back against my seat and study her. Everything about her expression suggests she's dying to ask me a question.

"What's on your mind, beautiful?"

"I don't know if I should say it."

I drop my glass in front of me and get up. I circle the table, pull out a chair and place it right next to her before taking a seat.

"Remember, we don't lie to each other."

"I'm not—"

"Holding back is the same thing," I set her straight.

"It's a little bold," she warns.

"I can handle bold."

"You made me a promise," she says.

"Can you refresh my memory?"

"I love the plans you have for tomorrow, however I think it's a shame to waste an entire evening when we could perfect my education."

"I don't follow."

"You promised that you'd teach me how to pleasure you. Although it's been an outstanding day and truth be told, kissing is becoming one of my favorite activities, there's still so much I'm in the dark about. That's just wrong."

"Is this the wine talking or Brielle?"

"They do call it liquid courage. It's a little bit of both I think."

"I'll let it slide this time, but we don't want to make it a habit. If you want something from me, ask. No matter how naughty, I'll give it to you. Don't hide behind booze to get what you want. Got that, beautiful?"

"Yes, sir."

"Now about perfecting your education—"

"I'm all ears," she says excitedly.

Poor little princess she has no idea where I'm going with this.

"It's only fair that I make your sweet little pussy tremble and drip again before we further your awakening."

"Oh, God. Can I survive your mouth on me again?"

"You really don't have a choice. We're here for another day. What do you think I'll be doing between eating, drinking and swimming?"

She laughs.

I get up.

"Are we going inside?"

"Your delectable body is for my eyes only. Although it's unlikely anyone will catch us out here because of all of the foliage surrounding the property, I'm not taking any chances."

"Okayyyy."

Brielle shrieks as I suddenly lean down and grab her waist. By the time I hoist her up and, throw her over my shoulder, she's laughing hysterically.

"Oh my God, what are you doing?"

"You seem to be in a rush to learn, this is a much faster way to travel," I chuckle.

When we get back inside the villa, I slip her off my shoulder and place her on her feet. Barefooted, Brielle is a small little thing—barely taller than my sister.

I bend my knees until we're at eye level. "I want to pervert you," I groan, pulling her tight. "Say yes," I command, my fingers caressing her blonde hair. I tug gently on her mane, making her gasp as I expose her neck. "Tell me you want me to shower you with as much pleasure as humanly possible." My teeth and my lips brush against the soft skin of her slender neck and she shivers.

"God yes."

I meet her hooded gaze. "I can push you way out of your comfort zone."

"Whatever you want, Easton," she whimpers before lowering her gaze.

The motion causes her long blonde hair to fall in her face. Before she's able to brush it away, I beat her to it. With care, I tuck the strands behind her ears, relishing in how soft they feel between my fingers. Fisting that hair while driving my hard cock inside her tight pussy as I take her from behind will be surreal.

"Fuck," I breathe out, adjusting myself.

"What's wrong?"

"*Whatever you want, Easton.* Those are powerful words to a man."

"I mean it. I love how you make me feel."

"You're such a good little princess."

I pull her tight and kiss her fiercely—like I haven't spent most of the day tasting her lips. She melts into me moaning her approval as she opens her mouth to greet my tongue. I cup her beautiful face as I deepen the kiss. After a few long, heated minutes, I slowly pull away.

"No," she protests.

"Less than twenty-four hours later and I find myself with a greedy little vixen," I tease. "I'm not done with you yet." I pause looking around the living room for the perfect prop for this lesson. "Let's use the big armchair near the window," I suggest.

She scrunches her nose. "How is that going to work?"

"Let's get this—" I pause. "What is that thing called again?"

"A beach caftan," she says.

"Let's get that sundress off you."

She laughs.

She pulls the dress over her head and lets it fall at her feet.

Damn.

Earlier she was wearing a sexy purple bikini. She must've changed after her shower. The orange one she's wearing now is goddamn dangerous.

"Off," I command with a finger wave.

"My God you're demanding," she complains with a huge smile.

Watching her strip out of her bikini is more erotic than I would've ever thought. Brielle is still oblivious to how sexy she really is. When she grows into herself, she'll be a force to be reckoned with.

My eyes brush up the length of her body before resting on her blonde triangle of curls.

What a fucking masterpiece.

I could see her in all her glory a thousand times and my mouth would water a thousand times.

Her naked body. Her smooth silky skin. Her pert little nipples, her perfect pink areola and of course the piece de resistance, her huge sensitive clit that loves to be sucked and licked.

"Aren't you going to get undressed?" she asks. "I haven't seen you naked yet."

I move closer and reach between her legs. "All in good time."

"Oh, God," she gasps holding onto my forearms as my fingers begin their exploration.

"It's about you for now. Are you ready for your lesson?"

"Yes," she mewls.

"Good. I want you to use me for your pleasure."

"I don't even know what that means."

"Last night I pulled those orgasms out of you. I want you to understand how it feels when you chase your own climax. I want you to climb on that big chair and place your knees on each armrest. Head facing the windows and butt facing me."

She looks positively petrified.

"What a lewd position."

"Exactly."

She doesn't budge.

"You get on that chair or we can go back out in the garden and keep talking. You want me to make you come or you want me to entertain you with another story? The choice is yours."

Cautiously, she moves towards the chair, climbs on it and assumes the position. When I gave her my command, I didn't expect I'd end up having a goddamn heart attack. The sight of Brielle opened so temptingly is what a guy's wet dreams are made of.

With a shake of the head, I snap back to reality and step behind her. I reach out and let my hands slide over her bare ass. She trembles and moans. The sound travels straight to my crotch, making my cock ache for more. *Not yet.* Languorously, I caress her in slow circles, teasing her supple skin. Without warning, I pull my right hand back and lift it above my head.

Smack.

"Ha!" she exclaims. "Did you just spank me?"

"Nah."

Slap, slap, slap, slap.

"That was a spanking," I set her straight.

My large imprint marks her ass as mine.

I never thought that being her first *everything* would induce such a feral surcharge, but it does.

"Oh God," she whimpers. "I felt the vibration all the way to my clit."

"Did you just talk dirty, Princess?" My hand rubs the redness away.

She turns her head so our eyes meet. "I think I just did," she bites on her lower lip.

"Keep it up. I love your dirty mouth."

"Is that the extent of our lesson?" she asks.

"Is that disappointment I hear in your voice?"

"Maybe."

"You want more?"

"Well, you were the one advocating you'd take me to the dark side. That was hardly a stroll in Wonderland."

"Oh, now you're really going to get it," I warn. "Eyes up front," I command.

I kneel in front of her and sit on the floor so that my back leans against the seat of the large leather chair. I slide down until my head is resting on the seat. I lift my head up just enough to bring my nose to her so that I can inhale her heady scent. *Thank you God for this incredible gift.* I close my eyes and moan at the heavenly smell of her innocent pink pussy.

All mine.

"I'm ready for you, my princess," I announce when I open my eyes again. She looks down at me from between her parted legs. Her bewilderment is amusing. "I'm going to stick my tongue out. It's your job to use it."

"East—"

"Brielle, don't make me repeat myself."

"I don't know if I can do this."

"A few strokes will have you changing your mind."

Although my tongue is ready for her, she doesn't lower her hips enough so that her clit makes contact with it.

"I'm not going to touch you. This is all your doing."

I present my tongue again.

She hesitates at first, but slowly she lowers her hips until I feel her fat little gem against my tongue.

Fuck.

She barely moves at first, but as the seconds tick away, her hips start to sway back and forth.

Good girl.

I keep things tame at first by simply letting her slide against my tongue. Soon, she picks up the pace.

I do the same.

My tongue swirls around her big clit and her legs start to tremble.

Now we're getting somewhere.

She switches from a back and forth movement to gyrating her hips in a circular motion.

I give her more and she lets out a long moan of pleasure.

"Mmmmm," I offer as a response.

"That feels really, really good," she purrs.

Her juices run freely into my mouth. They're sweet, slick and abundant—a reminder of my own painful need. It's punishment not to play with my hungry cock, but I know that the slightest touch would be my undoing.

My mouth is more demanding around her clit now. I lick it over, and over, and over again. With each lick, her fat clit swells sending me over the edge. The sensation against my tongue is fucking amazing.

"Dear God." Her loud plea echoes in the room.

Without being coaxed, Brielle starts bouncing her clit off of my tongue.

"Ou. Ou. Ou."

Jesus Christ.

My cadence grows at the same frantic rate as her bouncing. The lewd sounds my mouth makes as I try to keep up with her only serve to turn me on even more.

She lowers her hips nearly suffocating me with her pussy against my face.

That's what I'm talking about.

I lap at her with even more fervor.

I know I said I wouldn't touch her, but my cock is desperate for something a lot edgier. I bring my hand up.

"Easton," she cries out as two thick fingers slowly spread her wet pussy wide and slip inside to scoop her juices. I move my finger from her pussy to her forbidden hole and slide right in without an invitation. I don't go very far because she clamps down on me.

"Wha-what are you doing?" she stammers between heavy breaths.

"I'm making it good for you."

"But, that's .... that's... I don't even know where to begin," she pants.

"Do you trust me?"

She nods slowly. "Yes."

"That didn't sound convincing, beautiful."

"I trust you, Easton."

"Better."

"But that part is so—"

"It's a hidden pocket of pleasure. If it doesn't feel good, tell me and I'll remove my finger."

I fully expect her to demand that I stop defiling her this way, but instead, her gaze slides back up to the window.

Wow.

With extreme care, I start sliding my finger in and out of her hole.

"Oh, God," she moans.

Brielle's ass is impossibly tight. I can't imagine lasting long when I fuck her there.

Feeling the familiar tug at my balls, I know I need to make her come. I latch on and trap her between my lips.

"Yes, yes, yes. Oh, yes."

I suck her fat clit hard while pushing the finger that's trapped inside her ass downwards forcing her to give me what I want.

And she does.

"I'm coming, I'm coming, I'm—"

Her ass clenches so tight around my finger, I feel it all the way to my balls. The jolt causes me to lose an embarrassing amount of pre-cum.

"Mmmm," I hum in response. No way am I removing my mouth from her pussy.

"Oh. Easton. Yes." Each word is followed by her clenching her ass cheeks hard.

Fuck.

"Good Lord!" Brielle continues praying.

That must've been a hell of an orgasm.

Her wails and the way her body trembles under my hands as I lick up her juices, has me nearly coming in my sport shorts.

The more I make her climax, the more she tastes like a woman on my tongue.

"My God," she pants.

"Are you okay?" I ask before giving her pussy one last kiss.

"I'm not sure yet. I feel drunk and dizzy."

"Let's move on to the next lesson. That should sober you up."

"I'm not drunk on wine, I'm drunk on your mouth, Easton."

"I love hearing you say that."

"You have a formidable tongue, Mr. Winchester."

"I try my best, Your Grace," I smile. "Now, beautiful, we slide right into the next lesson."

"Don't I get a respite?"

I chuckle. "My princess needs a little nap?"

She laughs.

"You've been so eager to please me. After that little performance, I'm horny as hell. In other words, it's my turn."

"Okay, okay," she rolls her eyes. "I've been begging for it after all."

"Yes, you have. Get off the chair."

She does and stands in front of me.

Her cheeks are so rosy, her nipples are still on alert and her pussy is so swollen. *What a vision.* I just want to put my mouth on her again and make her come a second, third and fourth time. That will have to be part of a later program because my cock demands attention.

I stand up.

"On your knees."

She just stares at me.

It's then that I realize that given her innocence she wouldn't know what's coming.

"I assume you've never seen a man's cock before?"

"Never—" She stops. She swallows. Her cheeks turn pink. "Well, not until yesterday."

I frown.

"I caught a glimpse of Big Daddy's."

I let my head fall back and roar in laughter.

"So this is the first cock you'll see up close and personal?"

"Yes."

My cock bulges.

"That means my cock will be the first one you suck?"

Her eyes widen like saucers. She opens her mouth to say something, but nothing comes out.

I chuckle.

"Your next lesson starts now, beautiful."

"Oh, gosh."

"On your knees, Princess." I repeat.

Her eyes shift to the left then to the right.

"Now."

With a whimper, she slowly lowers herself down to her knees.

"I want you to lower my sports shorts and release my cock," I order.

Her eyelashes bat furiously, but she doesn't comply.

My jaw twitches.

"Tsk. Do you want me to put you on my knees and spank you again so I get what I want?"

She gasps. "You wouldn't."

"Try me."

She swallows hard before closing her eyes for a beat. I'm just about to make due on my promise when she opens her eyes again. She lifts her hands up and hooks them around the elastic on my shorts. With a slow motion, she lowers them. Since I'm commando, my long cock snaps against my stomach.

"Oh," she says.

I grin as I watch her eyes zoom in on my huge cock.

"You're so…" She pauses. She shakes her head and even frowns. For a minute, I think something is troubling her, but I'm dead wrong. "Your body is surreal. It's true it's the first time I've seen a man naked, but I've seen my fair share of smoking hot fitness models on social media." That makes me laugh. "You're absolutely gorgeous. It's unfair to other men to look this good."

Wow. "Thank you," I smile wide. I take care of myself, but hearing the compliment coming from her does something to me.

She looks up at me and something flashes in her eyes I can't read.

"What is it?" I ask.

"I'm not sure how to say it."

"Don't overthink it. I'll never judge you."

"I'm not sure why it makes me feel so incredibly sexy to be down on my knees looking up at you this way. Crazy, right?"

Her revelation startles me.

I've got myself a good little submissive.

"That could be a long topic to cover, but suffice to say that you're coming into your own. And that's a good thing."

She nods her approval.

I don't need more words from her. The glimmer in her eyes says it all.

“Ready for more?”

“Yes.”

“Open your mouth, Princess,” I say. My voice edges on the dark side. I’m impossibly hard.

“You’re going to—” she finishes her sentence by pointing to her mouth.

“Hence what I meant by my cock will be the first one you suck on.”

“I haven't got the slightest how this works. What if I screw up?” she asks worried.

I extend my hand to her cheek and caress it tenderly. “I'll guide you. I know I said it's my turn, but you'll enjoy it too. Trust me. We'll take it slow,” I promise her.

“Okay.”

“Good.”

I fist my cock and present it to her like an offering.

“Are you ready to part those pretty little lips for me?”

CHAPTER 16

Brielle

I moan, melting at Easton's filthy command.

I fix my eyes on his huge cock. His veins are popping like crazy. *Wow.* It's so powerful and hungry. Angry even. It's impossible to look away. His rock-hard cock pulses and juts out from under his sculptured abs. I can feel his eyes on me. Watching me. I look up at him in awe.

"You're enjoying the show?" he asks.

"It's so impressive. You're so impressive." My voice is so low. So raw. I barely recognize it myself.

"Thank you," he smiles. "Do you want to see a little more before you take my cock into your mouth?"

I nod. "Yes."

My whole body shivers with anticipation when he starts to stroke his cock slowly. A thick white milky moisture beads at the tip and trickles down over his swollen head and veiny cock.

"What's that?" I ask.

My God I sound so innocent.

"It's pre-cum. You do this to me, Brielle, because I want you so damn much."

I'm taken aback.

"I want to come inside your mouth." I feel his words all the way down to my clit. "Will you let me?" His brown eyes emanate such heat.

"I'm not sure I fully understand what that implies, but I don't think there's anything I could refuse you," I admit.

"Now you know how I feel about you."

To hear a man who could have any woman he wants—with far more experience than me—say that, melts my insides. I won't lie. It's such an ego boost.

He squats, fists my hair and brings my lips crushing into his. Our kiss ignites my soul. *My God.* When he pulls away, I grunt my dissatisfaction.

"I'll want to kiss you again after I come inside your mouth," he says before standing back up.

"Okay." I feel like a lovestruck teenager. I just can't get enough of him.

"Open up, beautiful," he commands.

There, on my knees, I part my lips for him.

I do it without shame. I'm far too excited to finally learn how to pleasure him to bother.

I want this. I really want this.

Easton slides his cock inside my mouth, and I moan at the saltiness of his pre-cum against my tongue. He's so big and so wide, his size stretches my lips as he fills my mouth. When he pushes his hips forward a little more, I turn my eyes down, too intrigued by his sliding cock.

"Eyes up!"

I look up at him on his command.

"Are you okay?"

I nod.

"Can I go deeper?"

I nod again.

He feeds me several more inches of his cock.

He's so hot, hard and demanding. When his cock pulses against my tongue, I moan around him.

"More?"

"Hmmm."

"Fuck, that feels good," he grunts swinging his hips back and plunging his cock into my mouth in one single stroke. He hits the back of my throat with such force, I gag.

Dear God.

"Sorry, beautiful. I'm a little too excited."

I pull away from his cock.

"I didn't see that coming, but I'll survive," I smile.

"That's my girl. Let's try this again."

When he thrusts inside my mouth, this time the gag doesn't surprise me as much.

"I'm going to let loose now," he warns.

I place my hands against his chiseled stomach readying myself for what comes next. I didn't expect his abs to feel this way under my touch. Everything about him says he's a real man.

Easton fists my hair and thrusts again. With more resolve this time. He makes true to his promise and doesn't hold back. He's unwavering. Punishing even. The way he dominates my mouth sets my entire body ablaze.

"What a fucking amazing view."

I lift my eyes towards his face.

"All mine to enjoy," he says with a side-smile.

I moan into his cock. I never tire of hearing him say that I'm his.

"Let's take things to the next level," he announces. "I'm going to pull out so that only my tip remains inside your mouth. I want you to swirl your tongue around my tip." I hesitate. "As if you were licking a lollipop."

Got it.

To my surprise, this is incredibly enjoyable.

"Poke your tongue inside my hole."

So much of his saltiness comes gushing in my mouth when I do.

"That's it, scoop up my cum."

I go at it with gusto.

"Oh, fuck yeah. You have an eager little mouth. I like that."

That fuels me into giving him more.

"The rest of my cock needs attention. Bob your head back and forth so your mouth is sliding up and down my cock. When you get to my tip, tighten your lips around it."

I feel a little awkward at first. After a few minutes, I find my stride.

"Take me in deeper," he commands as he starts rocking his hips back and forth.

And I do.

"That's it. Suck on that big cock, you dirty girl."

"Hmmm," I moan, closing my lips around his tip and suck, suck, suck.

"Are you ignoring my balls?"

His balls?

God.

What am I supposed to do with them?

"Cup them. Feel their weight in your hand."

I slide my hand down and close it over his balls before tightening my grip. "Gentle," he growls. "We don't want to hurt the family jewels, do we?" he chuckles. I soften my grip. "Much better. Caress them. Kiss them. Make love to them."

That sounds positively dirty. Then again, I am sucking on this man's cock. This is as filthy as it gets.

To my surprise, kissing his big balls is so erotic. I love how they pulsate against my lips.

"Shift the attention back to my cock," he orders.

I move my head back up, wrap my lips around his cock and bob my head back and forth. This time, the motion doesn't feel so awkward and my fear of choking around his cock has somewhat subsided.

"Faster!" Easton commands.

I inhale his cock and bob my head back and forth with more resolve.

"You're such a fucking dirty princess. You're eating my thick cock like a starved woman," he chuckles. Easton leans into me and pinches my left nipple so hard, I squeal as the intoxicating current travels down to my throbbing clit. "Look at your tits bounce," he says. "I can't wait to fuck them and mark them with my cum. Every part of you belongs to me. Don't ever forget it."

I answer with a whimper.

"Jesus, you're going for it."

I suck his cock at a furious pace. The more I suck, the more my juices drip between my thighs.

"Oh, shit, Brielle. You're making me lose my fucking mind."

Your dirty talk is doing the same to me.

I can only sob in response.

"I can't tell you how hard it makes me when you let out those helpless whimpers."

Against my will, I do it again. It's as if I have no control whatsoever over myself.

"I love watching you worship my cock. I could get used to having you on your knees like this. I might need a daily dosage."

"Mm-hmm," I nod.

"You want that too?" I hear the surprise in his voice.

With his cock buried deep inside my mouth, I hum an eager moan.

"You're so fucking mine."

I bob my head back and forth, delirious from his words.

"You ready for my cum, you royal dirty girl?"

God. Is it normal for me to relish how he calls me his dirty girl?

"I asked you a question. Are you ready to swallow my load?"

"Mm-hmm," I nod.

"Good girl."

I pull my head back slightly and close my lips around the tip of his cock like he told me before and I squeeze tight.

"Fuck!" Easton roars. My eyes fly up just in time to catch his eyes roll to the back of his head. The ecstasy I read on his face leaves me in awe. *My God, I never thought I could make a man react this way.* "Jesus Christ." He clamps the back of my head with both hands as he christens my mouth with a savage cry. "Oh, Brielle, baby." His massive, throbbing length spurts warm cum down my throat in a hot gush as pleasure ripples through me like a wave. To my surprise, his excitement causes my pussy to clench. Without even thinking, I squeeze my legs together and tilt my hips back and forth a few times. *That feels amaz— Ah!* Before I know it, I'm freefalling.

"Oh, God," I mumble around his cock. The buildup between my legs is overwhelming and oh so delicious. "Easton!" I cry letting his cock drop out of my mouth. "I'm—"

Mother of God.

My whole body shakes as a powerful climax takes over me. It's so strong, I have to hold onto him not to tumble and fall.

“I got you,” he says gripping my arms. “Hey, beautiful.”

I don’t answer. I’m still trying to catch my breath from that core-shaking orgasm.

“That was amazing.”

It was.

“You did good.”

I did?

“You really impressed me. I didn’t think you would swallow.”

Wow.

“You’re okay?”

I answer with something that’s a cross between a nod and a headshake.

“Talk to me.”

I meet his gaze. “I'm okay. I think.” My voice comes out in a faint whisper.

“You missed a few drops.” Easton reaches out and wipes the trail of cum dripping down my chin. “Lick it off my finger,” he commands.

He rewards me with a victorious smile when I do.

“That was pretty intense for you, wasn’t it?”

Embarrassment washes over me and I avert my gaze.

“No. Eyes on me. What just happened?”

I lock eyes with him again, but I don't answer.

“Brielle.”

“I didn’t know… I didn’t...” I pause.

“I’m listening.”

“I didn’t need to touch my clit.”

His eyes widen as realization sets in.

“Did you just come on your own?”

My cheeks flame up.

He leans down and scoops me up into his arms. Instinctively, I interlace my legs around his waist spreading the juices of my wet pussy against his stomach.”

“You’re dripping, baby.”

To hide my discomfort, I wrap my arms around his shoulders and snuggle my face into the crook of his neck.

“Did you just come?” he repeats.

"I did," I mumble against his skin.

"Look at me, Brielle."

It's a struggle for me to hold his gaze.

"You just squeezed your legs together, trapping your fat clit between your thighs with my cock buried deep inside your mouth while you were on your knees in front of me and you came?"

The amazement in his voice surprises me.

I nod.

"Fuck that's hot."

"I didn't even know my body could do that." I let out a shy laugh.

"You're perfect."

No one's ever said that to me before. Not even my parents.

"You're an incredible man. I feel lucky you chose me."

"Nah, you chose me."

Easton kisses me deeply and with his cum still coating my mouth I return his kiss with as much fervor. He sucks my tongue, stealing every one of my sobs and whimpers, swallowing them with greed. *God, I love how he does that.*

Too soon, he abandons my lips. "You'll have an out-of-body experience when you come all over my face while my eager tongue is mercilessly toying with your clit until you climax. Something tells me you'll enjoy a sixty-nine. A lot."

"Oh." His promise sends a tide of sensations running straight down to my clit like a shockwave.

"That'll be a lesson for another day. Come on, my dirty princess needs a shower. I'm going to wash every single part of you and then I'll inspect every delicious bit of your body with my tongue to make sure I did a thorough job. This might take a while," he grins.

CHAPTER 17

Brielle

It's a second lazy day for Easton and I in paradise.

Once Officer Pavlova was done with her morning inspection, we hit the pool. We lounged there until lunchtime. Between catnaps, I managed a few lengths of the pool. Easton just watched over me while reading his iPad. He chuckled every time I woke up.

We enjoyed another scrumptious lunch until I was too full to walk. After which, Easton suggested we play tourist for the rest of the afternoon. Just as we were leaving, Lilo and Sienna both texted me to make sure I was enjoying myself. Understandably, Sienna didn't ask too many questions. Lilo on the other hand, didn't hold back. Her texts were a bit more explicit. Her parting words had me in stitches laughing,

Enjoy the heck out of that hunk of a man. He's way more intriguing and a whole lot sexier than royal men. Do we have Americans living in Belzer? As delicious as Harlen is, I think he sees me as a kid sister. Not good. Anyhoo. Got to run, love. Si and I are going shoe shopping.

Easton patiently waited for me to finish with my furious text marathon with my best friends. Once I was done, we hopped behind the wheel of the Aston Martin to explore Elba with my officer in tow in the Range Rover behind us.

What a phenomenal day. It went by way too fast. I can't believe the sun is already setting.

"You weren't kidding when you said barbecue is your forte," I say putting another morsel of moist lamb into my mouth.

Easton asked the chef to marinate the meat and prepare the rest of the meal. He wanted to own the barbecue. That, he did.

"I think it's a rite of passage for all American men. I think there's a law that stipulates that if you don't master the craft by the time you're eighteen, you have to move to Canada or Mexico. I'd never be able to live north of the Niagara Falls and my body doesn't agree with Mexican food, so I had to learn," he chuckles.

"Oh my God, that's funny."

"I'm joking. Partially. I love Mexican. For us Winchesters, it's a family thing. My grandfather took barbecuing very seriously. My father made it a religion. I'm just following in their footsteps," he explains.

"Is it true that your grandfather wanted to name you after sexy Scott Eastwood's father?"

Easton chuckles. "Yes. My grandfather was obsessed with old cowboy and western movies. His favorite actor was Clint Eastwood."

"Sienna is completely in love with Scott."

"Don't remind me. She thinks I have the power to arrange a date with him. I'm good, but I'm not that good. First off, I don't have many contacts in that circle and second off, he's getting up there in age. He's too old for her."

"Says the guy who's eleven years older than I am."

"Ouch," he shakes his head. "Touché. But she's my baby sister. I'm entitled to be protective of her."

"Not to mention that Scott doesn't come across as the caveman type she's so desperately seeking," I say.

"I'm not going to even touch that one. I still don't know where Sienna gets those crazy ideas from."

"She's obsessed with the men of Anders. She thinks they're the hottest royals on the planet."

"Moving right along." I laugh. "To answer your question, yes Grandpa Ford, wanted to name me Eastwood. His first choice was Remington because it's the brand of a gun, just like our last name—"

"Winchester is a beautiful city south of London."

"Yeah, but Grandpa Ford never travelled abroad. I doubt he made the connection."

"I see."

"Anyways, Mom put her foot down on both selections. Dad came up with Easton as an alternative. He wanted a name like his—Hugh—that wouldn't have a nickname attached to it. Mom approved. So did Grandpa. When Sienna came along, Grandpa Ford wanted my parents to name her, Beretta—again keeping with the guns and westerns theme. Mom nearly had a heart attack. My father had to step in before Mom declared World War III on her father-in-law. My parents settled for a soft and feminine name, but Mom said that the minute Sienna came out and wailed in the delivery room, she knew she'd be a spitfire."

"She wasn't wrong. Sienna is the most spirited woman I know."

"You mean she's a handful." We both laugh. "I knew becoming my sister's surrogate parent would turn out to be challenging, but that girl has a way of testing my patience," he rolls his eyes. "Still, I'm a sucker. She's my sister and I love her."

"You did a phenomenal job. She's an incredible woman."

"Thank you for saying that."

"It must've been hard for you at such a young age. It's too bad you didn't have any other family members left to help."

"Ah. Sienna never told you about Scrooge Philip and Asshole Michael Timmins."

I shake my head. "No, she's never talked about them."

"My parents' will stipulated that Uncle Philip would become our guardian if anything were to happen to them. Dad was an only child and both of his parents had passed when Sienna was still a kid. Mom had been estranged from her older brother for years—we might have visited him three times—but he was the only family left. I had just turned eighteen at the time and I knew nothing about parenting, so I didn't protest. We left most of our possessions in rented storage. My parents had made arrangements for that."

"I can't imagine how devastating it must've been for you."

"More than words can say, Brielle. Losing my parents was the most debilitating experience of my life. It was pain like I had never endured before—granted I had a loving childhood, so what did I know about pain? Their death would have paralyzed me had it not been for the fact that I was all Sienna had left. I had to be strong for her."

"I didn't grow up in a tight knit family and love isn't a word we use, but I wasn't uprooted from my home at the tender age of seven. Thank God Sienna had you."

"Thank God we had each other." His words are solemn.

"What happened to your family home or were you renting an apartment?"

"My parents were careful planners. It was nearly a science with them. They had made all the arrangements with a leasing company in Portland to rent out the house until I turned twenty-five. Then, I could decide to keep it or sell it. Other than what I needed for university, the rest of the money from their life insurance was also locked until I turned twenty-five. My only valuable possessions were my laptop and a very long list of domain names my father co-owned."

"Domain names?"

"Yeah. It'll make sense in a minute. With a broken heart, we left the safety of Portland, Maine behind and we moved in with Uncle Philip in Queens, New York. The asshole made it very clear from day one that he wasn't happy to see us at his doorstep. He also made a point to let me know that rent was due on the first of every month and it was my responsibility for buying the food Sienna and I ate—he'd break my knuckles if he caught me eating *his* food. I also had to pay a portion of the electricity and water bill."

"Are you serious?"

He nods. "Needless to say, Uncle Philip and I didn't get along. My cousin Matthew and I barely talked to each other even though he was only a year older. On top of that, I was having a hard time adjusting to a new city and a new school. It was way worse for Sienna. I didn't feel we had any other choice at the time. My father was in computer engineering and I've been tinkering with computers and codes since I was this high. Although I had a mildly successful Internet business since I was sixteen, I didn't think it could sustain us. All that changed when Michael Timmins—my cousin Matthew's nineteen-year-old best friend—started taking interest in Sienna. The way he looked at her from the first encounter, gave me the creeps. I told my uncle about it, he scoffed and laughed. He told me that if he had to choose, it would be Michael since he barely knew us and despised my father. I figured Michael's fascination would pass—"

"But it didn't," I say.

Easton arches an eyebrow. That simple gesture says so much. "He didn't stop eyeing her, but you can't kill a person for looking at your sister the wrong way."

"Ah!"

"Joke. I did want to harm him, but refrained. So Sienna and I settled into this routine. Eight months after we moved to Queens, I came back from school to the dingy basement we called home and found Sienna in tears. She was shaking like a leaf. I asked her what had happened, but she couldn't even answer. She was so distraught. I asked her if someone had hurt her at school. She shook her head, but didn't offer much more. After a few minutes of coaxing, she finally opened up."

"Michael did something to her?"

Easton's nostrils flare and his eyes narrow to menacing slivers. "He grabbed her hand and placed it on his crotch promising her that he'd be her first and it would happen before she turned eight. Sienna didn't understand it all, but she was scared shitless. She knew that wasn't supposed to happen."

"That's horrible," I exclaim. "What a despicable human being. He assaulted and threatened her."

"Damn right the asswipe did. I was seeing red. The next day when I saw Michael, I rearranged his face with my fist. It was ugly. You'd think that my uncle would stand up for us given what Michael had done. Not a chance. He told me that my cunt of a sister and I were no longer welcome in the shithole he called his home because I had hurt someone who was like a son to him."

"What a callous idiot."

"Amongst other things," Easton sneers. "Needless to say, I packed our things and got the hell out of there."

"I can imagine how traumatized Sienna must've been."

"She was. For years. That's why you're hearing the story from me, not her."

Poor Si. I shake my head in disbelief. "Did you return to Maine?"

"No. I had finally managed to enroll in university and I saw the benefits of remaining in New York."

"So where did you go?"

"Adam Goldblum was the closest I had to a friend back then. We had finished a few assignments at his home so I knew where he lived. Unannounced, I showed up at his door flanked by my frightened little sister and two big duffel bags containing our worldly possessions. God was watching over us. Adam's grandmother lived in an enormous and luxurious home in the Upper West Side she refused to leave. Her husband of forty years had passed away two months prior, and she wasn't going anywhere—no matter how much her kids begged. Adam's family was worried about her and I desperately needed a place to stay. Bubbe Goldblum became our honorary grandmother for four years. She was incredibly caring and exactly what Sienna needed. Our presence also allowed her to move her attention away from her grief and her family could let out a sigh of relief because she was no longer living alone. It was a win-win for everybody."

"That's amazing!"

"It was. Since I had the peace of mind of knowing that my sister was safe, I was able to finish my university degree and take my software company to the next level. Adam and I have even partnered up on a few lucrative projects. Everything was going great and then just like that," Easton snaps his fingers, "our lives completely changed."

"What do you mean?"

"Do you remember the domain names I was talking about?"

"Yes."

"Along with being a computer engineer, my dad was a geek. I mean he ate tech stuff up. That's why early on he scooped up as many domain names as he could. Back then no one cared about them. And he was able to nab crazy domains like diet.com, blinds.com, weightloss.com and benz.com, to name a few, effortlessly. And he bought all the other country codes for top-level domains too—think diet.co.uk, and so on. They were worthless when he bought them, but he always made me promise to never sell them until the price was right. I didn't know what that meant, but I agreed. Then big corporations started to discover the Internet. Once they realized many of the coveted domains belonged to me, they started waving money in my face. Big fucking money. Unimaginable sums. That's how I made my first million before I turned twenty-one. It's been a joyride ever since."

"Wow. Your father was a forward-thinker."

"I'm really sad he didn't live to profit from his foresight."

"It's a shame," I agree. "Is Bubbe Goldblum still alive?"

"That feisty woman is alive and kicking," Easton laughs. "After I struck gold, I hinted at the fact that I should buy a place for Sienna and I. Bubbe Goldblum put her foot down. She insisted that my sister needed a female presence. That's why we ended up living with her that long. When we finally parted, it was to heart-wrenching goodbyes. Partially because, it was time to move on and I was getting ready to send Sienna to boarding school in the UK. I knew I'd miss our Bubbe. We owe her so much."

"Do you still keep in touch?"

"Bubbe got tired of winter. Her and three other girlfriends moved to Miami. They live in a luxury penthouse and they're having the time of their lives. One of her friend's sons is down there and keeps an eye on the crazy foursome. If I'm in Miami, I always drop by for a big hug."

"What a woman. What a story! You're truly a trailblazer." I let out a heavy sigh and allow my shoulders to slump.

Easton reaches for my hand. "Why the long face, beautiful?"

"I'm just born into money. It isn't very original."

"There's nothing wrong with that," he smiles.

"I admire you. You took what your father left you and built on it. And now you're sitting at the top of an enviable empire. On top of that, you took care of your sister."

"I'll always be there for her to protect her and take care of her. Well, until she finds her caveman."

I didn't see that one coming and I explode in laughter.

"After that point, she'll be his responsibility. That said, given how successful her own food blog is, I doubt she'll need a man."

"So you've been a parent for a third of your life," I say.

He ponders on my words.

"I guess you're right," he nods.

"You must be tired of being a parent."

I do my best to hold his gaze, but the warmth creeping up my cheeks forces me to avert my gaze.

"Don't look away." Just like that my eyes are back on him. "What do you mean?"

I find the courage to ask, "Do you still want kids of your own?"

It's a silly question really considering my mother's plans, but for some inexplicable reason, I have to know.

"I bypassed the diaper changes, late-night feeds, teething and terrible twos, but even with all my travels, I was there for most of the ups and downs of growing up—and those pesky teen years weren't a walk in the park. I'm well trained now. Why put all of that priceless education to waste?"

I laugh. "I love the way you put things."

"To answer your question, I do want kids of my own. I want a lot of them." His rich chocolate eyes bore into mine when he says that. For a few beats, neither of us speaks. We just stare at each other. "What about you?" He squeezes my hand a little harder.

His question catches me off guard.

"Me?" I even point at my chest.

"Yeah, you. Do you see any other gorgeous princesses sitting across from me?" I giggle. I know. It's not very royal-like, but Easton makes me feel as lighthearted as a child.

"As you know, I'm an only child. Had it not been for Lilo, I'd be this ill-adjusted human being." Easton laughs. "When you're a royal and you're already isolated, it's easier to have allies. I wouldn't want my child to be alone facing the world. I want to have a big family. I want tons of little feet running around me."

And I want it to be with a loving husband.

Easton's eyes burn into mine with a smoldering glare. "Interesting."

"That I want loads of babies?"

"No. That we want the same thing."

I blush so hard I have to bring the back of my hand against my forehead.

"It seems we do."

Pity we can't do anything about it.

CHAPTER 18

Easton

Brielle's questions about fatherhood flares this ancient, throbbing part of me that craves the idea of planting my seed inside her and watching her belly swell with my baby.

My half royal baby.

Our child.

I haven't even felt her pussy yet, but now, it's all I can think about.

Crazy, huh?

A couple of days ago, she was still an unattainable beauty I lusted over and now she's sitting across from me in nothing more than an orange tank top—yup, she's braless—and a pair of super-short denim shorts. I spent most of last night with my mouth on her, unless her lips were wrapped around my cock. She's a very quick learner. And the intimacy between us surprises me. I'm not one of those guys who run away from relationships like the plague. I've had a few solid ones in the past, but none strong enough to make me want to see my girl pregnant.

It's like life is playing this fucked up game on me with Brielle.

In any other situation, this baby scenario could be possible, but I'm no king or even a prince. Sure my colossal fortune tips into the multi-billions of dollars and my empire spans globally, but there's still so much missing.

I have no aristocratic blood running through my veins.

No army.

No subjects.

No noble lineage.

No crown.

And no throne.

I know there's so much I could offer Brielle. I'm just not sure any of it would meet her parents' expectations.

Why does this even cross my mind? I haven't got a clue. That's the thing with her, she makes me want things I never have in the past.

"I can't believe tomorrow is our last day in this little pocket of paradise." She changes subjects. "I don't want it to end."

"It doesn't have to."

She shakes her head and lets out a sad laugh. "All good things must come to an end."

"That's not how it works in my world," I say. "Do you have anything pressing in New York on Monday?"

"No. This is the last stretch for me at school. I'm working on a few dissertations and I was planning on updating my blog. Nothing exciting."

"Then stay here with me for another day."

"We can do that?"

"We can do anything you want."

"Then let's stay," she says excitedly.

"Great! I'll let the hotel know and make a few phone calls so my team covers for me. I'll also let Officer Pavlova know. Once that's done, I'm all yours again. That's if you still want me," I wink.

"Well, I don't think my education is nearly as perfected as you promised. It's best if we keep working on it," she says nonchalantly.

"You know I have to punish you for that dare."

Her eyes widen.

"Don't worry. Punishing you will only heighten your pleasure."

"Then by all means, don't let me stop you," she says. "In fact, punish me hard."

She has no idea what she's playing with. Brielle is the first woman I've taken things slow with in a very long time. Cindy Toffler was the last virgin I was with. That was twelve years ago. I'm usually far more unrepentant with my lovers.

I cup her face and fix my eyes on hers. "You're too keen for your own good."

"You're offering more pleasure. I'd be a fool to refuse."

Cheeky little princess.

"You're right." I pause. "It's time to push you way out of your comfort zone."

"You say that as if that's not what we've been doing for the last two days."

"Perhaps, but if you're begging for more, I'll give it to you in spades… and I'll give it to you hard."

I watch the blush blossom on her cheeks.

"Are you still in?" I challenge.

Her eyes are veiled with lust. "Yes," she purrs in response. "I'm all in."

My balls contract like little pendulums.

I told you she's a quick learner.

With every hour we spend together, she sheds her innocent persona and steps into the woman she was always meant to be.

"I want you to see what I see," I say.

"I don't understand."

"You're gorgeous when you're all made up. You're almost angelic when you wake up in the morning, but when you come… you look like a goddess. I want you to see why I'm so addicted to making you come."

"How in the world are going to make that happen?"

"Do you trust me?"

"Absolutely."

"Good." I stand up. "Let's go inside." I extend my hand to her and she takes it.

"Oh, is it a repeat of yesterday?" she asks as I drag her to the master bedroom.

"Nah. It would be too boring to do the same thing two days in a row."

"I could argue with that."

I laugh. "You liked yesterday?"

"Like is putting it mildly."

I stop right in front of the bathroom, turn around and place my hands on her shoulders. “Well, you’re going to love today's lesson.”

“Ohhh!”

“Come on, in you go,” I tilt my head towards the bathroom.

“We’re going to take a shower first?”

“Not yet. I need to get you dirty first.”

She narrows her eyes and purses her lips. She considers me for a beat. I do nothing to rush her. Eventually, she walks inside the bathroom. I turn on the bright light and follow right behind her.

“I want you to stand before the mirror,” I tell her.

She flashes me a cocky smile and strolls all the way to the counter. *God bless short-shorts.* She leans against it and crosses her arms over her chest. Her tits bulge underneath her tank top when she does that.

“No, beautiful. I want you to face the mirror.”

Her eyes widen and her mouth gapes open. “You can't be serious!”

“Is someone changing their tune?” The mockery in my voice is unmistakable.

“You want me to look at myself while you have your mouth on me?”

“Not my mouth. My cock.”

“You're going to take me? I thought you said—”

“At my place. Where it’s safe. When you're ready,” I finish her sentence. “I don't have to take your virginity for us to have a lot of kinky fun.”

“Kinky?”

I nod.

“I thought we were going for naughty. I don't know if I can handle kinky.”

“For God’s sake, woman, I came gushing in the back of your throat half a dozen times last night. Kinky shouldn’t worry you. On the contrary.”

“I guess the training wheels are off?”

“You better believe it.”

“If all this translates to pleasure, I'm not even sure why I'm arguing,” she says turning around.

I take a long step and stand behind her.

I meet her gaze in the mirror and we both smile at each other. The veil of lust I read in her eyes matches mine. I run slow hands down her shoulders and around to her breasts, taking their weight and kneading them over her tank top.

"I love your hands on me," she says leaning back and allowing her head to drop against my chest.

I place a soft kiss on her forehead. "And I love touching you. Look at that, another thing we have in common."

She laughs.

"Look in the mirror, Brielle. What do you see?"

"A princess and her American lover."

I lean down and bite her earlobe hard.

"Ah," she moans

"That's right. You're playing the game so well," I whisper before rewarding her. I suck her ear's tender flesh into my mouth and soothe it with my tongue. "And guess what?" I ask.

"What?"

"Your lover is eager to please."

Brielle holds her breath as my fingers slide underneath her tank top to find her nipples. My fingers feather over them first, then flick, pinch and tug them until they're so hard underneath my touch. I growl.

"God," she hisses.

"You're so fucking responsive."

"This is so sexy," she says.

"It's sexy as hell," I correct her.

For a few long seconds she watches me make love to her tits. The fact that her lower lip is trapped between her teeth only heightens the moment. The more she melts into my arms, the more my cock swells.

"I want you naked." Without waiting for an answer, I pull her tank top over her head and throw it over my shoulder. "There's too much covering your pussy," I tell her.

"You're so eager."

"I already warned you, Princess. It's understandable. Look at what I'm about to ravish."

She lowers her gaze.

"No. Your eyes are on me the whole time."

"Okay," she nods.

I undo the zipper on her shorts and slide them—and her panties—down her hips. They pool around her ankles with a soft rustle against the marble floor.

"Step out of them and kick them to the side."

On an exhale, her shorts land inside the bin.

"Who's the eager one now?"

"You're rubbing off on me," she says.

Good one.

Unrushed, I allow my gaze to sweep down her body, over her taut stomach, her hips, her slender thighs, until it lands on the blonde triangle of curls between her legs.

"Your eyes are burning my skin," she exhales.

I respond with a chuckle.

I keep one hand busy on her tits while the other travels down her stomach. As I close in on her pussy, she groans, arching her back, causing her naked ass to brush against me.

"What do you want, Princess?"

My eyes lower to follow the path of my hand.

"Yes."

I tilt my hips forward and grind my hard cock into her back. She lets out a strange little sound when I do it again.

"I'm sorry, Princess, but I don't think you understood my question. Do I need to—"

"Your fingers."

"But my fingers are already on you."

"Lower."

"How much lower?"

"Between my lips."

"Which set of lips?"

Yeah, I know I'm being a bastard.

She swallows hard. "My pussy lips."

"Fuck, I love hearing you talk dirty." I let go of her breast and let my hand slide down to her ass cheeks. "What if I wanted to touch you here?"

She squirms.

I leave the warmth of her pussy and clamp that hand across her stomach to hold her in place. “Where are you going?”

“Easton.”

“That's not a good answer to my question. Didn’t you like my finger there yesterday when you came?”

“That’s the problem.”

“I don't understand.”

“I think I liked it too much.”

“That's not a problem. That's a blessing. You have an amazing ass. I’ve been fantasizing about it for months. Yesterday's action only makes me want more.”

“How-how much more?” she stammers.

I don't answer her immediately. Instead, my fingers trail down.

“I want to come here.” I say tracing the cleft between her ass cheeks.

Rubbing her tight asshole sends an electric current straight down my spine.

She gasps at my touch and her knees go weak.

“You're going to take me there before you take my virginity?”

“Technically, your ass is also virgin,” I remind her. “I'm not going to fuck your ass, I just want to play with it.”

She watches in the mirror with wide eyes as I plunge my middle finger inside my mouth and move it back to her ass. Slowly, I slide it inside her tightness. She balls both hands into fists and slams them against the marble counter right before clenching her asshole around my finger.

“Oh, God, Easton.”

“Jesus,” I growl.

Her eyelids drift shut as she pushes backward onto my touch.

“Eyes on me,” I command.

I don't have to repeat myself twice.

“I fucking love your ass. Let me soil you there.”

She offers a shy nod.

“Was that a yes?”

“Yes.”

“Yes, what?”

“Soil me.”

"Those are beautiful words."

I withdraw my finger. Over her groan of protest, I say, "I need to get undressed for this."

"Oh, okay."

My t-shirt hits the floor followed by my sports shorts. Just like yesterday, I'm commando.

"Both hands on the counter," I tell her.

She obeys bracing her palms on the marble counter as she leans in close to the mirror.

The position is a gift. I lick my lips at the sight of her fully exposed.

She stares at my cock in the mirror.

I wink at her when her gaze meets mine.

I move to stand behind her again. "Eager to feel my cock?"

"Would it be wrong to say yes?"

"Not at all, beautiful," I smile.

"I still can't get over the transformation of your cock when it goes from flaccid to erect."

There's a charming innocence behind her words. I still have to wrap my head around the fact that I'm her first in every sense of the word.

"It isn't magic. It's all you. Can you feel what you do to me?" I drag the tip of my cock down her backside until I'm nestled between her thighs. "How much I want you? That's why my cock is this hard. And from the feel of it, you want me too," I say sliding my cock greedily between her slick lips.

"Honestly, it seems like I'm constantly wet when I'm around you."

"That's the way it's supposed to be."

"I like this. I like—"

"Finish that sentence," I demand.

"I like us."

"Same here, beautiful."

She offers a radiant smile.

I force one finger inside her pussy. Then a second. And pump in and out a few times. "I love how your tits sway every time I do this."

"Yes," she pants slamming her ass back against my hand, meeting with my thrust.

"Ready for more?"

She shudders and lets out a moan. "I am."

I'm just about to scoop up her juices to spread her slickness over my length when from the corner of my eye, I notice a much better option. I ease my fingers out, and with one last caress, I remove my hand from between her legs.

"Don't stop—"

"Patience," I scold.

I reach for the glass bottle with the intricate design that intrigued me so much when I saw it yesterday. I remove the lid and pour a generous amount of oil into the palm of my hand.

"Now we're really going to have some fun."

I rub my palms together and lather the oil all over her back, work my way down to her ass and in between her cheeks.

"Oh, that feels amazing. I could get used to this."

So could I.

Brielle stands before me with her blonde hair disheveled, without a trace of makeup, with her arms braced on the counter, her legs parted, purring like a little kitten under my touch.

A man can't ask for much more.

I savor this moment.

I take my sweet time watching her wiggle under my hands.

"You're so fucking beautiful."

"I'm the lucky one," she says locking eyes with me. I frown. "I hit the jackpot with my first lover. I could've ended up with an average bloke, but no, God gave me an Adonis. Chiseled to perfection, broad-shouldered and strong like an ox. Those washboard abs?" She lowers her gaze. "Wow." I chuckle. "He has a face to make angels weep. He's patient, kind and caring. And then there's the other side… the naughty lover who does things to my body I never even dreamt of. I'm sure many women have fallen for his charm, but he's here with me." She pauses. "It's good to be me."

Her confession leaves me in awe. At the same time, that first part upsets me. I don't want to be her first lover. I want to be her only lover.

Pushing away the thought, I say, "That's a tall order to live up to."

"I reckon you're already there. You have nothing to worry about," she gives me a slow suggestive smile.

There's a quiet confidence in her now. One that wasn't there before I had my tongue on her pussy.

"In that case, let's turn up the heat," I tell her.

I massage her cheeks as I slide my cock between her slit. I tilt my hips back and forth rubbing my hard cock against her. The combination of her body warmth and the slickness of the oil is indescribably heady.

Needing more, I fist my cock and rub it forcefully from her hole to her clit.

I nearly stop breathing.

This is the first time I've felt a woman's pussy bare against my cock. I've come to relish the weight of her clit against my tongue. I never expected it would feel this fucking amazing against my cock. The sensation of her fat nob flirting with my tip is insane.

"Press that royal ass against me, beautiful."

She does as she's told.

When she turns around to look at where our bodies meet, I nearly lose my shit.

"Oh, Easton."

"Uh-huh?"

"Uh-huh."

I lean forward, cup her chin and turn her head a little more so that I can dominate her mouth. We kiss passionately until we're both panting loudly.

Damn, I can't get enough of her.

"Give me your hand," I say as I pull away. She hesitates. "I'll hold you steady."

"Okay."

"This is all for you," I tell her forcing her hand to circle my cock.

"I love your cock," she says.

I lean forward and bite her shoulder.

"Say it again."

"I love, love, love your cock, Easton."

"Mmmm."

"And I love how hot it feels inside my mouth—especially your head. It's such a turn on to feel your veins throb."

"Jesus, baby, you're going to make me come too fast."

"Are you saying no more dirty talking?"

"Not unless it comes from me."

We both laugh.

I move her hand to the side and she places it back on the counter.

"Time for more."

She nods.

I press her cheeks together adding more pressure against my cock and I place my thumbs strategically to hold it in place as I glide over her ass fast and furious. It's so hedonistic, you'd think I was fucking her.

Brielle's mouth falls open and her skin flushes pink as I grind between her cheeks. The next few long seconds, I tease her with my wide, smooth tip. Greedily, I circle her puckered hole over and over again spreading my pre-cum there. I can't wait to stretch her and fill her. I have no doubt she'll have to call the paramedics the day I'm able to shoot my load up her royal ass.

She purses her lips together to suppress a sob as she arches her back and pushes back against me, trapping my cock between our oiled and sweaty bodies. Her skin glistens. As much as I want nothing more than to lean forward and lick every bead of sweat off her body, I don't want to break my stride.

"Tell me what you see when you look at yourself."

"Oh, God, Easton."

Slap.

"That doesn't answer my question."

"Mmmm."

"Answer me."

Her sob turns into a tortured moan.

Slap. Slap. Slap.

If I don't see her smile with content.

My princess likes it a little rough.

"Let's try this again. What do you see?"

"A person I don't recognize."

"I reckon," I borrow her word and she smiles wide, "she's always been inside you. So who is that person?"

"An uninhibited woman chasing her orgasms with her eyes on her lover."

"Well, she's not chasing her orgasm yet."

"Yes she is," she affirms.

"No, beautiful," I set her straight. "I have a formidable cock, but rubbing it between your ass cheeks will do squat for your clit."

"You're going to touch me?"

"Touch, what?"

We've come too far for her to still be shy about her body or certain words.

"My clit," she says in a soft voice.

"Speak up."

"My clit."

I shake my head. "No. You're going to do it yourself."

"Wh-what?"

"I don't want uninhibited. That's still too noble. I want you to leave your virtue at the door. I want you promiscuous. Lewd. Indecent."

"We've never done that before."

"I know. Time for another lesson." Without giving her a chance to think, I slide her hand from the counter and interlace it with mine. I travel between her legs in a slow sensuous motion.

"Ah!"

Her whole body jerks.

"You feel that?" She nods. "That's your clit."

"It's so hard."

"It's engorged with blood. I want to believe that I do that to you."

"You know you do."

"Good answer."

"God." Her eyes roll to the back of her head when I move my hand.

"It's only when you rub that little coil of tension that you lose your fucking mind. Got that, beautiful?"

"Yes."

"Together!"

"Together," she affirms.

I grab her shoulder with my left hand to control this ride. I tilt my hips forward and start gyrating in wild movements as I guide her hand between her legs. Our fingers skate over her clit. It's one thing to feel her juices dripping against my hand, but knowing that she's also feeling her slickness at the same time as I do is so fucking hot.

"Mother of God."

She took the words right out of my mouth.

"This is so good. So, so, so good," she chants.

I pick up the pace.

My ruthless fingers dance up, down, and around her clit. I play hardball circling, grazing, flirting, but never giving her the heavenly relief of full contact. Meanwhile my cock grows impatient as more of my pre-cum leaks while she squirms for more. Given her half-lidded eyes, I'm willing to bet that the tight bundle of nerves at the center of her universe is begging to explode.

"My cock belongs here," I growl.

"Claim me," she pants.

"Fuck, Brielle."

I do her cheeks good.

Every time my cock makes contact with her body, I have to coax myself to maintain the course.

This is so fucking hedonistic.

"My God, that sound is going to drive me crazy. It's so bloody sexy."

The slap of our bodies slamming together punctuates each one of her words.

A swear?

I love her foul mouth!

"There's nothing quite like the sound of two bodies grinding together seeking pleasure."

"Our bodies."

"Our bodies," I repeat.

Her arm trembles from the strain of holding herself up. I let go of my cock and wrap my arm high around her torso—right underneath her heaving breasts. The sensation of her tits brushing against my arm is pure filth. I tug her hips back a little more, forcing her small frame into a deeper bend, and I lose myself between her cheeks thrusting like a mad man.

I rub against her at a frantic pace. The agony of not being able to bury my cock deep inside her wetness splinters into a million points of sharp, shimmering pleasure.

Jesus Christ.

Her head lolls backward to rest on my shoulder. She lets out a string of inarticulate groans.

"Eyes on me," I remind her.

"You're a bloody tyrant," she throws at me.

My eyebrows hit my forehead. "You're finding your voice, beautiful. I like that."

She responds with a lazy smile.

I resume my mission.

My cadence is unrepentant now. I rub against her like I wouldn't be satisfied until her cheeks molded perfectly to my cock.

"Easton," she moans, and my name on her lips is dripping with sex.

She gets on her tiptoes. My cock jerks. The graceful arch of her back forces her tits to hang. The visual is mouthwatering. Her waist is impossibly narrow under my strong grip and the way her slim thighs tremble contracts my balls so nicely.

The woman staring back at me could grace the cover of Sports Illustrated Swimsuit Issue, but she's mine.

For now anyways.

My princess.

"I'm so close. I need—"

"Have I told my royal dirty girl she could come?"

The harshness of my question surprises her. It surprises even me.

She blinks furiously at me. "Err… No."

I have to bite off a smile at the slightly agonized expression on her face.

"But—"

"You should at least ask me nicely. That's what good little dirty girls do."

"Please, let me come."

As much as I want to prolong this and torture her a little more, the pull at my balls lets me know that there's only one way out for me.

My head tips back as my fingers dig into her hips. *Christ.* Every muscle in my body is taut.

"I want to hear you scream my name as you come. Can you do that?"

"Yes."

"Come with me, Brielle."

I press my hand against hers.

"Oh! I-I'm—" She can't even catch her breath to finish that sentence.

"Take your pleasure from me!" I bark.

"Easton. Oh, Easton."

Good girl.

I stop fighting for control and give in.

"Jesus Christ, Brielle!" I roar.

I come hard and fast, my balls slapping off her skin with every thrust and I mark her royal ass with my cum.

"Dear God," she groans again as her body trembles.

"Shit," I growl willing my legs to stop shaking as the last of my cum splatters up her back.

Her body goes limp in my hands and she collapses forward, dropping her head against the mirror.

"Are you okay?" I ask.

"Thank you, thank you, thank you," she chants as her body trembles even more.

I suspect the second and third waves of her climactic peak are rumbling through her.

No, thank you.

I'm far too mesmerized and spent to say anything.

CHAPTER 19

Brielle

I teeter between two worlds unwilling to let go of my dream. Of course, Easton is the leading man. And of course it's naughty. He's opened a veritable Pandora's box. I never imagined it could be this mind-blowing to be intimate with a man. If he can make me lose my senses straddled over an armchair with his mouth on me or make me come so hard bent over a counter—that it took me at least five minutes to catch my breath—I can only imagine what it will be like when he takes me and makes me fully his.

Easton.

My lover.

How am I going to learn to live without you?

I want so much more of him—the man who rescued me at a ball and whisked me away to a private island. The one who helped me become a woman.

The more I think of the handsome hunk sleeping next to me, the more turned on I am.

Slowly, I spread my legs open and I catch my breath as I slide my hand down my stomach until I reach my pussy. I'm so wet. And so warm.

God.

I delve my fingers into my aching pussy and tease myself a few times.

Yes.

My middle finger rolls in languorous circles over my clit—just like Easton taught me.

Mmmm.

I flash back to our smoking hot interlude in the bathroom yesterday and I have to bite off a moan.

That was so hot.

It's funny. He demanded that I keep my eyes on him, but he didn't have to. It was nearly impossible for me to move my gaze away from his gorgeous face.

Easton.

I love how you corrupt me.

Now I'm rubbing myself thinking of the raw carnal desire I read in Easton's eyes.

That was for me.

His kisses are mine.

His touch is for me.

His dirty talking is all for me.

His cum. For me as well.

My finger skates furiously over my throbbing clit.

Without him, I would never have had the courage to pleasure myself like this.

He's entirely responsible for the education of an innocent princess.

Ah!

My legs squeeze tight together and my middle finger blurs over my clit as I think of all the things I have yet to learn.

I want him to show me.

I want him to keep calling me his little royal dirty girl.

I want him to keep dragging me to the dark side.

Ohhhh!

The first soul-racking convulsion rumbles through me and I bite forcefully against my lower lip as I come undone.

Dear God.

My body is still shaking when another climactic wave washes over me.

Ah!

My heart pounds so hard, it's ridiculous.

I can't believe what I just did.

I catch my breath and open my eyes.

With my fingers still trapped inside my dripping pussy, I turn my head against the pillow to admire the man who's been pushing me to do dirty, inappropriate things.

Thank you.

He's fully exposed. My eyes caress the length of his muscular body and suddenly, a wicked thought crosses my mind.

I lift my head up. The clock flashes five a.m.

I remove my hands from my pussy and with great caution, I slide my body closer to his. His masculine smell invades my senses, and I close my eyes for a beat, wanting to take it all in.

He's too perfect to be true.

It's the crack of dawn and I can't wait for him to wake up.

What have I become?

Embracing the royal vixen in me, I go after what I want.

The heat spreads through my body as I lean forward, gently grab his cock and wrap my lips around it.

"Mmmm," he hums.

I tighten my grip around his hardening cock and bob my head up and down.

"Oh, yeah, beautiful."

His words fuel me.

I go at it with more fervor.

My eagerness betrays me.

Shoot.

I gag when his tip hits the back of my throat.

"Fuck, Brielle, you're hungry, baby."

I don't slow down.

"Wait. Give me a minute. You can't attack me like this," he says gently pushing me away.

With a small laugh, I pull away from his cock, a wide smile stretching my lips.

"Well, good morning to you too, Princess."

"Good morning."

He lifts his upper body, folds his right arm and drops his head against it. "Such a dirty little girl."

"I thought that was a good thing."

He reaches out and strokes my long hair. "And she's mouthy too. A few days with me and you're now this cheeky vamp?"

"I want you," I offer as an answer.

"Wow. No waffling. You just put it out there."

"You keep telling me to speak my mind."

"You're a great listener and a very quick learner."

"Thank you, sir," I beam.

"What exactly does Princess Brielle want from her lover this morning?"

"She wants him to play with her."

"That's tempting. Am I to understand that she wants me to play with her royal pussy?"

"Yes."

"I guess it's already been a few hours. That little pussy must be feeling pretty lonely?"

I offer him an expression that's somewhat a cross between a grimace and a grin.

"What was that?"

"Nothing."

Since it's no longer pitch black in the room, I can see his brown eyes squinting at me.

"What. Was. That?"

"I—" I bite my lip, blushing furiously and looking away.

Okay, so I guess I still have a little shyness left in me.

"Tell me," he says.

"My royal pussy isn't that lonely."

"Then why did you just wake me up?"

"Because your touch is very different from mine."

He sits up in bed, grabs me by the waist, lifts me up and places me between his parted legs. "What are you saying?"

"I'm saying that it should be your turn touching me."

"As in you've already touched yourself?" he asks carefully.

I nod.

"Words!"

"I touched myself, thinking of you touching me."

"When?"

"Just before I woke you up."

"No fucking way."

"I might be addicted to the sublime sensation of coming," I admit.

Easton growls.

"You're fucking perfect," he says.

He brushes my hair off my face before crushing his lips to mine. He groans, grabbing my jaw and kissing me fiercely. I return his ardor. As we lose ourselves in this passionate heat, his cock throbs hard between my legs. I place my hands around his neck and pull myself towards his body so that my pussy is right on top of his hard cock.

"Don't do that, Princess. You're going to get us in trouble."

"I just want to know what it feels like."

"*You* woke up on the naughty side of the bed this morning."

"I think I already admitted to that," I laugh.

"Yes, you have." An impressed grin teases his lips. "So what are we going to do about it?"

"I vote to explore things further."

"I like your moxie, kiddo."

"Well, we're both awake. We might as well make the most of it."

Chuckling, he brushes his thumb over my cheek. "My filthy princess shall get her morning fix."

"Hooray!"

He just shakes his head.

"What do you want me to do to you?"

I run my hand along his well-defined chest and relish the feel of the thick cords of muscle rippling beneath his warm skin. I love how strong he feels under my touch. "I don't know. You're the master teacher. I'm just the incredibly gifted pupil."

Easton laughs.

"I want to wake up like this every single morning of my life."

Me too.

For a few long seconds, neither of us speaks.

His words weigh thick in the room.

He gives me a little resigned smile.

I return it.

"We should focus on a lesson that will be mutually satisfactory," he says after a long stretch of silence.

"I thought all the lessons were like that," I retort.

"This one will be a little different. Italian roosters are still sleeping and I should be following in their footsteps," he jokes. I laugh. "As much as I want to shower my princess with pleasure, my brain hasn't quite caught up with the rest of me."

"We don't have to go for a vigorous lesson. It can be a lazy one."

"Great minds think alike."

He rubs my pussy and then gives it a slap.

"Ouch. What was that about?"

"Lazy doesn't preclude filthy," he explains.

"Oh! Now you have my undivided attention."

"On your hands and knees, dirty girl. Your head facing the foot of the bed."

I do as I'm told.

Without warning, Easton shoves his fingers inside my wetness.

I moan.

"That pussy is drenched."

I turn my head so our eyes meet. "I came really hard," I tell him.

Slap.

"I don't remember allowing you take your pleasure without me."

"But you were in the room."

Slap. Slap. Slap.

"Don't play coy with me, Brielle. You know exactly what I mean."

I flash him a devilish smile.

"The next time you decide to play with yourself, I want to watch."

"Yes, sir."

He chuckles.

"I've created a monster."

"Thank you."

"Funny."

Easton slides two fingers inside me again.

"Finally," I pant.

I expect him to play with me, but instead, he removes his fingers from my pussy and brings them to his mouth. With his eyes on me, he licks my juices off his fingers.

"My God that's dirty."

"You ain't seen nothing yet, beautiful," he warns. "Spread them wide."

I eagerly obey, opening my legs as wide as I can.

He slides down the bed until my pussy is hovering over his head. His strong hands grip my hips forcing me to sit on his face.

He parts my lips with his tongue before sucking my clit. The sweet pain sends shivers traveling all the way down to my toes.

"Yes," I hiss with my eyes closed.

When he flicks and teases my clit, I nearly scream.

I lower myself even more against his mouth as he strokes around my clit. I'm dying for him to pull me into his mouth and suck me hard until I lose my mind. But he doesn't.

Just like that, he stops.

"What happened?" I complain.

"If I take care of my princess, I expect her to take care of me." I frown. "My cock is begging for your lips."

When I turn my head around, his mighty erection salutes me.

"It's bigger than it was yesterday."

"That's because it hasn't come yet. Stroke it a few times and see what happens."

I laugh.

"Let's get back to the order of the day," he says.

"I agree!"

"Together."

I nod. "Together."

I turn myself around to face his stiff cock.

Wow.

My mouth is already watering at the sight and my nipples tighten so much I can't tell if it's pleasure or pain. I don't think I'll ever be able to get over my fascination for his thick long cock.

I'm still deep in admiration when Easton reaches for me. His hands splay across my hips and he pulls me down until my whole pussy is spread open across his face again. I whimper with each vibration of his feral groans. He's going to make me lose it the way his teeth graze and nibble at my pussy, almost pushing me over the brink of pleasure before he alternates and sucks my clit.

God how I love his mouth.

I close my eyes to feel each revolution of his tongue around my clit. I'm in Nirvana and then just like that I feel his hand on my ass cheek.

Slap.

Huh?

Below me, he lifts his hips up, urging me to take him in.

"Got it," I say.

I wrap my fist around his cock before lowering my mouth around his beautiful cock. I push my head back until his tip is the only part of his cock still trapped inside my mouth. I swirl at it with my tongue, relishing every single lap. I love that I know this drives him crazy. Aware that I'm ignoring his balls, I slide my free hand down until I'm cupping his balls. I gently pull at them as my hand strokes them.

"Mmm-hmm," he grunts, yanking his hips up.

That boosts my confidence.

I open my mouth wider and take more of him. With a steady head bob, one hand slips up and down his cock while the other hand remains cupped around his balls.

He inhales sharply.

This is amazing.

I won't profess to being a professional at sucking cock—after all I'm on day three of my training—but the way he reacts is intoxicating.

How can an inexperienced princess unravel her prince?

My prince?

God. How I want that with all of my heart.

Focus.

I pull back again, drawing his cock slowly out of my mouth, before swirling my tongue over its head, toying with him. The more I tease him, the more voraciously he eats my pussy. I tremble under his assault.

"Mmmm." We both moan at the same time.

His cadence grows wild, eager and desperate. It's cruel and so utterly sinful at the same time. Then he wraps my clit with his mouth, and I whimper around his cock. I close my eyes lost in the sweet way he's eating my pussy.

Yes.

He rubs my clit quick and hard. I squeeze my legs around his head, aware I'm seconds away from coming undone. When he slides a finger inside my asshole, my whole body starts shaking and I know I'm holding on by a thread.

Dear God.

"My royal dirty girl is close." The dirty talking again. "Her fat clit is pulsing against my tongue and it's making me want to lose my shit. I want your throbbing pussy to come hard for me."

I hum my response, nodding at the same time with my lips still wrapped around his cock.

"Got that?"

I let go of his cock. "Yes."

"Good. Now give me what I want."

He wraps his mouth around my clit once more and sucks harder and harder while pumping his finger in and out of my ass.

Oh fuck, I'm there. I'm so there.

He growls against my clit and I dive right off the cliff.

As my climax mounts spiraling up to my brain like a geyser, I lose my grip on his cock. I tilt my head back engulfed by the first wave of my orgasm ripping through me.

"Ohhh, Easton," I whimper.

Closing my eyes, I grind against his face. I'm shameless and impulsive in my pursuit. The sensation of coming all over his mouth–his face–is so perverted, it nearly stops my heart. After a few long pleasurable seconds of bliss, I go limp. I collapse face first against the bed with my ass sticking in the air. I'm spent.

I'm still panting hard in an attempt to catch my breath when I hear Easton say, "On your back."

I look behind me. He's on his knees with his hand fisting his cock. I get a full view of him stroking himself slowly in front of me.

When did he have time to slide from under me?

"Didn't you hear me?"

"I did."

"What are you waiting for?"

I obey.

He slides closer to me and positions himself to straddle my chest. And just like that, he's over me. Dominating me.

"Ready for your next lesson?" he grins.

I run my hands up and down his muscular thighs. "I'm not sure. I thought you said it would be a lazy lesson. This looks intense."

"Let's just say you got me all worked up. And this next lesson is about me claiming another part of you. Are you up for that?"

"I'm up for anything you have to teach me," I smile.

"You're very agreeable, Princess. I like that about you."

There's so much I like about you.

He moves his hand up and down the length of his long hard cock for a few strokes before leaning forward. With his free hand, he rubs the dripping tip over my bottom lip.

"Lick it," he commands.

I slide my tongue out, licking the pre-cum drizzling from his cock.

His half-lidded eyes are veiled with lust and that wicked, sexy smile causes my clit to throb again.

He responds by strangling his cock even harder releasing more pre-cum.

I'm completely mesmerized.

What an unforgettable view.

I cross my legs and clench hard, gyrating my hips in a circular motion and chasing another orgasm.

Easton's eyes shoot down at me. "No you don't," he growls.

I whimper.

"You want to come again?"

"Yes."

"We do it my way."

"What do you want me to do?" I ask in a desperate voice I don't even recognize.

A few days ago I didn't even know what an orgasm was. Now, I can't live without them.

"Show me how you touched yourself while I was still sleeping, beautiful. Play with your clit. Come with me," he rasps.

He shuffles back so he can watch as my hand slides down to my pussy. He licks his lips when I push a finger inside; squeezing his cock hard when my thumb flicks at my clit.

Seeking pleasure at my own hand is one thing, but doing it with his eyes riveted on me is so hot, so filthy.

"I... I... I'm going to— God—"

I'm so turned on and so slippery, that it doesn't take me long to lose control.

My pussy tightens greedily and clenches in wild pulses.

"Ohhh," I sob.

I come so hard I think I've transcended into another world.

Mother of God.

I open my eyes just in time to catch Easton as he cups his balls with one hand and strokes furiously with the other.

The veins on his cock are angrier now then ever.

"Keep your eyes on my cock."

"I wouldn't dream of looking away."

"Fuck, Brielle," he pants. "You don't know what it does to me to hear you say stuff like that."

He's squeezing, pumping his cock to the point where I'm sure he's going to rip it right off his body. The cadence is relentless.

"Tell me you want my cum on you."

I nod. "I do."

I can't even believe I'm begging for this.

He's going at it with such resolve that his massive balls clink together every time he pumps his cock.

Amazing.

A long thick string of cum seeps from his tip and drips onto my tummy and we both watch its descent.

"I'm near, beautiful."

The expression on his face is a combination of pure bliss and extreme pain.

"I'm coming, baby."

Suddenly, his balls contract.

"Jesus fucking Christ," he growls.

Easton squeezes his cock as he spews his cum all over my breasts, covering me with his climax. There's so much of it that some cum lands on my chin and my cheek. I have no doubt he's also christened my hair.

I've never seen anything like this.

With one last growl, he collapses on top of me, pressing his hands against the mattress to avoid crushing my body. He wraps one arm around my waist and flips us over so he's lying on the bed and I'm now on top of him.

"Now your cum is all over me," I complain. "I thought you said it was about claiming another part of me. Seems like you've claimed me from head to toe," I laugh.

"You're precious," he chuckles.

I drop my head against his chest and listen to the rhythmic sound of his heartbeat. I love when he nestles me in his arms like this.

He kisses the top of my head and tightens his embrace. "I hope that wasn't too much?" he grunts between breaths.

I slowly lift my head and meet his gaze.

"No."

"So you're okay?"

"I'm more than okay."

I want to remain locked up on this secluded Italian island with this incredible man for the rest of my life.

"Yes. You. Are," he says amused.

I let out a soft laugh.

"Can I keep you hostage?" he chuckles.

Did you actually hear my prayer, God?

CHAPTER 20

Brielle

"You're back!" my cousin exclaims when I walk into the kitchen.

"Hey, Lilo."

"How was lunch with Sienna?" I open my mouth to respond, but she lifts her hand up. "Wait! There's a lot to talk about. We can't do this without drugs."

"Drugs?"

"I dropped by Sprinkles and bought their strawberry triple layer cake. Sugar is the must-have drug for a heart-to-heart between friends."

"Ohhh!"

"I know, right?" she grins.

"In that case, drugs it is!"

"Brilliant!" she cheers. "Sit. I'll be back in a second," she waves me over. "Tea?"

"Absolutely!"

While the water is boiling, my cousin walks to the refrigerator and comes back with a delicious looking cake.

"Strawberries and pound cake? What's there not to love?"

"Indeed. Our favorite," she winks.

A few minutes later, Lilo is sitting across from me.

"Oh my God, I can never get over how amazing this cake is," I say biting into the moist dessert.

"I could live off this alone," Lilo laughs.

"Ditto."

For the next few minutes, we savor our dessert in silence. Once we're done, we wash it all down with strong British tea.

"That was phenomenal. Thank you," I say.

"It was my pleasure. So, back to my original question, how was lunch with Sienna?"

I stop scraping my plate for the last few crumbs, drop my fork and meet my cousin's piercing gaze. "Life can be so funny."

"What do you mean?"

"It's been the three of us since we were twelve and we always promised each other that when we started seeing a guy, we'd tell each other everything—"

"Yikes."

"Exactly. I can't do that with Sienna. I can't tell her all the things I did with her older brother. As curious as she is, she's fully aware that she can't ask too many questions—that would be awkward and morally reprehensible."

"Of course. Talk about too much information."

"To answer your question, it was great seeing her again, but it was a little weird at times because we were both skirting around the issue. I'm just grateful that she seems to be genuinely happy for me."

"She hasn't stopped talking about it since she found out. And you're right, she's thrilled her brother found an amazing woman," my cousin smiles wide. "You may not be able to tell her everything, but lucky for you I'm a great listener. What happened over the weekend, woman?"

I burst out in laughter. "How long have you been waiting to ask me that?"

"Well, you arrived late last night and you left before I did for your morning classes. The only reason I didn't bombard you with text messages while you were away is because I didn't want to distract you from your sexy weekend with your *American lover*." She says that last part with a theatrical voice.

"You're too much."

"Yeah, yeah, yeah. Start talking, cousin."

"It was absolutely amazing, Lilo. Better than any of my fantasies. Easton is a wonderful man."

"Details. I want details. Tell. Me. Everything." She pounds on the table between each word. Plates, cutlery and cups rattle on the table. Her little outburst even causes our water to spill.

"Calm down, woman," I scold.

"Newsflash, you're the only one amongst the three of us who has actually seen a man's…" Lilo looks around the kitchen before leaning into the table. She places a hand near her mouth and shifts her eyes from left to right. "Penis," she finally whispers.

Nevermind the fact that her officer—who is standing guard at the front door—is far from earshot and both of our ladies in waiting are out shopping.

"I think you should start calling it, cock."

She leans back against her seat as if I punched her in the chest. "Advice from a woman with loads of experience," she nods. After a few pensive seconds, she says, "Cock it is. So how was his? Big? Small? Curvy? Circumcised? Uncircumcised—"

"Cut. Uncut." I correct her.

"You're a wealth of information now," she observes.

I bite off a smile. "You're killing me."

She doesn't miss a beat. She leans forward and grabs my hand. "Describe it," she demands.

I raise a surprised eyebrow. "What's gotten into you?"

"You don't see it?"

"See what?"

"You look completely different today."

"In what sense? It's still little ol' me."

"No! No, no, no," Lilo shakes her head. "You look like a woman." To be fair I feel different. "If I can't have what you have yet, I want to know everything."

"All right, you win," I say lifting my free hand up in surrender. "Let me start from the beginning."

"Sounds good to me."

"Elba was paradise on earth, it was like a tease. I didn't want it to end. Can you believe I already miss him?" I feel myself blushing.

"You guys connected?"

"We did. Even though we grew up in different worlds and in different countries, we have so much in common. I feel so comfortable and so safe with him."

"I've always liked Easton," Lilo says.

I like him a lot. "As for his cock, it's perfect—like the rest of him. It's so manly. I don't have much to go by, but I think his is fairly big."

"Did you go all the way?" she cuts to the chase.

I shake my head. "No, not yet. We started with the ABCs."

"Oh yeah. I like him even more. He's taking his time with you," she says knowingly.

Lilo can be so hilarious.

"Yes. That's exactly what he said."

"Were you nervous?"

"That's putting it mildly. I was certain my awkwardness would be a turn off. I mean how many women has Easton had so far—"

"Lots, I'm sure."

"That was a rhetorical question."

"Oops. Sorry."

We both laugh.

"I'm not daft. He's an incredibly good-looking man. He's eligible and he's very wealthy. Of course, women would be attracted to him—"

"But he made things happen to be with you," my cousin reminds me.

There I go blushing again. "He did. He was the consummate gentleman. His constant encouragement made me feel sexy and boosted my confidence."

"He was the perfect one to be your first."

"Yeah," I nod.

"Was he a gentleman the whole time or was he a little... naughty?"

"You've expanded your vocabulary," I say impressed.

"I've been preparing myself for this conversation." She crosses her arms over her chest and flashes me an expression of pride that says it all.

"He was *very* naughty."

"Ohhh, girlfriend, do tell."

For the next few minutes, I tell Lilo everything. I don't leave anything out. I've been dying to share my sexy adventure with someone and I'm not about to put the brakes on.

It's a veritable verbal diarrhea until Lilo interrupts. "Royal dirty girl?"

"I know it sounds a little demeaning—"

"Not at all. I can't believe how wrong, yet so incredibly right, royal dirty girl sounds."

"That's exactly how I feel."

My cousin places the back of her hand against her forehead and tilts her head back ever so slightly. She places her left hand against her heart and says, "Oh when, oh when, will I find a man who will call me his royal dirty girl? God, FYI, I'm very ready for this." No, Lilo isn't at all dramatic.

We both lose it.

"Can I continue now?" I ask once I've regained my composure.

"If it involves more royal dirty girl action, by all means."

I just shake my head. She's enjoying this more than I am.

I resume my tale and recount the rest of the details of my wanton weekend with my lover.

"Mother of God," Lilo says fanning herself when I'm done. "That sounded positively perverted."

"In more ways than one."

Lilo suddenly jumps to her feet. "Hail, Your Royal Bawdiness! I bow to your greatness. And to that filthy tale."

"Oh, stop it. Sit down." I turn beet red.

"Are you kidding me? What you described is every girl's ultimate first time. Of course I have to celebrate."

I let out a long sigh. "I guess you're right. The last few days were surreal. No. It was far more than that. I'm not using the right words. It was more like an epiphany and an apogee rolled up into one," I say.

"The education of an innocent princess."

"Touché. I've kicked the virtuous woman to the curb and I don't have an ounce of shame about it. On the contrary. Easton allowed me to come into my own in the most graceful way possible."

"Mmmm," Lilo hums.

"Can I tell you a little secret?"

"What are cousins for?"

"Don't ask me where this comes from—"

"Trust me, I won't. You were saying?"

It's my turn to look left and then right to make sure we're still alone. "I can't stop thinking of him spreading my legs, and burying every single inch of his very long and thick cock inside me—taking my virginity. By accepting my gift, we'll be forevermore connected."

And now, my body craves Easton's touch.

Lilo's mouth drops open.

"No matter what, I'll hold a little part of him inside me," I continue. "And you know what else I've been thinking about?"

"No." Her eyes widen even more.

"With a little luck, I might get pregnant, which means I would be of no interest to Prince Haakon." There. I said it.

Lilo burst out laughing. "That would totally screw up your mum's plans. My mum said that your mum keeps going on, and on, and on about becoming the Queen's mother. Your mum says it's such an honorable title. Something about elevating the image of our country. We already have a queen. And a beloved king—a man everyone admires. It's as if she forgets you'll become Queen of another country. One more backward thinking and substantially poorer than ours—and that doesn't even account for Prince Haakon's recent eye-popping spending sprees."

"She's so obsessed that she doesn't care if I succumb to a silent death trapped in a loveless marriage," I lament.

"What does your father have to say?"

"Daddy doesn't like the idea one bit. He thinks Prince Haakon is a leech—"

"Well, he is."

"True. Mum's claws come out every time Daddy says anything. He said that a few days ago, Mum was in a particularly pissy mood. She shut him up by telling him to go back to screwing his disgusting whores. He hasn't broached the subject since."

"Back to you getting pregnant. I love the idea of you putting your foot down and fighting to be with the one you choose, but doing it this way would be unfair to your child," Lilo reasons.

I purse my lips and shrug.

I know it's childish, but I'm angry that my fate is sealed without my consent.

Lilo gets up and walks around the table to me. She kneels and grabs both my hands in hers as she sits on the floor. "There has to be another way out of this mess."

I avert my gaze.

"Bri, trickery is unbecoming of you. As much as I vehemently oppose these ancient protocols, I don't think you want to use a child to get out of an unpleasant situation."

"Can you think of anything else?" I challenge. I know she means well and I hate the sarcasm in my voice. "The clock is ticking. It's my future and sanity we're talking about here."

CHAPTER 21

Easton

"Knock, knock, knock," I say rapping my knuckle against the ajar door. "Good afternoon, Miriam."

"Good afternoon, Mr. Winchester," my secretary says lifting her eyes up from her iMac.

"I hear you've been cracking the whip around here during my absence."

"Someone has to steer these young lads in the right direction. Had I not put my foot down, they'd be here twenty-four hours a day. That's simply unacceptable," she says lifting her chin up defiantly.

I call Miriam Stockley my secretary but she's so much more. She runs my New York office with military precision. She holds a degree from NYU Stern School of Business. In other words, she's as sharp as a whip. After giving birth to her twins, Miriam became a stay-at-home mom. After five years as a full-time mom, she was ready to get back into the fray. I was lucky to scoop her up.

"You won't hear an argument from me. I know I set a bad example," I say.

As rewarding as this industry is, the hours are punishing. With the time differences, there's always a financial market bustling about somewhere in the world. Not to mention that with the Internet, it never stops. That's why I have offices around the world. I won't lie, I'm a workaholic, but without my multiple offices, I'd never sleep. That said, like attracts like. The people who want to work for me have as stringent work ethics as I do.

"Well, I've said it before." Here it comes. "Once you settle down, you'll have to change your ways."

"I'll keep that in mind."

That's my usual standard answer.

"You've done a great job with Sienna and I'm sure you'll want to be present for the milestones in your children's life."

I frown.

That's a new one. She usually leaves my sister out of it.

"I saw her a few days ago at Pierre Victoire. She was having dinner with Princess Blakely," she explains. "What a charming young lady. They both are."

"Ah, I see. Princess Blakely is adorable and thank God Sienna turned out okay," I say.

"She certainly did." Miriam pauses. After a few short seconds, she adds, "Perhaps I've said too much."

"Yes, you have, but I won't hold it against you," I wink.

She'll find a way to weave this into another conversation.

"How were the meetings in Switzerland?" she changes the subject.

"Swiss bankers want to know how they can get in on the action. In other words, these last three days were incredibly productive. Good things are coming our way," I grin from ear to ear.

"They always do. You have the golden touch."

"Nah. It helps that I got my start as a software developer for financial companies. I understand the ins and outs of these markets in a way few people do. Cracking codes for that many years gives me an edge."

"It certainly has. I guess that's why we attract so many high rollers… and royals." She sighs on that last part.

"Another one?"

"Yes, and this one is particularly insistent. He called on Thursday right after you had left for the weekend and hasn't stopped since. Carla," that's the receptionist, "is about to lose her mind if she has to repeat herself one more time. I tried to reason with the chap and make him understand that you were in important meetings and therefore, out of reach, but it was to no avail. This one is going to be a handful. Just because he's a prince, he thinks that he can jump the queue."

Six months ago, Prince Zoran Zvonimir from the Kingdom of Vojislava wanted in on the action. The man is loaded, but he expected my staff to jump every time he snapped his fingers—which was all the fucking time. After several warnings, I rewired his money back to his account and severed our ties. I refuse to work with assholes.

"Who's the royal this time?"

"Prince Haakon of Wallon from the Kingdom of Brihon."

"Come again?" I almost choke.

"Prince Haakon," she repeats.

How the fuck did that happen?

"The flashy manwhore prince?"

The words fly out of my mouth before I can catch them.

Miriam laughs.

"Allow me to correct you, sir, it's the flashy manwhore aristocrat turned saint."

"Why do you say that?"

"I asked Elian to run a thorough background check on him since I figured you'd want to have a dossier before you call him. As much as I hate to admit it, I'm sort of a royal watcher and I was quite intrigued by Prince Haakon's recent transformation. Elian confirmed my suspicions."

Elian van der Wiel is a Dutchman living in the Cayman Islands. He's also the guy I turn to when I want to find hidden dirt on potential investors. Everyone boasts to have a clean slate. Elian is the one who confirms that. I have some mad computer skills, but Elian and his team of hackers can find a needle in a haystack.

"And?"

"It was the judicious work of a magician."

"Merlin the wizard?" I mock.

"Better than that. Elian says that when people hire top publicist Geordie Ollie Goodger it's because they have a lot of skeletons in their closets or they want to polish their image—many times it's both. Wizard Goodger creates the perfect illusion."

"I'm not surprised the manwhore prince would resort to that. His reputation is atrocious."

"But there's more."

"I'm all ears."

"The prince has been throwing his money left, right and center. Even buying a multimillion-dollar yacht big enough to house a helicopter. He sold both the boat and the chopper last month for a pittance. Then he turned around and bought a ridiculously priced mansion in Beverly Hills. I wouldn't touch Prince Haakon with a ten-foot pole, but of course, it's your decision."

Interesting.

"Get the prince on the phone," I demand.

Miriam's eyes bulge out of her skull. "Are you really considering this? Prince Zoran was a nightmare."

I shrug. "I'm curious. I want to know what Haakon is made of."

"All right. Everything Elian was able to dig up is on your desk. The zip file was also emailed to you."

"Thank you. I'm sure there's more for us to discuss, but it'll have to wait for the next couple of hours? I want to deal with this first."

"Not a problem." She opens her mouth to say something, but hesitates. "Why do I sense there's more?"

"Because there is," I say simply before heading to my office.

* * *

Brielle and I spent three incredible days in Elba. I might not have fucked her pussy or her ass yet, but I've done everything else to claim her as mine. The last few hours on our private oasis were bittersweet. We both knew it would inevitably come to an end. Facing reality was a lot more difficult to accept. This was another instance where I wished she were just a girl who happened to be my little sister's best friend or that I was born with a noble title. It would be so much easier.

Since she flew back to New York, we've been texting each other nonstop. Every night while I was in Switzerland, we had video chats on WhatsApp. It's been like we were living in our own little world.

And Miriam's news has burst that bubble.

She may not have met him yet, but Brielle is promised to him. The fact that Prince Haakon would choose my investment company over others is an uncanny coincidence. One I'm displeased with.

After carefully going over Elian's file, Miriam patches me through to the prince.

"Prince Haakon, this is Mr. Wright returning your call."

"For God sakes, it's about time," he barks so loud that I have to pull the phone away from my ear. *You have no fucking manners.* "I thought I was going to have to cut short my dignitary functions in Australia and track you down."

"I—"

"I'm a very busy man, Mr. Wright."

And I spend my days knitting and petting my cat.

Not even a minute into this conversation and I already want to hang up.

"Now that I have you on the phone, I'm ready to talk business, Mr. Wright."

Oh yeah, you don't know about Mr. Wright yet.

It's something I started because I made it big in this industry when I was still very young. After I made tens of millions by selling my father's domains, I became an angel investor. I made a once-in-a-lifetime bet on a tech company that exploded. Six months later, I did it again. Two months after that I had picked another winner. After my hat trick, everyone in the financial world wanted to know who had funded those start-ups. I became the anonymous angel with the Midas touch. That's how I ended up making my first billion by twenty-six. It was a gravy train after that. I was lucky. On the flip side, the attention was overwhelming. Craig Wright allowed for some privacy and protected Sienna. I didn't want people to be able to find my bio by doing a Google search. I use my alias until investors have been properly vetted, they've signed a pile high of nondisclosure agreements and another slew of legal documents and they've been invited to a remote island—like Elba—for an investor weekend.

"I'm sure my secretary told you that I was away."

"She did, but this was a very important call. I was expecting her to track you down."

"That's not the way we operate around here," I tell him. "Not to mention that with the number of investors we have, no one on my team would get any work done if they spent their time chasing after me."

"How many of your clients are future kings?"

Arrogant pig. "How can I help you, Prince Haakon?"

"Well, the obvious, of course."

"Which is?"

Nope, I have no intention of making this easy for him. I don't know him and I already hate his guts.

"I want to multiply my money."

From what Elian found out, you don't have much left. "What exactly did you have in mind?"

"I'm looking for big returns. I'm talking twelve hundred percent at least."

That's statistically impossible, you moron. "That's very ambitious."

"From what I understand, you can make it happen."

"I'm not a miracle worker. I'm just really good at what I do."

"And that's exactly why I want to work with you." He let out a frustrated sigh. "It's impossible for me to figure out what your minimum investment is." *Two million dollars.* "But I'm in."

"It's our mission to look after our investors."

Our investors quadruple, quintuple and even sextuple their money at light speed.

"And I want to be one of them," he asserts.

If this asshole prince is short on cash, why is he knocking at my door and more importantly why is Brielle's mother so keen on marrying her daughter off to him?

"Why invest with my company? There are others out there."

"True, but everyone in the financial market world says that you, Mr. Wright, are the undisputed king of venture capital. You've made the Forbes' Midas List three years in a row. I want to work with the best. Why wouldn't I? You are the best. That's why I'm calling."

"My counterparts show impressive results," I argue.

"It's a well-known fact that nine out of ten startups will fail. How many tank each and every day in Silicon Valley? You are one of the rare ones able to spot that one winner a mile away. I'll soon be crowned King of Brihon at the tender age of thirty-three. A king should work with a king. A king can respect and trust another king."

Too bad I can't say the same about you.

"I see."

"So, what's the minimum investment to get in?" he asks.

"This is between you and I?"

"Of course. You have my word. I won't breathe this to another soul."

I never allow phone conversations to get to this point, but I'm itching to know what kind of game this asshole is playing.

"Twelve million dollars," I say.

Prince Haakon coughs on the other end. "What?"

I'm sure you heard me. "If you don't have the—"

"I have it," he blurts out. "Well, I will soon."

"I don't understand. You either have the money or you don't."

"I am to take a wife just after I become king."

This guy sounds like a fucking robot.

"Congratulations." *Not.*

"Thank you. I'm excited. My wife-to-be is young, gorgeous and her kingdom is extraordinarily rich. Soon to be *my* kingdom."

"So you're coming in as a couple?" I ask.

He explodes in laughter. "Of course not. This isn't going to be that kind of marriage."

"What do you mean?"

"My wife will have her place and that will be taking care of our home and children. End of story. I don't need her meddling in my affairs."

Why is he revealing such personal things to a stranger?

"You're using her money, but you're not involving her?"

Brielle deserves better than this backward-thinking dimwit. Who the hell still has such a low opinion of women these days?

"Brihonites don't have a favorable impression of the man who will soon rule their nation. Many of my subjects feel that since my parents' divorce and subsequently my mother's death—may she rest in peace—I've gone astray. My older sister is more interested in taking care of her large family than becoming queen. She renounced the throne. She has eight children, which is unheard of in our lineage in recent generations. She doesn't need any more responsibilities. My grandmother bypassed my father for the kingship because he remarried a divorcee, one few Brihonites like. So, there's only me as the rightful successor to the throne. Most Brihonites think that I'm a spoiled brat and a manwhore—"

"Are you?"

"We're both men, Mr. Wright. We both have dicks that need attention. When you're a prince, you lead a charmed life. I have access to anything I desire—including an endless supply of gorgeous women. Why would I deprive myself from sampling their goods? And I have. A lot. Shamelessly so."

Rich.

"I've lived my life in the spotlight. What can I say? I love being the center of attention. I know I'm not a very handsome man—I'm lanky, pasty white, ginger and severely balding. Despite my obligatory military service, I'm not very fit, but the title… the title changes everything, Mr. Wright."

"I wouldn't know," I say.

"I suspect not. You may be king in the financial world, but that's just a symbolic title. Mine, is a birthright—one my wife-to-be and I will be able to pass on to our children. That's priceless and limited to only a few chosen ones."

That comment is dripping with contempt.

"I needed an image change, hence becoming somewhat of a recluse. That's also why I started this stupid foundation to help the people of Gambia—"

"The smallest country on the western part of the continent."

"Perhaps, but thanks to me, everyone now knows this African nation. They've even named a major street in my honor."

No, you're not a self-centered prick. "I see."

From Elian's report, Haakon influenced his grandmother, Queen Gertrude, to substantially raise taxes, threatening to tax air if he had to. Brihonites unwillingly footed the bill for the Gambia fund. He cares more about being seen than his people. If there's a camera anywhere, you're sure to find Haakon grinning like an idiot. His endless selfies are nauseating.

"The next step in rejuvenating my image and winning the trust of my people is to marry a woman who will become my queen. I found her. And her mother swears she's a virgin. Bonus. That will win me extra points with my people." *I can't believe my ears.* "Her mother is so eager to be able to wear the title of mother to the Queen, that she would be willing to grant me any wish. So, the twelve million dollars you request is only a phone call away. In fact, I'm so eager to get in I'll throw in twenty-four million so my money grows faster. When can we meet in person, Mr. Wright?"

Fucker.

CHAPTER 22

Easton

"I don't care if he comes in with thirty billion dollars, I'll never work with that jackass," I spit out.

I'm so infuriated, I can't fucking breathe.

When I hung up the phone with the royal dick, it took everything in me not to clear the top of my desk—including my iMac and the three other very expensive computers I use for trading—with the back of my hand in revolt.

Fucking Prince Haakon doesn't know *my* Brielle and already he's intent on disrespecting her. He's promoting her virginity like it's a badge of honor. *Show a modicum of decorum, asshole.* He wants to use her as a baby factory to spit-shine his tarnished image as he robs her country blind.

Jesus Christ.

I can't believe this is the best Princess Janika can do. There has to be other candidates. Better ones. Ones with scruples. Ones that might give Brielle a chance at happiness. Not that conceited jerk.

And what about Prince Janek? Doesn't he care about his daughter? I know Brielle said her parents can't stand each other, but how can they pawn her like this?

Haakon has no intention of loving Brielle.

I could love her.

Where the hell did that come from?

That conversation turned my stomach around and now I can't even think straight.

I pace around my office like a caged animal, willing my heartbeat to regulate, but it's to no avail.

"What a vile piece of shit." I scowl, something dark welling up inside of me.

I stick my hands in my pockets because if I don't I'm going to break every window in this office.

I was quietly brooding on the idea of offing the idiot prince. I was actually going over my head the list of potential investors who might connect me to a member of the mob.

I growl low.

This is nonsense.

It's unlike me to want to harm someone.

I look at the time. Four o'clock.

I already know that I'm so angry, I doubt I'll be able to get any work done until I get this out of my system.

"Fuck you, Haakon, she isn't yours yet," I growl.

I grab my iPhone and dial Brielle's number.

As I wait for her to answer, I coax myself to calm the hell down.

"Easton!" she says when she picks up.

"Hey, beautiful. How are you?"

"Great! You're back?"

"Yeah, I got back a few hours ago. I'm at the office." I pause. "Are you at your place?"

"Yes. I got in not long ago."

"Are you alone?"

She hesitates. "Lilo has her internship this afternoon at an art gallery. She won't be back until ten. Iyanna and Philippa—Lilo's lady-in-waiting—are running errands. Why?"

"Can you stall Iyanna and Philippa and ask them not to come back until much later?"

"Why?" she asks again.

"Do you want to see me?"

"I can't believe you'd ask me that question."

"One should never assume."

"Yes, I absolutely want to see you. I've missed you."

"We're on the same page, beautiful. I'm dying to see you too," I tell her. "Sienna is at the penthouse. We could do a hotel, but it might take me a while to find a room in a five-star one. Your place is much faster."

There's a short pause. "You should've said that from the beginning." I hear the excitement in her voice and I can't help but smile.

She's mine.

"Who's guarding your door?"

"Officer Mordanova."

"Blakely's new bodyguard?"

"Yes."

"I don't know her very well."

"What do you have up your sleeve, Mr. Winchester?"

"I miss both sets of your lips."

"I don't even know what to say to that."

"Say yes, beautiful."

"I'll warn Officer Mordanova of your pending arrival," she laughs.

"That's my girl. See you soon."

"I can't wait."

"Neither can I."

* * *

"Good afternoon, Officer Mordanova," I say as I approach Brielle's door.

She's as menacing-looking as Officer Pavlova. I guess it makes sense since she was also part of the Russian Special Forces. I usually get a faint smile from Officer Pavlova, Blakely's second bodyguard is all business.

"Good afternoon, sir. The princess is expecting you."

"I believe she is."

"Please, go ahead," she extends her hand.

"Thank you."

I don't even have time to ring the doorbell than the door flies open.

"Easton, it's good to see you again," Brielle says in a formal tone.

"Brielle, likewise." I match her formality.

"Thank you so much for bringing back my wallet. I can't believe I left it at your place while I was *studying* with Sienna earlier today."

I'm a little thrown off at first. "I was in the area and I figured you'd need it," I say when it clicks.

"The least I can do is offer you a cup of tea."

I bite off a smile. "It's always a good time for tea."

"Indeed it is."

Brielle looks over my shoulder.

"Thank you so much, Officer Mordanova," she says.

"Of course, Princess."

"Please, come in, Easton," she tells me.

I step inside her penthouse and wait for her to close the door before whispering, "How are you going to explain the fact that I might be here for a couple of hours?"

"Her shift ends in fifteen minutes," she whispers back. "We're in the clear after that because Officer Pavlova takes over at five." She grabs me by the hand and rushes me down the hallway to the kitchen. "Blakely hasn't spoken to her bodyguards or her lady-in-waiting about you yet. She will. I doubt they'd say anything to mother, since she's always so short with them and treats them like imbeciles, but why take a chance."

"Good. Then I'll be completely vetted when I need to stop by for an afternoon fix?"

"Something like that," she winks. "How was Geneva?" she asks walking to the stove.

"I guess we're really having—"

Whoa!

Holy Jesus.

I got so distracted by her little ruse that it's only now that I take note of her mouth-watering outfit. My eyes sweep up and down the length of her body in appreciation.

She.

Looks.

Smoking hot.

My princess is wearing a fitted pink short-sleeved knitted top that offers a slight peek of her taut tummy and does wonders to showcase the gorgeous roundness of her breasts. The pièce de résistance is a pair of elegant lace shorts—in a different shade of pink than the top—with a drawstring that elicits misbehaving. Her hair falls in soft curls to the middle of her back and a pair of fashionable studded earrings frames her perfectly painted face. She completes the look with a pair of peep toe nude high heels.

In other words, she could stop traffic.

"Easton?"

I look up and meet her gaze.

"You're staring."

"Fuck Geneva," I say when I can speak again. "In that outfit, my business trip is the last thing I want to talk about."

She laughs. "You're too funny."

"No. I'm as serious as a heart attack."

"You like it?" she asks doing a little twirl.

The view is so tempting that I cock my head to the side to take it in again.

I shake my head.

"You don't?" The confusion on her face is amusing.

"No. I fucking love it." I close the gap between us and fist her long blonde hair. "Tell me, Princess, that you didn't go to school dressed like this."

"I didn't. I wore prim and proper university attire," she jokes. I laugh. "This is for you. I changed after your call. I wanted to look pretty."

She's well past pretty.

I grin like a fool. "This is for me?"

"Yes," her grin is as wide as mine.

"Cheeky Princess. If the wrapping is this seductive, should I assume it's the same for what's hiding underneath?"

She flashes me a defiant glance. "You mean the lingerie?"

"What else?"

She lifts her hand up and wiggles three fingers. "Three words. French. Pink. Soft lace."

I growl.

This woman is such a fast learner, she's quickly becoming an honor student.

Slap.

She yelps when my hand connects with her ass. "You don't like French lace?"

She's playing with me.

"You said three words, but you used four words."

She laughs.

"I missed you so much I can't count anymore."

Her revelation takes me aback.

"Well, I missed you so much that I've been sporting a perpetual hard on for the past three days," I say as I palm her breast, groaning at the feeling in my hand. "And you know what?"

"What?"

"The sexy outfit just made it harder."

"I can take it off, if it'll make you feel more comfortable."

"Brielle!" I warn.

"What? I was just trying to be helpful. That perpetual hard on part sounds painful."

"Not as painful as this."

Slap.

"Ouch."

I rub her sore spot. She purrs. "Better?" I ask.

"Yes."

"Good. About my impossibly hard cock… I have to feel your pussy."

I love it when her cheeks flush.

I've gone without sex for weeks and even months at a time, too focused on work and on taking care of my sister to even bother with pussy. That said, I've never done so many filthy things to a woman without fucking her. Don't get me wrong, I love coming down Brielle's throat, and marking her body with my cum gives me such a high, but nothing compares to a warm slick pussy.

"Your fingers or your mouth?" She's so eager.

"That won't do. My cock."

"You're going to take me here?"

"No. We'll do something similar to when I grinded against your ass. Except this time, you'll be doing the grinding."

"Oh. You never cease to surprise me."

I chuckle.

“Take your heels off—the same applies to the shorts—and get on the counter,” I order.

“Here? In the kitchen?” Her eyes go as wide as saucers.

“Yes. I’d hate to disappoint you.”

“Why don't we go upstairs to my bedroom?” she suggests.

“If we do, I might not be able to contain myself. I’ve said it before and I stand my ground. I want your first time to be special. You’ve got a little community living thing going on here. We may not have that much time.” She laughs. “You’re high up enough that we don't have to worry about being caught by nosy neighbors, even if the blinds aren’t drawn,” I say, looking around me. “This is the safer way. And still pleasurable,” I grin.

“Something tells me I'll never be able to look at this kitchen the same way ever again after today.”

“You can bet on it.”

She takes a step back, kicks her shoes off and removes her shorts.

My eyes are transfixed by her dainty little feet. As much as I love those high heels, they’ll be a hazard against the marble countertop.

“The top.”

She pulls her pink top over of her head and flings it to the side.

“Oh, Brielle,” I say, drinking her up.

The sight of the soft pink bustier and the lace panties against her tanned skin makes my cock pulse.

“They’re brand new,” she explains.

I take a step closer to her and bring my hand up to her cheek. I stroke gently with the back of my fingers. “Who were you thinking of when you bought this combo?” I ask in a dangerously low voice.

“You, of course.”

“Good answer. What were you hoping for when I finally got to unwrap my present?”

“That you’d make me feel like I did when we were in Elba.”

“You want me to make you come, Princess?”

“Oh, yes please.”

“Have you touched yourself since you’ve been back?”

She shakes her head vehemently. “You told me not to.”

"That's right. Good girl. You remembered that your orgasms belong to me."

"They do," her voice comes out in a quivering tremor.

"Up you go," I say, helping her hop on the counter. "On your back."

She obeys beautifully.

I pace around the counter, my blood at a dangerous boiling point because God knows how much I want to protect her and fuck her like a fucking animal at the same time, so that she feels marked. Taken. Mine.

I stop and inhale her headiness.

Damn.

She smells like she's ready for me.

The mixture of her arousal and her expensive perfume has me all riled up. But then it gets better. My eyes drop to the middle of her parted legs where her protruding clit is visible, begging to be touched, flicked and sucked.

"You look like a feast in this position, beautiful."

I lick my lips as if I were a predator about to devour her.

"I feel so vulnerable."

"Just the way I like you."

Her lips form an O.

I approach her, tuck two fingers into the waistband of her panties and start pulling them down, but I halt all movement when I take another whiff of her inebriating scent. I lean forward and kiss the smooth rise of her pubic bone over the pink lace and grab the lace fabric with my teeth.

"Dear God," she pants as I drag her panties all the way down to her painted toes.

I let the lacy fabric drop to the floor and lean forward to ravish her lips. When I pull back, I can't help a smile of satisfaction seeing her smeared pink lipstick. That carefully applied shade is now everywhere. I reach out to clean it off, with my eyes locked onto hers.

"Three days with you and now I can't get enough of you," I admit before dropping a soft kiss against her lips.

"It's the same for me," she murmurs against my lips.

"I can't tell you how much I want to eat you—"

"Yes, please," she hisses.

I love how she takes my words as a promise.

I pinch her nipple over the fabric of her bra as a reward.

"Ah!" she gasps.

I do it again.

She whimpers.

"I want you to come with my cock between your pussy lips," I tell her.

She nods breathlessly.

My blue-blooded dirty girl is so beautiful right now, I don't have the heart to discipline her and demand words. If this is all she can give, so be it. I'll let it slide this once.

"Lose the bra," I command.

I expect her to sit up, but instead, she wiggles her way out of her bra against the counter. She throws it at me, but I duck.

"What are you trying to do? Kill me with lace?"

We both laugh.

I place my hands on her hips and slide her down, right up to the edge, before spreading her legs as far apart as the counter will allow. I let go of her, but she protests.

"Where are you going?"

"I gotta pull my cock out," I chuckle.

She giggles. "It wouldn't be as much fun without it."

"Your words are truly an epiphany," I joke.

I don't bother removing my suit jacket or my tie. Instead, I fling my tie over my shoulder so it lands against my back. I've always loved fucking a girl while wearing a suit. There's such dominance in the act.

"You look so good in a suit—I mean really good—it should be illegal, but you look even better out of one."

"So you like what you see?"

"No. I bloody love it."

I shake my head and smile at her smart repartee.

I slide my zipper down and pull my pants and boxer briefs to my knees. My cock snaps to my stomach. Every vein pops like crazy. I'm so hard I feel it all the way down to my swollen bulbous head. With my legs partially shackled, I move forward until my cock is level with her pussy. I fist my cock and pump it a few times as I watch my flared-out purple head turn nearly blue. I cup my balls and squeeze tight, torturing myself a little before I give in to pleasure.

"Fuck," I pant.

I need this.

I need her.

Brielle's hooded grey eyes are riveted on me. "That's so sensual."

"I'm just going to play with you."

"Please."

"I think it's important for you to know that I'm clean."

She looks at me with a puzzled expression on her face. "What does that mean?"

It's amazing how innocent she is.

"I've never been with a woman without using a condom and I get tested regularly. Since you're a virgin, of course, you're clean. It's really to put your mind at ease more than anything else since I won't be taking things too far."

"Thanks for telling me," she offers a shy smile.

I don't know why, but I hold my breath when I press my cock against her dripping pussy.

Holy Jesus.

My head falls back at the surreal sensation.

"Christ," I grunt, pressing my hardness against her parted lips.

"Dear God," she hisses.

"Brielle, baby, your pussy is going to be the end of me."

"Mmmm," she hums.

"How does it feel?" I ask.

"Oh, Easton," she whispers. "I—ohhh—this—this feels… I don't even know how to describe it. It's that good."

"I hear you."

I've done a lot in my life, but this is fucking hot.

For a few long seconds, I tease her in languid circles, stroking my engorged knob around her. This is so fucking erotic. Needing more, I glide my cock down through her pussy lips to her ass, nudging the little puckered hole.

"Easton!" she cries out, shooting up on her elbows.

"Don't worry. I'm not going in. I just need to feel it." That comes out like a prayer.

She shivers.

"Okay?"

She nods.

"I need to hear you saying it."

"I trust you."

Music to my ears.

So I do it again. Gliding mercilessly against her clit, her virgin dripping pussy and the bud of her tight asshole.

She mewls, she moans, and yeah, I'm in heaven. What makes this even better is that our eyes are locked to the place where we're joined. Both of us are in silent contemplation as my tip presses against her warm entrance and slowly slips inside.

Her pussy clenches against my tip.

Jesus fucking Christ.

No sooner than I'm in, I pull out.

A second more and there's no going back.

As much as feeling her skin-against-skin awakens a primal need for more, I made a promise to her. No matter what, I'm determined to keep it.

She gives me an agonized expression that I'm certain matches my own.

"Go deeper," she begs.

My eyebrows hit my forehead. "My dirty girl wants to play with fire."

She gives me a one-shoulder shrug.

"Are you on the pill?"

She shakes her head. "No."

"Then I'm not going deeper."

"A few more inches aren't a big deal," she offers.

I beg to differ.

"You can pull out in time," she insists.

What's gotten into her?

"It's not enough that you're spread open and that I'm using you in such a shameless way, you're forcing my hand? Tsk, beautiful, that's not the way things work between us. This is as much of me as you'll get. You got that?"

"Okay."

"We're on the same page?" I press.

"Yes, we are."

"Can I go back to pleasuring my princess now?"

"Please." There's something unreadable that veils her eyes.

"We're good?"

"Yes."

I know there's more.

"Something is up. You want to talk about it?"

"No. Everything is fine."

She starts rubbing her pussy up and down my cock, and all thought escapes me.

"Stop," I growl. "If you're going to be a bad princess, you're going to chase your own climax."

"What?" she exclaims.

"I was going to make it easy on you, but you forfeited that privilege."

"But I love feeling your cock inside me."

Two seconds and she can't live without it?

Sure, I have a formidable cock, but come on.

"That makes two of us. Still. This is as far as we'll go," I repeat myself.

She responds with an afflicted look.

"Sit up!" I command.

I don't know what's going on, but I'm going to get it out of her.

"Spread them wide." She does. "You're going to use my cock like you did your fingers when we were in Elba. I don't want you to stop until you come your pretty head off. You hear me?"

"Is this your idea of a punishment?"

"Oh, Princess, keep it up and I'll be redefining your understanding of the word punishment."

Her eyes go wide.

"Yeah. You think you dictate this? Think again. My cock. Your pussy. Now."

She fists my cock and looks up at me.

"Go on," I tell her.

Slowly, she brings my cock to her pussy.

"Shit," I groan as I feel her lips part around my cock.

When she starts stroking her clit with my cock I think I'm going to die. It feels so different with her hand wrapped around me like this.

Both of us just stare down at this sight—the communion of two bodies.

"That sound is just pure filth."

She's talking about the slick noises.

"Filth can be a good thing," I say.

"Indeed," she smiles.

She pushes my cock against my stomach and angles her body so her pussy slides against the underside of my pulsing cock.

"Faster and put more pressure against your clit."

When she picks up speed, I bite my lower lip to avoid grunting loudly. Her cadence becomes erratic as she rubs my cock up and down every inch of her sweet little greedy pussy without ever taking me inside her wetness. Her moans fill the room with every stroke.

Fuck this is good.

"My dirty girl. My princess. My goddess, you're taking such good care of me," I hiss before leaning forward, crushing her lips and forcing my hard cock against her.

"Oh, God… I'm coming," she says against my lips.

"Are you going to come hard for me?"

She nods.

"I didn't hear you."

"Yes, I will," she pants.

"In that case I want to watch you get yourself off. Use me at will to rub that royal pussy into a frenzy until your juices come gushing all over my cock."

"Dear God, is there no end to the dirty talking?"

"None whatsoever."

She bucks her hips and starts moving faster and faster until her eyes close and she tilts her head back with her lips parted. She squeezes my cock so hard, I growl. And then she loses it. Her whole body shudders and I feel every vibration all the way down to my balls.

"Easton—"

She drops her head against my shoulder. Her body convulses under the climactic waves. When she lets go of my cock, I grab it and start jerking wildly. It doesn't take long for my orgasm to course through me.

"Oh, Christ, Brielle."

My warm cum explodes and lands in hot white streaks across her stomach, her thighs, her tits and even the tips of her hair. When I look down, I realize I'm in the same predicament.

There's cum everywhere.

Shit.

It's on my shirt, my navy blue jacket and dripping on my pants. Not even my Italian shoes have been spared. In our passionate exchange, my tie slipped back into position and it's also covered in cum.

Not good.

I already know there's no way I can leave this penthouse looking like I just fucked my girl six ways from Sunday.

I'll need an escape plan.

I embrace her and close my arms around her a little tighter as I drop a soft kiss on the top of her head. She's so limp in my arms.

Our heavy breathing reverberates against the kitchen's walls. I suspect she's also struggling to get her feet back on the ground.

Yeah, you came hard.

We stay like this interlaced into each other for a long while. Neither of us wants this to be over. I know I don't.

Out of the blue she says, "I'm yours, Easton." Her voice is so faint I'm sure I misheard her.

"What did you say?" She looks up at me and hesitates. I brush my lips against hers. "Say it again."

"I'm yours."

She says that with such sincerity, with such naked honesty, that I scoop her into my arms and kiss her with everything I have.

"Where did that come from?" I ask when I pull away from her.

She shrugs. "You told me so."

"And you believe it?"

She nods, then swallows hard, as if her mouth is dry. "With all my heart."

I came here to remind her who owns her.

Who claimed her innocence first.

And who will be the first one to fuck her pussy. And her ass.

And to make sure that no matter what, the only name she'll ever want to scream out when she comes is mine—even if it's in her head.

It was about asserting my dominance and my stake over a man who doesn't know her, let alone deserve her. An ingrate who has no business putting a ring on her finger.

I didn't expect that her words would flare up the possessiveness and jealousy that blinded me after my call with Haakon.

"Damn right you're mine." I pause. "And I'm yours."

"Oh, God, Easton—" She shakes her head as if she's having a conversation with herself. "You are?" she finally asks.

"Yes, Princess."

She blinks up at me. "How do we—"

"Shhh." I place two fingers against her lips. "Let's focus on the now."

She gives me a sad smile.

"What's up with the frown? I thought I just took good care of you."

"You did. You're right. Why fret over the future?"

"That's my girl."

Her smile is a little brighter this time, but not by much.

Honestly, I don't have the answers. We're from two different worlds and I don't want to come between her and her parents. She'll resent me in the long run.

My heart is beating fast in my chest at the thought of her belonging to another man.

What I feel for Brielle is new to me.

I don't even know how to call it.

I've been in relationships for weeks—months even—and never felt anything close to this.

Although I haven't put a label on it, what Brielle and I share is far from casual, but there's still that insurmountable barrier.

CHAPTER 23

Brielle

For the past blissful week and a half, Easton and I have seen each other every single day. It's incredible that even though he keeps pushing me further out of my comfort zone and amps up the naughty level whenever he can, my virginity is still intact. He held true to his promise. I've objected many times, but he reminds me that there's no rush. When he says that, it gives me hope. It helps me believe that what we share could possibly last for longer than a heated season.

We've become quite creative about finding places to meet. He's been back to the penthouse a few times and we've used a number of the conference rooms at his office in the most unlawful way. It's not that we're hiding anything from Sienna, it just feels awkward being over at their place when she's there. It's not like Easton and I are sitting in front of the telly watching a film and eating popcorn. I have no doubt she knows that, but why rub it in her face? Sienna has been very understanding and she's still on my team. This only makes me love her more.

I've also become a bit of an expert at dodging my mother's calls and text messages about Prince Haakon. She thinks the prince and I should connect before our official dinner. I disagree. The only tool I have in my arsenal is to use my workload at school as a shield. Iyanna and Blakely are in on it. The same goes for Officer Pavlova. They've been allies in my quest to keep my Pollyanna glasses on. Nothing is official yet. I'm sure if I really hate the man, my mum will back off. I hope. I agreed to meet the prince so that she can stop yapping my ear off.

My workload is only a partial lie. It was my decision to attend summer school to speed up my degree. Sienna and Lilo followed suit. All that to say that I have quite a lot of papers to finish. That's why I'm locked up inside the penthouse on a beautiful sunny day instead of being outside.

"I need a break," I mumble, rubbing my tired eyes.

I'm just about to get up to go to the kitchen for dessert and a cup of tea when my phone rings. I grab it, already giddy.

"Hey, beautiful!"

"Easton!"

"I know we spoke this morning, but I wanted to check in with you before I leave."

"I'll never get tired of hearing your voice."

"Same here," he laughs. "You're still at it?"

"Yup. Other than a few breaks here and there, I've been sitting at the dining room table since seven o'clock this morning."

"You're a real trooper."

"That's what I keep telling myself, although I'd much prefer going for a stroll or running to a yoga class instead of being cooped up in here."

"Priorities first, Princess."

"Right. Are you at the airport?"

"Yes. I'm sitting inside the private jet. We're on the tarmac waiting our turn. We're minutes away from takeoff."

He hasn't even left yet and already, I miss him.

"Were you able to confirm if you'll have to stay longer in Stockholm?"

"I'm still waiting on that start-up to confirm, but it sounds like I might have to be there five days instead of three."

That sounds like an eternity.

"I'll miss you."

"Not nearly as much as I'll miss you."

A smile, one of optimism, crosses my face. "I love hearing you say that."

"It's true. You know it. In the last week and a half I've grown accustomed to seeing you every day. I'm sure in the next few days I'll feel the void."

His confession tugs at my heart.

"I already know it's going to be a brutal week for me," I confess.

"That makes two of us, beautiful. We'll be on WhatsApp every night?"

"Absolutely!" I cheer.

"And we can text each other whenever we feel the need to connect."

"And I intend on doing exactly that," I say lifting my chin up in determination.

"I don't have much time left, but I have a question before I go."

"I'm all ears."

"Tell me, Princess," his voice goes down by many octaves, "how many times are you going to pleasure yourself while I'm away?"

"Oh, gosh."

"That doesn't answer my question, beautiful."

"I'm not."

"You're not what?"

"I'm not going to touch myself."

I've gone from not having self-pleasure as part of my vocabulary to enjoying when Easton demands that I play with myself in front of him. To say that I've come a long way is an understatement.

"That's right. And you know why?"

It's my turn to lower my voice although I'm the only one in the penthouse. "Because you own my pussy." I can't help but grin.

"Damn right I do. And the rest of you. The only time I want to see your fingers deep inside your sweet little princess pussy is when we're on video. That's the only time you're allowed to work your royal pussy until it squirts all over your fingertips. Got that?"

"Loud and clear!"

Even when he's kilometers away, his dirty talking gets me so wet.

"Good," he chuckles. "My girl is such a good pupil."

"That's only because she has the best teacher in the Big Apple."

"Excuse me?"

"I mean the best teacher in the world."

"Much better." We both laugh. "All kidding aside, it's time for me to go, Brielle."

So soon? "Okay."

"I'll touch base the minute I land."

"I can't wait."

I hang up with the man who's turned my world upside down in the best possible way. I let out a heavy sigh as I bring my iPhone to my heart and hug it as if I was hugging him instead.

Even though Lilo has tried to coax it out of me, I refuse to admit that I've fallen for Easton Ellis Winchester. It's ridiculous. I know. It's only been a few weeks. How can I possibly feel this way about him? At first, I thought it was my innocence playing against me. It's not. I reached that conclusion a long time ago.

He may not have a kingdom, a crown or a throne, but I would call him my king. I want Easton to be the shepherd to my heart. If I were just a regular girl, it would be a fairly uncomplicated situation. Alas, I come with aristocratic baggage. And it weighs a damn ton right now. I never thought the royal blood flowing through my veins would one day end up choking me.

Bollocks.

I shake off my momentary despair and decide to take a note from Lilo's book.

"Sugar. I. Need. Sugar."

* * *

After polishing off two slices of the almond pound cake Sienna baked and brought over yesterday, I soothe my soul with two strong cups of tea. Now that I'm perked up again thanks to my sugar high, I'm ready to dive right back into my homework.

For the next two hours, I'm so focused, I surprise myself. The problem is that I'm now cross-eyed.

In desperate need of a body break, I decide to go up to the rooftop—with Officer Pavlova in tow—to get some sun. Fifteen minutes later, I feel like a new person.

"Back at it!" I pep myself up as I enter the penthouse.

I barely have time to sit down behind my Mac laptop when my phone rings. I don't recognize the number.

"It can't be Easton. He hasn't landed in Sweden yet."

I'm just about to ignore the call when it hits me.

"Maybe he's making a Wi-Fi voice call!"

Overjoyed to hear from my lover so soon, I click on the video button not even thinking twice.

"Hey—" *That's not Easton staring at me.* "I'm sorry, I think you have the wrong number."

"Princess Brielle?"

"Yes," I say cautiously.

"Forgive me for not sending a text message prior to calling you, but I was eager."

"I'm sorry, but have we met?"

"I'm Prince Haakon."

What?

"How did you get my number?"

"Your mother suggested I take the initiative."

I can't believe she did that.

"I see."

"I guess you didn't recognize me."

I shake my head. "No, I didn't."

"I've been told I look different in person."

No kidding. You look much older than your photos, mate. "Don't we all."

"Absolutely not. You're as beautiful as the photos I've seen of you online and the ones your mother sends me."

"She does that?"

"Yes. Daily."

I'm stunned.

"I'm sorry about that. I'm sure you must have other things to do with your time than—"

"Not at all. In fact, I look forward to them."

"Right."

I avert my gaze.

"Am I catching you at a bad time?" His question brings my eyes back to the screen.

"I'm in the middle of studying."

"Ah, yes. You have two years left on your degree?" he asks.

"A year and a half," I correct him.

"You're nearly there."

"I am."

My answers are wooden.

I can't even bring myself to offer him the slightest of smiles. I'm still in shock that my mother would betray me like this. How dare she go behind my back and give out my phone number without my consent – and sending him photos? Dear God!

"Well, I thought your mother had a brilliant idea. I wanted to reach out so that you feel a little more comfortable when we finally meet."

That's unlikely to happen. "Okay."

The mention of the inevitable makes me want to vomit.

"I'm in Australia right now, but I'll be back in Europe soon. I promised Princess Janika I would stop by for a visit. She mentioned you'd be coming from New York to Belzer for the occasion."

"Yes." *But I really, really, really don't want to.*

"It was supposed to be an informal thing, but your mother is making a big deal out of it and in the end, I'll bring my grandmother, the Queen, and a few other family members."

Great. Not. "My mother has already warned me of your visit. She didn't tell me you were coming with an entourage."

Sarcastic a bit?

Absolutely.

"Warned you?"

"Yes."

"That sounds fairly threatening considering you'll be my wife soon. You'll have to warm up to me."

Cold sweat trickles down my back.

"We haven't even met yet, Prince. Maybe you won't like me when you meet me in person."

Please God, hear my prayer.

"I already like what I see."

I wish I could say the same thing. "Right."

"Listen, Brielle, people of our rank and stature understand that marriage is a business arrangement. Nothing more. Nothing less. Some of us are lucky enough that we're able to tolerate our significant other.

Some of us might go as far as to say that we genuinely like the person we were obligated to marry. The rest of us endure."

I see he's been drinking the same Kool-Aid as mum.

"You're much older than me—"

"That's a good thing—"

"That's not where I was going with that."

"Humor me. You were saying." He even does this annoying hand gesture.

Jerk!

I usually love video calls, but right now, I hate them.

"The press has made it clear that you enjoy life at its fullest—"

"You mean I'm a self-confessed player?"

"Something like that."

Manwhore is a word they used, but we'll go with player.

"Surely, in all those years, you must've met someone who you wanted more with." *Yes, I'm fishing for a way out.* "What about that actress? What's her name again?" I snap my fingers a few times, but nothing pops to mind.

"That was ages ago." *As in four months?* "It's water under the bridge now."

"Fair enough. Maybe it didn't work out with her, but maybe *she's* out there. Do you really want to miss out on your chance to meet the one you were supposed to be with?"

He rolls his eyes and lets out this choked sound. "Brielle, don't tell me you believe in fairy tales."

That's dripping with contempt.

"Love isn't a fairytale," I argue.

He narrows his green eyes at me and brings his phone close to his face. The move is so intimidating that I jerk back in my seat. "And at the tender age of twenty, you know that firsthand?"

Oh, this conversation is sliding straight down to the gutters of hell.

"I know people who are in love." That's the best I can come up with.

Many of my former and current commoner classmates tell me how they long to find a love that parallels that of their parents'. So it is possible even if loving relationships in my circle are a rarity.

"Good for them. That's not how it's going to work between us. This is strictly business," he repeats. My stomach drops. "We'll let the dust settle once I take on the kingship and then we'll get married. You'll rear my children, you'll respect me and you'll always be ready when I want to have sex—regardless if you can stand the sight of me or not."

May I barf now?

I stare at Haakon's unattractive face for a second before bursting out laughing. "You're serious?" I ask in disbelief.

"I'm dead serious. I already have our marriage all planned out." *Excuse me?* "Love is for pathetic losers, like commoners. We're better than them. We were born into unspeakable privilege and wealth. Who cares about love? We can buy anything… and anyone, we want."

"How can you say that?"

"Enough with this love rubbish," he snaps. "This sort of arrangement isn't without precedence in my country or yours."

I don't even know him and already he's lost his temper. I can just imagine how short his fuse will be once I'm trapped in a marriage.

My opinion means nothing to him. He operates in the same fashion as my mother does. *They* should get married. Clearly, they have a lot in common.

"If you agree to become a docile and obedient wife, life will be good. If not, we'll have a marriage centered around the children—and favorable photo opportunities—"

"Wh-what does that even mean?" The words tumble nervously out of my mouth.

"We want my subjects to think we are a happy couple. It's good for politics. The press will play an important role in our relationship."

"What?"

"As I was saying, we'll keep up the façade until you ask for a divorce."

"A divorce?"

What a cruel man.

"Yes. My parents broke the mold on that one. It's no longer as taboo as it once was in Brihon. Once I give you your marching papers—"

"That's what you call it?"

"Well yes, I'll have dismissed you as my queen and my wife."

For the love of God, he makes this sound like a job. Not a very pleasant one at that.

"To continue my point, once the ink is dry, you can live wherever you want, do whatever you want. You can even get remarried if you want." *Thank you, sire, for your immense generosity.* "You're young, so you might still hold up nicely." *Buzz off.* "Of course, we'll have a prenup." *My father has far more money than everyone in your kingdom combined.* "Just keep in mind that once the divorce is pronounced final, you'll have to leave my manor, but the children stay. They'll have my surname and my blood will run through their veins. They will be mine."

"My blood will be running through their veins as well," I protest.

"You'll merely be a queen by marriage, not by birthright. Other than bringing them into the world, you won't have much claim over them."

I swallow a snarky reply.

His words are stone cold.

"So if I decide I don't want to leave my children behind, I'll be a prisoner?"

"Perhaps, but it will be one of the most luxurious prisons known to mankind."

I hate you.

"Getting you pregnant will be fun." *Huh?* "It's been a while since I've banged a virgin. I'm looking forward to our wedding night."

You're repulsive.

That trite comment makes me see red. I'd rather stab a steak knife into his crotch than let him come anywhere near me. I'll live with the consequences.

"Should I assume your ass is also untouched?" he continues when I remain stunned into silence. "I hope so. I love ripping a tight virgin ass in half. And you're so lucky because your husband-to-be is very, very well *equipped* for the job." His eyes drop. I assume to his *equipment.*

My mouth parts open in shock. A wave of revulsion passes through me, and for the first time in my life I'm this close to spitting out *fuck you* in a person's face. Alas, my upbringing wins and I just shoot daggers at him with my angry eyes.

"You're a virgin front and back, right?"

"I refuse to dignify that with an answer," I manage.

"Suit yourself. Your mother assures me you are. I'm sure she'd never steer me in the wrong direction since she's so eager to marry you off to a king." His smirk becomes wider. *My mother is a piece of work.* "I know some princesses remain virgins until they wed by getting their assess fucked. I hope you aren't one of them. I might have to return you and give your mother a good spanking. I can do that when I become king." He lets out an awful laugh. "That was a joke."

No, you're the joke, mate.

"I have to go," I blurt out as I feel the first onset of a terrible nausea mounting from the pit of my stomach to the back of my throat.

"Pity. So soon? We were just getting to know each other."

No, you were spewing rubbish and I'm about to get violently ill.

"I have a pile high of homework to do and you've given me so much to…" I choose my words carefully, "think over."

"I'm glad you see it that way. I just called to say hello, I never imagined we were going to be able to iron out so many important things. Well, on this parting note, remember, Brielle, a political marriage is a healthy marriage because both parties know exactly where they stand. I'm so excited about our future."

I don't even bother to answer, I just hang up the call.

I sit there for a few long seconds fuming in anger.

"Arghhh!" I yell, throwing my phone across the room and shattering it in a million pieces.

What a great analogy for my poor broken heart.

And then Easton's face flashes in front me.

I bring my hands up to my throat as a panic attack hits me.

Oh God.

I can't breathe.

I hate these archaic constraints.

Suddenly, the walls of the penthouse seem to close in around me, a black haze blinds me. I drop to my knees and I start to wail.

"As God is my witness, I'd rather slash my wrists and bleed to death than ever become that demon's wife!" I yell between fits of rage and sadness.

Then I realize there's something unfathomably worse than dying—never seeing Easton again.

Please God, save me.

CHAPTER 24

Brielle

"Iyanna texted me and begged me to come back. She said it's an emergency!" Lilo blurts as she bursts into my bedroom and the door slams open, startling us both. My eyes fly up. Hers move to where the door makes contact with the wall. "Sorry about that," she says. "What's—" her jaw drops when she takes me in. "My God, Bri, what happened?"

"It's... it's... it's..." I hiccup. "Oh, my God, Lilo, my life is over. I want to die," I burst into tears.

She rushes over to me and sits next to me on the bed. "What happened?" she repeats. She brushes my wet hair off my face and caresses my cheek with the back of her hand. "Talk to me, Bri."

I can just imagine what I look like. For the past hour I've been crying uncontrollably and that's in between rushing to the loo to puke my guts out.

"I don't want to live anymore," I wail.

"What is it?" She shakes me so hard my hair goes flying all over the place. "Is it Easton? He no longer wants to see you? Did he break your heart? I swear I'm going to find him and give him a piece of my mind if he did this to you."

"Nooooo! Easton is perfect!" I burst out crying.

"Then what is it? You're freaking me out!" Lilo yells so loudly I jerk.

"Bloody Prince Haakon of Wallon from the Kingdom of Shit showed his true colors," Iyanna says. When I look up, she's leaning against the doorframe with her arms crossed over her chest and with that same sullen expression on her face that's been there since she found me crying face down on the bathroom floor.

"What the hell did he do? Was the prince here?" Lilo is frantic.

I take a deep breath in and will myself to calm down long enough to say, "My mother is pushing her agenda."

Lilo's eyebrows knit together. "I don't understand."

"Mum gave Prince Haakon my phone number. I answered the call without recognizing the number thinking it was Easton calling from his Swedish number. That's when my world came crashing down like a castle of cards. I had the most traumatizing conversation of my life with a disgusting man I feel I'm being sold to."

"What did he say?"

"Perhaps I should go," Iyanna suggests.

"Stay," I tell her. "You already know the story. Without you arriving when you did, I would have already jumped from the rooftop."

"Are you sure, Princess?" she asks. "I don't want to overstep my boundaries."

I extend my hands to her. She comes running over. "Iyanna, you're far more than just a lady-in-waiting or an assistant, you're a friend."

"I am." She brings my hands to her lips and drops a soft kiss against them. "And friends don't let friends marry repulsive assholes." The harshness of her words slices through the room. Both Lilo and I are surprised. "What?" she challenges.

"I've never heard you use that kind of language before," I say.

"But I'm right, am I not?" she insists.

"There's no other way of describing such a vile person," I agree.

I lean to grab a tissue, but it's empty. It's the second box in a matter of an hour.

"Let me run and fetch you another box," Iyanna says before I ask.

I give her a grateful look. "What would I do without you?"

She's back in a flash. "I just regret I was out when the asshole called. I would've interrupted that call and I wouldn't have held my tongue."

"I wish I'd never had to go through that. I'm still shaking in anger," I say.

"Now that we've all established that the Prince of Shit is reprehensible, please can you tell me what happened?" Lilo demands.

I wipe the flood of tears off my face and tell my cousin everything. I start with my pleasant conversation with Easton before telling her all of the horrible things Prince Haakon said and how he viewed our future marriage.

"What a pig. How dare he threaten to keep your children. Only a monster would say something like that."

"Exactly," Iyanna says.

"He's worse than a monster, Lilo. The crude jokes he made about the things he intends to do when he becomes King are chilling. This man won't be a fair king. He'll be a tyrant. He'll rule by instigating fear in people. From what I sense, his kingship will be nothing more than a dictatorship."

"Which is why you can't marry him," Iyanna says.

"Mum—"

"These old conventions are just that, old. They don't apply in our world anymore," Iyanna interrupts.

"They're relics like so many of the artifacts in the Museum Of National Treasures in Belzer," Lilo chimes in.

"Your mother is holding onto them like a life jacket. It makes absolutely no sense," Iyanna continues. "My mum," – that would be Contessa Calixta Aurelia Elise Hoffräulein – "told me in confidence that your father asked her to speak to your mother. Mum says Princess Janika is blinded by a force no one can fight. No one understands her motives given that Prince Haakon isn't exactly a prize."

"I'm sorry, but not only is this utterly stupid, but it's plain wrong," Lilo states. "You and Easton were made for each other."

"Hear, hear," Iyanna agrees.

She doesn't know everything, but my lady-in-waiting knows enough.

"Prince Haakon is the opposite of the man Easton is—"

"They couldn't be more different," Lilo interjects.

I offer her a warm smile. "Easton's mere presence leaves me flustered—even when he's God knows how many kilometers away, I still feel him. He cherishes me. He's patient with me. I feel safe with him." I pause. "I felt violated the entire time I was on the phone with Prince Haakon. That last comment about me being a virgin was testament to his black heart. And any man who would force a woman to choose between misery and her children deserves to be castrated."

"Amen to that!" Lilo shouts lifting her hands above her head.

"For the last few weeks, it's been heart-stopping moment after heart-stopping moment with the most wonderful man on this planet and now I'm faced with a grim future. They say God works in mysterious ways. Sometimes I question that. Why would God sacrifice me this way?"

"God isn't the one behind this mockery. Your mum is." The expression of revolt on Iyanna's face says it all.

I let out a long heavy sigh. "Even after I called her and told her word-for-word what Prince Haakon had told me, she stood firm. She says that first encounters can be a little awkward sometimes," I confess.

"That's rubbish." Yes, you guessed it, Iyanna voices her opinion.

"Even now with reality staring her in the face your mum refuses to listen?" Lilo asks.

I nod. "She won't budge."

"Then don't show up at the altar. Run away," Iyanna says. "I'm sure your father will back you up financially and your blog is very successful. You can live anywhere you want. I'll come with you. So will Officer Pavlova and Officer Stanton. No one wants to be around your mother's sour attitude."

"You're too sweet," I tell her.

"Just like Iyanna," Lilo says, "my mum tried to talk to your mum. She told my mum to butt the hell out and stay out. Mum was furious and promised to never speak to your mother ever again."

"She keeps insisting that after the first dinner with the prince, I'll see him in a different light and I'll like him," I say.

"My arse you will," Iyanna sneers.

"You're a whole different person today," I say, a bit taken aback.

"If I knew who to hire, I would commission a hit on the Prince of Shit's head. That would force your mother to back off," my lady-in-waiting admits.

I'm shocked by her words, but at the same time I'm so touched. It's my turn to take her hands into mine. "I admire your loyalty, but I won't allow it to get to that point."

"Killing yourself isn't an option, Princess," Iyanna retaliates.

"I doubt I'd be able to go through with it. It was all talk, stemming from desperation," I set her straight. "I need time to calm down and find a way out."

For a few long seconds, no one speaks.

"Go meet him," Lilo says with a pensive look on her face. My head snaps in her direction.

Iyanna's jaw drops. "You can't be serious?"

"At least you'll have ammunition to tell your mother this is a bad idea. You can say there's no chemistry between you and the prince. I think that'll give you a leg to stand on," she offers a sympathetic smile.

"I appreciate your suggestion, but I doubt it's going to work. Mum's parting words were, *"Suck it up, Brielle. There are worse things in the world than to marry an unattractive and slightly repugnant king."*

"She's contradicted herself! One minute she says you'll like him and the next she tells you he's shit!" Iyanna shouts.

"Your mum is over the top. My parents were also in a sort of arranged marriage, and it's true they barely speak to each other anymore, but they don't hate each other. Your mum hates your dad—with a passion—and she's not shy about cutting him off at the knees any chance she has."

"I know. Daddy isn't a saint, but he doesn't deserve that."

"No one deserves to live with such a vitriolic— It's best if I don't finish my sentence," Iyanna says.

"I absolutely agree with what Iyanna isn't willing to say." Lilo nods, her lips pursed together. "At this rate, your mum and dad are going to kill each other with their constant exchange of condescending words."

"I totally agree," I say.

"Why would your mum want the same crappy life for you?"

"It defies logic, Lilo."

"I have to quote the French, *Il y a anguille sous roche*. There's more than meets the eye, Bri."

I look up at my cousin. "That's what Dad says. He says that usually, he's content to let Mum fly off the handle and find a safe place in the manor to hide, but this is beyond him."

"I'll repeat myself. Meet the Prince of Shit. You can then tell your mother that you lived up to your side of the bargain, but that's as far as you're willing to go—regardless if you end up being a disappointment as a daughter," Lilo says.

That's one of Mum's favorite insults. She knows it makes me feel guilty when she says that. I've never felt like I could live up to her expectations. That's just a daily reminder.

"If she still insists, I'm with Iyanna. Run away. You'll have access to your trust fund when you turn twenty-five. I'm certain your dad will back you up in the meantime. If not directly, through Prince Joachim and Princess Birgitta—your grandparents aren't very fond of your mum. And Prince Joachim wouldn't hesitate to involve his father, King Dagget, if needs be. Your blog is more than sufficient to sustain you. So, you might have to downgrade a bit. Maybe you'll have to go someplace far away where you'll be out of reach of your mother's claws. One thing is certain, I'll never be able to live with myself if I don't push you to fight this with everything you have," Lilo says with a determination I've never seen before.

I ponder on her words. "Okay. Maybe that dreadful dinner is the first step."

"Yes." Lilo says.

"I don't know," Iyanna says shaking her head.

"I'll follow Lilo's advice," I tell her.

"Your call," she shrugs.

"Neither of you can breathe a word of this to Easton or Sienna."

"But—"

"Lilo, promise me," I insist.

"Okay." The reply doesn't come immediately, and when it does, I can tell she's against it.

"Iyanna?"

"Princess—"

I shake my head. "No. Just promise me."

"Bollocks."

I cock an eyebrow.

She averts her gaze. "I'll keep my mouth shut."

CHAPTER 25

Easton

The flight from Manhattan to Stockholm is nearly eight hours. Of course Brielle has been on my mind since I hung up with her.

My little princess.

In the very short time we've been seeing each other, I've become addicted to the way her lips taste—both sets. My decision not to fuck her yet has opened the door to so many possibilities. Surprisingly, having to rely solely on naughty play isn't such a bad thing.

My cock hardens as her sweet scent fills my nostrils.

Fuck.

As promised, I called Brielle, but she sounded off. I may not know everything about her, but we've grown close enough that I'm able to read her mood. Just like when we were having a little dirty fun in her kitchen, I could feel she was hiding something, but it was impossible for me to coax it out of her. I called Sienna to ask her if anything was up with her best friend, but she said that as far as she knows everything is fine. I'm not buying it. I didn't become a multi-billionaire by being able to sense which companies would fly high and which would bust without relying on my gut.

"What the hell is going on, Princess?" I ask myself as I pace around the hotel suite.

I've been possessive of Brielle from the instant I kissed her, but now after so many days of us being together, I'm like a starved tiger who finally has its prey—don't you dare touch what's mine.

Just like in my business, once my mind is set on something, I'll move mountain and earth to make it happen. Dating comes easy when you're wealthy, young and fit. So getting the girl has never been a problem. With Brielle it's different. I always knew it would be tricky, but now that she's mine, I wonder how I'm going to keep her. I'm flying blind here—something that's never happened to me before.

"How do you keep the girl you were destined to be with when you don't fit into her world?"

Frustrated, I plop myself at the desk and open a browser on my Mac laptop. I do a quick Google search on Prince Haakon. The number of results is staggering. I bypass Wikipedia, People magazine, two leading UK celebrity papers and royal watcher HELLO! magazine. I click on one of the lower results on the first page—those are often chock-full of good info. The headline screams at me. 'PRINCE HAAKON LURKÖPING TRAVELS WITH OWN BED, LINEN, TOWELS AND TOILET SEAT, NEW BOOK REVEALS. PEOPLE OF BRIHON FOOT THE BILL.'

"What a loser."

I click on another link on that same site and the next headline is as much of a joke. 'PRINCE HAAKON, AKA THE ROYAL FUCK-UP OF BRIHON, STRUGGLES TO PLEASE HIS GRANDMOTHER, QUEEN GERTRUDE. DOES HE HAVE THE BALLS TO BECOME KING?'

"That dickless asshole will be a terrible king," I mumble.

The next link is about Haakon's father, Prince Clemens of Wallon. 'WHERE "UNPOPULAR" PRINCE CLEMENS WENT WRONG.' I scan it quickly and it has to do with how the prince's media-hounded farce of a divorce with his now deceived wife Princess Diandra caused the Queen to bypass her own son for the sovereign seat.

"What a messed up family." I shake my head. "Brielle will be miserable. She's such a pure soul. If she marries that idiot, they'll contaminate her."

I'm fuming. Once again, my first instinct is to break everything around me. Instead, I will myself to calm down. I tap my Montblanc fountain pen angrily against the desk, trying to make sense of Brielle's mother's motives.

Doesn't she love her daughter?

"I need answers."

I grab my phone and dial my secret weapon when evaluating celebrities who want to invest in startups. The world of show business is all smoke and mirrors. Canny publicists are masters at creating an impenetrable image. My source pokes holes through those well-crafted fronts.

"Hey, Clara, it's Easton," I say as I type her blog URL.

"If it isn't my favorite American bloke," she laughs.

"Oh, I don't like the sound of that, sugar plum. Have you been cheating on me?"

"Every single day."

We both laugh.

"I'm on your blog and I can see business is booming for ShowBizDaily.com," I chuckle.

"What can I say? Too many celebrities willing to fuck up and too little time. Who would've thunk that one day, I'd be doing this full-time?"

I met Clara Bowen seven years ago at a party in London. Those were the days I was building my presence there. We went out on three dates, but quickly realized that we'd be better off as friends than lovers. She's a Brit and she used to work at one of the top gossip rags in the UK. She got a tip on a juicy story, but her then editor refused to run with it stating that it was too risky for the paper. Clara disagreed. She was running her blog part-time back then. It was nothing much to talk about, but she decided to jump in fearlessly. She quit her job, pursued the story and blew the whistle on a major scandal. Since then, her blog is one of the top ten most visited showbiz and gossip sites on the Internet.

"And you do it well," I say.

"A compliment?"

"You say that like I never praise your work."

"Yeah, but if you're opening the conversation with that, something is up. What can I do for you, mate?"

"Straight to business," I laugh.

"Time is money as you Americans say."

"Fair enough. I need your professional opinion on someone."

"A celebrity wants to ride the startup speeding train?"

"No, this guy is royalty."

"Didn't Wizard Elian come up with anything? He's an expert at cracking the royalty code," Clara says.

"He did, but this guy is a bit of a media whore. Well, actually he's also a manwhore, but he relishes the attention he gets from the media—good or bad. I think it's his own way of validating the fact that his title trumps anything else."

"Who are we talking about here?"

"Prince Haakon of—"

"Run away as fast as you can," she blurts out.

"I gather you're not a fan?"

She lets out a long sigh. "We all get that being born royal opens the door to unimaginable privileges, which most of us will never get a taste of, but Haakon takes it ten steps further. The man thinks the taxes his people pay are to fund his playboy lifestyle. That's just wrong."

"Yeah, I gathered that from the few articles I've read online."

"That's what happens when you allow a child to grow up without boundaries. And discipline. And proper punishments."

"His parents' divorce?"

"Exactly. The Queen pushed Princess Diandra out of her kids' lives. Haakon's big sister, Princess Wilhelmina Artura Liseea of Paddock, turned out okay. That's not the case for the prince. Haakon is abominable. Prince Clemens was too busy renewing ties with his long-time lover Caramya Rosalind Shandersand to give a toss about his son. The result? An ungrateful rich kid who is completely out of control."

"The making of an asshole manwhore," I sneer.

"According to my sources, the unattractive prince has seen more pussy than a retired gynecologist. We're talking about absurd numbers here."

"I'm not surprised. No little Haakons running around?" I ask.

"None that I know of. It seems that the only thing Haakon is capable of doing right is to wrap it up tightly."

"Or he's shooting blanks."

She laughs.

"Forgive me for asking, Easton, but those questions seem to transcend the kind you'd ask about a potential investor. Why do I sense this is personal?"

"You're good—"

"Bite your tongue, mate. I'm the best."

"I won't argue with you."

"So are you going to answer me?"

"It's very personal."

"What in the world would a loser like Haakon have in common with a guy like you?"

"Princess Brielle Elise Madeleine Strasberg of Exton."

"I don't understand, Easton. That girl has such a clean slate, it's ridiculous. No matter how much they dig, none of my sources are able to find anything on her. She's flirting with sainthood."

"Let's just say her and I are more than friends," I admit.

It's not like me to lay my personal life on the line like this, but I need Clara's help.

"Wow. The elusive Easton Winchester gets caught in a mighty royal net."

"You have a way with words, Clara."

"So what's the deal between you and the chaste princess?"

Over the next few minutes, I tell Clara as much as I can without compromising the intimacy I share with Brielle.

"My God, those conventions are prehistoric," Clara says when I finish.

"I couldn't agree with you more."

"Well, I shouldn't be surprised."

"Why do you say that?"

"We're talking about Princess Janika Levyna Strasberg of Blackcheldale, a.k.a., the princess with a bitter *and* black heart."

"That bad?"

"That's how the manor's staff refers to her behind her back. She's miserable, spiteful and mean. Oh, and I forgot to mention her penchant for vodka martinis."

"A functional alcoholic?"

"She's as dysfunctional as they get."

"Brielle is the complete opposite," I say.

"Clearly, she takes after her father's side. Prince Janek is a lot more easy-going. Thanks to years of marriage to Janika, he's lost his jovial personality, but he isn't a mean prick."

"I've been mulling over some of the information Elian collected on the selfish prince and I've done some basic Google searches—"

"Despite the smiley photos, the Lurköping clan isn't close. I'd be willing to bet that they hate each other. Diandra's motherly love was good for Haakon. Now that she's gone, he's a lost cause. Add to that a series of recent melodramas and you have a recipe for disaster. The tension between the Queen and Clemens' long-time-lover-now-wife is palpable. Her disapproval of her grandson's philandering ways is well-known."

"I get the gist of the family dynamic, but there's something bothering me. After hearing what you just said and after reading a few articles, things make even less sense."

"Like what?"

"First off, I would think that Princess Janika would have higher standards for her daughter than Haakon."

"I think she's too self-absorbed to care."

"It seems to be more than that, Clara, but there's something more pressing."

"Shoot."

"Why would a self-confessed playboy sell brand-new pussy magnets a few months after acquiring them?"

"You're referring to Haakon's former twenty-seven million-dollar fifty-meter superyacht and the two-million dollar EC120 Colibri Hummingbird helicopter?"

"Exactly. And he sold them at a loss to buy an outrageously expensive mansion on the other side of the planet."

"Interesting that you'd ask. That transaction is still very recent—the ink has barely had time to dry on the legal papers—"

"In other words you're following the story?"

"You know me well, mate."

"What's your take on it?

"Do you really want to know?"

"I wouldn't ask if I didn't."

"Do you have half an hour?"

"That much?"

"That's the abridged version," Clara says.

Shit.

* * *

The deluge of information Clare shared was jaw-dropping to say the least. Haakon is a piece of shit. After hanging up with her, I call another one of my contacts.

"Bryce!"

"Hey, Easton!"

"How's business?"

"Too many crooks, too little time," he laughs. "How about you?"

"Too many startups, too little time… and not enough seed investors." It's my turn to laugh.

"So in other words, you're rolling in dough?"

"It takes another billionaire to know," I joke.

"Ain't that the truth?"

We both laugh.

"How can I help you?" Bryce asks.

Bryce Van Der Linden owns Linden Corp. He has nearly a decade and a half on me. We met through a mutual client—a high roller. Since then, I've called on him many times. He's my secret weapon when all else fails. I reach out to him when Clare and Elian come up empty handed… or when my gut tells me there's more—like it is now.

"If I was in the market to sell an obscenely expensive yacht and helicopter for some quick cash, who would I call?"

"Are you in trouble?" I hear the concern in his voice.

"No. I'm talking about a potential client."

"Money laundering? Or are we talking about a dot com whiz kid? Those are the ones buying yachts like it's candy. Even A-list celebrities are now renting instead of buying. The upkeep alone is ridiculous."

"He's a royal."

"You've piqued my curiosity. Who are we talking about?"

"Prince Haakon."

"I've vaguely heard about him. If he's royal, haven't you already reached out to your trusted sources?" Bryce asks.

"I have, but there is still so much about this guy no one can dig up. Elian doesn't have a full picture. Neither does Clare. That's a problem." I pause, weighing my words. "This is more personal business."

"A woman?"

"Yeah."

"Sounds serious."

"It is, Bryce."

"Wow. I never thought I'd hear you say those words."

"It's always when you least expect it, right?"

"So they say. Thank God, I'm still immune," he chuckles. "Talk to me, Easton. I need more to go by if I'm going to help you."

Over the next few minutes, I tell him everything I know and what Clare discovered.

"I figured since yachts and helicopters are so pricey, they must leave a trail of money," I conclude.

"You're right. There are only a handful of people qualified to act as a middleman in those types of transactions. I'll get my team to start digging."

Bryce is the leader in cyber-intelligence. The man's team pinpoints a minute detail everyone else misses and traces it to any corner of this planet. Hackers don't stand a chance. Swindlers will be exposed. Thieves will be brought to justice. The more complex and puzzling cases get Bryce's group of top code crackers excited. He's saved me a lot of money—and headaches—in the past. I hope he can fill in the blanks.

"So you think you'll find more dirt on the crooked prince?"

"You wouldn't bother to call if you didn't think I could."

I sigh a breath of relief.

This man's confidence is humbling.

"Thank you," I say. "I appreciate it."

"Not a problem, Easton. I'm already rubbing my hands together. I can't wait to follow the money trail … when we're done with him, the asshole prince won't have a leg to stand on."

From your lips to God's hears.

CHAPTER 26

Brielle

"Wake up! Wake up! Wake up!" Lilo yells, bursting into my room.

I bolt upright in bed.

"What? Is the building on fire?"

"Worse!"

I look around the room.

Nothing.

I even sniff in a few times.

Smells pretty normal to me.

"You aren't making any sense, Lilo."

She approaches my bed. "I was up early enjoying a lazy Wednesday morning on the rooftop since I don't have any classes today. I had just finished flipping through the pages of the latest edition of Ideal Home and decided to visit their Facebook page to watch a cool DIY video. But when I landed on my newsfeed, my jaw dropped and I started to panic."

"What in the world caused that reaction?"

"This." She hands me her iPad.

I read the headline in shock.

'FORMER PLAYER PRINCE HAAKON TO MARRY THE BEAUTIFUL PRINCESS BRIELLE OF EXTON. STAY TUNED!'

"Is this a joke?" I ask.

"I visited three different celebrity sites and two royal ones. They're all chanting the same hymn."

"That's not possible. For the love of God, we haven't even been in the same room."

"I'm going to state the obvious here and assume you knew nothing about this."

"Lilo, I'm in as much shock as—"

"Oh my God, the Prince of Shit started a shit storm!" Iyanna shouts rushing into my bedroom waving her iPhone in front of her.

"I just saw the news," I tell her.

"Why would he go to the press before he even asks for your hand in marriage?" Lilo asks.

"To put pressure on me," I say at the same time as Iyanna says, "To put a collar around her throat."

Her explanation is far more accurate.

"What an unscrupulous man. He's sending the message that he owns you," Lilo says.

"Exactly. Now that it's public, it becomes a lot harder for me to say no," I say in a pained voice.

"No, it doesn't," Iyanna protests.

Her face is beet red in anger.

God, do I ever love this woman's loyalty.

"Do you think your mum knew Haakon was going to pull off something this sneaky?" Lilo asks.

"I'm willing to bet my trust fund on it. That woman's hands are dirty," Iyanna answers before I do.

"She's right," I say. "I stuck my head in the sand like an ostrich when I should've been more vigilant."

"Why would you say that?" Lilo asks.

"I should've known that Mum was too quiet. She hasn't called or texted in the past three days to pester me about the impending dinner with Haakon. I assumed—wrongly so—it was because she had found a staff member at the manor to harass." I shake my head. "I never imagined that my own mother was ally to a much bigger coup."

"Let me start making arrangements for your escape, Princess," Iyanna says getting off the bed. "If I start now, we could be at the—"

An incoming call interrupts my lady-in-waiting. My heart sinks.

I look down at my night table and my heart sinks even further.

"Who is it?" Lilo asks.

"Mum."

I bought a new phone a few days ago. Since the SIM card was still intact, I still have the same phone number.

"Oh, no." Iyanna and Lilo say in unison.

"What are you going to do?" Lilo asks.

"Normally, I'd hide under the covers, but I have a thing or two to say to my mother."

"Okay, we'll be in the kitchen. Come down the minute you hang up with her," Lilo tells me.

"I will."

Once they leave my room, I answer my phone.

"Mum—"

"Brielle, honey, you're the darling of the media today. I'm so proud of you," she coos.

Honey? Proud?

What is she up to?

CHAPTER 27

Easton

When I see a tall elegantly dressed man in a three-piece suit scanning the room, I stand up.

"Thor, over here," I wave my friend over.

He approaches me commanding the attention of everyone sitting in Matsalen—the two Michelin-starred restaurant where we're meeting. It's not that hard when you're built like an athlete, you look like a movie star and you have that regal air about you. The fact that most women sitting in the restaurant give him a once-over isn't surprising anymore. Thor is a force.

"Mate, I got on my jet the second I could. I've been in back-to-back meetings in New York for the last four days," he says shaking my hand.

"No problem. I'm glad you could make it," I say, patting his shoulder. "Please sit."

"Thanks."

He unbuttons the jacket on his gray pinstriped suit and takes a seat. I sit across from him.

"You were assigned a room, right?" I ask.

"Yes. I was. Thanks for that. I didn't even need to get my secretary involved. It's not an easy feat to get a room last minute at the Grand Hôtel."

"You're right. We were lucky. A group of Japanese businessmen were checking out yesterday as I was enquiring about a room for you. Freja, one of the clerks at the front desk, has a thing for American accents. I was able to snatch a luxury suite for you before it was assigned to someone on the waiting list," I chuckle.

"Bless, Freja. She's the one who checked me in and escorted me to the restaurant. She couldn't stop talking about you."

"What can I say? I break hearts wherever I go."

"Tosser."

We both laugh.

"I know it's only lunch but I need a drink," Thor says, "I left NYC in the middle of the night and I have so much on my mind I barely slept on the plane."

"It's been nonstop for me since I got here three days ago, I'll join you. Until half an hour ago, I was stuck in a meeting."

I spot our waiter and call him over.

"Yes, sir. Are you ready to order?" he asks when he gets to our table.

"Axel?"

"Yes, sir, that's right."

"We haven't looked at the menu yet, but my friend and I could use a drink," I tell him.

"Certainly. What can I get you?" the waiter asks.

With a hand gesture, I invite Thor to order first.

"I'll have a vodka neat. Ice cold, please."

"Absolutely, sir. And what will it be for you, sir?"

"I'll have the same."

"Very well. May I suggest a platter of smoked salmon with your drinks? Of course, it's local."

"Why not?" I say.

"Absolutely," Thor says.

"I'll be back shortly," our waiter says.

"Thank you," Thor and I answer in unison.

"Those are some cracking numbers, mate."

"They're unbelievable."

"This Swedish startup is a real gem. Although Krems Technology has only been in America for six months, they're leaving the competition in the dust." Thor doesn't waste any time.

"I told you."

"With an IPO, this could explode. The returns could be mind-blowing."

"That's why I called. They still need—"

I cut my sentence short when I notice Axel pushing a trolley our way. In a matter of seconds, he's displayed the appetizer and set our drinks in front of us. With a slight nod, he makes his exit.

"Cheers!" Thor says lifting his glass.

"Cheers!" I parrot.

We both take a few sips of our vodka and move on to the platter of smoked salmon. After a few bites, I speak again.

"As I was saying, Krems Technology is nearly there. We still need some seed money for a few infrastructural changes I think will make the difference between several hundred million dollars and tens of billions."

"No matter how much you need, I'm in," Thor confirms.

"I knew—" I can't speak anymore.

I don't think I can breathe.

"Easton?"

"No fucking way," I say when I catch the images on the big screen TV. I even blink a few times to make sure that I'm not seeing things. "No fucking way," I repeat as realization sets in. Although the volume is muted, the images flashing in front of me don't lie.

"What is it?"

Thor turns around.

"Jesus Christ," he says when his head snaps back to me.

Haakon's smirking face makes me want to throw up.

"Can you translate the caption?" I ask.

I already know what it says, but for some reason I need the confirmation.

"Haakon announced his pending wedding to your girl this morning."

Thor and I have been in constant contact since the weekend in Venice. He knows about my princess and I.

"This must be some sort of joke. As far as I know, she hasn't even met him yet."

"Call her," Thor says.

I pick up my phone and dial Brielle's number.

"She isn't answering."

"Try again," Thor presses.

I get the same result the second time around.

"What about Sienna? Does she know anything?"

I text my sister and luckily she fires back a response.

I pull my eyes away from my phone and meet Thor's inquisitive gaze. "No. Sienna said she hasn't spoken to Brielle since last night. I asked her to drop by her penthouse. Sienna will call me when she gets there."

"You're sure the princess wasn't playing you for a fool, mate?" Thor asks.

I jerk back shocked by Thor's insinuation. "Brielle?" I shake my head vehemently. "No. I can't even believe you'd say that."

"I'm just checking. You're my mate and I have your best interests at heart."

"I appreciate that. Brielle would never do such a thing. I'm certain of it. That said, I'm not sure what's going on here."

"Brielle never brought up Haakon?"

"She hasn't mentioned his name since we were in Elba. There was a moment a few weeks ago in her kitchen where I sensed she had questions about us, but I didn't allow her to continue, because I didn't have answers for her. We were on WhatsApp until she was ready for bed last night and everything seemed fine. And now she's all over the news and linked to that asshole."

"Haakon is bad news."

"This is fucking irritating and I can't even get a hold of her."

"Does she have a landline? Perhaps her mobile is on mute because of all the media attention."

"Good point. Let me text Sienna. I'm sure she must have it."

As I type a text to my sister, a tall and very attractive woman approaches us. Both Thor and I glance up at her. She stands out. I assume she's making her way to the back of the restaurant, but she stops at our table.

"I'm sorry to interrupt your lunch, Mr. Winchester," the beauty with an accent says.

I know her?

I drop my phone on the table. "I apologize, but I can't quite pinpoint how we know each other."

"It's me. Officer Pavlova."

My eyes bulge out of my skull.

"Officer Pavlova?" I repeat in shock.

CHAPTER 28

Brielle

I should've known that putting my foot down wasn't going to be the end of it. I just never imagined that I'd be dragged back home kicking and screaming. Since getting on the private jet, I've lost track of Iyanna. I was told by Mum's bodyguards that my lady-in-waiting was on a different flight. This makes no sense. Two different planes heading to the same destination? To make matters worse, I seem to no longer have any service on my mobile. I've asked—even begged—the guards to use their phones to call Iyanna and Lilo, but they refused. To say that I'm infuriated, is an understatement.

As the black Benz slows down in front of our manor, I'm shocked by the number of vans and people rushing about.

"This can't be my home," I mumble.

When the car comes to a stop, the guard sitting on the passenger's side jumps out of the vehicle and runs to my door. He opens it and extends a hand. I ignore it. The only reason I'd touch him would be to slap him.

I grab my Chloe Crush handbag and the large leather Louis Vuitton tote I managed to stuff my laptop and iPad in before I was forced to leave my own home. I get out and circle the car until I'm standing in front of the trunk.

"I'd like to grab my luggage, Officer Guzik," I tell the guard.

"We'll have one of the stewards bring your suitcases up to your room, Princess," he says.

"Why can't I just grab them now?"

"Instructions from your mother, Princess."

Now I'm really angry.

I turn on my heel and stomp past the swarm of people until I reach the front door.

"Princess Brielle, it's good to see you again," Brúnn, our long-time butler says, slightly bowing his head.

"It's good to see you too, Brúnn."

He opens the door for me and as I step inside my home, he whispers in my ear, "I wish it was under better circumstances, Princess."

"So do I," I say sadly.

I pull myself together and continue on my mission.

I storm inside the house searching for my mother.

I find her talking to Vendela, one of the staff, in the main dining room surrounded by an explosion of bouquets and clouds of colorful puffy evening gowns.

"Mother!"

"Oh, honey, you're here," Mum says getting up and dropping the piles of dresses that were on her lap into Vendela's arms. She rushes to me with her arms wide open. She attempts to hug me, but it's awkward because she's not used to showing any form of affection.

"What's going on and who are all these people?" I ask, pulling away from her.

She shrugs. "It's nothing—"

"It's a mini production. What do you have up your sleeve?"

"I thought we'd kick things off by selecting the perfect floral arrangement and I asked the best fashion designers in Belzer to submit their top designs."

"Why did you do it? Why did you leak this improbable news to the press?"

Forget about niceties. I need to get to the bottom of this.

"What makes you think I had anything to do with it?" she asks.

She said the same thing when I spoke to her yesterday. She's still sticking to her lame story.

"So you didn't know?" I press.

"Well, not exactly. Prince Haakon did consult with me for fact checking purposes."

"Fact checking?"

"Yes, I had to make sure the press had the proper spelling for our names and that they had recent photos to feature with the article. We took such lovely family photos earlier this year, it would be a shame not to use them. You look so beautiful on them," she says. I can detect the tinge of pride in her voice.

Really?

"So you helped Haakon—"

She shoots me a cold stare. "*Prince* Haakon," she corrects.

I roll my eyes. "In other words, you've been in on this from the beginning?"

"I don't like your tone, young lady."

I use a different approach. "You've never been one to beat around the bush. One thing about you, mother, is that you always take full responsibility for your actions, regardless of what other people think. Your reluctance to answer me makes me wonder if *Prince* Haakon has you in his back pocket."

It's not like me to be manipulative, but since Mum holds a PhD in the subject, it's an art I understand well.

"I'll have you know that no one pulls my strings," she spits out. *You fell for it.* "Prince Haakon was overjoyed after your conversation. He couldn't shut up about how beautiful and poised you were. Fit to be queen, he said. I did such a great job with you."

Never mind the reality.

Nursemaids took care of me from when I came into this world until I went to boarding school. Mum couldn't be bothered getting her hands dirty.

"He just knew it was right between the two of you," Mum continues. *He's an idiot.* "The prince wanted the world to partake in his joy."

"I'm just a puppet in this show since nobody deemed it important to warn me in advance of this media junket. Is that it?"

"Well, one good thing that came out of the prince's initiative is that he mentioned your little blog. I'm sure it will be good for business," she sneers in the most condescending way. "Enjoy it while it lasts."

Unbelievable.

"That's your answer?"

I'm at a loss for words.

"You still don't get it, do you? This is inevitable. The sooner you accept it, the better it will be for everyone concerned." She approaches me. Each step is calculated. Although we're the same height, Mum makes it a point to prance around the manor in four-inch heels. I'm wearing flats. I look up and meet her amber eyes. "You say nothing has been made official yet. Well, consider this fortuitous media blitz the nail in *your* coffin."

I can't believe she just said that.

"Is that why you had those brutes, you call guards, drag me here?"

"What do you think?"

"Where are my officers?"

She takes a long step back and crosses her arms over her chest. She purses her red lips. No matter the time of the day, her Maleficent makeup is impeccable. "Officer Pavlova is putty in your hands. The same goes for Officer Stanton. I've made sure that their supervisor dismissed them. We terminated their employment while you were sleeping. Less drama that way. No teary goodbyes."

"What?" I shout.

"Since you're stepping into a new role, I decided you needed security fit for a queen."

"You fired my officers?"

"Yes." She gives me a self-satisfied smile—a smirk really—and starts stalking around the room. "They've already left New York, Brielle. God knows where they are by now. Two less people on the payroll."

"What has gotten into you?" I ask in a low voice.

"Prince Haakon cut short his official Australian tour. He wants to strike while the iron's hot. He's flying home as we speak. He thought we should move things up. I agreed. The dinner takes place in four days."

"But Dad left at five o'clock this morning for Hong Kong on business."

"Exactly. What a lucky break," she flashes me an evil grin.

My God. She's been planning this for a long time.

"He's my father and I want him there."

"He's useless!" she shouts. I flinch. When her eyes meet mine, I don't recognize the woman standing in front of me. It's like she's possessed. "He'll only instigate an argument with Prince Haakon or Prince Clemens. It's best if he isn't present."

"I don't—"

"You are not going to bring shame to this family, Brielle." The anger in her voice is unmistakable. "Come hell or high water, this dinner will take place," she says in a voice that doesn't welcome objection.

I just stare at her. I'm so dumbfounded that I don't have any ammunition left.

Something crosses her eyes and suddenly, she's grinning. "We're going to enjoy a fabulous meal—just you and I." She claps her hands together. *Huh?* "I've asked the chef to prepare one of your favorite dishes for lunch—veal schnitzel."

Talk about Dr. Jekyll and Mr. Hyde.

"What?"

"Lunch, Brielle," she snaps.

Well that didn't last long. She's back to her old self.

"We can't make all of these important decisions about the dinner and your wedding on an empty stomach. Run along and freshen up. I'll expect you in the gardens in fifteen minutes."

"But, Mum—"

She ignores me. "Officer Canterwick," I didn't even notice him standing behind me, "please escort my daughter to her room and don't let her out of your sight. I also want two guards posted at her door twenty-four seven. Every step she takes, I want someone following her. Anyone who disobeys my orders will get their walking papers. Understood?"

"Absolutely, Princess." Officer Canterwick bows. "Princess, after you," he says turning his focus on me.

CHAPTER 29

Easton

I'm still staring in disbelief at Brielle's bodyguard. I guess she notices.

"I know I look a little different," Officer Pavlova says with a laugh. The woman actually laughed. That's a first.

So far, I've only seen Brielle's bodyguard in a black pantsuit with either a white shirt or a black one. She always wears the same shoes—black army combat boots. Her hair is always pulled back tight and she never wears a trace of makeup. The woman standing in front of me could easily double as a supermodel. She's ditched her trademark black in favor of a feminine soft purple crisscrossed top. She's paired it with a fitted white skirt that hits her below the knees and a pair of high heels in the same shade as her top. The accessories complement the look. Her makeup is soft and feminine and her hair is far longer than I ever imagined. *Wow. Officer Pavlova is a knockout.*

"You don't even look like the same person. The transformation is uncanny—" Then it hits me. "Wait a minute," I say, rising to my feet. As I do so, I'm aware that I'm calling attention to myself and creating somewhat of a scene in thc restaurant. "I'm sorry, Officer Pavlova, but it just dawned on me. What are you doing here? How did you find me? Is Brielle with you? Did you hear about the news?"

I bombard her with questions.

"No, sir. I'm here alone. Princess Janika dismissed me from my functions earlier this morning."

"What? You're no longer Brielle's bodyguard?"

"No."

I open my mouth to ask a question, but remember my manners.

"Please, have a seat." She does. I do the same. "This is my friend Thor Lidström."

"Pleased to meet you, Officer Pavlova," Thor says.

"The pleasure is mine, Mr. Lidström," she says shaking my friend's hand.

"Would you like a drink? We're both enjoying a glass of vodka," I say.

She shakes her head. "No thank you, sir. I never drink when I'm on duty."

I frown.

"Princess Janika might have given me my marching papers, but as far as I'm concerned, I still answer to Princess Brielle," she says in a solemn tone.

"Officer Pavlova, what's going on here?"

"Let me start from the beginning," she says

"Please do."

"Princess Janika had a small army of her guards escort Officer Stanton and I to the airport at four o'clock this morning. The guards banged at our doors at three-thirty. We had exactly thirty minutes to pack under the watchful eye of an armed guard. We were then put on a private jet to Norway."

"Armed? Norway?"

She nods. "When a colleague lets you know that he's carrying, it's usually not a friendly visit. Those royal guards were sent with a specific mission in mind and clearly they had no intentions of getting caught. Why Norway? I suspect it was to throw us off. I might not have family there, but I have good friends there—former military married to Norwegians—who were able to help me."

"My God," I say.

"I didn't get a chance to speak to the princess to tell her what was going on. My phone was confiscated the second the guards busted through our suite. Luckily, I always have two concealed backup mobiles, which Princess Janika knows nothing about."

"Where is Brielle now?"

"Lady Iyanna—"

"That's Brielle's lady-in-waiting," I tell Thor.

"Got it," he nods.

"I'm sorry to have interrupted you, Officer Pavlova."

"Not at all, sir. As I was saying, Lady Iyanna has my other numbers. It's a security precaution that I demanded since she's always with the princess. Lady Iyanna told me that guards woke them up at five o'clock this morning. They were to take them back to Belzer under this emergency that none of the guards were forthcoming about. They simply said it was vital for the princess to get back home."

"You buying it?"

"No. Something is up or else I'd be on that plane with Princess Brielle instead of here with you. Lady Iyanna also told me that Princess Janika has Princess Blakely under lockdown at the penthouse—"

"What happened to Blakely's bodyguards?"

"Now it makes sense why Princess Blakely's bodyguards were summoned back to Belzer for urgent training. They left two days ago. Officer Ratajkowski—the head of security for the Royal Family in Belzer—insisted on it. When I questioned him, he told me that my turn would come soon. I thought it was protocol so I dropped the subject."

"Did Lady Iyanna say anything else?"

"She didn't have much time, sir. She used a ruse—her period," Thor and I chuckle, "to use the loo. She made a beeline to the office upstairs to make a quick phone call from the landline before they were escorted out. Iyanna confirmed they're in Belzer now. She's with her mum. She was able to text me. She told me that when one of the guards caught her making that call, he yelled at her before striking her across the face."

"A guard who hits a woman?" Thor asks. "Rich."

"The bastard is lucky I wasn't there. Iyanna told me who he is. I'll make sure to take care of him the first chance I have. Iyanna told me that after she was found, the guards cut all of the lines in the penthouse. None of this sits well with me."

"What the hell?"

"I'm sorry to state the obvious, but this sounds like a kidnapping."

My head whips in Thor's direction. "Who the hell kidnaps their own grown child?" I ask stunned.

"It's been done before, mate. Brielle is hardly the first princess to oppose an arranged marriage. Some families don't take lightly to opposition," he says.

"I have to side with Mr. Lidström," Officer Pavlova says. "My job is to keep Princess Brielle safe and keep my mouth shut. That doesn't mean I don't hear things. I know of Prince Haakon. Since no one is safe from Princess Janika's wrath at the estate in Belzer, most of the staff hate her. Lady Iyanna did mention that some of her fellow staff members were asked a few days ago to prepare for something big. No one knew what it was. The news that exploded on social media this morning explains it all. Princess Janika was lining up the ducks."

"All that for a marriage to a man Brielle doesn't even know?" I'm dumbfounded.

"For Princess Janika, appearance is everything. The woman would go to war to preserve her pristine image. Furthermore, how many women in the world will ever be able to hold the title of the Queen Mother."

"Unbelievable," I shake my head in disbelief.

"You'd be surprised what still matters amongst royals, Easton. I should know," Thor says.

"I'm sure you do."

"To answer your earlier question, Princess Brielle mentioned your trip to her cousin and Lady Iyanna. After so many years in the Russian Special Forces, I can track anyone down. Given your status, I started with the best hotels in Stockholm. It only took me two calls to find you. Once that was done, my friend Galina Zvilnis stopped by the best shop in Oslo to buy me a new wardrobe. She helped with the makeup and hair. I was then able to catch a flight incognito. The trick is to hide in plain sight. Princess Janika's guards would never be on the lookout for someone who looks like this," she indicates her outfit. "This gives me ease of movement."

"Mission accomplished! So you knew I was in Stockholm and you knew which hotel I was staying at, but how did you know I was at the restaurant?" I ask.

"That's pure luck. When I arrived, I intended on leaving you a message and then sit in the lobby and wait for you. When I mentioned to Freja that I was looking for you, she assumed I was your guest. I didn't contradict her. She escorted me here."

"Thank you so much for tracking me down."

"Not at all. It's my duty to protect Princess Brielle."

"From her own mother?"

"I'd say that after that little covert stunt Princess Janika pulled, your girl definitely needs protection," Thor says.

I really didn't need to hear that.

"Once again, we see eye to eye," Officer Pavlova nods with a smile. "Princess Janika is the least of my concerns."

"If not her, then who?" I ask.

"I know former colleagues who were on the inside of the Kingdom of Brihon until recently. I made calls and asked them to sniff around."

"And?"

"They're still at it. That said, they did have a lot to share. They know of the many skeletons Prince Haakon hides in his closet. I'll give my life before I allow that man to touch the princess I serve."

"Officer Pavlova you're scaring me," I tell her.

"Forgive me, sir, that wasn't my intention. It's just that I believe—and forgive me for overstepping my boundaries here—that you care for the princess."

"Very much so," I admit.

"Prince Haakon has some fairly twisted perversions. Very unhealthy shit," Officer Pavlova says.

"Jesus Christ," Thor grunts.

"Motherfucker," I growl.

This story is beyond me.

"If he touches her, he'll soil the princess. I won't allow that to happen." Officer Pavlova's words give me chills.

"I don't want that to happen either. I'm not one to advocate violence, but I swear to God, he touches her and he dies."

It fucking pisses me off that I wasn't there to protect her.

"I'll help you hide the body," Thor chuckles.

Brielle's beautiful face flashes in front of me. *My princess.* Her long blonde hair, slender body, luscious lips and radiant smile. And then there's that wonderful personality that makes her even more attractive than she already is.

"What do we do?" I ask, her serene image fresh in my mind.

"Kidnap her back."

Thor's answer shocks me. "Wh—what?"

"I was thinking along the same lines," Officer Pavlova says. "I can have some people in place in Belzer by end of day."

"I can help. I have years of Krav Maga training under my belt and a black belt in karate. No one fights like Israelis. After all, they're no strangers to conflict," Thor states.

"Whoa, people. What the hell are you talking about?"

"Sir, time is of the essence. Lady Iyanna warned me of a dinner with Prince Haakon that takes place in four days in Belzer. Everything points to the fact that an official engagement would follow."

"Over my dead body," I grunt.

I rub my face with the palms of my hands. Too frustrated, angry and confused to make sense of things.

Then my phone chimes in. When I look down at the text flashing on my screen, my dread deepens.

It's Clara.

No doubt you've heard. I was collecting data before touching base. This is bloody urgent. Call me now.

Another message follows. This one from Bryce.

There's a good reason Haakon bought that mansion. We need to talk.

CHAPTER 30

Brielle

The minute I arrived back in Belzer, chaos—and sorrow—carved a permanent place in my heart. Most times overshadowing my anger at my mother. *How could she do this to me?*

She says I'm free to come and go as I please, but that's a lie.

She broke my iPhone and handed me a flip phone saying I didn't need more than that. She cut off the Internet in the manor, which means I have no contact with the outside world. Lilo and I haven't spoken to each other since I left Manhattan. And let's not forget the menacing-looking guards at my door who follow me everywhere I go.

She's holding me hostage in my own home.

She won't admit it, but the writing is on the wall.

By some miracle of God, Mum is still oblivious to what Easton and I share. I thought maybe she had me followed, but no. Obviously, I didn't tell her anything. I don't need another excuse for her to be furious at me and make me feel worthless.

In other words, these have been the cruelest four days of my life. It feels like my soul—and my heart—is in the lost and found. When things become unbearable, I go to that serene place in my head where I can pretend I'm still with Easton.

That keeps me going.

He's been on my mind, etched into my skin, his last kiss still a lasting memory on my lips. When I feel that all hope is gone, I think of him.

My king.

He's been playing the main role in my dreams since the last time I saw him.

"I can't wait to see you again," I mumble to myself as I catch my sad reflection in the mirror.

But first and foremost, I have to get out of this prison.

Before dinner is over, I'll let everyone at the table know that I have no intentions of marrying Prince Haakon. Regardless of the consequences, the axe drops tonight on this farce.

Since my father got back yesterday, a lot has changed. He's taken control back, which means there has been a lot of arguing. Daddy is beside himself. He can't wrap his head around how Mum blindsided him. It's been nasty between the two of them. Mum told him to get the hell out if he didn't agree. He told her he wasn't going to leave me here alone with her demented plans.

Daddy caught wind of my escape plans. He put a hard stop to them. He told me if my mother insists after tonight, he'll deal with her. He wants the satisfaction of bursting her bubble when I tell her no in front of the Prince of Shit and his family. In other words, tonight should be interesting.

I shake my head and snap back to the moment.

"The dinner is an hour away," I remind myself. Reluctantly, I apply the finishing touches to my makeup.

There's a knock at the door. I don't bother getting up from my vanity.

"Princess, a package arrived for you," Iyanna says walking into my bedroom.

I look up and meet her eyes in the mirror. "I'm surprised my mother didn't intercept it."

I didn't see Iyanna for an entire day after arriving. When I finally saw her, I was shocked by the nasty bruise on her face. Even now with makeup, the black and blue mark is still quite obvious. At least the swelling is down.

I was furious.

My mother brushed it off stating that Iyanna wasn't following orders.

Rubbish.

I'm not sure who's responsible, but the guard who hit Iyanna ended up in the hospital. Something to do with a violent fight at a bar a few nights ago. Apparently, he's in pretty bad shape.

"Oh, come on, Princess. She's way too obsessed to let this slide. She did inspect it before allowing me to bring it up to you."

"Who is it from?"

"I'm not sure. If you open it, you'll find out."

"I'm not interested in another gift you and I both know we'll end up returning."

"Maybe this one is different."

"In what sense?"

"Princess, trust me. Open it."

"I don't have time for games."

She doesn't respond.

I extend my hand. "Okay, hand it over."

I snatch the box, undo the ribbon and the wrapping before lifting the lid off the box.

"Montblanc pens," I shrug when I catch sight of the expensive German luxury pens. "So what if these cost fourteen hundred dollars each. I'm not keeping them," I insist.

"There's a note," she says.

I roll my eyes and open it.

Dear Princess,

May you enjoy a long and happy marriage. You'll be the most beautiful queen in recent memory. Please accept this token as an object of my admiration. Congratulations.

—A faithful subject.

"It's standard, Iyanna. And boring. I've read at least two-thousand just like this one today alone."

"Perhaps the second note might be a little bit more interesting," she says.

I look down at the box on my lap. "What second note?"

"This one," she says pulling an envelope that's tucked inside her bra.

I give her a suspicious side-glance.

"Open it," she presses.

"You're acting mighty strange," I tell her.

"Not at all."

When I open it, I frown as I read it.

Princess,

I hear your father got the Internet reconnected and he's replaced your mother's guards with his. Still, I wasn't willing to take a chance. Two of the Montblanc pens are real. The third one isn't—the one without the diamond in the cap-top. It's a custom USB key. Put the key inside your laptop. The rest is self-explanatory.

—Someone to watch over you.

I look up at Iyanna. "What's this?"

"I think the note explains it well," she says.

"Iyanna," I warn.

"Princess, please do as the note says," she implores.

"You're behind this?"

"Maybe."

"Does Daddy know?"

"No." She doesn't offer more.

I let out a long sigh and consider her seriously.

"You should *really* check what's on that USB key before the dinner," she insists.

I cock an eyebrow at her, but now I have to know what's on this key.

I get up, walk across the room and plop myself in front of my laptop. I insert the key and double-click on the only folder that's on it. I double-click again on the file that says, 'Read me first'. I then move onto the Word document that's named, 'Read me next'. I scroll down and my jaw drops.

"Dear God," I say.

I turn around to face Iyanna. Her expression is unreadable. I continue scrolling down. After fifteen minutes of opening folder after folder, I turn around and face my Lady-in-waiting again.

"I don't think the dress Mum selected for the dinner will do," I say gingerly. "I need something that will make a statement. I want to make sure Prince Haakon has his eyes on me the entire evening."

Mum spent hours upon hours going through the mountain of dresses she commissioned. In the end, she selected something that I hated, stating it was fit for a queen. Since I don't care anymore, I didn't argue.

"May I suggest the one you bought a few months ago when you were in Miami?" Iyanna says.

"Great minds think alike."

It's her turn to cock an eyebrow.

CHAPTER 31

Brielle

Mum went all out.

The dining room is decorated with such opulence. There are dozens upon dozens of bouquets and candles everywhere you look. All in white. It was a last-minute change. Mum says it's important to send a subliminal message that I'm still intact.

Whatever.

We sat down and the waiters finished serving another round of champagne. Mum is sticking to her trademark vodka martinis. Her third so far. She's on her best behavior tonight.

Daddy is sitting at the head of the table. Queen Gertrude is sitting at the other head. Guards, stewards and waiters line the walls. Mum is sitting to Daddy's left. I'm sitting to his right. Prince Haakon is sitting next to me. I really should say he's nearly sitting on top of me. He's so close, I feel like I'm suffocating. Prince Olaf—Prince Haakon's uncle—is sitting next to Mum. Prince Olaf and Mum seem to have been wrapped up in an interminable conversation since he walked into our home an hour ago. Throughout the table, other family members from Prince Haakon's side are present.

Since Mum was so impolite with Lilo's mum and she had my cousin under a stupid lock-down, they didn't bother to show up. Daddy's siblings send their regards, but apologize for not being present—they prefer not to be in the same room as my mother. Speaking of the devil, Mum was never able to explain why her family couldn't attend. She mumbled an incoherent excuse. I just shrugged it off. I don't care enough.

Already, I'm bored out of my mind.

"On behalf of my family, I would like to thank you, Prince Janek, for receiving us into your home," Queen Gertrude says.

"Not at all, Queen Gertrude. Janika, Brielle and I thank you for honoring us with your presence. It's been such a long time since our families have been in the same room."

"Indeed. It's incredible what war can do to two nations," Queen Gertrude says.

"It's a good thing those century-old wars that divided our kingdoms are behind us," Daddy says.

"Hear, hear!" the Queen agrees lifting her glass.

Everyone at the table follows her example.

"Well, I for one, would also like to thank Prince Janek for opening his home to us and more importantly for giving me his daughter's hand in marriage," Prince Haakon says.

"You never asked me, therefore I never gave it." Daddy's words are as sharp as a razor. "This arrangement was made through my *lovely* wife." The room goes silent. Daddy flashes Prince Haakon a smile, but his eyes are cold. "But those are semantics, right?"

"Absolutely!" Prince Haakon is quick to agree. "What's important is that we're all here."

"Isn't it?" Daddy says.

Mum looks at him suspiciously.

"I know I've said it before, but Princess Brielle, you look stunning in that dress," Prince Haakon says.

I open my mouth to answer, but Mum beats me to it. "Thank God we don't have any official photos tonight. I don't think it's appropriate for a future queen to be seen in red. It's a bit much and sends the wrong message. I had selected a beautiful soft pink dress for Brielle, but once again, she prefers to ignore my wise advice."

"You do realize that once she becomes queen she can overrule you. Perhaps it's a good thing that she's starting now." I nearly choke in laughter at my father's response.

"Well, thank you for that reminder, Prince Janek," my mother sneers.

"My pleasure," Daddy says in a mocking tone.

She gives him the evil eye, but he just stares straight at her, forcing her to shift her gaze.

"Personally, I like the red on you. It brings out your blue eyes and your blonde hair," Prince Haakon compliments.

"Thank you," I say simply.

"She's absolutely gorgeous," Queen Gertrude smiles.

"Thank you, Queen Gertrude," I say, lowering my eyes to my champagne flute.

"Not at all, child. Don't be so shy. Own it. Everyone has been buzzing about you since the news went viral. Although I'm not as healthy as I once was and who knows how long I still have on this earth, I'm happy God granted me this day. I just hope I'll live long enough to meet the great-grandchildren you'll gift me with."

"You will," Prince Haakon says. "Don't worry, Grandmother, Brielle and I will rival Wilhelmina and Prince Carl," he winks at his sister. She just rolls her eyes.

"Let's not rush things, I'm too young to be a grandmother," Mum says.

Of course, this is about her.

"Princess Janika, it's best if she starts young," the Queen says.

"Twenty is too young," my mother retorts. *Is she actually putting me first?* "I'm not even forty yet. For God's sake, I can't have toddlers running around calling me Nana. It will only make me feel ancient." *No, I was wrong.*

"I disagree," the Queen quips.

"Ladies, I think the kids are going to make that decision," my father pacifies.

"You're okay with us having a large family?" Prince Haakon asks me.

I lace my fingers together and take a deep breath in. "What did you have in mind?" I ask him.

"I wouldn't be opposed to six kids. Eight, if your health allows it," he tells me.

"I see," I nod.

"You're okay with that?" Prince Haakon presses.

"Wouldn't that be too much to handle?" I ask.

"Not at all. We're rich." *No, mate,* we're *rich. Your kingdom is struggling*. "Money is no object." *Because you think you'll get your hands on* my *fortune.*

"That's not what I meant."

"Oh, Brielle, stop talking in codes and just say it," my mother snaps.

I choose to ignore her.

I turn my body so I'm facing the Prince of Shit. "If we have six children, wouldn't that really be nine for you?"

"Wh-what?" Prince Haakon's face suddenly drains of all color.

"It's simple mathematics. Six plus three equals nine," I smile.

"I-I don't know what you're talking about," he says.

"For the love of God, Brielle what's gotten into you?" My mother asks. "What kind of conversation is this? You're disrespecting our guests."

I turn around to face her. Her eyes are burning with anger. "You're right. Perhaps I should be more explicit."

My answer throws her off.

I reach for my clutch sitting on my lap and pull my phone out. I do a quick search, turn the volume up and place it on the table.

"What are you doing?" My mother's fury is mounting.

"It will all make sense in a second," I tell her.

There's a round of hush-hush muffles throughout the room. I look up and the Queen looks positively petrified.

I select a MP3 file and press play.

"Fuck! That big cock of yours."

"Fuck, your pussy is hungrier since you got pregnant, Megs."

"Harder, Haakon. Fuck me harder."

"Jesus, your tits are so heavy, Megs. I'm going to titty fuck them later."

"I want you to fuck my ass. It's been too long."

"I don't want to hurt our baby."

"You won't. I need to feel you up my ass."

"I love it when you talk dirty. Don't worry, I'll pump some royal love potion up your slutty ass."

"God, I love you, Haakon."

"I love you too, Megrhana and I love our baby."

Prince Haakon jumps to his feet. In his rush, the chair topples behind him. A steward is quick to pick it up. "Stop that right now!" he yells.

I do. No point in wasting any of this.

"Don't you dare speak to my daughter that way," Daddy growls waving a menacing finger at him. "This is my house and I make the rules. I want to hear the rest."

"So do I," my mother says in a calculated voice.

Members of Prince Haakon's family are all as white as ghosts.

"Brielle resume that audio." Daddy's voice carries weight and gravity to it.

"Okay!" I say, pressing play.

"You can't marry that stupid princess."

"I have to. It's the only way to save my kingdom. It was so easy to play Brielle's mother for a fool. She thinks she has the upper hand. Stupid bitch. Soon, I'll get my hands on a shit load of money."

"You wouldn't need them if you hadn't wasted all your money on frivolous—"

"You mean like the mansion you demanded I buy you in Beverly Hills?"

"The baby and I need a place to stay."

"A large apartment condo or townhouse would have done the same."

"It's the least you could do. I'm your girl."

"Megrhana, we've already talked about this."

"Brielle is a dumb virgin. What does she know?"

"We'll have to keep our affair a secret until Brielle gives me an heir."

"But you have an heir growing in my belly."

"That's not the same. I need heirs of royal blood."

"I should be Queen. I'm the mother of your first born—"

"I'm coming, Megs, baby."

"Come, baby. I love your big fucking cock, Haakon."

"I'm going to fill your slutty cunt with more royal seed."

"Oh God, fill me with that potent seed. I wish I could get pregnant every time you shoot your load inside me."

"Take my seed, bitch. Fucking take it."

"Oh, yeah. I want another baby after this one, Haakon."

"We'll have more kids. Lots. Brielle is so innocent, she'll never know and by the time she figures it out, she'll be in too deep and her kingdom will be under my control. Oh, fuck, Megs, here I coooooome!"

I stop the audio and heave a sigh of relief.

It's over.

I look around the room and you wouldn't believe the look of fright on everybody's faces.

Except for my parents. They're both totally shocked.

"Well, I think we get the gist of it," I say in a triumphant voice. "I have loads of photos and videos if anyone cares for more."

No answer.

After what seems like an eternity, Queen Gertrude speaks. "Where did you get that?"

"It was sent to me. Someone was concerned that I was walking into a marriage that was doomed from day one. Oh, one thing to keep in mind, is that on the audio Megrhana talks about one baby, but since then she's gone to the press to confirm that after her ultrasound she's expecting triplets."

"You were playing me for a fool, Prince Haakon?" my mother asks.

Mum's expression changes from that of the perfect hostess to the menacing one I'm used to.

"Princess Janika, you can't believe fake news. It's rampant nowadays."

"Fake news?"

"Yeah."

Prince Haakon flashes Mum an idiotic grin.

Mum responds with an icy stare and what I can only describe as a smirk.

"For argument's sake, let's go with your story. Let's pretend you didn't call me a stupid bitch to that cheap slut you were shagging." Don't let the calm voice fool you. Mum is beside herself. "Are those babies fake?" she asks.

"This is propaganda!" Haakon retaliates.

Does he even know what that means?

"Have a modicum of decency and grow some balls, mate. That was hardly an answer," my father growls. "Are you having triplets with that woman or not?"

"I can assure you, Prince Janek, this is a mistake."

"Is that why you're so red you look like you're going to pop an artery?" my father questions.

"Surely—"

"Oh stop it, you idiot. That was your voice. No one here is stupid other than you," Queen Gertrude snaps.

"Did you know about this?" my mother asks the Queen.

The Queen shrugs.

"I'm sorry, I didn't get that. Was that a yes or no, Queen Gertrude?" my mother presses.

"Ruchella Megrhana Marples has been a thorn in my side for the past month. I've done a good job at managing her, but my media-whore of a grandson decided to make a big splash without consulting me first. I assume that aggravated Megrhana—who's convinced she should step into my shoes. As absurd as that sounds. She said she had leverage. I thought she was bluffing. I guess I was wrong."

"You knew this woman was expecting triplets?" my mother asks.

"No. That's news to me."

"But you knew she was pregnant?" my mother insists.

Wow.

Queen Gertrude lets out a heavy sigh. "As I've said, she's been a pest."

"How could you?" my mother spits out. "Your grandson is tainted and you didn't think it was a good idea to warn me?"

"Don't you dare get on your high horse, Princess Janika. You were so blinded by your pointless mission that you were willing to sell your daughter's soul. I wouldn't agree to marry my worst enemy to my disgraceful grandson, let alone my only daughter," the Queen sneers.

My eyes shift to my mum's, but she averts her gaze.

Yeah, I'd do the same thing too if I were standing in her guilty shoes.

"So you played us and now you're the one being played by this Megrhana," my father concludes.

"Hmph." The Queen offers my father a one-shoulder shrug.

"Was that an answer?" my father presses.

"Partially," the Queen says before letting out a long sigh. "I knew the B-rated American actress—and I'm being generous here—would irritate the hell out of me, I didn't expect it would be to this extent. She's a money hungry and vulgar whore without a drop of talent. What makes it dangerous is that she's desperate for validation. She was able to sink her claws into my grandson and now she's a problem we can't get rid of. If this MP3 is already in the hands of the media, we'll never be able to downplay it. It's going to turn into a real circus." The Queen leans against the table. "All because you couldn't control your willy, Haakon."

The room is silent under the weight of the shocking revelations. Even though, mentally, I was ready for this, my heart is pounding like crazy and my body is trembling.

There's only one thing left to say.

I stand up. "This farce of a wedding is off."

"You can't do that. I've already made it public!" Prince Haakon shouts, grabbing hold of my wrist.

Four of Daddy's guards surround Prince Haakon in a blink of an eye.

"Let go of me before I slap you," I grunt.

He removes his paw.

"Brielle, come on—"

"You're wasting your breath," I tell him.

"Don't do this." He grabs my arm again.

My father jumps to his feet. "Touch her again and I'll have one of my officers beat you to a pulp."

"I-I didn't mean to—"

"You're a pee on, Haakon. You aren't worthy of my daughter, our kingdom or my fortune. I would sooner burn everything I own to the ground before I let you ruin it."

I've never seen Daddy this angry.

"Royals have kids out of wedlock all the time. It's no secret that *you* haven't been faithful." Prince Haakon doesn't know when to quit.

My father gives him a condescending glance. "Perhaps, but I was smart enough to wrap it up so that I don't soil our name—and lineage—with bastards."

"Prince Janek—"

"Shut up, you fool."

"We should wait for everybody to calm down before making hasty decisions, Prince Janek. There might still be a way for this to work between our two families," Queen Gertrude says.

My father offers the Queen a smile, but when he squints his blue eyes at her and when that smile turns into a grimace, you know it's not going to be pretty. "Really?"

"Well, yes."

He tilts his head back so he can look down his nose at her. "Desperation doesn't look good on you, *Gertrude*."

Daddy turns and faces my mother. "Janika, you brought these leeches into our lives because you wanted a meaningless title? Princess wasn't goddamn enough?" Daddy never swears in front of guests. "Nothing ever is for your royal bitchy self."

"I—"

"How many times did I tell you it was a bad idea?" He shakes a menacing finger at her. "You were so bloody obsessed. You were going to marry off our only daughter to this loser?" Daddy is yelling now.

Mum jerks against her chair.

"Janek—"

"I know you hate me, but Brielle? I though you loved your own child. I was wrong."

"Janek, please—"

Daddy lifts a hand. "Spare me, woman."

"Haakon, you're a repugnant asshole." Daddy's focus is back on the prince. "Every breath you draw in my presence annoys me." Haakon holds his breath, but quickly turns beet red. "You're annoying me right now. I can't believe your grandmother knew of this. I wouldn't put it past your family if every single person in this room knew about this mockery and they were willing to keep it a secret. Not that I had any intentions of giving my blessings for this marriage—I wanted to see how far Janika took this farce—but I'm grateful to whoever was watching over my daughter. Thank God for that person for exposing you as the vile individual you are. Now, you all have two options, you can leave my home immediately or you can be escorted out. The choice is yours." He turns his attention to his Officer in Command. "Officer Özkal, make sure there's no rubbish left in this room by the time I come back downstairs."

Officer Özkal takes a step forward and bows. "Of course, Prince. Consider it done."

My father extends his hand to me. "Come on, sweetheart, let's get out of here. The stench in this room is wretched." I run towards my father and grab his hand. "We'll need to get the manor fumigated first thing tomorrow."

It's only as we step out of the dining room that I realize Daddy left Mum behind.

* * *

I barely have time to process everything that's just happened when I hear Iyanna's voice. "Princess, over here," she waves.

"Give me one second," I tell her. I look up at my father. "You had a lot to say," I laugh.

"This unexpected outcome ignites the fuel of hatred between the Kingdom of Brihon and ours." He takes both my hands into his and brings them up to his lips. He drops a soft kiss against my fingers. "You're too precious to endure a marriage that kills you a little every day. Don't say yes until he's the right one and you love him. Blue blood or not. As long as he's an honorable man, he respects you and protects you. You hear me?"

I fight back tears. "Yes, Daddy."

"Good. When you do, I'll welcome him with open arms."

"Thank you for standing up for me."

"Go on, Iyanna is waiting. I have a few important phone calls to make. I'll catch you later."

"Okay," I say.

I watch him run up the stairs before making my way to Iyanna.

"It's over!" I say.

"It's about bloody time."

We both laugh.

"I have a car on standby. Officer Pavlova is outside waiting for you. Officer Stanton in already in the passenger seat."

"What? They're here? How did you manage that?"

"I have my ways," she winks.

"You're the best."

"I did have a little help." I frown. "Your guardian angel wants to make sure you're okay," she says.

"You mean the person who gave you that USB key?"

"Yes."

"I don't know how you got connected to this person, but thank you from the bottom of my heart," I tell her, hugging her.

"I told you, Princess. Friends don't let friends marry assholes."

We laugh again.

"You've been a true friend. Is my guardian angel here?" I ask, looking down the corridor.

"He's in Belzer. Officer Pavlova will take you to him."

"Oh, it's a man."

"No, Princess, it's *your* man."

"Easton?" I ask in a feeble voice.

"Like I said, *your* man."

CHAPTER 32

Easton

The stress of the last two days has robbed me of my sleep. Still, there's a flood of energy coursing through my veins right now. I'm jacked up by the idea that I'll be seeing her again.

Memories of the last time I was with her assail my senses.

"Brielle."

I'll never forget the feeling when I saw her beautiful face flash next to Haakon's on the big screen TV. I swear I stopped breathing for a second or two. I've known for a while now that my feelings for my princess were far more intense than for any other woman before her, but in that instance—when I thought I might have lost her—something in my heart shifted. Something new. Something overwhelming.

I stand in front of the open French doors overlooking the Regalia Gården. Iyanna suggested I stay in a secluded place—away from Princess Janika's reach. Since all of this is fairly last-minute, Iyanna reached out to her contacts. Princess Blakely's summer home in Berheim—two hours away from the capital—has been my hideaway since I arrived in Belzer. Officer Pavlova and Officer Stanton have been staying in the guards' quarters. The Erkerhus Fortress has been our little headquarters—the place where we planned our attack.

My phone pings and I pull it out of my pocket.

It's Officer Pavlova.
We're pulling up in front of the castle, sir.
I'm ready for her.

Iyanna and a legion of maidens helped prepare the expansive dining room. Everything is fit for *my* princess. The full moon hanging in the sky is more than I could've asked for. The way it casts a flood of light inside the room while shining bright on the Regalia Gården sets the tone. Although the gardens sparkle like diamonds, they pale in comparison to Brielle's eyes.

When I hear heels clacking against the hardwood floor behind me, I know she's here. As I listen in as she walks towards me, I make out another set of footsteps receding. Officer Pavlova. Even without those clues, her sweet scent is a precursor. Already, her expensive perfume fills my nostrils.

"I missed your smell, Princess," I say, turning around.

"Easton," she says.

She readies herself to run towards me, but I lift my hand up to stop her. "Don't move. Let me take you in." She's breathtaking.

Seeing her again sends adrenaline rushing into my blood.

I approach her slowly and my eyes caress the slender curves of her body. I stand in front of her for a beat before walking circles around her.

She laughs as her head whips around to follow me.

"See something you like?" she asks.

"What an impudent princess!"

She purses her painted pout and cocks an eyebrow in response.

Damn.

Just like that my mind goes straight to the gutter and I can only think of those lips wrapped around the head of my thick cock, sliding up and down.

I'm as hard as a rock.

Even though my desire for her is indescribable, somehow I find it in me to remain gallant.

"You're as beautiful as ever, Brielle."

"Thank you. You're not so bad yourself."

"What this? It's just a suit," I say, pulling the lapel of my bespoke gray jacket.

"Not on you. It's a masterpiece. You wear it incredibly well."

I stop my pacing and stand in front of her. "Well, thank you for the compliment. I'm just trying to keep up with you," I wink. "Everything you wear always looks stunning."

"What this? It's just a dress." She borrows my words.

"Not on you. It's a vision. You wear it—and everything else—incredibly well."

We both laugh.

"No tie?" she asks continuing our game.

"Nah. It's too hot tonight for that. No sleeves?"

"Nah. I'm too impatient to feel your hands on me."

"Fuck, baby." I take a long step forward. She rushes towards me and jumps into my arms. "I missed you so much, Brielle."

"I missed you too, Easton." Her breath hitches. "I missed being with you."

I crush her lips with mine. I kiss her to make up for the last seven days. She returns my passionate kiss matching my wild tongue strokes.

"I've been counting the minutes until I was able to do that again," I say, pulling away from her.

"I've been waiting for a kiss since my last one."

"Greedy, girl."

"Can you blame me? My American lover is hot as sin, muscled like a soldier and he always takes good care of me."

I smile.

I reach out and cup her cheek. She allows her head to fall in the palm of my hand and she closes her eyes.

"You're all I've been thinking about since I left New York." My voice is rough and needy.

Her fingers grip my shoulders. "Every day felt like a punishment," she says.

"It's the same for me, but we're here now."

"Thank God."

I drop her to her feet and drink her in again.

"I stand by my words, that is one sexy dress."

Brielle is wearing a flowy hot pink dress with a delicate bow at the neck. Her long blonde hair falls in rich waves. As usual, her makeup is on point. Her diamond earrings with pink stones in the center illuminate her gorgeous face. The second she walked into the room, my eyes zoomed in on her towering black heels. The little silver studs add an element of edginess to an otherwise elegant outfit.

"I changed," she offers.

"I'm sorry, I didn't get that."

"This isn't the dress I wore for dinner. I would've sent the red one I peeled off my body two hours ago to be cremated, but Iyanna talked me out of it. Instead, I sent it to the drycleaner. I want Haakon's prints and smell erased forever."

I laugh.

"So this is just for me?" I smile.

"Yes."

"What's hiding underneath it as well?"

"It's always just for you, Easton," she flirts back.

God knows I want to ravish her plump lips again, but not yet.

"I'm glad to see no one laid a hand on you."

"No. Thank God."

"Yeah... it would've gotten physical if anyone had touched a beautiful strand on your head."

"You would've done that for me?" she asks.

"I would've done anything for you. I already did. Why do you think you're standing here?"

"I wasn't sure when I was going to see you again." Her voice breaks.

"The countdown started the second Officer Pavlova tracked me down in Stockholm. It took us a little time to get our ducks in a row, but there was no way I was going to leave you here."

"She found you?"

"There's so much for me to tell you. Let's go out on the balcony. It would be a shame to miss out on such a perfect night."

"I agree. This is a gem of a property—from the castle to the grounds. We have an outstanding summer home, but Lilo's is spectacular."

"It's one of the most incredible places I've ever stayed at."

I grab her hand and together we walk out on the balcony.

"What a stunning view. Even at night," she says.

I turn around to face her and sweep my eyes up and down the length of her body. "I couldn't agree with you more," I smile.

"Something tells me you aren't talking about the gardens."

"Don't get me wrong, they're okay, but nothing compared to the girl standing next to me."

"You're full of compliments."

"I'll shower you with more once I tell you the story."

"I can live with that," she smiles. "I can't believe my mother dismissed my officers without even telling me. How in the world did Officer Pavlova find you?"

I start when Haakon first contacted me and tell her everything.

"I'm grateful for your officer's dedication. I couldn't have pulled this off without her help. Officer Pavlova was critical, but so was Thor—"

"Your friend from the ball?"

"Yes. He was with me in Stockholm when I heard the news. I nearly had a heart attack."

Anger bursts through my body as the images of the press coverage come rushing back. I will the feelings down like I have for the millionth time in the past four days.

"I had nothing to do with it. It was a huge shock for me too," she says.

"I have no doubt. That's why it was so crucial to get you out of that mess. Officer Stanton, Iyanna, her mom, Princess Blakely and a number of people who respect Officer Pavlova and who were concerned about your wellbeing were also part of the team."

"My God," she says bringing her hands to her cheeks. "All that for me?"

"You wouldn't believe how many people in Belzer absolutely love you, Princess."

"I don't know what to say."

"Your mom isn't as popular and I'm sure it comes as no surprise if I tell you that most people can't stand the sight of Haakon—present company included. In a very short period of time, we had a small army. Iyanna warned us about your father's refusal of an escape plan. If he was going to ensure that you didn't end up becoming Haakon's wife, I was okay with that. Regardless, I had to get that information to you. I wanted to expose the asshole. More importantly, I wanted your mother to back off. So it was a question of getting the USB key in your hands before dinner. Since I wasn't sure if your mom had Iyanna followed, we used her mother. She met with Thor and then she gave Iyanna the pens."

"But how did you get the information?"

"Clara Bowen. We go way back. I also got help from Bryce Van Der Linden."

Over the next few minutes I share with my girl my relationship with Clara and Bryce.

"Megrhana was furious after Haakon's little publicity stunt went viral. She sought revenge. She called the top blogger in the industry. That's how Clara got her hands on that information before everybody else. When I opened the file and took note of its content, I was blown away. And disgusted. I wanted to break that asshole's jaw for his duplicity. I held back because I knew the crushing public humiliation he was going to endure would be much better than broken bones," I growl. "Bryce discovered a long list of unscrupulous things Haakon has been wasting his people's money on. No wonder he keeps demanding the Queen raise taxes. It's an aberration she'd indulge him with a second thought. I'm just glad you will never be part of that hot mess."

"Thank you so much for looking after me."

"I would've rather died than to stand back and watch Haakon marry you."

"I would've taken my life first."

"Shhh," I place two fingers against her lips. "Don't say that."

"I was desperate and I thought it was my only way out," she says.

"It's over. It's just the two of us again."

"A princess and her American lover," she smiles.

I take her in my arms and embrace her. I drop a soft kiss on the top of her head.

"About your American lover—"

"What about him?"

"What if he wanted an upgrade?"

She places her hands against my chest and pushes away from me. She looks up at me and knits her eyebrows in confusion. "Is that an American saying?"

"No, beautiful. It's my way of asking you to be my girlfriend."

"Ah!"

"I told you, Princess. You're mine." My voice is so solemn it's unrecognizable even to me. "I'm in Belzer to claim you back."

"I feel like I've been your girlfriend since Elba."

"You don't know what it means to me to hear you say that. I've been exclusively yours since then—well, since Sienna's birthday, although it took me a while to act on it—but with this wedding bullshit, I didn't know if it's something I could've asked, but now—"

"Yes! A thousand yesses, Easton. I want to be your girlfriend. Officially."

"That's music to my ears, baby."

"Can I make a request?"

"Of course. Anything. I'll give it to you."

"Make me completely yours. I want to feel you inside me."

Whoa, I didn't see that coming.

"Brielle—"

"I'm all woman, Easton. I'm no longer the innocent girl you saved in Elba. I know you said we would wait until we were at your place where it's safe and when I'm ready, but this castle is a fortress and I have some of the best guards in Europe stationed downstairs. It may not be yours, but I feel safe here. And I'm ready. I want this. I want you."

That makes two of us.

Her lack of hesitation lets me know that she's dead serious. What I read in her eyes confirms the sincerity of her declaration. Gone is the rosy-cheeked innocent princess that I used to lust over.

My eyes linger on her a beat longer. "You're sure about this?" I've been dying to be inside her since the ball, but a gentleman always asks twice.

She lifts a determined chin. "I am."

"You've come completely into your own?"

"I know who I want."

"You want me to ruin that sweet innocent pussy?"

"Yeah. What are you waiting for, boyfriend?"

Holy shit.

"Those are dangerous words, Princess."

She slides her hands underneath my half-unbuttoned white shirt and I groan. "What? That I want my king to claim me?"

"You know what this means?"

"Yes."

"What does it mean?" I press.

"It means," she says, stroking her fingers across my chest, "that my boyfriend is going to fuck me."

I growl with satisfaction.

"Once I take that part of you, you're mine forever. There won't be any doubt who you belong to."

She studies me for a long beat.

Her blue eyes are sparkling.

"And that's a problem how?"

I pull her close and lean forward. I drag my teeth up her slender neck and she moans for me. I taste the soft skin on each one of her bare shoulders before my hand travels to the hem of her dress. Without warning, I move my hand between her thighs until I cup her pussy. A growl rumbles in my throat when my fingers slide underneath her panties. Her wetness is a gift. I was hard before, but now I'm stiff as all fuck.

I touch my lips to her ear. "I guess it isn't any problem at all. I see you're ready for me." She gasps and collapses against me when I slide two fingers into her. I kiss her exposed neck as I pump my fingers a few times inside her dripping pussy, enjoying the slickness of her juices on my hand.

"Oh Easton," she whispers.

Fuck, I've missed this so much.

"You're so wet it's unreal," I tell her.

"I told you," she says, clenching her pussy around my fingers, "I know what I want."

Slap.

"Bad Princess!"

"Ouch." She frowns up at me, rubbing her butt. "My boyfriend can be so mean sometimes," she rolls her eyes with a smirk.

"Say that again."

"My boyfriend can be so–"

"No, just the first part."

"My boyfriend?"

"Yes! Again!"

"My boyfriend."

"Again."

"My boyfriend."

"Good, I like the sound of that. As much as, *my girlfriend*."

She smiles wide. "So do I."

"I had a whole elaborate dinner ready, but I can't wait, Princess."

"I don't want to wait."

CHAPTER 33

Easton

I lead my girlfriend back into the dining room and down the hallway, my hand never leaving hers. After four days in this castle, I know it well.

"Where are we going?" she asks.

"The home spa."

"Wouldn't a bedroom work better? Or a sofa? Are we going to have a relaxing steam bath before you take me?" she laughs.

"Funny. I want you, and I want to take that part of you, but I want to be considerate."

"Towards me?"

"Not just you, but also our host. I'd hate to be a terrible guest by getting Blakely's bed soiled."

"Ah. Good idea."

"Getting rid of towels and replacing them with new ones is easier than having to buy a new bed," I chuckle.

"Lead the way, my king!"

"I'm glad you approve, my queen."

My hand tightens on hers as we go down three sets of stairs. When we reach the basement, we keep walking until we stop in front of a set of glass doors.

When we walk inside the spa, I turn up the ambient temperature, switch the lights to a dim setting and I select a playlist of songs sure to get us in the right mood.

"Look at you. It's like you've been living here forever," she laughs.

"I'm guilty of having enjoyed this spa too many times since I got here."

"I don't blame you," she says, walking around the room. "It's one of my favorite spots in the castle."

I grab her by the waist and pull her to me. "This is good?"

"Yeah."

"If we were at my place it would—"

She brings two fingers up to my lips. "Easton, I love how you care about me, but this works."

"You're sure?"

"I'm positive."

I lean forward and let my lips graze her ear, "You're perfect."

"So my lover keeps telling me."

Slap.

"Ouch!"

"It's *boyfriend* now."

"I know. I wanted to see how you were going to react," she laughs.

"You're impossible. You like provoking me because you like feeling my hand against your ass."

"Guilty as charged," she smiles wide.

I just shake my head at her. "We're going to use one of these mosaic tile lounge chairs. I'll pile some towels on top of it to make it as comfortable as possible. Call it our little love nest."

"I like the sound of that."

It doesn't take me long to set the scene. Lilo's plush white towels will cushion the hardness of the chair.

I turn around to face her. "Do you want a drink? Champagne?"

She shakes her head. "No. I don't want anything. Just being here with you calms me."

I close the gap between us. "It might hurt a little."

"I know."

"Oh, shit."

"What?"

"I didn't plan for this. I don't have condoms."

"I do!"

"Wh-what?"

"They're in my handbag upstairs. I'll be right back."

"Wait."

She's already gone.

What the hell just happened?

A few minutes later, I hear her heels clacking against the marble in the hallway.

"I'm back!"

"Is there something I should know here?"

"You're surprised I came ready?"

"Slightly."

"When Iyanna told me you were here, I knew tonight would be the night. There was no doubt in my mind about it. While I was getting ready, I asked her to drive to the pharmacy and get me what I needed."

"No way."

She gives me a one-shoulder shrug. "Just because we're virgins doesn't mean we're dumb."

I laugh.

She opens the palms of her hands. "Since neither Iyanna or I know anything about sizes, I told her to grab the large, extra-large, extra-extra-large and the 'beyond huge'. I didn't bother with the small and medium because I don't think they'd fit," she grins.

"You're hilarious, but good call on the last two."

"You're okay with me taking the initiative?"

"Why would you even ask that?"

"I'm not on the pill—"

"You did the right thing, beautiful. We have plenty of time for that."

"You mean kids?"

I glide my thumb against her lips, smearing the remainder of her lipstick. "Yeah. Kids."

"My lover. My boyfriend. And my baby daddy? Yeah, that would be too much in one shot."

I roar in laughter. "Baby daddy?"

"Without the Internet, I got bored. Iyanna is a big celebrity watcher so she brought me a stack of old magazines. My vocabulary has expanded quite a lot."

I lose it again.

"So, what size are you, my king?" She doesn't even allow me time to compose myself. "Easton, work with me," she says when I'm still laughing.

"Okay. I'm good. You have to stop cracking those jokes out."

"I'm not trying to be funny," she winks. "So, back to the matter at hand—pun very much intended."

"'Beyond huge', obviously."

"Good Lord. I was afraid you were going to say that."

"As if you've never had me down your throat choking on my beyond huge cock."

"Sometimes being oblivious isn't such a bad thing."

"You're going to enjoy every inch of me."

"Promise?"

"Promise."

"Good. Because there's no money-back guarantee on these," she looks down at the condoms she's still cradling in her hands.

I grab both her hands into mine causing the packets to tumble to the tile floor. "Come here."

She doesn't resist.

I run one hand up her side, feeling her warm body under her dress and the swell of her breast with each breath. It's almost more than I can bear. I never thought it was possible to miss someone this much.

"I'm going to make up for the last week we were apart," I say before kissing her collarbone.

"Yes, please."

"That's my girl."

I crush her lips with mine and I unleash the pent-up hunger I've been suppressing. My lips are firm and demanding, teasing her desire. I nip at her lower lip, forcing her to open her mouth for me, and I plunge in, my tongue stroking hers.

Fuck.

She gasps when I yank her up in my arms, march us towards the mosaic tile lounge chairs and set her down.

"Oh, we forgot the condoms," she says taking a step forward.

"I'll grab them. Take the dress off."

My words stop her in her tracks.

"Wait."

"Don't make me repeat myself."

"Don't you want to do the honors?"

"You do it. If I touch it, I'll rip it off you. It's too perfect on you for me to destroy. Not to mention, that it makes me hard to watch you undress for me."

"Duly noted, but I need help with this zipper," she grins.

"All right."

I brush her cascade of hair down the front of her shoulders before pulling down her zipper. I take a long step back. I don't trust myself.

"That wasn't so bad. You can control yourself."

"Cheeky, Princess," I shake my head. "Off."

She removes the dress and lets it pool at her feet.

I groan looking at her standing there in her lacy lingerie.

It's not the first time I've seen her like this, but every time it gets to me.

"Jesus. Those are sexy as fuck. You're making it hard for me to take you gently. I want to rip the lingerie off you and take you like a wild animal."

"Oh."

As much as I want to feel the softness of her hot pink lingerie under my touch, it's best if I take it slow. I'm just a man, there's only so much I can handle.

"Remove the bra."

She wiggles her way out of the bra, releasing her beautiful breasts. She winks before playfully throwing the bra at me. I catch it and toss it over my shoulder.

"One more piece of fabric and that royal pussy is mine. Off."

She smiles.

Slowly and with her eyes on me, she pulls her lacy panties down her legs. The tease is excruciating. She's just about to remove them when I stop her.

"Throw them to me."

She does.

I catch them and bring them to my nose.

Finally.

"One week without you," I groan. "I wanted to smell you so much it haunted me. It's like I was going out of my mind."

"God, Easton."

Brielle stands there in all her glory.

Her perfect body.

Her delicious slender curves.

Her silky smooth skin.

Her pert rosy nipples.

Her cute as fuck clit.

Her virgin pussy.

Her sweet ass.

All mine.

"Shoes off."

She flicks off her high-heels and kicks them to the side.

"Drop that hot ass on that chair."

She obeys.

I toss the panties over my shoulder, walk to her and drop to my knees. I lock eyes with her for what seems like an eternity. She doesn't flinch. I study my beautiful princess fully aware that I'm about to make her my queen.

I place my right palm against her chest. "On your back."

I lean forward, capturing a pink nipple in my mouth and suck hard. Languorously, I tease her by moving my tongue from one breast to the other. "I love your tits, baby."

"And I love your hot mouth on my tits," she says, moaning for me.

I halt all movement and lift my head to meet her eyes.

"Did that just come out of your mouth?"

"You're a bad influence on me, Mr. Winchester," she laughs.

"Good. Keep it up."

She laughs.

I resume my mission.

I nibble her nipples again and she gasps, bucking her hips against me wildly, like she's lost all restraint. I'm already impossibly hard, but her reaction turns me on even more. Every little mewl she lets out, makes me fear that I might lose my shit with her tits in my mouth.

Unable to wait another minute to feel her, I plunge two fingers inside her pussy and she lets out a delicious shuddering moan. *Fuck.* I scoop up her juices and without warning glide my fingers deep inside her ass. There's a part of my brain that's dictating that I take it slow, but there's a stronger force pushing me to ravish this woman in the most immodest way. I listen to the latter.

"Dear God, Easton!"

"Imagine my big cock fucking your tight virgin ass, Princess."

She's so tense.

"Don't worry, your pussy first." I wink.

"I don't think I'll ever be ready for that. I can handle your fingers, but I don't think I can handle more," she says.

"I beg to differ, but like I said, not today. Open wide for me."

"Huh?"

"I've barely touched you and already you're in a daze."

"You do that to me."

"In that case, I have my work cut out. Your legs, Princess," I say, waving my hands at her trembling thighs. "Spread them open."

"Oh, yeah."

I look up and our gazes meet before I lower my head towards her pussy. I inhale the sweet scent I've obsessed over for days before blowing hot breaths.

"God!" she screams when my mouth kisses the tip of her engorged clit.

The contact of my eager mouth against her silky wet pussy is nearly too much to bear.

I growl when I plunge my mouth between her lips and she bucks into my face.

Oh, yeah.

I nip, tease, flick and toy with her.

"Mmmm," I hum when I latch on to her protruding clit.

Brielle clamps both hands against my head, nearly suffocating me as she rubs against me.

Fucking beautiful.

"Oh, Easton," she moans.

That's it. Take what's yours.

While my mouth takes good care of her clit, I gently circle her asshole with my fingers, toying with her. When she's ready for me, I slide my tongue down through her pussy lips and push it into her ass.

"Jesus Christ!" she hisses.

I feel her raise her head, but I push her right back down against the chair.

No, you don't.

"I need more, beautiful."

"More?" she pants.

"I want you to sit that royal pussy on my face. Grind against me. Use me. Fuck yourself with my tongue. Gush your juices down my throat," I growl. "Oh, I also want to taste more of that pretty little ass as well."

"Easton, that was too much."

"You'll be singing a different tune when you're coming your head off." I wink. "Get up. We need to switch positions."

She doesn't move.

"I'm waiting."

She moans, but slowly, I get my way.

Once I'm on my back, she straddles me and scoots forward.

Already, I know she's leaving a trail of her slick juices on my suit.

"Ah," she muffles as her sweet pussy settles over my mouth.

I growl.

One hand goes to her ass, holding her tight as my tongue pushes deep into her sweet wetness.

It doesn't take long before she starts grinding against my face.

Yeah, baby.

I go to town.

I offer her unrestrained access to my voracious tongue.

She uses it without an ounce of prudishness.

Good girl.

Every time her clit rubs against my tongue, the vibration pulsates all the way down to my aching balls.

"Ahhh," she lets out, tilting her head back.

My eyes are on her, watching her take pleasure.

"Dear God," she gasps, reaching out to cling onto something, anything. She settles on her long mane. She interlaces her fingers into her blonde hair and moans. She rocks back and forth, back and forth, chanting my name. "Easton, Easton, Easton…"

I gorge on my girl's sweet pussy and her puckered little asshole like my life depends on it. I fucking devour her.

She groans and grunts like a woman possessed, bucking her hips faster as more and more desperate sobs fall from her lips as I take ownership of her pussy.

"Please make me come, Easton. Please," she begs me.

Can you believe that her eyes are daringly holding my gaze?

I caress her inner thighs in response.

She sways her hips frantically against my face, taking what's hers.

"Yes, I'm so close," she pants.

She whimpers loudly, throwing her head back. Her long hair tumbles down the tips caressing my legs, her cries crashing over me.

She's nearly delirious. She's panting and gyrating her hips against my mouth.

I give her what she needs.

My tongue laps and laps and laps.

Damn.

My hands palm her sweet ass squeezing tight as my lips press hard over her hard clit.

"Yes, I'm there. I-I'm there!" she cries out.

CHAPTER 34

Brielle

"Ahhh!" I cry out as my climax hits me.

I come so hard I think I'm going to lose consciousness.

"Oh, Easton!" I yell out as I succumb to the pleasure.

I tremble uncontrollably in his hands as my orgasm charges through my body like an electric current.

Dear God.

My pussy juices gush like a river. Easton laps at me determined not to let one drop go to waste.

The sound is intoxicating.

That was mind-blowing.

I try to catch my breath, but my heart is beating too fast. It feels like it'll jump out of my chest and run a lap or two around the spa.

What an incredible lover.

"Are you okay, beautiful?" he grunts between breaths.

"I'm not sure. Ask me in a minute. I can't think right now," I laugh.

"That good, huh?"

"You already know the answer to that," I say with my eyes still closed.

I feel him move out from under me, but since my eyes are closed shut, it's only when I feel him hover over me that I know he's close.

"If my princess doesn't talk to me, I don't know what she needs."

"Your princess doesn't need anything at all right now. Maybe just a kiss."

"I can manage that."

When he takes my mouth in his, I taste myself on his lips.

It's a first for me.

Wow.

He drops his forehead against mine. "Are you ready?"

"Yes."

"Don't be brave, if it hurts you tell me. Everything stops. We can try another day."

"I really want this."

"Brielle, did you hear what I said?"

"Yes."

"I want this as much as you do, but I want it to be pleasurable. A little pain is inevitable, but I don't want your first time to be so painful that it's off-putting."

"Okay. I promise I'll tell you if it hurts too much."

"Good girl."

He kisses me again. With abandon this time.

I lose myself to him and his need.

"You're still dressed," I tell him between kisses.

"You want me naked?"

"How else is my boyfriend going to ruin my pussy?"

His eyebrows hit his forehead.

"A week apart and I barely recognize you. You're lucky that I missed you so much and I don't want to waste a minute punishing you for that smart mouth of yours."

"It's hardly fair that I'd get punished for wanting my boyfriend this much."

"I love it when you say stuff like that."

He pulls away from me and strips out of his tailored gray suit, kicks off his expensive shoes and pulls off his trousers and boxer briefs in one fluid movement.

I never get tired of seeing this man naked.

I just gawk at him as he peels his socks off and throws them to one side.

Not very lady-like—I know—but can you blame me?

I may be lacking in experience, but in my opinion Easton is a work of art.

I'm unable to peel my eyes away from his chiseled chest. His well-defined abs are calling for my touch and his muscular biceps are begging for my kisses. Don't even get me started on his sculptured V muscle. I brush my eyes down the length of his body and follow the line of dark hair extending from his bellybutton down to his beautiful cock—nine inches of erect goodness. Thick, straight, with a dark purple head. His balls hang proud underneath his cock. He's ready.

Definitely 'beyond huge'.

He walks to where the condoms are still scattered across the marble floor. I can now admire him from behind.

As if the man wasn't blessed enough, there's his ass.

Oh my God, what an ass.

Firm.

Muscular.

Taut.

One day I'll muster up the courage to bite that ass.

He picks up one of the condoms, turns around and flashes me a devilish glance. He tears the packet with his teeth, sheathes his massive erection and walks back to me.

God was really good to you.

And I get to enjoy every scrumptious inch of him.

Lucky me.

"If you keep eating me up with your eyes like that, you're going to feel self-conscious," he chuckles.

"I'm admiring," I tell him. "I sometimes struggle to believe that you're mine."

"I feel the same way about you, beautiful."

I answer with a ridiculously wide smile.

"We're doing this?" he asks.

I lie back on the lounge chair and beckon for him to join me.

"No hesitation on my part."

"Is that so?" he chuckles. He approaches me and stands over me with his closed fists at his waist. "I might get used to this assertive Princess," he says straddling me.

I reach up and grab his erect cock.

"I'm ready to feel you inside me, Easton."

His brown eyes hood as they lower to the sight of my hand circling his cock. He tilts his hips forward as he lets out a feral growl.

"Fuck, beautiful. This is going to be so good between us."

"I agree."

I'm fearful and excited at the same time. It's a weird pull and push feeling. Like nothing I've ever experienced before. Easton awakened the woman in me, and he's about to claim her fully.

"We're going to take it nice and slow."

"Okay."

For some reason, I forget to breathe when I say that.

He slides his other hand down my thighs. "Spread them wide for me."

And I do.

Easton lowers himself and places his left hand above my head against the lounge chair. He grabs his cock by the base and places it right at my entrance. He slides his tip between my lips. The huge head of his cock caresses my pussy and teases my clit in a languorous motion that nearly drives me out of my mind. As he glides up and down my slit, I realize how wet I still am from my first orgasm.

Unbelievable.

I expect him to plunge right inside me, but instead he says, "Remember our agreement?"

I frown confused.

"You tell me if it hurts."

I nod. "I will."

He holds my gaze for a beat longer, almost as if he was looking for any signs of hesitation.

I nod again. "I promise," I say.

Even though I want this, it doesn't prevent my voice from coming out shaky.

"Good."

Slowly, Easton pushes the head of his cock into my tight virgin pussy, stretching me around his cock.

That takes my breath away.

I grit my teeth and my hands claw at his forearms.

That does little to tamper the searing feeling of being torn in half.

The next thing I know, I cry out in pain.

Easton halts all movement.

"Fuck. I'm sorry, baby," he says.

"It's okay," I pant. "You're a lot to handle," I offer him a small smile.

His cock is so big, so wide, so overwhelming and so different from his fingers or his tongue.

"We can stop."

"My mind is certain of this, my body might have a few more reservations but I'm sure it'll come around."

He laughs.

"Slow and steady," he says with a nod.

"Okay."

Easton pushes inside me again. And again. And again.

Each inch is an excruciating feat.

"Jesus Christ," he mutters, shoving in another few inches. "I knew you'd be tight, I just didn't expect it to be *this* tight. I don't want to hurt you. Can you still handle it?"

"Yes."

"Okay." Easton works his hips feeding me more and more of his cock. "Fuck, you're too tight," he repeats. Sweat gleams on his shoulders and chest. I'm as sweaty as he is.

Another shove.

Another inch.

Another tear and I cry out again.

I dig my fingers into his forearms in an effort to ride the pain. It's in vain.

"Oh, God!" I cry out again.

"I'm almost there, beautiful. Just breathe for me," he coaxes.

"Okay," I repeat because there really isn't much more to say.

As much as I try, I can't help but shake.

The pain is far worse than what I expected. It's like nothing I'd ever experienced before in my life. Not even a pretty bad ski accident in Switzerland many years ago where I broke my leg can compare. Breathing in and out doesn't seem to help much.

Easton continues to work his hips back and forth and then without warning, he shoves inside me with a determined thrust and just like that, he pushes through my resistance.

My body shrieks in pain and so does my mouth.

Thrashing my head to one side, I pull my lip between my teeth and bite down hard.

Mother of God.

"You're so fucking tight," he says.

"And you're so fucking big!" I fire back.

Tears swell in my eyes, but I blink them away.

Everything we've shared so far has been so intense, so perfect and so beautiful. I expected this experience to be the same. It's not.

I've only known pleasure with my boyfriend.

This feels like my pussy is being ripped in half.

"The worst is behind you, beautiful."

My eyes fly up to his gorgeous face. It's as if he could read my thoughts.

"Really?"

"Really. I'm going to move a little faster and a little deeper now. You'll definitely feel me, but it shouldn't be as painful. If it is, tell me."

"Okay."

I watch in fascination as the ridged muscles of Easton's flat stomach contract. He draws himself out and then thrusts back inside me. He penetrates me this time around with unwavering force that I grit my teeth as he fills me up.

"How does it feel?" he asks.

"You're so deep." My voice trembles when I say that.

"Not really. Your tight little pussy is like a vice. As much as I want to stretch you out and fill you up by sinking myself to the hilt all the way inside you, I won't. There's plenty of time for that."

"I love it when you say that."

"What?"

"That we have all the time in the world now."

"We do. You're fully mine now," he grunts in my ear as he continues to force his way in and out of my virgin pussy. "No one else will ever be able to have that part of you, Brielle. It's all mine," he repeats.

I moan at the possessiveness of his words.

Easton pulls out of me, keeping only his tip lodged in me. He sweeps his gaze down to where our bodies are fused together.

"There are certain things you can only give once. Thank you for giving me this gift, Princess."

I follow his gaze and jerk back surprised by the sight of my own blood glistening on the condom, smeared across his stomach and his thighs. My own body is also marked by blood.

Wow.

"That's proof that we were meant to be together." His comment pulls my eyes up to his. "And guess what?" It's a rhetorical question since he doesn't allow me to answer. "I'm fully yours now, Princess. I don't want anyone else. I just want you."

I'm at a loss for words.

I'm used to Easton, the guy who unravels me with his dirty talk.

This solemn confession leaves me in awe.

"I don't want anyone else either," I tell him.

Easton lays his whole body over mine and kisses me with unrestrained passion. I respond with as much fervor.

He starts driving in and out of me with abandonment.

The pleasure I was hoping for doesn't come, but there's something else. Something I haven't felt with him before. It's an intense connection. Maybe this is what they mean by communion of the souls.

In and out.

In and out.

In and out.

Easton fucks me in a slow steady cadence.

The slick sounds of our naked bodies pressed together, his sheathed cock stained with blood pumping in and out of my pussy and his low grunts is a symphony to my ear.

I don't think it's possible for us to be any closer, but Easton wraps me even tighter in his arms. His face is right next to mine. His chin is tucked into my shoulder and his heavy breathing caresses my skin as he fucks me. He feels so heavy against me, but I don't dare to tell him. I don't want to break this embrace.

"I don't have much left, beautiful," he growls in my ear. "You're going to come for me?"

"Yes," I respond, even though I doubt very much I'll be able to climax. All I can feel is his body above mine.

"Together."

"Together," I repeat.

I'm not exactly sure how this is going to work. There's no room between our sweaty bodies for his fingers—or mine.

That doesn't seem to deter Easton. He pumps into me like a piston. And I take it.

"Fuck," he grunts. "Princess, come all over my cock," he pants.

"I—"

Suddenly, a familiar tingle curls up at the pit of my stomach.

Easton angles his body and presses down hard against my clit. With each thrust, his body grinds, awakening all my senses.

Ooooh.

I dig my fingernails into his ass and squeeze hard, forcing his weight against me.

It's a ripple at first. And then it hits me.

Even through this pain, I can climax.

Dear God.

"Easton. Oh, Easton," I chant over and over again as my pussy burns around his cock. I come apart stitch by stitch, my pussy pulsing in tight staccatos.

Having his thick cock buried inside me intensifies my orgasm.

As the second climactic wave washes over me, I buck against him, pulling him closer.

"God. Shit. Brielle. Baby."

His words sound raw and urgent.

"Oh, fuck!" He lets out another deep roar.

As I watch him take his pleasure from me, I can't help but smile.

I did that to him.

Without warning, Easton catches my lips in a blazing kiss. I respond as best as I can to his overwhelming passion. As he devours my lips, he continues to drive himself deeper inside me, grunting into my mouth as he pours his release inside my pussy.

I'm no longer a virgin.

"You're fucking perfect," he moans covering my face with soft kisses. "And you're fucking mine."

I can't help but giggle like a silly girl.

The tenderness of his kiss, a stark contrast with the way he just claimed my innocence.

I can only belong to him now.

Thank you, God.

After a few minutes, I find the strength to open my eyes again. When I do, I meet his tender gaze.

"Hey, beautiful. You're still with me?"

"Barely," I smile.

"Well, at least I didn't kill you after our first time."

"That would've been a Shakespearean tragedy."

We both laugh.

"I think we've had enough drama lately to last a lifetime," he says.

"Hear, hear."

He kisses me softly on the lips and says, "I'm going to pull out now. It might hurt a bit."

"Oh, okay."

With one swift movement, he yanks his cock out of me.

"Ouch!" The void and pain make me cry out.

The sudden absence of his warmth makes me shiver.

"Sorry, beautiful."

"I'll survive. I think."

He flashes me a warm smile. "Let's go take a shower. I need to pamper my princess."

"Yes, please," I laugh.

He removes the condom and tosses it on a towel on the floor. When my eyes sweep down his body, I'm shocked by the sight. The dried blood against his white skin is jarring… but I guess no more disconcerting than what I see on my own body.

Wow.

"Come on," Easton picks me up in his arms. Instinctively, I nestle my head in the crook of his neck.

He strides towards the shower dropping soft kisses against my forehead along the way.

I could stay like this forever.

He drops me to my feet and sets the water temperature.

I feel extremely vulnerable for some reason. I think he senses that.

He pulls me against his warm body. "Let's get under the water." His breath caresses my cheek. "The warmth of the water will soothe your body."

"Okay," I nod.

I've forgotten how amazing it is to have the water run against my skin as his hands glide against my body.

"Is the water okay?" he asks soaping my back.

"Yes, it's the perfect temperature."

"Good."

"I love that scent," I say inhaling the perfume of the lotus flower shower gel.

"Hmm-mmm," Easton hums. He's taking this so seriously. "Turn around, I need to take care of the rest of my princess' sexy body."

I obey.

Instead of using the shower pouf, Easton gropes my breasts with both hands.

"Hey. Hands off," I protest.

"I need to make sure every beautiful part of you is cleaned," he grins.

"Right," I laugh. "We haven't taken a shower together since Elba. I've missed that."

"Same here."

Easton makes due to his promise. He washes every last bit of me. I wince internally when his hand glides between my legs. *Will my pussy ever recover?* He even washes my hair. I love how his fingers massage my scalp. I swear the guy is a professional. Of course, it's only fair that I return the favor. Feeling his defined muscles underneath my hands is such a turn on. If my pussy weren't so sore, I'd be begging for his cock again.

"This is so good, I'm tempted to suggest we stay under the water for the next hour."

"Your skin is already red as is, beautiful," he laughs. "Time's up!"

A quick towel dry later and we're back lying down on one of the mosaic chairs. Soft chill-out music seeps from the speakers and the lights are low. The perfect mood for a perfect evening. I don't know how long we lounge like this for, but I don't care. I'm in heaven. When Easton pulls me closer to him, I purr. I love the feel of my naked legs intertwined with his hairy ones.

"Does it still hurt?" he asks holding me in his strong arms.

"A bit. Okay, more than a bit—"

"I'm sorry," he repeats.

"I'll get over it."

"You should've said something—"

"Why? And rob myself from seeing your face when you came inside me? No way. That was way too hot."

"Don't worry, I'm sure I'll have that look every time I come with you."

"I like knowing that," I smile.

"I tried to control myself, but I've wanted you for too long and you responded so well, beautiful. You bring out the caveman in me."

"I didn't know you had one of those hiding inside you."

"I didn't either until you."

We both burst out laughing.

"So I wasn't terrible?"

He places two fingers under my chin and tilts my head back until our eyes meet. He stares at me long and hard. *God, I was awful.* Worried, I avert my gaze. "Look at me," he commands.

I can't.

"Brielle." My name is a low growl, a warning.

I meet his gaze.

"It was your first time, so you have to cut yourself some slack."

"Oh, no. It was a dreadful experience, wasn't it? Just say it. No need to sugarcoat it."

"If you were that terrible, do you really think I'd come that hard?"

I shrug. "I guess not."

"Remember the first time you gave me a blow job?"

"Yes."

"It was a little awkward for you."

"To say the least."

"And it got easier and more enjoyable?"

"*Way* more enjoyable," I smile wide.

"And now you're a freaking pro," he laughs.

"Well, thank you, sir." It's my turn to laugh.

"It's the same for this. We'll take it easy for tonight. We won't go at it again, but tomorrow, we're getting back on that saddle and I want you to ride me like a cowgirl rides a stallion," he says with resolve.

"That's a tall order."

"Not really. Since I intend on enjoying your pussy at least four times a day, every single day, you'll get a hold of this in no time."

"Sounds like my sex life will be off the charts. The commute, on the other hand, not so great."

"I have a solution for that."

"I'm all ears."

"Move in with me."

"What?" I jerk in his arms.

"I want to live with my girlfriend."

"Are you serious?"

"Sienna can have the penthouse and I'll buy a bigger place for the two of us. I've already started looking at houses in Belzer. That way we'll have a place of our own when you want to come back and visit."

"I don't know what to say."

"If you think things are moving too fast—"

I place two fingers against his lips. "No. I want this. I just didn't expect it."

"You live with an entourage in New York and I live with my sister. Sneaking around for a few weeks was fun, but I don't want to do that forever."

"Neither do I."

"We'll talk to your father about securing the services of your officers. I don't want him to get upset at me for not protecting his little girl. And, I don't need King Dagget sending his guards after me for unknowingly breaking a protocol. I won't profess to understand all this royalty business, but I'm not taking any chances with you. This past week has taught me a valuable lesson—I refuse to let anything happen to you."

"Wow. No half measures with you, Mr. Winchester."

“No, never. Your status made me hesitate in going full force after what I wanted. But that's behind us. I had an incredible life before you, Brielle, but you’ve made it so much better. I need you in my life every single day. I want to go to sleep with you nestled in my arms and I want to wake up with my arms wrapped around your waist. That's if you want that too.”

“A thousand times, yes.”

Unable to contain the flood of emotions overpowering me, I burst into tears.

Easton pulls me closer to him. “What’s wrong, Brielle?”

I'm too choked up to answer.

“Come on, talk to me, beautiful.”

Still nothing.

He drops kisses on my forehead, my cheeks and my trembling lips. Gradually my body stops quivering and I can speak again.

“I didn't think it was in the cards for us. I thought the story of the princess and her American lover was a short-lived one,” I sniffle.

Easton wipes away my tears. He grabs my chin between his fingers and forces our eyes to meet.

“Silly Princess, don't you know that's not how the fairytale ends.”

CHAPTER 35

Brielle

2 years later

Oh yeah, there's so much you don't know yet about what happened after the dinner with Prince Haakon and the reunion with my man.

Easton and I spent the night at Lilo's summer home. The next day I went back to my parents home to test the waters and see if it was too early to tell my parents Easton and I were a couple. When I walked into the manor, it was like World War III had erupted. My mother was in a fit of rage and very drunk. Daddy was nowhere to be found. There were broken dishes everywhere. I quickly turned around and ran out of there.

After dinner, Daddy went up to his office to make some calls. When he then went back downstairs, he told Mum he would be breaking with Belzerian traditions. He wanted out. You can imagine that the news shattered my mother's perfect image and she wouldn't hear of it. Daddy packed his bags and moved to another manor we own an hour away. He waited patiently for Mum to go on one of her trademark pampering weekends in Bulgaria. The minute she was out, he jumped into action. He fired her security team and her two secretaries—they were all under a gag order. He then changed all the locks in the manor and brought in a team of professional movers to pack my mother's belongings and ship them to her parents' home. When Mum was done with her three-day R & R weekend, she was faced with the stark reality of her situation. The credit card had been cut off and there was no chauffeured car waiting for her outside. Daddy didn't stop there. He had his lawyers present her with divorce papers at the spa.

You can imagine that Mum fought tooth and nail, but in the end, it came down to the prenup. After twenty-one years, my mother forgot she signed off on a clause that stipulates that the marriage would be terminated if she were to put my father's wealth or companies at risk. Daddy's lawyers found a clever way of weaving the Haakon fiasco against Mum—after all, the idiot prince was pretty forthcoming about his less than honorable intentions.

Six months after he was a free man, Daddy met the lovely—and so beautiful—Duchess Nadja Malena Lindfjeld from the Kingdom of Daavík at a charity event in London. Don't get me wrong, under all those layers of anger, Mum is a stunning woman. That said, Nadja is Daddy's future. She's a forty-two year old divorcée. She has two adult sons—both serving in the Daavíkian Royal Navy. Unlike Daddy's, her divorce was civilized.

Nadja changed my father. He looks twenty years younger. He lost an insane amount of weight. He no longer drinks excessively and he's given up chasing women. Yup, my father is a one-woman man now. Daddy's morphed from being a cliché—a rich moody prince who was stuck in a disastrous arranged marriage—to becoming a fun and jovial guy. Thanks to Nadja, I've rediscovered my father. She left her kingdom and moved in with him a year ago. It's the first time I've ever seen him happy. Amen for small favors.

Mum is still miserable.

I grew accustomed to her constant badgering and verbal harassment. It's one thing when she was putting me down, and belittling my blog and accomplishments. It's completely different when she puts Easton down just because he wasn't born a royal. That's where I put my foot down. Her attitude is just stupid. He's much more of a man than Haakon will ever be.

Still, I made efforts to maintain somewhat of a relationship with Mum until she became violent. In one of her drunken stupors, she turned on me when I showed concern about her wellbeing. Easton—my man … my gorgeous, sweet, fearless and protective warrior … the man I love with all my heart—stepped forward to shield me from her wrath.

That was the last time I saw her. We've been estranged for a year and a half now.

Unable to withstand the humiliation of being labeled the first royal divorcée of Belzer, she left the country soon after that incident. She moved to Estonia. She has a lot of family there. Since this whole Haakon mess blew up in her face, Mum had to be content with a small settlement. Not that she's suffering. Her family is very wealthy. The last I heard, a vodka martini was still her best friend.

Oh, well.

EPILOGUE 1

Easton

My girl and I are sitting in the back of a chauffeured Bentley on our way to The Colony Grill at the Beaumont Hotel in Brown Hart Gardens. I flew her to London for a four-day getaway. It's uncharacteristically hot so the streets are bursting with activity. It's hard not to be enveloped by the bright lights and the exuberant energy of people rushing to their favorite hangout spots. Brielle is completely transfixed by the nightlife. I beckon her attention. I lift her hand and drop a soft kiss against it.

"You look beautiful. Then again, I don't know why I'm surprised anymore."

She's wearing a sleeveless short black cocktail dress with a seductive V decorated with beautiful white pearls. She paired it with a stylish clutch and satin high heels with a crystal buckle. Both are elegant and black.

She gives me a brilliant smile. "Thank you. It's date night!"

"Is it still date night when we're traveling?" I tease.

"Bite your tongue, mister. Fridays are sacred. Date night is important."

"*Every* night with you is important, Brielle."

Since we've been together we've had this tradition. As much as I can, I try to be in New York for the weekend and arrange my schedule accordingly. It isn't always possible, but when I'm in town, it's something to look forward to given how busy we both are.

"You're full of compliments," she says.

"Ten years from now, I'll still be full of compliments." I tap the tip of her nose with my finger.

"So you think this thing between us is going to last?"

"You couldn't get rid of me even if you tried. It'll always be Easton and Brielle."

"I've been told."

"Nah. You just know where I stand when it comes to you, Princess."

She blushes.

"I still can't believe Officer Pavlova and Officer Stanton are both sick. What are the chances?" she says, changing the subject.

"We're still okay. My officers are equally capable," I wink.

"Of course."

"I feel for Officer Pavlova and Officer Stanton. Food poisoning is a nasty business."

"Indeed. It's just that they've never been sick. Those women are tanks."

"Stop worrying and enjoy tonight."

"I'm sorry. You're right."

It turns out that living with a princess demands a certain level of logistics. I had to beef up my own security. It's part of the package deal of dating royalty. I'm now considered a potential target if anyone wanted to bring harm to my princess. Officer Selezneva—sitting in the passenger seat—and Officer Carradine—tailing us in a Benz—are my shadows.

"We're here, sir," our chauffeur says.

"Excellent. Thank you, Jonathan."

The car has barely come to a full stop than Officer Selezneva jumps out, opens the door for Brielle and extends her hand. "Princess," she says.

"Thank you," my girlfriend says.

"You'll text me when you're ready, sir," Jonathan says.

"Absolutely," I nod. "It shouldn't be anytime soon. Tonight is all about my girl. I don't want to rush things."

"Of course. Have a good evening, sir."

"Likewise, Jonathan."

I get out of the car, circle it and pull Brielle into my arms. I drop a soft kiss on her forehead. I've never been one to give into overt displays of affection in public; when you're constantly walking around with a shadow or two, you're extra careful.

We walk hand-in-hand to the restaurant with Officer Selezneva trailing behind us. Officer Carradine already has the door open for us.

My God these women are efficient.

"Thank you," I say with a nod.

"Of course, sir," she answers.

"Mr. Winchester. Princess Brielle. Always a pleasure to see you again," our hostess greets as we arrive at the front desk.

"Amanda, likewise," I say.

"It's been too long. We haven't been in London in months," Brielle says.

"Indeed," Amanda smiles warmly. "But you're here tonight and that's all that counts, right?"

"I couldn't agree with you more," Brielle says.

"In that case, let me see where you'll be seated."

"Thank you," my girl and I say in unison.

"Hmmm," Amanda hums.

Brielle looks up at me and knits her eyebrows together.

"Hmmm," Amanda hums again.

"What's wrong?" Brielle asks.

"I'm a little stumped," Amanda says.

I take a step forward. "Is there a problem?"

"I'm afraid so, sir."

"What is it?" I ask.

"It seems we have your reservation for tomorrow Saturday, not for tonight. And glancing at the number of reservations, it seems we're booked solid until the last service."

"Oh, no," Brielle utters.

"That's not possible. My secretary made the reservations two months ago. And it was specifically for Friday night."

"I really do apologize. I have no doubt you're right, sir. There seems to have been some confusion on our end. We've just updated our computer system to a new software and it's been a bit of a challenge to say the least. Some reservations were dropped and some others seem to have migrated on their own."

"What are you saying, Amanda? Do we need to find another place to eat tonight?"

"I really hope not," Brielle says.

Our hostess lifts her hand up. "Oh no, sir. Princess. Please. I won't hear of it. If you'll allow me just a few minutes, I'll make it right."

"Okay," I nod. "That sounds good."

"May I invite you to wait in the lounge? It'll be much more comfortable. I'll send some champagne over. The best in the house, of course."

"I appreciate that," I tell her.

Brielle and I make our way to the lounge with our bodyguards in tow.

Soon after we're comfortably seated, a waitress rushes in with a bottle of Dom Pérignon Vintage. Once she's filled our glasses, she rushes out.

"Cheers!" I say, lifting my glass.

"Jubel!" Brielle cheers in Belzerian.

We both take a long sip of our champagne.

Wow!

"Not that it makes up for the possibility of not being able to dive into my favorite dessert, but I must admit, this champagne is lovely," she says dropping her glass on the table in front of her.

I chuckle. "I agree. This is exceptional."

"I can't believe our date night might get derailed because of a silly computer glitch."

"Nothing is definite yet," I remind her.

"Yeah, but it's not like you can just materialize a table. Unless they intend on adding a table somewhere in the corner of the kitchen or in the lobby or the loo, how are they going to accommodate us?"

"Why don't you enjoy the champagne and let Amanda worry about it?"

"You seem overconfident."

"We're good clients. A place like this prides itself on loyalty. I'm sure Amanda will do right by us."

"Fair enough," she says reaching for her glass again.

A few sips later and Amanda walks into the lounge with a huge smile stretching her face.

"This looks promising," Brielle says.

"Told you."

"Mr. Winchester. Princess. I apologize it took me so long, but I think I found a way to accommodate you."

"A cancellation?" Brielle asks.

"Unfortunately, no. That said, one of the private rooms that's closed—because we're set to start renovation on Monday—will be ready for you in the next few minutes. You don't have to worry. It doesn't look like a construction zone. We had made the decision to keep it closed over the weekend to make it easy on us, but since we made a mistake, it's only fair we rectify it."

"Good news. Thank you, Amanda," I say.

"Are you sure?" Brielle asks. "We don't want to be any trouble?"

"Rest assured, Princess, I wouldn't have it any other way. Neither would management."

"In that case, that's great news."

And that brings a huge smile to my girl's face.

"I'll be back to get you when everything is ready."

"Once again, thank you, Amanda."

"It's my pleasure, sir."

Then she scurries off.

"A large private room is a bit over the top," Brielle says once Amanda leaves the room.

I lean into her and whisper in her ear, "I like the idea of a private room. I've been traveling so much lately. I miss you. Every part of you. Why wait until later to make up for lost time. We can get started much sooner."

She pulls away from me. "Easton Winchester, bite your tongue. I'd never do anything like that."

I lean into her again. I know the officers are standing guard outside and they most likely can't hear me. Call it a habit. Since living with my girlfriend, I've had to resort to whispering my dirty talk when we're out. "You said the same thing when I suggested we do it on the balcony at our penthouse."

Her eyes widen like saucers and she turns beet red.

"If I recall correctly, you're the one begging for it lately," I grin from ear to ear.

"That was different. We have privacy. Not to mention with all the tall shrubs, it makes it easier to give myself freely without feeling like a prostitute. Anyone could walk in on us in the private room."

"Not if we lock the door."

She just shakes her head.

"You're unbelievable." She pauses and squints her gray eyes at me. "That wicked gleam in your eyes scares me."

"It should."

"Easton," she admonishes.

"Calm down. I'm just yanking your chain."

"I love that expression."

She laughs.

A knock on the door calls for our attention.

"Mr. Winchester. Princess. If you'll follow me," Amanda says.

"Excellent," I say getting up.

All four of us trail behind Amanda as we make our way through the restaurant. It's the usual formation. My girlfriend holding my hand. One officer in front of us. Another following us.

"She wasn't kidding. This place is packed," Brielle says in a low voice.

"I'm glad she found a solution," I tell her.

Out of the blue, Brielle starts laughing.

"What?"

"Nothing," she responds, lifting her eyes to the ceiling.

"What's going on inside that pretty little head of yours?" I ask, narrowing my eyes.

"It's nothing," she says again.

"Your smile suggests otherwise, Princess. Indulge me."

"I could just imagine us all dressed up sitting at McDonald's wolfing down our Happy Meals because it's nearly impossible to find a table this late in London on a Friday night."

"Silly Princess, don't you know that's when money comes in handy? We're not going to step inside McDonald's and sit. We're going to send Jonathan. He buys the goods. He comes back with the goods to the car. We wolf down the goods in the car. That's the only decent way of doing it," I joke.

"You're hilarious. I can't tell you how much I missed you."

"Not nearly as much as I missed you," I tell her.

She brings my hand up to her lips and drops a soft kiss against it. I barely have time to enjoy the contact against my skin than already she's rubbing off the red lipstick print she left behind. "I wouldn't want to stain your crisp white shirt," she says.

"You're too precious."

"We're here," Amanda announces.

"Thank you," Brielle and I say in unison.

Amanda opens the door.

Officer Carradine steps inside the room.

I extend my hand. "Princesses first," I bow.

"You're such a gallant man. I think I'll keep you."

"You better," I laugh.

Brielle walks in.

Suddenly a chorus of voices shouts, "SURPRISE!"

"Ha!" Brielle staggers back and slams right into me.

"It's okay," I tell her catching her in my arms.

She turns around to face me. Her eyes are as big as saucers. "What's going on?"

"I think it's self-explanatory."

"You're behind this?"

"That would be a yes."

"You tricked me? This isn't date night? We aren't in London for a lover's getaway?"

"Not technically."

"Why didn't you tell me? I could've had a heart attack."

"First off, I think you're too young for that. Second off, how else was I going to get you here and get all these people here without you knowing? You're so connected with your family and friends, you would've smelled this a mile away."

She turns around and scans the room. Her eyes bounce from left to right with her mouth gaping open. She's taking in every single beautiful face staring at her. I lean into her just in time to catch her eyes land on the large banner hanging across a bare wall. "My Girl Rocks the Fashion World," she reads aloud.

"CONGRATULATIONS!" the crowd shouts this time.

"Oh my God," Brielle says as realization sets in. "All of you are accomplices? You all knew. No one even dropped a hint."

"That was the whole point of us yelling, surprise," Lilo shouts.

"I could've acted surprised."

Everyone in the room laughs.

"Right," a few people say.

I just shake my head.

Brielle has the worst poker face on the planet.

My girlfriend takes a shaky step inside the room and walks straight to her father. "Daddy, I spoke to you a few hours ago. You made me believe you were in Belzer. How could you?"

"Your boyfriend made me do it," Prince Janek says, lifting his hands in capitulation. "The bloke left me no other choice. He was so headstrong about this night. I wasn't going to be the one to let the cat out of the bag. Sorry, sweetheart. I had to side with the American on this one," the prince chuckles.

Our favorite people in the world are present. The level of security in this room and surrounding this hotel is ridiculous. I'm pretty sure the President of the United States would be envious. I couldn't imagine this day without Brielle's grandparents or her great-grandparents—the Queen and King Dagget. In other words, along with the reigning sovereign, the three other people in line to the Belzer throne are all under one roof. Getting this day orchestrated was a real tour de force. It took several months of careful planning. Without Miriam, Nadga, Iyanna, Blakely and Sienna's help, there's no way I would've been able to pull this off. It goes without saying that the management and staff at The Colony Grill were in on it. They put so much manpower on this. My friends Thor and Harlen are also present.

Our friends and family are gathered here because my girl is a rising star. Since graduating at the top of her class six months ago, Brielle has been devoting herself to her blog. Over the last month, the New York Times Style Magazine, Style New York Times, Le Figaro France and Porter Net-A-Porter.com, named Brielle Fashion Blogger of the Year and indisputable trailblazer because she single-handedly put

Belzer fashion on the map. Well, I guess I should say her mother had a hand in it as well. In a sea of pastel tulle and frilly dresses Princess Jenna had commissioned, there were quite a few gems. Once the dust settled, Brielle made it her mission to use the newfound interest for her blog—thank you very much, Haakon. It doesn't stop there. Her influence has been so transcending that the MoMA, New York will have a big exhibit in two months to celebrate the best Brielle's country has to offer. Of course, my girl is the guest of honor. I'll definitely be standing by her side on that day.

"Oh, my God, Easton, you're incredible."

"I'm so proud of you, beautiful." I embrace her in my arms and kiss her tenderly.

Our friends and family start to whistle, cheer, clap and some even stomp their feet.

I pull away from my girl. "Oh, stop it, you guys," I scold. "There are two other people who didn't want to be left out," I tell Brielle shifting my focus back to her.

Brielle extends her head. "Who? Everyone is here."

I nod at Officer Carradine to open the door.

"Almost everyone."

Two familiar faces walk into the room.

"Oh, my God. Officer Pavlova. Officer Stanton," Brielle shouts running to her bodyguards. "You're not sick. You tricked me as well. Where's the love?" she laughs.

"We had strict orders from Mr. Winchester to play along, Princess," Officer Pavlova says.

"Yeah, our hands were tied, Princess," Officer Stanton says.

"It's a big day of celebration and Officer Stanton and I wanted to be part of it. I hired some backup so that I can be free to enjoy this evening with you, Princess."

"I'm so lucky to have you two," Brielle says choking up as she embraces the two women who would give their lives for hers.

"It's an honor to protect you, Princess," Officer Stanton says.

"Thank you from the bottom of my heart," Brielle says. "Don't go anywhere. I have to say hi to everyone, but I'll be back."

And she's off.

I follow right behind her and do the same.

My sexy girlfriend makes her way around the room kissing and hugging every last person here. I thought I was going to have to restrain her because she covered King Dagget's face with a couple hundred kisses before hugging him so hard, I was certain she was going to break the poor guy. Those two have such a special bond.

I'm a big fan of the King. Believe it or not, I met with him, Prince Joachim, Brielle's grandfather and Prince Janek a couple years ago before we moved in together. I wasn't sure if our relationship was going to cause a rift in her family because I'm not a royal. King Dagget said, if he could approve the first ever royal divorce—one that was long overdue—he'll gladly welcome a good man with solid values with open arms. He said he nearly died when he found out Brielle's mom wanted to bring Prince Haakon into his family.

Speaking of the devil, the only person missing tonight is Princess Janika.

She refused my countless invitations.

Prince Janek and Princess Blakely tried to reason with her, but she won't budge.

It's her loss.

She has an exceptional daughter, but she doesn't see it.

She's so blinded by stupid conventions that she's missing out on the best things life has to offer—the people who matter most.

Despite her mother's betrayal, Brielle tried, but it was in vain.

When it looked like her mom had hit rock bottom, she suggested rehab and seeking counseling. Her mom lost it on her. Thank God I was there. I had to stand between Princess Janika and my girlfriend, daring her mom to even try to lay a hand on her. I'll protect Brielle no matter what—especially against her own mother.

Oh, here's something else you don't know, Princess Janika blames Brielle for her divorce. When she spat that in my girlfriend's face, I had to bite my tongue not to explode in laughter.

Talk about sticking your head in the sand.

The divorce is her own doing.

You must be wondering what happened to the idiot Prince and his slut of a girlfriend.

Lots.

After I received King Dagget's blessings, Brielle held a press conference to tell her side of the story. It was a real media frenzy. Luckily, the press sided with my girl. That said, Haakon's stupid stunt paid off big time for her—hence why we're here tonight.

Things didn't quite turn out as expected for Haakon.

After his disgrace, Queen Gertrude stripped him from the kingship and granted the title to her third child and second son, Prince Sven, who was only sixth in line to the throne. He has a solid marriage and four well-adjusted kids of his own. Unlike Haakon, his life isn't marred with drama.

Haakon was pissed off and made no attempts to hide it.

It only gave ammunition to the press to further ridicule him.

Haakon and Megrhana got married two months after that dreadful dinner. Megrhana wanted to walk down the aisle before her baby bump became apparent. The press couldn't shut up about that wedding. Not because it was extraordinary. And not because it was classy. Because it was a real circus. She wore an asymmetric red dress that was so short in the front it was indecent. He wore a red tuxedo with black satin lapels. It goes without saying that he also wore a pair of red and black shoes. Head to toe red when you're ginger? Not a good idea. Queen Gertrude nearly had an aneurysm. Photos of her rolling her eyes during the ceremony peppered the rag papers and websites. It was quite hilarious.

Haakon and Megrhana have already been divorced for a year now.

Yep. Freaking amazing.

Megrhana had a really hard time giving birth. After the babies were born, they had to sedate her because she had lost so much blood and she was in severe pain. Under the Queen's order, the Skahemmet Hälsocenter hospital in Göranbacken, Brihon brought in a nursing mother to feed the triplets while Megrhana was recuperating.

That's when the countdown started for the talentless actress.

Haakon walked in one afternoon at the hospital to check up on Megrhana to find Tremond Dockett kissing his wife on the lips. His wife was kissing Tremond back with as much passion.

Tremond is Megrhana's manager. And he's her first cousin.

Thanking God for this miracle and seeing a way out, Queen Gertrude ordered an immediate paternity test and demanded a quick turnaround. The triplets weren't Haakon's kids.

Yeah, that's some pretty twisted shit.

Tremond and Megrhana have had a sordid hidden relationship for years. When Haakon took interest in Megrhana at a charity event, she thought she had won the lottery. Tremond went along with it because of the potentially huge payday. Too bad he couldn't keep his hands off his cousin.

So Megrhana might be a B listed actress with a string of mediocre and terrible defunct TV series under her belt, but she managed to pull the wool over Haakon's eyes.

I almost feel sorry for the bastard. Almost.

Thank God Brielle was never part of that family.

What a mess.

Good riddance.

I scour the room with an appreciative glance and can't help but smile. The vibe is so high. As I take in the smiling faces, I'm humbled. This turned out exactly as I'd hoped. Better even.

All this for my girl. The woman I love with all my heart.

After her round of kisses and hugs my ebullient girlfriend approaches me. The devilish glee in her eyes speaks volumes.

"You!" she shakes a warning finger at me.

"What?"

"You're lucky I love you so much or else you'd be in trouble. I can't believe you went behind my back like this," she says.

"It's because I love you so much that I did."

I'm just about to kiss Brielle when Amanda shouts, "Is it time for champagne yet?"

"What do you think, guys?" I turn to take the question to the crowd.

There's a collective rowdy, "Hell yeah!" "Oh, yeah!" and "Yes, please!"

It's party time!

* * *

The last four hours have been off the charts.

The band is doing a pretty darn good job entertaining us. The champagne is flowing freely and the atmosphere in the room is electrifying. And of course, we've been stuffing our faces silly.

The Colony Grill is as American as apple pie—all the way down to the cuts of meat served with French fries, sweetcorn chowder, mac & cheese, coleslaw, New York style hotdogs and meatloaf. Tonight, we all feasted on a purely Americana menu. The parade of dishes was outstanding. From the look of satisfaction on everyone's face, it was absolutely delicious.

Happy guests. Happy host.

Brielle lost her mind when the staff rolled in two tables weighed down with everything you can ever desire to create your own custom sundae. Everyone went a little overboard and indulged—including King Dagget.

The music suddenly fades into silence and the bandleader—who also happens to be the guitarist and singer—approaches the microphone. “Well, ladies and gents, it's been a pleasure, but the band will take a short break. Don't go anywhere, the night is still young.”

“Crush Uproar are such amazing musicians,” Brielle says.

“They're incredibly talented.”

“How did you find them?” she asks.

“That's Miriam's best friend’s nephew. From what I understand, Scott has been playing the guitar and singing since he was three. He even has a degree from the Manhattan School of Music. It's in his blood. Miriam showed me a few videos of him and his band on his YouTube channel. I was so blown-away, I hired him on the spot. I flew him and his band to London to perform tonight.”

“You’re such an amazing boyfriend.”

“I try my best, Princess,” I say.

She laughs. “You're incorrigible.”

“It's easy to be an amazing boyfriend when you have the best girlfriend on the planet.”

“Officially, that was cheesy… but very sweet,” she smiles. “Thank you. I'm surrounded by my favorite people in the world. What more can a girl ask for?”

“I’m pleased you enjoyed the evening. Tonight was all about you, beautiful.”

"Well, everything is perfect."

"Hey, while the band is on a break, do you want to thank everyone for coming out tonight?"

"Brilliant idea! Will you come up with me?"

"Nah, you go. I'll come join you in a minute. I need to run to the restroom real quick."

"I can wait for you to come back," she says.

"People don't want to hear me talk. I'm just the guy behind the incredible woman."

"But I want to thank you in front of everybody."

"And you will. I'll be in and out before you know it. I'm a guy. It doesn't take me half an hour to use the restroom."

She swats my arm. "I'll have you know that beauty takes time," she lifts her chin up with defiance.

"Sure. Whatever you say, doll," I grin from ear to ear. "Go up there and make a speech. It's good practice for MoMA," I tell her.

"I like how you frame that. It makes it a little less threatening."

"You have nothing to worry about. You're a natural."

"Thank you for being so supportive."

She leans into me and I can't help but take her lips in a soft kiss.

"Go on," I say, breaking our embrace.

As she makes her way up to the podium, I steal away from her and make my exit.

I carefully leave the door slightly ajar.

When I step into the hallway, five eager pairs of eyes are staring right at me.

"Ready?" I ask in a low voice.

All five heads nod.

"Let's give it a minute," I say.

Tap, tap, tap.

"Can everyone hear me?" Brielle asks.

"Yes!" the crowd shouts back.

"The wonderful man who made all of this happen will be right back. Nature called." There's a round of laughter. "But in the meantime, I wanted to thank you from the bottom of my heart. There are no words to express how happy I am that all of you came out tonight to celebrate little old me. Everyone flew from faraway… I can't believe you'd do that for me."

"You're worth it, sweetheart!" Prince Janek shouts.

"That's our cue!" I tell the five people standing behind me.

They nod again.

I pull my phone out and fire off a quick text.

"Other than my family and my friends, my blog was the only thing of significance in my life. Well, that's before Easton." Another round of laughter. "I never imagined—"

Clink, clink, clink, clink.

"Why are you doing that, Daddy?" Brielle asks.

Clink, clink, clink, clink.

The entire room starts to clink their glasses with their cutlery.

"What's going on?" I hear the nervousness in her voice.

I step inside the room and Jodi, the violinist, starts to play.

As I approach Brielle, Scott and the other musicians follow behind me.

Brielle looks completely startled. Panicked even.

She hasn't clued in yet.

Her beautiful gray eyes search mine.

Suddenly, she brings her hand up to her face.

She got it.

I approach my girl grinning like a fool.

I step up on the podium and grab her hands, well, I try to grab her hands. She's so emotional, she refuses to uncover her face.

Brielle cries her eyes out.

I just smile at her.

Our family and friends are now gathered around, phones out filming the joyous moment.

I shift my eyes to the left to make sure the professional film crew is capturing every moment. Sure enough, everything is as planned. They meshed with the rest of the guests all evening long waiting patiently for their cue.

The musicians stop playing.

With the soft whispers of the violin, I drop to one knee.

The room erupts in cheers and claps.

Officer Pavlova breaks from the crowd, approaches the podium and hands me a small red box. With a small nod, I thank her. She smiles wide at me and I find myself returning her smile. I turn my attention to the beautiful woman standing in front of me. I take her left hand and she doesn't resist.

"I know you, my queen. If I had kept this on me during the evening, you would've found it and that would've ruined the surprise," I say, shaking the little box.

"You tricked me twice in one evening Easton Winchester?" She fiddles nervously with her hair.

"Maybe," I grin.

"So this isn't about my blog?" she asks between tears and laughter.

"Sort of. It's about the woman behind the blog. The one who stole my heart."

"Oh, God." She fans herself with her free hand.

"On my sister's eighteenth birthday, when I finally noticed you were all grown up, there was no going back for me."

"I can't believe this."

"Brielle, I knew from the second you removed your mask in Venice that I was in deep. You changed my world with one kiss. I wanted to show you that tonight. I wanted this day to be special, romantic and unforgettable. I can't imagine doing this without our *village*."

There's another round of cheers in the room.

"Every day I spend with you, I'm more and more certain that God spent a little more time on you."

"That's so sweet. I love you so much, Easton," she says.

"I love you so much too, beautiful. That's the thing. Falling in love is easy. Having sex is even easier—"

"Wait a minute there, son. That's my little girl you're talking about."

Her father's comment catches me off guard.

"I apologize, Prince Janek. I'm trying to make a point," I tell him.

"You're lucky I like you, son."

"Thank you, sir."

"I'm pulling your leg. I've been dying to ad lib. Carry on," he winks.

I smile wide.

"As I was saying… Love? Easy. Sex? Super easy. Bumping into someone that sparks your soul? That's very rare. I have that with you, Princess. And I want that for the rest of my life. I want to be yours forever. Princess Brielle Elise Madeleine Strasberg of Exton, will you be my wife?"

"Yes, yes, yes! I love you so much, Easton. Yes, I want to marry you," she says.

"I love you more than words can say. I'm so happy with you, Brielle."

"You're my everything."

Her joy overflows—just like mine.

I let go of her hand and open the red box.

"Mother of God, that's beautiful."

"You like it?" I ask slipping the ring on her finger.

"Easton, are you serious? I love it," she says lifting her hand to eye level.

"Sienna and Blakely helped me pick it. It also passed the test with Iyanna and Nadga," I tell her.

She does this face and wags a parental finger at her best friends. They just grin back at her while giving her the thumbs-up.

I got Brielle a six-carat rectangular cushion cut set on a platinum ring with brilliant round diamonds decorating the shanks. It's stunning on her.

"Everyone tricked me."

"Yeah, but what a happy ending."

"I couldn't have said it better."

I pull her close to me and turn to face the crowd.

"She said, yes, you guys!"

"I did!" she yells flashing her ring to the crowd.

"She's going to become Mrs. Winchester!"

"And you'll become Prince Easton Ellis Winchester of Exton," Prince Janek shouts back at me as he steps up on the podium.

What?

His words come as a shock. It never crossed my mind.

"I gave you my only daughter's hand," *I know it's old-fashioned, but I wanted all my Ts crossed for this one,* "and you also get my kingdom, son. Welcome to the family."

He grabs me in his arms and gives me a hearty embrace. He rocks from side to side for a few long seconds. I can't help but feel emotional. When he lets go, I notice he wipes away a tear. I won't lie, I do the same.

Wow.

I grab Brielle and wrap her in my arms again and whisper in her ear, "Thank you for allowing me to love you and protect you from this day on."

She dissolves in tears.

God, I love her.

My Brielle.

My Princess.

My queen.

The mother of my heirs.

My forever.

EPILOGUE 2

Easton

A week later

After a week away with my fiancée, I'm back at the grind. I considered working from the penthouse to stay close to Brielle so I could fuck her at will to make up for the forced celibacy this past week, but since I have a lunch meeting near the office, I reluctantly pulled off the bandage. Although it was an enjoyable time in the Hamptons, my girl and I had to be on our best behavior because we weren't alone.

I sip the last gulp of my double espresso latte when my phone rings.

"Hey, Xavier," I say, accepting the call.

"Easton, mate. Should I already be calling you Prince Easton?"

"Not yet, but it's never too early to start practicing."

"Wanker," Xavier exclaims. "I was just calling to congratulate you. Rumor has it you popped the question last Friday."

Thor and Harlen are my closest friends, so they were present. That said, I was asked to keep my list of invites tight, given the high stakes. Alas, Max, Nikolaj, Bryce, and Martin weren't on the list. Had the engagement party taken place in Belzer—with an army to protect the King—things would've been different.

Xavier Keller is Max Keller's cousin.

"No rumor, dear friend. It's all fact."

"You didn't chicken out?"

"Not a chance. I got the girl. She's mine forever. The best part is her father isn't sending the Belzer army to track me down like a fugitive."

"You get to live and keep your head on your shoulders."

"Thank God for small favors."

We laugh.

"Were you still able to have fun considering the level of security?"

"With three generations of royals present under one roof, in a foreign land, the security put that of the President's to shame."

Xavier whistles.

"Asking a princess to become my fiancée, means this is my new normal for me. Same as the shadows that follow me everywhere."

"Better you than me. Since stepping off the pitch, I no longer require security guards. Now that I'm in New York and I can move around practically incognito, I feel your pain. Having bodyguards sometimes feel like having nursemaids."

He means nannies.

Xavier Keller is a former star European football player, with a plethora of trophies in his name. Although born in New York City, he spent years in London—hence the accent. After cutting his teeth in the business world working with Nikolaj von Henningsen and Martin Gallagher, he's taken over the COO position of the fashion company Max inherited from his Brazilian uncle. Max decided to keep the control under the Keller name by nominating Xavier.

"For the right woman, you'd be willing to have two beefy guys shadow your every step," I tell him. "Heck, for the right woman, you'd be willing to do pretty much anything."

"You sound like Max."

I laugh.

"How was the house?" Xavier asks.

"It was perfect," I tell him. "I couldn't have asked for more."

Max offered his luxurious mansion in the Hamptons as an engagement gift. Brielle, her family, Sienna, and I spent a week of leisure there. Although Brielle's family is used to the finer things in life, they were quite impressed by the summer destination of choice for affluent New Yorkers.

"Good."

"The only problem is now my fiancée wants me to buy a house there."

"I'm sure you have enough loose change between the cushions of your sofa to purchase a mansion *cash*."

"You're probably right," I chuckle. "Since it's been just my baby sister and me for a long time, I never saw the point in buying a house in that upscale seaside community. I'm so in love with Brielle and making her happy is my top priority. I might have to grant her wish. Like I said, for the right woman… you know the rest."

"You're *royally* pussy whipped, mate."

"Don't think the pun has gone unnoticed," I observe. "For the rest, I'm man enough not to even bother denying it. What can I say? Brielle is my queen."

Xavier laughs.

There's some noise in the background on Xavier's end.

"Easton, there's a knock at my door," he says. "Can you give me a second?"

"No problem. I'll wait."

A minute later, Xavier is back on the phone. "That was our HR director. My nine o'clock interview just arrived."

"What a way to kick off Monday," I sneer. "I gather you've had no luck so far?" I ask.

"Not really," he says. "We're looking for someone who is qualified, ambitious, and a go-getter—"

"Those traits are as common as yellow taxis in a city like New York."

"Indeed, but we're looking for more. We need someone who can easily integrate with the rest of the team. The fashion division might turn in multibillions of dollars a year, but since the majority of the operations are in Brazil, the New York office feels like a tightknit family. Whoever we hire must fit in. So far, we've interviewed a lot of people who profess to be team players, but in reality, they were Doberman dogs disguised as a cuddly Bichon Frise, and only revealed that side of their personality when asked the right question."

I laugh. "That's a hilarious analogy."

"Alas, it's the truth. Some questions trigger the most surprising answers," he adds. "Furthermore, we'd like to find a candidate who's open to traveling to Brazil. Can you believe I had a candidate—who couldn't be more than twenty-five—tell me to my face she doesn't travel to Third World countries because there's zero hygiene and the potential to get sick from polluted, or even worse, contaminated, water is too high. Here's the kicker. She's a second generation Mexican American."

"Are you kidding me?" I balk.

"I heard it with my own two ears," Xavier says. "She's never been outside of the United States. She's never even been to the West Coast."

"We're too young to ridicule the generations that follow us, but come on."

"Thank you," Xavier agrees. "You're lucky in your business you don't have to deal with hiring a lot of people, since you work mostly with freelancer consultants."

"True, but on the downside, I'm not exposed to sexy as fuck bombshells with *plenty* of *luscious* curves with nice *juicy, plump* asses," I say, mimicking Max.

Xavier chuckles. "Stop making fun of my cousin, Winchester."

"Max's obsession puts him in a position to be ridiculed."

"There's so much I could say about that, but I don't have time for a dissertation. I have to go."

"Go get 'em, tiger!" I tell him.

Xavier

The moment I end the call with Easton, a text message from Deidra Summers flies across my screen.

> **Deidra:** I'm running late. The stupid city-wide construction is a bitch. You'll need to hold the fort until I get there.
> **Xavier:** Copy that. How long do you think it's going to take you to get here?
> **Deidra:** If I weren't wearing sky high heels and a pencil skirt, I'd power walk. Since I have no plans on breaking my ankles, I'm at the mercy of traffic. If I had to guess, I'd say another twenty minutes or so.
> **Xavier:** I'll get acquainted with Miss Mitchell until you get here.
> **Deidra:** Try not to charm her with your sexy accent.
> **Xavier:** I can't be responsible for things that are out of my control.
> **Deidra:** Speak American like the rest of us.
> **Xavier:** I've been living abroad for too many years. I'd have to dust off my American accent from the recesses of my mind. That would demand far too much mental gymnastics.
> **Deidra:** Rolling my eyes.
> **Xavier:** It's best if I get to it. I wouldn't want to make Miss Mitchell wait.
> **Deidra:** Fingers crossed she's the right candidate.
> **Xavier:** From your fingertips to God's ears.
> **Deidra:** LOL

I drop my phone on my desk, a smile still tucking at my lips. Deidra is Curve Envy Fashion's VP.

She's been here well before me. In fact, she used to work in my cousin Max's investment division. She's played an instrumental role in turning our uncle's struggling company around, taking it from being stuck in the red to a very profitable venture. Our uncle Arturo Barros was steadfast in his determination—top quality trumps everything. Sadly, that motto was his demise. Quality in of the utmost importance, but not if it's sinking you like the Titanic. Uncle Arturo kept quiet about his financial woes until the very end. It's only when Max inherited the company after his death that the truth came out as bright as a neon sign. Uncle Arturo had been bleeding money for a long time, but instead of reaching out for help, he was resolved in his decision to do it *his* way. Given Deidra's contribution, some might say my position as a newly appointed COO is nepotism. It's true Deidra is almost family since she used to date my cousin Gabriel until she became infatuated with a woman, but unlike me, she doesn't have blood ties to the President and CEO—Max—or the CFO—my older brother Zane. That said, you won't hear her complain about being passed for the promotion. In fact, she insisted on remaining exactly where she was. Since Gabe, she's dated a handful of women *and* men. After her last messy break-up with a woman who cheated on her with a Broadway actress, she decided she wanted a baby solo—with the help of a fertility clinic. Biological clock and all. Shouldering more responsibilities isn't something she's looking forward to. She's already warned Max she intends on taking at least six months off to enjoy her new baby when the time comes. Translation, it was a win-win situation for both of us. She isn't interested in world domination. I, on the other hand, am dying to establish my reputation by making my mark *off* the pitch. World domination tops my list—in the fashion world, anyway.

Time to meet Miss Mitchell.

I stand up, tuck my phone into my trousers' pocket, stroll to the chair where I left my suit jacket, slip it on, snatched the iPad off the small circular conference table, and exit my office. I stalk toward the small conference room located on the opposite side of the floor, near Zane's office. Hiring an executive assistant Deidra and I will share turns out to be a lot more challenging than I expected. So many candidates look good on paper—amazing, in fact—but when you meet them, you feel there's a disconnect. Like Deidra said, fingers crossed Emma

Mitchell puts an end to our search. We haven't been searching that long, but I must confess, interviews are one of my least favorite responsibilities as part of the COO position. That said, my cousin entrusted me with the position, so I have to suck it up.

When I walk into the conference room, Emma Mitchell jumps to her feet.

"Good morning, Miss Mitchell," I say, extending a hand.

"Mr. Keller, it's a pleasure," she says, shaking my hand.

"Likewise," I say.

I wait for recognition to hit her, but Emma maintains a neutral expression.

She isn't a hardcore football fan. Good.

I pull my hand from hers, and just are at the seat. "Please, sit down."

The slender brunette smiles wide before taking a seat on the modern made in Italy white velvet high back wingback chair.

I place the iPad on the coffee table, unbutton my suit jacket, adjust my tie, and take a seat on the silver-gray sofa—also an import from Italy. Deidra can sit on the chair opposite to Emma.

There's a proper conference table in the room, but we prefer to hold interviews in the sitting area. The fashion division is much smaller than the investment division, and we like to keep things friendly.

My eyes drop to the empty cup in front of Emma. "Would you like another coffee?" I ask.

Smiling brown eyes meet my hazel brown ones. "No, thank you, Mr. Keller. One cuppa is enough. As a true British transplant, I've already had two cuppas of tea this morning."

"You can take the girl out of Britain, but you can't take Britain out of the girl?" I joke.

"Guilty as charged," she laughs. "I've been in New York for two years now, and Little London is still my *pieds-à-terre*. Furthermore, I'm not ashamed to beg for a care package from back home any chance I get."

I chuckle.

"Water?" I suggest.

"I'm fine. Thank you," she says. "I must say, this is the first interview where I've been offered coffee and biscuits." The Brits call cookies, biscuits. "Exceptional coffee and scrumptious biscuits, may I add."

"We take coffee very seriously," I tell her. "It's in our DNA. As for the biscuits, it's only civilized."

She giggles.

"Another notch to the company," she replies.

She's witty. I like that about her.

"Shall we get started?" I ask.

"I've been looking forward to this interview for weeks. I'm ready." She's practically bouncing off her seat.

I look down at the iPad and start with the first interview question on the list.

"What would you say is the number one strength you bring to the position?"

And... here we go.

Twenty minutes into the interview, and I'm praying for Deidra to get here soon.

Emma has this habit that's becoming quite distracting. Every time she finishes answering one of my questions, she crosses and uncrosses her legs in a deliberate fashion. The come hitter look in her eyes doesn't go unnoticed.

I loosen my tie and clear my throat.

I have an issue with her wardrobe selection, but her CV, qualifications and answers are quite impressive.

If only Deidra was here, I'm sure Emma wouldn't dare expose this much skin. I could bring it up, but that opens to misinterpretation.

Another stellar-on-paper candidate that turned out to be a disappointment in person.

Pity.

If Miss Mitchell thinks she can flirt her way to the top, this isn't the company for her.

"I'm sorry," Emma says, "it's really hard for me to pretend I don't know who you are." My eyebrows ride up. "You're Xavier Keller for God sakes. *The* Xavier Keller."

Until now, she hasn't given the impression she knew who I was.

She played her card close to the chest.

Sneaky Emma.

She brings her hands to her chest, like an excited kid who's granted three scoops of ice cream for dessert. "My entire family nearly died when I told them who I was interviewing with."

"Emma, I'm just an executive these days. I'm no longer a—"

"You'll always be a legend," she declares. "Just because you traded your jersey for a suit, doesn't diminish your greatness."

Okay, clearly, I'm in the presence of a fan.

"I'm flattered," I say.

"Are the rumors true?" Her tone is suggestive.

"Which rumors?" I ask.

"You know…"

She lowers her eyes for a beat before meeting my gaze.

"No, I don't know," I tell her. "Please enlighten me."

She cocks an eyebrow and purses her lips in response.

As if that's a bloody answer.

My patience is wearing thin. "Miss Mitchell—"

"Your appetite…"

"My appetite for…?"

She stands up abruptly.

"What are you—"

The question dies on my lips when Emma undoes the sash at her waist of her purple wrap dress, exposing her naked body.

"Your appetite for pussy," she says.

My head jerks back in surprise.

Her tits are on full display.

She came to an interview without any underwear on?

Blimey.

When I said we like to keep things friendly, this isn't what I was referring to.

"Look," she points to her bush. "X Marks the Spot," she sings songs.

Involuntarily, my eyes lower to her pussy.

And don't you know it, the first letter of my name is staring at me.

Jesus Christ.

"I got a special waxing job yesterday… just for you," she adds, her tone jovial and light.

I didn't even know that was a thing.

I can safely say, no woman has ever done anything this ludicrous before.

I pull my eyes away from the indecent sight, and stare up at Emma. *What in the actual fuck?* "Th—this is harassment," I trip all over my words. I'm usually an eloquent man, but I didn't see this one coming. Not by a long shot.

"Not if it's mutual," Emma says. "And I really, really want you to fuck me, Xavier," she tells me in a nonchalant tone that laughs in the face of the gravity of the current situation.

"This was premeditated," I accuse.

"Of course, it was," she tells me. "Trapped in a conference room with the sexy bachelor forever and pro footballer Xavier Keller? You bet I'm going to take full advantage of *you*."

Interviews are usually taxing, but this is a bloody nightmare that threatens to give me a fucking headache. We're looking for an executive assistant. Not a big fat scandal. This was supposed to be straightforward, not the making for a sexual harassment case and potential lawsuit.

Bloody hell.

I drag my palm down my face and let out a long, exasperated sigh.

"I bet you make the sexiest come noises. Oh, my God, your come face must be *sooooo* sexy."

I'm not going to lie. I'm completely out of my depth here.

Think fast, Keller.

I glare at her, my mind spinning to find a solution out of this land mine without everything exploding in my face. No matter how you look at this situation, I'm at fault. I'm a man in a position of power. No one will care if Emma is the skank throwing herself at me. At the end of the day, all anyone will remember is I'm fully dressed, and she's buck naked.

Crossing the pond, I was prepared to be anonymous. After all, football—aka, soccer—doesn't have the same clout as other team sports in America.

I expect this kind of in-your-face carnal display of overt sexuality on the pitch, not in a conference room. It's par to the course in my former profession. In my experience, football groupies are willing to do outrageous things to secure bragging rights. Fucking a famous footballer is equivalent to winning the Heisman Trophy in American football for those women.

Just when I think things can't get any more out of hand, they do. Emma slides a finger between her pussy lips and brings her drenched digit to her lips, cleaning off her juices, moaning suggestively.

"I'm so wet for you," she tells me. "Apparently, you're well endowed. I want to find out for myself. Mark me, Xavier. Pretty please."

Emma is so out of line, it's pathetic.

"Miss Mitchell, there is a grave misunderstanding—"

"No misunderstanding on my part, Xavier," she turns around and bends over, flashing me her pussy and asshole, "I think I'm crystal clear in my intentions." She has the audacity to point a frantic finger at her pussy.

She's absolutely bonkers.

I want to put that stupid dress on her body before physically removing her from the conference room, but any physical contact, and I'm doomed. Even approaching her would be suicidal. No, it's best if I stay exactly where I am and try to knock some sense into her from a far.

"Emma!" I shout, my irritation audible in my growly voice. "Enough—"

Suddenly, the door to the conference room flies open, interrupting me, and Deidra rushes in.

"I'm sorry, Xavier, I'm—"

She stops midsentence and freezers in place. Her blue eyes ping-ponging from mine to the naked woman bent over.

I open my mouth to speak, but she precedes me.

"What the hell is going on here?" Deidra demands.

* * *

Who's The Next Billionaire?

I'm furiously writing the next two scorching hot billionaire romance stories in the series.

Psst… Max's cousins, Xavier and Zane, are so, so hot! And they LOVE curvy women!

I'm still writing Xavier's story, but you can pre-order it now. Don't mind the date on Amazon. It will be published way before December 2022. The date is simply a place holder.

Get it now: A Very Bossy Billionaire

Great news! You can binge-read Zane's story now!

Zane's romance is a decadent Christmas billionaire romance featuring a sassy redhead with plenty of curves and a tall glass of water, aka a stupidly hot billionaire.

Get it now: A Very Fake Christmas

Psst… you can read a sneak peek of A Very Fake Christmas at the end of this book.

Do you want more of Easton?

If you're dying for more of the tall, dark, and handsome billionaire, you'll find him in another one of my saucy tales.

The soon-to-be Prince Billionaire has a starring role in **Billionaire Mogul—Beckett**.

Beckett's romance is part of a binge-worthy **Billionaire Hotshots** world.

The series is so unputdownable, you'll lose sleep over it. And no, I'm not sorry about it.

Beginning the naughty adventure now!

Billionaire Mogul—Beckett kicks off the series with a sinful dating the boss office romance.

Get it now: Billionaire Mogul—Beckett

Psst… you can read a sneak peek of

Billionaire Mogul—Beckett at the end of this book.

Reviews are a beautiful thing!

It only takes a few minutes to leave a review,
which makes a huge difference for an indie author like myself.

Leave a review for:
Billionaire Factor—Easton

Scarlett's Book Banter!

Dear Sexy Reader,

It was a pretty regal ride!

Thanks so much for coming along and thanks for reading all the way to the 'Scarlett's Book Banter' page.

Easton and Brielle's story was challenging to write because this was my first royal romance and it was the first book where my female lead was a virgin.

I can't tell you how many books I read as research. The story lines always seemed to be very similar.

I wanted mine to be different.

More importantly, I wanted my story to be believable. Not an easy task when the female character has a couple of bodyguards as shadows while she explores the many facets of her sensuality.

Here's another challenge, I wanted the steamy scenes to be naughty, but I wanted to wait until the end before Easton claims her. I didn't expect Brielle would be bold enough to entice him into taking her. It makes sense after what she had to endure with her awful mother and the prince of shit.

Easton and Brielle's passionate love story is much more layered than I had envisioned. It's full of twists, turns and surprises. It's the kind of unexpected adventure that keeps you turning the pages.

There's more of these hotter than hell New York billionaires. The series continues with one of Max Keller's cousins.

Zane Keller is very tall, devastatingly charming, stupidly handsome, and he has a phenomenal singing voice. The sexy billionaire will leave you breathless. The man is 6'6 and he's intense. Just like his cousin, he loves, loves, loves women with plenty of curves.

Zane's swoony Christmas romance book will rock your world. You'll have no other choice but to read this page-turner in one sitting.

Get it now: A Very Fake Christmas

(Remember, you can read a sneak peek of A Very Fake Christmas at the end of this book.)

Easton has a feature role in Book 1 of another one of my series.

We're crossing America and heading to LA for a delectable and naughty adventure!

Nothing feels more incredible than starting a new series… especially when you're guaranteed it's going to be SCORCHING HOT!

Billionaire Moguls Series

Illegally hot billionaire playboys. Unapologetic seducers. Powerful men who always get what they want.

These billionaires are demanding, domineering, and darn-right delicious.

Proceed with caution… you won't get enough of these Billionaire Moguls.

Billionaire Mogul—Beckett kicks off the series with a sinful dating the boss office romance.

Beckett's romance is part of a binge-worthy **Billionaire Hotshots** world.

Get it now: Billionaire Mogul—Beckett

(Remember, you can read a sneak peek of
Billionaire Mogul—Beckett at the end of this book.)

Much love,

Scarlett Avery

P.S. When a reader writes a review, an author angel gets their wings.

P.P.S. I keep writing because of your hunger for my stories. Thank you for your fervor, love, and loyalty.

P.P.P.S. For access to an EXCLUSIVE Storyboard, go to the next page!

****

Get the Storyboard for Billionaire Factor—Easton!

Thank you for purchasing this romance!

I've created a cool storyboard to share the many things that influenced me during the time
I was writing this story!

Trust me, you're going to love the extra tidbits.

When you sign up on my list, you'll receive an email with further instructions!

Sign up TODAY!

www.RomanceBooksRock.com

***If you've already signed up to my list from previous books, you can visit the same page to download the Secret Chapters and/or Storyboard for this romance. ***

****

Sneak Peak of A Very Fake Christmas

CHAPTER 1

Zane

I enter the Evangelista Lounge located inside the Bymark Hotel as crooner Frank Sinatra sings, *'Let it snow! Let it snow! Let it snow!'*

'Tis the season!

Eight days to Christmas.

No surprise, there's a queue to get seated.

Three groups of people stand in front of me—a couple embracing, three women decked up to the nines, and five men in sharp suits, sporting pricey watches. As I wait, my weary eyes sweep around the space for potential threats.

The coast is clear.

Reassured I won't have to deal with the embarrassing drama I had to endure the last time I was here, I relax.

Thank God for small favors.

I scan the room once more, but this time it's to determine if I should consider another one of the lounges in the hotel. Between office parties and impromptu get-togethers to celebrate the Christmas season, you'll be pressed to find a popular location in Manhattan that isn't crazy busy. It doesn't take me long to spot a few tables that seem to be ready to clear.

Good.

I pull out my phone and shoot Carl Tucci a quick text to let him know I'm early. Carl is a friend and MBA alumni from Columbia University who moved to Arizona four years ago. Distance and hectic lives aren't the best to maintain a close friendship even with technology, but I keep in touch with Carl more than I do with other grads who still live in New York. He's in town for business with his wife in tow.

My phone rings.

"Hey, buddy," I say, answering the call. "No need to rush. I'm twenty minutes early. Monday was wearing me down, so I bailed early from work."

"I'm sorry, Zane. I don't think I can make it," he replies.

"What happened?"

"I had to cut my meeting short. Debra texted me between bouts of puking sessions to let me know the baby was having a field day today."

"Poor Debra," I sympathize. "Give me a sec," I say. "I'm going to step outside so as not to disturb other patrons." It's only good manners not to force people to listen to your conversation.

"Okay."

With a few long strides, I'm standing outside the lounge.

"Not that I have first-hand experience, but a number of women from work have complained about the whole 'morning sickness' thing," I continue, pacing back and forth. "Apparently it can last all day and it's pretty rough sailing."

"It is," he confirms. "And you're right, 'morning sickness' is a lie. Unlike cappuccino, which goes out of favor by lunchtime, morning sickness can occur morning, day, and night. That's why my beautiful wife is barfing her brains out at seven p.m."

I cringe at the imagery.

"Priorities first, my friend," I declare. "Take care of Debra. I know your schedule is jam packed while you're here, but maybe we can do lunch tomorrow if Debra is feeling better?"

"Actually, I was going to suggest an early morning breakfast before my meeting. Debra can stay in bed while we meet. I don't want to put any pressure on her."

"Understandable."

"I'll be back in New York in March, and I'll make sure to bring her with me. You can meet her then."

"Sounds good," I say. "Let's meet here. There are few top-notch restaurants that serve the best continental breakfast options in town."

"Done! I'm sorry again for the inconvenience."

"Please. I hear the baby dictates, not the parents, so stop apologizing."

We chuckle.

"See you tomorrow, Zane."

"Catch you tomorrow, Carl."

I end the call, tuck my phone in the inside of my suit pocket, and head back to the lounge as a wave of patrons leave. When I enter, the maître d' waves me over.

I've never seen him before, and I breathe a sigh of relief.

Chances are he doesn't know what cluster fuck of a mess transpired the last time I was here.

After the niceties, I speak. "I reserved a table for four, but my friend just called to let me know that his wife is ill and he can't make it. That said, I'd still like to have a drink."

I'm here and I'm not leaving without injecting booze in my veins. It was that kind of a day.

"I see," he responds, lowering his brown eyes to the iPad screen. "Would you consider a seat at the bar?" he asks, meeting my gaze.

"Absolutely!"

"Excellent," he says, extending a hand, inviting me in.

"Thank you," I say with a nod.

As I strut towards the bar, a tall blond man waves me over before indicating a seat at the bar.

I tilt my chin in recognition, a smile creeping on my lips.

"Rick," I say, taking a seat on a high stool next to a Black balding man. The guy is engaged in an animated conversation with a Black woman clad in an eye-catching purple blouse with an elaborate oversized bow, sitting next to him.

"Mr. Keller. I thought you had moved out of state," Rick chuckles. "It's been a while."

"I've been laying low," I tell him.

"Of course," he nods. His green eyes shift left, then right before settling on me. "Man, your ex knows how to leave a lasting impression––and not a good one at that."

"Don't remind me," I grumble. "Let's not talk about her."

"Your wish is my command," Rick says. "What's your poison for tonight?"

"A vodka tonic, please."

"Do I open a tab?" he asks.

"Yes, I'll need more than one drink to ease this day," I tell him.

"I'll be right back with your drink," Rick says, turning towards a row of top-shelf bottles.

The last time Carl was in town, I suggested the Bymark Hotel. He loved it so much, he wanted us to meet here because he wanted his wife to experience the opulence the Bymark has to offer. The hotel—pre-renovations—looked very different when he lived in New York. Without his insistence, I probably would still be MIA. I wasn't sure what to expect showing my face here again after my smoking hot, but certifiably mental short-lived-ex-girlfriend fucked things up for me.

I clench my teeth as images from the cringe-worthy confrontation come flashing back.

So much fucking drama.

What a nut case.

Good riddance.

The movement of a hand appearing seemingly out of nowhere jerks me back to the present.

Rick sets my drink in front of me.

My eyes zoom in on the tumbler before meeting his blue eyes.

"Thanks," I tell him.

"It's behind you, man," he says with a wink, as if he's able to read my mind.

I simply nod.

I take a long sip of the vodka tonic, my thoughts still racing.

It's been two months and my ex should be a distant memory, but I find myself looking over my shoulder one more time.

I don't recognize any familiar faces.

Satisfied, I return my attention to my drink.

Not only have I been avoiding the Bymark like the hotel was contaminated, I've also been avoiding women. I needed to purge my system for a while. As a result, I eliminated unwanted drama in my life. Alas, I also eliminated the pleasure of losing myself between the plush thighs of a sexy lover.

I need to get laid.

Now!

Fuck jerking off.

I'm desperate for a warm and inviting pussy.

It's been too long. I'm done.

I drain my drink in a few gulps, a sudden urgent need coursing through my veins. I slam the tumbler on the bar a little more forceful than intended, the sound catching Rick's attention.

"Another one?" he asks, motioning to my empty glass.

"Not yet," I tell him.

"Flag me when you're ready," Rick says.

I nod. "I will."

He shifts his focus to a newcomer who sits next to the woman wearing the purple blouse.

I stand up, intending to give myself a little privacy as I consider the list of past hookups that speak my language—a drama-free, illicit night of raunchy sex with no strings attached.

I'm just about to shoot off a few texts when I lift my eyes.

A jaw-dropping sight temporarily stops the rhythmic beating of my heart.

Holy fuck.

A striking redhead stands in front of the maître d's stand. They're engaged in a back-and-forth conversation for a few long seconds. When the maître d' extends a hand, the woman's eyes lift up, looking past me.

The beautiful siren nods and sashays in my direction, swinging her hips left to right, strutting across the lounge like she owns the damn place.

Fuck if I don't want to be the one to check off her Christmas list.

My gaze follows the sensual sway of her wide hips, almost hypnotized.

Her luscious curves threaten to give me a heart attack.

She's wearing heels, but she's much taller than the average woman.

I'm guessing five-feet-ten or five-feet-eleven, barefoot. Still short compared to my six-feet-six frame.

With each step, I take her in.

Her sexy-as-fuck body is clad in a mouth-watering outfit.

Jesus.

I do a quick mental inventory, going through the catalog of our collections to find out if the bombshell is wearing Curves Envy Fashion—the plus-size high-end fashion label I co-own with my cousins and my brother. I give up the search. One, we have way too many items. Two, this woman is doing things to me and preventing me from thinking straight.

She's the kind of voluptuous temptation capable of making a grown man drop to his knees and thank God for his beneficence.

Patrons stop mid-conversation to admire her.

I don't blame them.

I'm as riveted, shamelessly staring. I couldn't look away even if you paid me a cool billion.

For a long beat, I stand stock-still, staring at the gorgeous vixen, my cock twitching in my pants, my heart pumping blood at a maddening speed, my head suddenly filled with very naughty visions of me fucking the hell out of this woman from behind, so my body can slap against her full ass with every hard thrust.

Lord have mercy.

The redhead glances left to right, as she captures every straight man with a pulse and functioning dick's attention with her self-assured stride.

With each elegant step in my direction, my heartbeat spikes.

Wow!

As Smoking Hot Redhead waltzes by, her cascade of long, straight hair swinging with each step, her gaze drifts toward me. She flashes me a shy smile, her hips keeping in rhythm with the upbeat Christmas song I don't recognize.

My cock salutes her, and I respond with a cocky, lopsided smile.

Fuck that beautiful hair.

Fuck those wide hips.

Fuck that radiant smile.

Hot damn, woman!

I only snap out of my trance when I notice her heading towards the empty stool next to mine.

As if pulled by a powerful magnetic force, I rush back to my seat as I shove my phone into my pocket.

Come to Daddy, sweet thing.

Get it now: A Very Fake Christmas

Sneak Peak of Billionaire Mogul—Beckett

CHAPTER 1

Beckett

Even though I'm sleep deprived and my balls are still aching from last night's wild sex marathon, I have to report for duty.

Adulting isn't an option when you're the CEO.

After greeting the security team standing guard at the gate, I step into the building, take the elevator, and head to the executive floor. Since it's early, the place is blessedly quiet.

As I stride to my office, I can't help but smile. There's always a sense of immense pride that washes over me when I trail the hallways of the five-story Culver City building my business partner and I own when it's empty like this. Photos in black frames of our milestones and achievements line the walls.

Our vision.

Our creativity.

Our boldness.

Our empire.

Our freaking dream come true.

We built this.

I enter my office, not bothering to close the door. I remove my gray suit jacket and place it carefully on the back of one of the guest chairs.

My phone rings.

Already?

I fish it from the pocket of my jacket and check the name on the screen.

"Good morning, Valerie," I say, accepting the call.

"I'm not sure it's going to be a good morning, boss," she says in a little voice.

"Are you okay?" I ask.

"I am."

"Did something happen to the kids?"

"No. Everyone on my end is safe and sound."

"Okay, so why the gloom and doom?" I ask.

My executive assistant Valerie Hurst is usually a cheery person. I don't recognize the person on the other end.

"Are you heading home from LAX?" she asks.

I was on my private jet at five this morning after three nefarious days in Sin City. Technically, I was there to work, but at night, all bets were off.

"I just walked into the office," I tell her. I round the desk and take a seat. "There's too much for me to catch up on to waste time in traffic. Not to mention, I have to head out to a meeting with the agency in a couple of hours."

"I gather you haven't checked social media?" Valerie asks.

"No."

"What about the entertainment news?"

"No."

"The newspapers?"

"No!" I stress. "What's going on, Valerie?"

"You might need to hire a new publicist. Fast!"

The former publicist who had been with me forever, hung up her PR boxing gloves to become a full-time mom upon the arrival of her fifth child. After a month of working with her replacement, I couldn't handle the woman's overdramatic nature and bitchy attitude. I fired her ass.

"Why?" I ask.

"I was about to turn off the TV as I was rallying my three rambunctious boys to get them into the van so I could drop them off at school, when the news broke."

"What news?"

“It has to do with…” she hesitates.

“Spit it out, Valerie.”

“It has to do with a woman you were with while you were in Vegas. The radio host was going on about it. Apparently, it’s spreading all over social media like wildfire.”

I frown into the phone. “The media has a shit fit because I was with a woman?” I chuckle. “It must’ve been a slow news night for them to focus on something as mundane as two people hooking up.”

“It’s more than that, Beckett. You’re going to need an expert who’s able to reframe this delicate situation before it turns into a blood bath.” Valerie has me worried.

“Delicate situation? Blood bath?”

“It seems you pissed off someone with a lot of weight and leverage.”

I flash back to my time in Vegas, my thoughts scrambling to make sense of what Valerie just divulged. I’m stumped.

“None of this makes any sense, Valerie!”

“Turn on your computer and do a search.”

I do just that.

I secure the phone between my shoulder and my ear. With quick fingers, I type my name in the search bar.

“What the hell?” I growl.

Screaming headlines flash on my screen.

It’s never a good thing when you see *BREAKING NEWS!* in front of your name on countless results.

‘BECKETT CHRISTENSEN STOLE MY DAUGHTER’S VIRGINITY!’

‘BECKETT CHRISTENSEN CORRUPTS PASTOR’S DAUGHTER!’

‘SEX SCANDAL MIGHT CAUSE BECKETT CHRISTENSEN TO LOSE IT ALL.’

‘EIGHTH RICHEST PASTOR IN AMERICA GOES AFTER CEO ROCK STAR.’

I blink.

I blink again.

I'm incredulous.

"What the fuck?" I grumble.

"I'm on my way," Valerie's voice breaks through my hazy thoughts. "In the meantime, I'll call security to make sure they beef up their presence. I'm sure paparazzi and reporters will surround the building in no time. Fucking piranhas."

"Good idea," I say. "Thanks for having my back."

"Always, Beckett."

"I'll see you when you get here," I say.

"See you soon."

I drop my phone on the desk and stare at the screen in disbelief.

Las Vegas is always a blast… even when it's for business.

I was in Sin City for the Monday night finale of a show I'm a co-judge on. The after party was over the top. It was all very PG because the room was swarming with reporters and celebrity bloggers. Last night, I was the MC at Bella Lusso's extravaganza televised fashion show. I ended the night on a bus packed with gorgeous supermodels clad in skimpy, expensive Bella Lusso lingerie, driving up and down the Las Vegas Strip. Of course, it was all in the name of publicity. A smoking-hot Brazilian bombshell model with dark eyes and long, dark hair caught my attention. After the ride, I went up to her room. If this modeling career doesn't work out for her, she has a future as a Cirque du Soleil artist. Man, that woman was flexible. It'll be a few days before my body recovers.

Where does pastor's daughter fit in?

I hooked up with her on Tuesday night. The woman has a gargantuan sexual appetite.

I exhale and pinch the bridge of my nose.

Coffee. I need strong coffee.

Although, I'd already had two cups on the jet, after that conversation, I need to shoot more caffeine into my veins. Drinking hard liquor at this early time of the day is ill advised.

I push away from my desk, ready to stand up when a violent tornado bursts into my office—aka my good friend and business partner.

"What the fuck, man? Seriously?" Rhys Hartford shouts, waving an iPad over his head.

"Did I make the front page of the entertainment section?" I sneer sarcastically.

"In every newspaper, on every entertainment website, and on every fucking celebrity blog, Beckett!"

"There's no such thing as bad publicity, Rhys," I tell him.

He shakes his head.

He shuts the door with the heel of his foot and stalks towards me, his blue eyes burning with a mix of anger and annoyance. He drops the iPad on my desk and does a slow clap.

"Once again, your penis is the star."

"Sorry yours doesn't gather nearly as much interest," I volley. I'm pissed off he'd accuse me without knowing the facts.

He places a hand at his waist and tilts his head back slightly, staring down at me.

His stance means business.

I stand up so I'm at eye level.

I'm a couple inches taller than he is, which plays in my favor.

"When *I* fuck a woman, it doesn't make the front pages of the entertainment section," Rhys says between gritted teeth. "For some reason, when it comes to you, your dick always ends up an international sensation."

"Well, it's a pretty formidable dick. Perhaps yours doesn't measure up," I retort.

"Don't make me pull out a ruler, Christensen," he shoots me a defiant side gaze. "Your forbidden Vegas escapade trumps everything out there. And you're trending under #ZelBeckEpicFuck. No one is talking about *our* company, Beckett. It's all about *you*, the bad boy with the insatiable sexual appetite. A virgin *and* a pastor's daughter? There were no other damn choices?"

"Listen, Rhys, I take full responsibility for my actions, but one thing is certain, Zelda was no virgin," I poke an angry finger at him. "I'm willing to back it up with my entire fortune."

"That's not what her father claims," he quips.

"This is a publicity grab on the pastor's part," I counter. "Zelda is as much of a virgin as I'm about to be canonized as a saint."

"Why would her father risk his reputation if it wasn't true?" Rhys challenges.

I'm about to retort when a memory surges.

"It all makes sense now," I slap my forehead with my palm.

"What are you talking about, Beckett?"

"Zelda was adamant. Fucking her pussy was a dealbreaker. Her father claims she's a virgin, but it's semantics—"

"What does that mean?"

"That woman's ass is well used, looser than many pussies I've fucked. She gets fucked in the ass to pretend she's still untouched."

Rhys lifts his hand. "Too much information."

"I'm not going to sit here and be accused," I retort.

"What about last month's presidential fuck with the President's daughter? What was your excuse again?" He's being facetious.

"I have none," I deadpan. "Trust me, her father's *former position* was the last thing on her mind as she was begging for my cock."

Always aim higher, is my motto.

I graduated from *almost* fucking the former Vice President's daughter and her two best friends in a club in London to fucking the former President's daughter. Honestly, that almost foursome in London could've cost me everything. If it wasn't for the fact my three playmates invited a few friends—who only party with drugs—to join us without my knowledge or consent, my dick might've put me in some hot waters. Going on pure instinct, I bailed out just as a reporter was making his way to the room where the fun was happening. It was a close call… way too close for comfort.

"In my defense, she kept insisting *once you go to Texas, you never go back*," I add.

That woman knows how to show Southern hospitality.

Rhys shakes his head and lets out a sarcastic laugh.

"What?" I demand.

"I get this isn't your first real taste of success, but it is for me," he reminds me not for the first time. "And right now, your dick is fucking it all up—for me, for you, and for all the hard-working and dedicated employees who believe in our vision. You owe them more than that," he jabs the air with his index finger.

We stare at each other long and hard like two silverback gorillas about to engage in a brawl, his blue eyes burning into my own.

Alpha versus Alpha.

"Beckett, you're the CEO of a multibillion-dollar company," he continues when I don't speak. "I'm the lucky bastard who gets to ride this along with you. You need to start thinking with your other head."

"I can multitask," I counter.

I hold his defiant gaze.

The fury dissipates from his eyes, replaced by an air of defeat.

This company is his *raison d'être*. Sometimes he forgets it's also mine.

I plow my hand through my thick brown hair and take a seat on the edge of my desk, my gaze never leaving his.

"I wash my hands of Zelda. She's lying. That said, I'll curb my appetite for the next week," I concede. "By the time I get back from New York, this fake scandal will be water under the bridge."

He lets out a forced breath.

"That won't do," he informs me.

I knit my eyebrows together. "What are you talking about?"

"I want more than words, Beckett."

"You want me to sign my pledge in blood?"

"A little too medieval for my taste," he snickers. "If you don't have any skin in the game, you'll have forgotten about this conversation by end of the day. God knows what kind of debauchery you'll indulge in while you're in the Big Apple."

"I won't—"

"Please don't insult my intelligence," he interrupts. "You love women. I get it—"

"And you don't?" I shoot him an incredulous stare.

"My fucks never end up becoming liabilities," he defends. "Yours often do."

"What do you expect from me, Rhys?"

He narrows his eyes. "A challenge."

"A challenge?"

"You keep your cock under lockdown for the next thirty days."

My eyebrows hit my forehead. "Come again?"

"No sex for a month."

"I know it's way too early for you to be drunk, but for the record, what's coming out of your mouth is preposterous."

"If you value this company as much as I do, you'll take me up on my challenge."

"You're crazy."

"Since you fired your personal publicist, allow me to step into the role. You need an image rehab, Beckett."

"Fuck off."

"Just because you'll be on the east coast, doesn't mean the media won't be after you," he ignores my protest. "This story won't die down anytime soon. You abstain from temptation for the next month and the spotlight moves to another scandal."

"Please. This is LA. Another celebrity will fuck up before lunch," I sneer.

"Yeah, but Zelda's father is just getting started. It's clear he'll keep fanning the fire. He'll be on CNN tonight."

Fuck.

"I'll counter on WNN." Wire News Network's Enews, aka WNN's entertainment program, has always been good to me.

"Your focus needs to be on the company. Not on a misguided pastor dead set on protecting his slutty daughter's long-gone honor."

Wait. What?

"You're taking my side now?"

He flashes me a cocky grin. "#ZeldaNotSoVirgin is trending faster than #ZelBeckEpicFuck. So is #BackdoorZelda."

I explode in laughter.

"You're not off the hook that easily," he warns.

"You can't be serious about this challenge, Rhys."

"I am." The smile is gone. "You lie low for a while… and you get a nice prize for your effort," he says, tapping me on the shoulder.

I'm skeptical, but I bite.

"What kind of prize?"

"My most valued bike."

My eyes grow wide.

It takes me a minute to recover.

"You're willing to part with your Legendary British Vintage Black?" I enquire.

"The one and only," he confirms.

Rhys has a stellar collection of expensive bikes, but in the world of motorcycles, he struck gold. He may not have much left from his first career, but he was able to hold on to a coveted ride released in 1948. It has an estimated value of four hundred thousand dollars. That baby is pure mechanical genius.

"It shows you how much this company means to me," he adds. "I hope it's the same for you."

I consider him carefully.

"Abstinence for a rare gem?" I ponder. The first word leaves a bitter taste in my mouth.

"Yes." Rhys's cocksure grin irks me.

"You think I can't do it?"

"Prove me wrong, Christensen," he challenges.

"You're so certain of yourself."

"I am," he says with supreme confidence.

I shoot him a side gaze. "Your bike as bait?"

"Pretty much."

"Thirty days?" I know I keep repeating myself, but I'm weighing the pros and cons here.

"Four *very long* weeks," he stresses.

I nod, pensive.

"You can only engage with women in a professional or friendly manner."

"I can do that." Something tells me my eagerness will come back to bite me in the ass.

"Let me make sure we're on the same page here," Rhys says. He lifts a hand and fans his fingers out. "One," using his other hand, he points to one of his fingers, "your cock can't be inside of a woman's pussy. Two, same for her ass. Three, it also applies to her mouth. Four, titty fucking is cheating. Five, handjobs aren't a way around the rules. I doubt you'd waste your time putting your mouth on a pussy if you aren't getting anything in return. So, that's a non-issue. And I don't have to mention kissing since you never do." By the time he's done with his long list of stipulations, my jaw is hanging open.

"Any questions, Christensen?" he asks when I'm still dumbfounded.

"I can't even get a blowjob?" I ask, sheepishly.

"Not unless you're flexible enough to suck your own cock." I roll my eyes. "You can jack off as much as you want."

I glare at him.

Fuck, it's like becoming a born-again virgin.

It's not like I have an issue with jerking off. I love stroking my cock. The problem is, I've never gone that long without sex.

My mind is spinning.

"You're not man enough, Christensen?" he dares.

It's going to take me a few weeks to find a new publicist, so keeping it zipped up is a good idea. Not to mention, he damn well knows I've never been one to back down from a challenge.

His triumphant grin grows wider.

Fucker. No way am I letting you have the upper hand.

"I can totally live without pussy for a month!" *I think.* "You're on!"

"Good! Let's shake on it."

And we do.

"Just so you know, I'm not worried," he says, his hand still in mine. "That bike will remain in my secured storage facility where it belongs."

I laugh. "I wouldn't count my chickens—"

A knock at the door interrupts me.

"Come in," I shout.

Valerie pokes her head in.

Her features are tense. Somber, even.

"What's wrong?" I ask.

"Yeah, what's going on?" Rhys asks.

"Sorry to interrupt, but something else came up," Valerie informs us. "There's a life-and-death situation you need to be aware of."

Good Lord.

What a morning.

Get it now: Billionaire Mogul—Beckett

****

Next In The Series

New York Billionaire Factor Series

Expect these hotter than hell billionaires to stop at nothing to seduce the women who have a hold on their hearts.

Billionaire Factor—Bryce
Billionaire Factor—Nikolaj
Billionaire Wedding Factor—Nikolaj
Billionaire Factor—Max
Billionaire Factor—Easton

Billionaire Max Keller's cousins, Xavier and Zane Keller, kick off a spinoff series. Both stories are intoxicating and unputdownable, featuring sexy as sin billionaires and sassy heroines with plenty of curves. The other books in the series are equally addicting.

Very New York Billionaires

You'll find my **entire catalogue** and **reading order** on my site:
www.ScarlettAvery.com

****

ABOUT THE AUTHOR

USA TODAY and Amazon TOP 21 bestselling author Scarlett Avery unapologetically pens all-consuming love stories featuring sexy as sin billionaires who have the determination of a thousand warriors. Her kickass heroines are smart and sassy. And you should always expect edge-of-your-seat twists.

Scarlett's stories are intense and passionate, emotional and steamy, and always leave you begging for more.

Her books have been featured in USA Today's Happily Ever After.

Manufactured by Amazon.ca
Bolton, ON

25457433R00196